# The Marked Queen

LEGENDS OF CORALIA

# The Marked Queen

### KATE JENKINS & MORGAN MOREAU

Published By: 4 Horsemen Publications, Inc.

4 Horsemen Publications, Inc.
PO Box 417
Sylva, NC 28779
4horsemenpublications.com
Info@4horsemenpublications.com

Cover & Typesetting by Autumn Skye
Edited by Jen Paquette



*Library of Congress Control Number: 2024951131*

*Paperback ISBN-13: 979-8-8232-0767-6*
*Hardcover ISBN-13: 979-8-8232-0768-3*
*Audiobook ISBN-13: 979-8-8232-0770-6*
*Ebook ISBN-13: 979-8-8232-0769-0*

# Dedication

For David, who refused to vote for Collette
because Captain Peter Blair exists.
For my co-author Morgan who banned the phrase
"and there was a letter."
For my parents, for putting up with my consistent
chatter about these characters.
For Nom, Kala, Emerson, Adriana, Liz, and Bex for all the
love and support. You guys are amazing, and I adore you.
For Jim Henson. Without his stories and his characters, I
wouldn't love fantasy the way I do.

~~ Kate

For Gavin, Avery, David, and Finley, who will do big things.
For Alane, because we didn't take them to the beach.
For Grey, who wears fine things well.
We'll always talk it through as a crew.
For Tracy, who sends me Canadian things.
For Robby Lewis, who is gonna get us in trouble! He can
blow it out his tubenburbles.
For Katie, because I "made" her write a torture scene.
For the Toms. Welling, Ellis, and Payne, collectively.

~~ Morgan

# Table of Contents

# Cast of Characters

**Agnes Aballe:** Human. Queen's Maid.

**Alba:** Elf. Palace Servant.

**Aphros**: Nereid, King of the Nereid people

**Rhoslyn Almeida:** Human. Sister of the Earl Veitel.

**Wrenn Almeida:** Human. Earl Veitel. (Deceased)

**Aurae:** Nereid. High Priestess.

**Borin:** Human. Guard. (Deceased)

**Cadan:** Riken's Army Commander

**Carac:** Human. Guard. (Deceased)

**Ceto:** A Nereid advisor to Aphros.

**Garibald Crobán:** Lord. (Deceased)

**Tolan Dethenal:** Half-human, Half-Elf. Palace cook and for-pay arena fighter.

**Jayden Drake:** Nereid. Duke and Ambassador.

**Alaoin Bialaor Eiero:** Human. High King of Fythias.

**Xavier Eisenhart:** Human. Head of Riken's Guard. (Deceased)

**Lady Cecelia Elrick:** Human. Wife of Lord Elrick. (Deceased)

**Lord Elrick:** Human. New Captain of the Guard, Minor Lord. (Deceased)

**Farner:** Young soldier in Riken's army.

**Faron:** Elf. Member of the Fythias Court.

**Thomas Fletcher:** Human with magic. Arrow maker and political activist.

**Collette Venora Josselyn Gaillane:** Human with magic. Queen of Coralia.

**Gaillard:** Human. Works for Ian.

**Gisela:** Elf. Palace Servant.

**Gwane:** Human. Child worker in Wildrun.

**Cremisius "Crem" Hawke:** Human. Commander of the Queen's Guard.

**Diana Hawke:** Human. Palace cook.

**Heilo:** Nereid. Steward to King Aphros.

**Mallan Hialti:** Regent of the Azmarin Empire.

**Howle:** A Veteran of the King's Guard.

**Ian:** Human. Tavern owner in Galel.

**Barris Ilthane:** Human. Barron of Pontus Bay.

**Indir:** Elf. Survivor of the Urhadell massacre.

**Jarin:** Human. Guard. (Deceased)

**Kenrick:** A young guard.

**Alexander "Pops" Leassitor:** Shifter. Retired Mercenary

**Larent Leassitor:** Shifter. Mercenary.

**Nora Leassitor:** Shifter. Retired Mercenary.

**Lynessea:** Nereid. Wife of Lord Barris.

**Morrley:** Human. Works for Ian.

**Nieven:** Elf. Survivor of the Urhadell massacre.

**Nawalya:** Elf. Mercenary.

**Rowan:** Human. Guard. (Deceased)

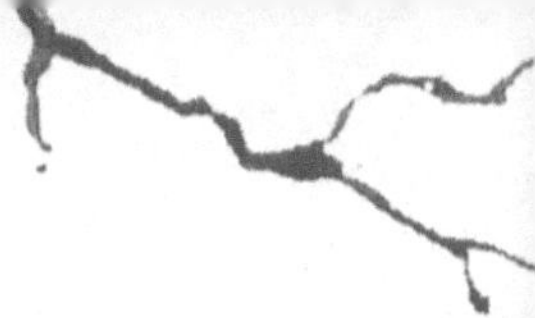

**Rulf:** Human. Guard. (Deceased)

**Sadon:** Human. Guard. (Deceased)

**Sara Whyldon:** Human with magic.

**Sargarus:** Human. Former King of Coralia.

**Riken Saullet:** Human. Baron of Wildrun.

**Arian Tal'Dela:** Elf. Mercenary.

**Brath Thancred:** King of Azmarin. (Deceased)

**Rion Thorax:** Human. Furrier.

**Amélie Vassetre:** Half-Elf: Daughter of Sabine and Faron.

**Elyna Vassetre:** Half-Elf: Daughter of Sabine and Faron.

**Éric Vassetre**: Half-Elf. Secretary to Alaoin. Son of Sabine and Faron.

**Sabine Vassetre:** Human. High Minister of the Fythias court.

**Zephraim Villot:** Human. Earl of Norbrick. Brother to the Queen.

**John Whyldon:** Human. Captain of the Queen's Guard.

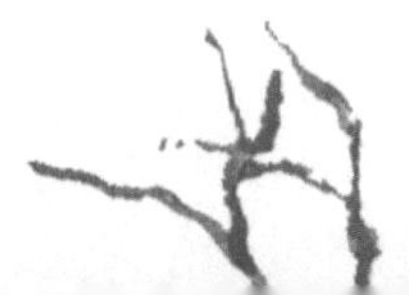

Azmarin Empire
Qvenall
Barcomb M
Myrefall
Coralia

Other Locations
Catillatio: The Capitol of the Azmarin Empire.
Gulf of Galel: Gulf bordering Galel and the Azmarin Empire.
Sherrose Caverns: A cave system in Quenall.
L'orilan
Fyithas
Pontus Bay
Galel
Nereid Kingdom
Veitel
A'lierdeen
Wildrun
Farner
Branlin

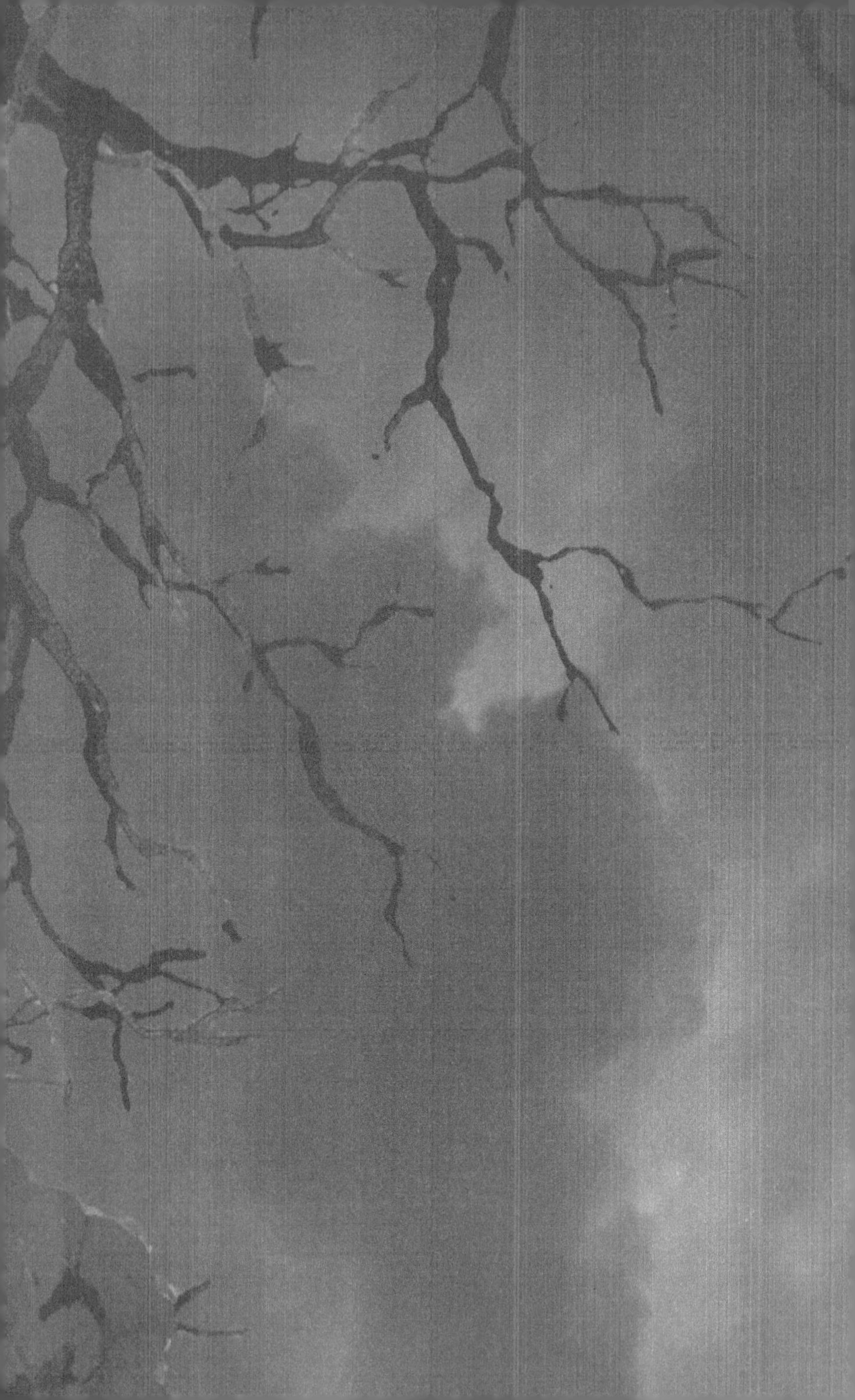

# Chapter One

The wooden platform gleamed in the morning light. Like the surrounding buildings, the bright harbor, shaded with pastel colors of blue, white, and coral, depicted the beauty of Nereid life for all to see. Aphros smiled to himself, listening to the comforting splash of waves and feeling the breeze on his face. His ashen curls swayed in the wind, almost dry since arriving on land an hour before to greet his guests. His scales glittered under the bright sun, proudly and brilliantly proclaiming him a Nereid king. He inhaled, taking in the salty fragrance with an appreciation he could hardly describe.

In the distance, the expected ship rocked in its moorings as the passengers descended. Aphros stood far enough back he could not yet make out faces, though he thought it fairly obvious the woman with shoulder-length chocolatey hair flanked by a group of men must be Queen Collette.

Though slight of frame, her taller stature and strong shoulders and arms told him she would be a formidable foe should things turn violent, and Aphros knew at some point attacks would come to the kingdom.

"They made good time," Aphros observed.

"The weather and sea have been cooperative," Ceto replied from beside him, beaming with excitement. Her golden eyes seemed to grow larger with every step Collette made to close the distance between them. "The Goddess Galene wanted them here."

"She did," Aphros agreed, smiling to himself. "And your excitement is palpable. You have been out here long before I." Ceto was dry and well groomed, characteristics one could not always associate with the woman. She preferred her time below the surface, and when she appeared on land, it was last minute, and water usually dripped from her vivid red hair. Her earlier return to the island, after spending time on the now-docked ship, left Ceto with strong opinions regarding Collette, a fact Aphros quickly learned. "I believe you are much more taken with the queen than even Jayden."

"A person who takes on the world to seek justice deserves recognition, do they not?"

"They do," Aphros replied with a nod.

Ceto turned to look at him more fully. "I believe she has earned the great honor of being Marked."

"Has she?" Aphros said. His gaze left their slowly approaching visitors, and he took in Ceto with curious warmth. "I do understand the depth of your affections for Coralia's true queen, but affection does not warrant the honor."

"No, you are right," Ceto said, her face contorting into teasing consternation. "Risking her life to save those at the labor camp, including Nereid, does warrant consideration. She didn't just help others fight off guards. She stood face-to-face with the leader, and she let him assault her so the newly freed prisoners and children had a chance to escape." When Aphros did not respond, she quickly added, "And look what she did for Jayden!"

"Jayden can provide the recommendation for the events in Quenall if he wishes," Aphros replied, though he tended to think Jayden should make the same nomination.

Aphros looked back at the docks, watching the visiting queen laugh with two of her companions. By Galene, her youth practically screamed for recognition. Such youth should not have been subjected to the violence of an overthrow and promised war. He sighed and nodded. "She should be honored, I think. So many would have turned their back or passed the task to another."

Ceto beamed again, clapping her hands together in renewed elation. "Can I do it?" she asked, leaving Aphros to wonder if she would start jumping up and down if he agreed.

He rubbed his chin, feigning thought as Ceto practically vibrated around him. "Perhaps, should she accept, you might be allowed."

Ceto responded by throwing her arms around him, an act only slightly less enthusiastic than he'd anticipated. "You are the best king!"

"Because I indulge you?" Aphros asked with a grin, his gold eyes mischievous.

"Indulgence is necessary," Ceto insisted as she released the king.

"It is," he agreed. Motioning toward the slowly approaching party, he asked, "Should we go meet them?" A nod from Ceto, and the two descended the platform and made their way to the docks. The Nereid king smiled as the features of their guest came into focus.

Collette's youthfulness resonated with Aphros. Though he'd known her to be a mere twenty-five, the wide eyes and full cheeks sprinkled with freckles illustrated how shameful the treatment she'd experienced by her people had truly been. The struggle was unfair, and he would make sure her experiences going forward came with support.

"Welcome," he said, his voice jovial and expression warm. "It is so wonderful to finally meet you, Queen Collette." He gave a bow resembling a nod, and his grin grew when she did the same.

"I cannot tell you how pleased I am to meet you and to be here," she replied. She was flanked by two men, a blond elf and a human with russet hair.

Behind her stood the rest of her party, elf and human alike. The ginger one might have been part giant from the look of him. Intrigue rose in Aphros. He would have to inquire about the composition of the group. He smiled again as Jayden made his way forward.

"Your Majesty." Jayden bowed with a flourish, his dark wavy hair falling forward in the effort. "I told you I would find her, cousin."

"So you did, Jayden," Aphros said, genuinely pleased both with the success and seeing his cousin looking so well. Breaking decorum, he offered the other man a brief but welcoming hug, a gesture returned just as eagerly by Jayden.

When the embrace ended, Jayden stepped back so he could stand near Collette. "Did I miss anything while I was gone?"

Aphros shook his head. "Just more confirmation from people on the inside of the stirrings in Coralia. We can go into more specifics once our guests have had time to settle and rest."

Jayden nodded and motioned Collette forward. When the two rulers were side by side, Aphros offered his arm to Collette. "Let me escort you to your accommodations while here," he offered.

He led the group along from the docks to the raised platform and along a stone path. They passed homes and businesses all made from a bright sandstone, some painted, though most remained a brilliant white. As they walked, he made an effort to point out places of note and others he found interesting. The small island made the walk equally small, and soon they arrived at the palace.

Comprised of four floors, the white stone building topped with a coral roof stood as the prominent feature of the town. Though rectangular, the estate gently curved toward the back, a feature Aphros knew could not be detected from their current position. No one could call the royal residence a castle, but a palace it was all the same. Each of his guests and more would be provided comfortable accommodations. Rooms enough for all present guests and a dozen more, a sizable kitchen and dining area, artillery storage, and spacious meeting rooms would serve the group well.

Passing a couple of guards as they strolled in, Aphros pointed out a carving above the entry. "The goddess Galene," he said, earning a smile from the other ruler. Her genuine interest and the close proximity Ceto kept further soothed any lingering worries the Nereid king held.

As they arrived in the entrance hall, Aphros relinquished Collette's arm, turning to the group. "Ceto, will you alert the staff? They can make sure our guests are shown to their rooms and have everything they need to relax."

"Of course," Ceto said, and she sprinted away without complaint.

Aphros chuckled, a hand pressed to his abdomen. "Ceto is quite impressed with you," he informed Collette. "So much so, she has requested we bestow you with one of our highest honors."

Collette's brows raised in surprise, almost as though she could think of no action in need of such acknowledgment. "Oh?" Collette asked.

The sudden silence from the rest of the group behind them demonstrated just how closely the people who arrived with Collette had been keeping an ear open.

Jayden, for his part, just raised an eyebrow but looked unsurprised. Aphros was already half-convinced his cousin would request the same.

Aphros nodded. "Indeed. The Nereid have a tradition of Marking those who have shown courage or strength or have otherwise acted in a manner worthy of note. From what Ceto reports, you put yourself at the mercy of a man who wishes to reestablish Merscale trades and who was also responsible for murdering and imprisoning innocent people. I also understand you were hurt in the process."

A small growl issued from the blond male elf standing near Jayden, accompanied by an unhappy look aimed at Collette. Simultaneously, the man with russet hair burst into laughter. Aphros wondered about the dynamics.

"Oh," Collette repeated, the word now more understanding rather than questioning. "I did not realize I'd done anything worthy of recognition." Her brown eyes darted to the russet-haired man, amusement shining in them.

"I'd wager the people you helped feel different," Aphros said. "All the same, it is an honor we offer to you, but you may take the time to consider, of course. If you are receptive, then you will meet with the priestess."

"Thank you," Collette said. "I shall think it over, and perhaps we can discuss it later?"

"Of course," Aphros replied.

Ceto returned, the palace steward and a couple of servants in tow. "Ah, Heilo," Aphros greeted his steward. Heilo was an older Nereid woman with thick, curly black hair she kept cropped just below her ears. She wore a stubborn no-nonsense expression, though it did nothing to hide her warmth and willingness to care for their guests. "Would you see our guests to their suites? I know they will want to eat and rest. Please make them comfortable."

"Aye, my king," Heilo said. She inclined her head and turned to Collette. "Your Majesty," she greeted. "Do I need to send anyone to the ship to gather belongings?"

"No. We traveled light and carried what we have with us," Collette replied.

"Then we will also get a list of things you might need," Aphros spoke up. He waved a dismissal to Heilo, insisting the Coralians be shown their spaces. "Jayden, a word before you also get some well-deserved rest."

Jayden nodded before stepping toward Aphros, who waited until they were alone again before speaking.

"You must explain the dynamics I just witnessed," Aphros insisted. He put an arm around his cousin's shoulders and led him farther into the palace toward a private office where they could catch up.

"Which dynamic are you most interested in?" Jayden asked, his eyes shining with amusement.

"Whatever you feel is important or amusing."

"Well," Jayden began as they entered an office. He closed the door behind them as Aphros saw himself to the wet bar. Bottles of dark rum waited to be sampled. "They are all very protective of the queen, but several of them are sleeping together or fighting. It's an interesting mix."

"Tell me more," Aphros requested as he sat out two glasses before uncorking a bottle of heavily spiced rum.

Jayden took a seat and waited for Aphros to hand him a glass. Once it was in hand, he lifted the glass in a silent cheer and took an appreciative sip. "Well, to start, Collette is with the russet-haired man. You know, the one with the easy smile. His name is Larent, and he is a shifter from what I understand.

There's some tension around his shifting, but no one has gone into details. At least, not around me." Another sip and Jayden continued. "The relationship is new, but they seem to care deeply for each other."

"So you didn't know Larent from your time in Quenall?" Aphros asked.

"No, but I did passingly know the half-elf with the dark hair. The muscular one with a scowl who hung back by the giant red head. His name is Tolan, and he is the one Collette ordered to help me safely leave Quenall when everything went wrong. He was with her then. Apparently, he left the party abruptly and without warning before she was injured. This was sometime after they left Azmarin from my understanding." He paused to drink again, a cross expression on his face. "He abandoned Collette at one of the worst times in her life, and Larent was there to pick up the pieces. From what I've gathered, there were already problems with Tolan's attitude before he left."

"Then we shall be wary of him," Aphros said, his gold eyes narrowed in thought.

Jayden nodded and continued. "The giant redhead is a man called Rion. He's a furrier and a former member of Collette's guard. He is also one of her former lovers. They seem to have parted on better terms."

"So three men in her direct travel party are either current or former lovers," Aphros summarized as he took a seat with his drink. "Good for her. She'll need the stress relief. Fythias won't be joining for a couple of weeks yet. Who knows when Coralia will declare formal war?"

Jayden laughed. "True. I don't think she's currently sleeping with all three, but who knows?" He shrugged and took another drink. "The two blonds, Arian and Thomas, are together." Jayden looked slightly put out by the news. "Thomas is the man I told you about who would stand outside the palace and speak out against Collette's policies."

"Does he not support her?" Aphros asked in interest.

"He does," Jayden confirmed. "But I think he believed her too gentle in her approach."

Aphros accepted the explanation. Collette could choose who she surrounded herself with, who she trusted, but he wanted to know what he could.

"Have you proposed joining Thomas and Arian yet?" he asked his cousin, changing topics.

Jayden rolled his eyes. "Too soon. Also, they appear to be monogamous."

"You never know," Aphros said. "Queen Collette seems to be surrounded by partners." He sipped from his rum, relishing the flavor. "Anything else I should know?"

Jayden buried his head in his free hand. "She is not with all of them," he reminded his cousin. "As for Arian and Thomas, despite how unbelievably attractive it was, having Arian threaten me for touching Thomas, roundabout way or not, tells me I will not be invited for any after-hours activities."

Jayden shook his head again, getting back on track. "The female elf Nawalya is an undertrained seer. She was also with the older male guard captain Whyldon. They are no longer together. From what I understand, she had a vision of Collette's death, and she did not share the information. Which is all water under the bridge for the queen."

"Why do you think Collette would forgive so easily when others have not?" Aphros asked.

"Collette, despite her considerable strength, is also very soft and caring from what I've observed. From my time in Quenall, I found her rather isolated by her position and her politics. Having friends, people who care about her, but are willing to own their mistakes, I think, means a lot to her. Nawalya comes

across as truly sorry from what I've seen of her actions toward the queen. As for the captain, if you spend some time around Collette and Whyldon together, it becomes very obvious just why he is so upset his lover did not tell him Collette was possibly in danger," Jayden said with a cryptic little smirk.

Aphros narrowed his eyes. "Are you suggesting what I think you're suggesting?"

Jayden gave his cousin, his king, a neutral look. "Depends on what you think I'm suggesting."

Aphros rolled his eyes, but he decided to indulge his cousin for a moment. "Are we supporting someone who doesn't technically have a legitimate claim to the throne?"

"Well, we could support the bastard who wants our people murdered for jewelry, or we could support the woman who has somehow made great changes while not being a true child of Sargarus." Jayden paused to take a drink and pour himself another. "I think I did not recognize the connection before because Captain Whyldon always behaved so formally when I was in Quenall. The restraint no longer exists, and I have witnessed a close, affectionate relationship while traveling with them."

Again, Aphros gave his cousin a tolerant look. "I think it's obvious who we have to support and who we should support. But we need to be aware of the possible resistance arising if ever the information of her parentage leaked."

"True," Jayden conceded. He took another drink. "I overheard a conversation I wasn't supposed to. They believe Collette isn't fully human," Jayden admitted with slight reluctance.

"A Coralian leader who isn't fully human…" Aphros said. "I never would have guessed." Aphros sipped from his drink. Nothing he now knew deterred him from his planned support, but complications existed now. "If either is exposed, we will have to make sure we can protect her."

# Chapter One

"Agreed, and I should also point out she has healing magic," Jayden said as Aphros took a drink.

The king choked on the rum, but he managed to set the glass down and glare at his cousin after the sputtering was under control. "You ass."

Jayden shook with laughter, having to put his own glass down so as not to spill on himself.

"You know these are all things I need to know."

"I am telling you, am I not?" Jayden asked once he calmed down, his expression innocent.

"I'm going to send you back to Coralia," Aphros grumbled.

"There is a rather attractive redhead there and a growing rebellion, so a return is not the threat you consider it to be."

"I wouldn't be sending you away to punish you. It would be to preserve my nerves."

"Did I tell you she did her magic in front of people at the labor camp? I'm willing to bet the news will spread like wildfire. Are my chances raised even more?"

Aphros rose from his seat to refill his glass. "Hiding magic is difficult," Aphros said, less surprised by the magic than some of the other revelations. "And if she revealed her magic after dealing with the fight Ceto described, she probably felt like she had no choice," Aphros guessed. "No wonder Ceto recommended her."

"I am recommending her as well," Jayden said.

"Can you justify it?"

"She put my safety ahead of her own several months ago, and now she saved not only her own people but several Nereid who believe Coralia is their home and will not abandon it," Jayden said simply. "She's more than earned the honor, and I doubt the priestess would argue."

"Then we should talk with the priestess," Aphros replied.

"Can we hold off until tomorrow? I'm exhausted and would like to sleep in my own bed tonight. Beds at taverns and inns are so uncomfortable," Jayden complained.

"Of course," Aphros easily agreed. "The priestess will want to talk with Collette, and I doubt she'll be up for such discussions."

Jayden gave Aphros a thankful smile before finishing the rest of his drink. He stood, a little unsteady thanks to the strong drink, and he made his leave.

# Chapter Two

Riken closed his eyes and took several deep breaths as he prepared for the coming confrontation. No other word existed for his meeting with Rhoslyn. Before arriving in Quenall, he'd gathered she was angry with him. He couldn't blame her, though he knew he needed to approach their pending confrontation with facts.

The facts, as he understood them, were numerous. He knew his beautiful Rhoslyn now ruled Coralia with Zephraim only acting as a figurehead. Likewise, the marriage between the king and queen existed in name only, and Riken hoped the change would leave more room for him in Rhoslyn's life. Lady Elrick was dead, and everyone believed it was a lover's quarrel gone wrong. Xavier died by Rhoslyn's hand after he had tried to assault her in her own rooms. Rhoslyn knew about his mishap with Collette. Most unfortunately, Rhoslyn had refused to see Riken outside of a formal meeting since he arrived.

Yes, their meeting would not be easy. He would need to apologize for much. Never in his life had he made such errors in judgment, and if any were to find him guilty for his errors, he would rather it be his goddess than any other.

Opening his dark eyes, Riken ran a hand through his wavy black hair then reached out with his free hand and knocked twice on the door to the meeting room. His other hand was wrapped tightly around the cane he would be forced to use for the rest of his life thanks to Collette shattering his kneecap.

"Enter," came Rhoslyn's reply, her voice level, though lacking in warmth.

Riken took another deep breath before twisting the handle and entering. The room was one he never thought he would get to see since King Sargarus died. Smaller than the council chamber, but more richly furnished, it more resembled a large office or small library except for the raised dais on the left where Rhoslyn sat on a heavily decorated, comfortable-looking lounge chair. Her silky cinnamon hair, fair skin, and cunning green eyes drew him in even if her expression warned of her temper.

Riken hobbled over to her, trying to conceal the severity of his limp. Arriving in front of her, he bowed deeply, ignoring the half-elf servant girl standing in wait and Zephraim who was seated against the far wall, a book in his hand.

"Riken," Rhoslyn said in greeting with a complete lack of her usual happiness to see him, "what do you need?"

She looked beautiful and ever so regal in a deep green dress. Her cinnamon hair was pinned up and her crown adorned her head. She also looked more aloof and angrier than Riken had ever seen her, causing all his words to dry up in his throat.

"Yes?" Rhoslyn prompted impatiently.

"I came to report my failure, Your Majesty, and to beg for your forgiveness."

Rhoslyn did not reply for several moments, instead tilting her head to study Riken as though she wasn't quite sure what to make of him. "You do need to fully explain the reports in your letters," she decided. "And Xavier, of course."

Riken lowered himself slowly to one knee in a sign of respect, though it was much harder than he felt it should have been. "There is nothing I can say to wash away the stain of Xavier, nor the actions he took against you. He was always loyal to me, and I was unaware of his more deviant behaviors until my commander Cadan made me aware. Had I known, I never would have left him with you."

Riken had never paid attention to Xavier's less-than-pleasant aspects. Those not-quite-human women Xavier targeted had not mattered. That his first true indiscretion was not only their queen but Riken's beloved made him glad Xavier was dead and gone. "There is no excuse for my lack of judgment, and I will accept any punishment you deem fit."

"I should send you back to Wildrun," Rhoslyn said, her voice growing colder with each word. "But from your letters, you have failed me there." She stood and walked over to where Riken knelt. "Explain to me again how you had Collette in hand, and she managed to escape."

Riken did not raise his head but kept it bowed in subservience and sorrow he had never shown Collette or Zephraim. In truth, had either of them berated him, Riken would have raged against the treatment. Rhoslyn alone had the power and the right to judge him for his failures. The Mother knew he had failed her and their kingdom.

"I was arrogant and overly certain of my success. I left all but three of my men at our resting place and rode onward to the labor camp. I did not know Collette was there until she approached us. I ordered her arrested but got too close. I allowed Collette to taunt and enrage me. She then attacked me, shattering my kneecap. Collette's allies killed two out of the three men with me. She allowed Cadan to take me from the camp. I am sorry I have failed you."

"Why would you be so careless?" Rhoslyn asked. "She managed to sneak out of the castle prison under the noses of every person in the palace. You thought four men would be enough to subdue her?"

"I didn't know she was there. I was just going to check on the status of the new camp, and when I saw Collette, she was alone," Riken trailed off. "There is no excuse for my stupidity."

"No, there is not," Rhoslyn agreed. She looked at the half-elf girl and snapped her fingers. Quickly, she approached Rhoslyn, picked up a pitcher, and poured a drink into a matching goblet. When she finished, she bowed and backed away, never making eye contact.

Rhoslyn turned her gaze back to Riken. "How do you plan to rectify your errors in the future?"

"By listening to the sound advice of Cadan, and yourself, and not underestimating our enemies."

"Fine," Rhoslyn decided after another long period of silence. "We shall meet again soon." Her words drew only the briefest of glances from Zephraim.

Riken nodded and rose shakily to his feet, head still bowed. "Is there anything else my queen wishes of me?"

Rhoslyn shook her head. "No. I think that is all for now." She sipped from her wine. "You should take better care of your injury, Riken. Perhaps meet with the palace physician."

Riken raised his eyes to look at Rhoslyn. "As you wish, Your Majesty." He bowed once before turning on his heels as best he could and limping out. He would head to his rooms, summon the physician, and wait to see if Rhoslyn would come to him or summon him.

# Chapter Two

*Riken,*

*You may come to me. My anger has waned.*

*Rhoslyn*

*Her Royal Majesty Rhoslyn, Queen of Coralia,*

*I am excited to begin our discussions of lending aid to Coralia in their efforts to apprehend the outlaw queen Collette. The false rumors of her death provided her too much of a lead on both our kingdoms, and I know you yearn to put a stop to her efforts. I will make plans to visit you in your kingdom in the coming weeks. I am still trying to organize the empire after King Brath's untimely death.*

*If needed, I can send aid ahead of my visit. I know there are many questions in your kingdom given the state of rebellion you have experienced. I am not unwilling to help shut down any and all problems. You simply need to ask.*

*Your Servant,*
*Mallan Hialti*

As Agnes hurried to the caves, she pressed a hand against her ample chest, encouraging her lungs to open and allow her to breathe better. The dash from the palace down to the caves took a lot out of the old woman, but the physical pushback did nothing to deter her from delivering her news.

She arrived at the entrance, a little windswept and disheveled from the physical exertion, but feeling more positive about

17

the future than she ever had before. She uttered the current code to a guard hidden just inside the concealed entryway, and when allowed to pass, she slowed her gait to something more manageable for her age.

By the time the older woman made it into the open main cavern, she'd caught her breath, though her excitement had only risen. She spotted Diana, the beautiful blonde former palace head cook, sitting at the makeshift table, though upon spotting the older woman, she rose from her seat and went to greet her.

"Agnes, we weren't expecting you," Diana said, her large eyes roaming over Agnes as though she had arrived injured.

"I know, but I have news!" Agnes said, her voice quivering with elation. "Great news!"

The announcement was enough to draw attention from Howle and Crem, who were off to one side of the cavern going over what appeared to be a map.

"What's happened?" Howle asked, now approaching the women. His long black and silver dreads swayed as he rushed over.

"She's alive!" Agnes announced joyously.

Crem and Howle looked at each other, then to Diana. Hope hesitantly sprouted in their gazes, obscuring the weariness they so often wore.

"How did you come by the news?" Crem, the former commander of the queen's guard, asked as he joined them. He ran a hand over his closely cropped brown hair, the action emphasizing his overly large ears.

"Lord Riken has returned! He can barely walk. He reports she attacked him in Galel."

Howle, true to his name, howled in laughter upon hearing the news. "By the Mother, lass, tell me he tried ta arrest Collette, and she beat him bloody. Give me more details."

Crem rolled his eyes and asked, "Did he say where he found her? Who she was with? Anything?" From the way his eyes lit up, Agnes knew hope was truly rekindling in the former guard commander.

The older woman smiled as Diana grasped her hands, jubilant from the news. "I can only report what I and Gisela overheard, but it seems as though she was near Wildrun, freeing the prisoners at an unsanctioned labor camp. Riken came upon her, intended to bring her here, and she attacked him." Agnes's pride over the girl she'd cared for since birth couldn't be contained. "Riken said she was with Mers, elves, and he suspects, Captain Whyldon."

"If Captain Whyldon still draws breath, he is with the queen," Diana asserted.

"I think so, too," Agnes agreed. "And it sounds as though she's gathered support on her own."

"Did Riken report this to Zephraim or Rhoslyn?" Diana asked.

"Both, though he was considerably more apologetic in speaking with Rhoslyn."

"After his own man attempted to assault Rhoslyn, I assume he groveled," Crem said, the worry lines back.

Agnes nodded. Barris hadn't been able to leave the castle much since Rhoslyn had taken over. They were all concerned, and Riken's return would only strengthen her reign.

"With confirmation of the queen being alive, we can reinvigorate the resistance," Diana reminded them all.

"Yes, we can." Crem gave Diana a soft grin. "Any news on Barris or Zephraim?"

"Lord Barris reports he is keeping a lower profile while he figures out a path forward," Agnes replied. "He believes Rhoslyn suspects him of nothing, but he would like for her to maintain the opinion a little longer."

Crem nodded, eyes shining in something akin to triumph. "Thank you, Agnes. News of her survival means everything to us."

"Thank the spirits she's alive," Agnes replied. She squeezed Diana's hands again and bid farewell to the men before making her exit.

# Chapter Three

Ian tread through the city with care, red hair glinting under the bright spring sun. Despite being human, and therefore at less risk, he was there on behalf of Queen Collette. Tasked with finding Cremisius Hawke and his friends, he had the task of delivering news of her ongoing survival and coming up with a plan to rescue Sara Whyldon. Neither task scared him as Ian had spent the past months technically committing treason depending on who was asked, but he knew he was in unfamiliar territory.

Walking down one of the many cobblestone streets, Ian kept an eye out for any friendly faces. He kept a low profile, doing nothing to draw attention to himself. The act allowed Ian to observe the people around him. Some held the distinct hunched body language of fear. In others, he saw something casually cruel, sneers and haughty expressions reminding him far too much of the inhabitants of Wildrun. Their presence told him how the locals were viewed and treated by the self-appointed monarchs.

Fortunately, among a smaller collection of Quenall locals, he saw glimmers of hope. These people did not look away, even though they didn't acknowledge him as he passed. Ian smiled as he realized news of Queen Collette had already reached Quenall.

Continuing through the city, Ian grew disheartened to find he recognized almost no one, and those he did know wouldn't know anything useful. After hours of no luck, he decided to seek out some of the more disreputable folks he knew when he spotted a hooded figure leaving the busier streets for a quiet one. Deciding it couldn't hurt to follow, Ian pursued.

He managed to follow the figure for several blocks, keeping his presence hidden among the others, though he eventually lost sight of them. Cursing, Ian spent a few seconds looking for where the person might have gone, only to end up face-to-face with the hooded figure and their blade.

"Why are you following me?" the hooded figure growled in a harsh, deep voice. Still, Ian recognized the voice as belonging to Cremisius Hawke. Having met the former commander during Queen Collette's birthday celebration the prior fall, Ian was unsurprised by Crem's lack of recognition. Ian knew Crem had helped hundreds of people that day, whereas the people who made impressions with Ian were much more limited.

Ian fell back on his tavern voice and manners, behaviors meant to soothe a customer ready for a fight. "My name is Ian, and I was looking for you, truthfully. I have a letter from Captain Whyldon for you," Ian explained with a smile. He reached for his side pouch slowly and pulled out the letter. Whyldon's neat, decisive scrawl across the front of the folded parchment spelled out the name "Cremisius Hawke."

Crem greedily snatched the letter from Ian's hand, giving him an apologetic look after the former commander realized what he'd done. Ian just shrugged and waited as Crem ripped open the letter and scanned its contents. Slowly, the tension in Crem's shoulders slackened, and hope bloomed in his gaze.

# Chapter Three

*Crem,*

*We are as well as can be expected. I suppose rumors of her death have long circulated in Quenall, but make no mistake, our queen is resilient. She has recovered from the injuries which demanded she stay hidden over winter, and she is ready and willing to do what is needed to rescue us all from our suffering.*

*We will be with the Nereid for now, but rest assured, Her Majesty plans on righting everything as quickly as possible. For now, Ian is with you to help. Don't lose hope.*

*John Whyldon*

"Thank you for this," Crem said after scanning the letter a second time. "Come. Let's get us both somewhere safe."

Ian nodded. "I would love that after my long journey here."

Crem nodded in agreement, and he led Ian toward the outskirts of town. As they walked, Ian could see the ex-guard had questions, but instead of pushing, he waited for Crem to speak.

"Whyldon's letter is sparse, but it says they are headed to the Nereid kingdom, and they are as well as they can be." He cast a glance at Ian. "How true is the last statement?"

Ian considered the question for a moment. "From what I saw, he isn't lying. The whole group he travels with looks tired, especially the queen. They carry a fire with them, though. A hope."

Crem nodded again. "We were told she was alive not long ago. Lord Riken arrived, and my people informed us, but I don't think I truly believed it until I saw it in Whyldon's handwriting."

"Lord Riken demonstrated honesty. No matter how horrific a person he is, from what I've gathered, he doesn't lie." In truth, Riken was moral, at least by his own set of beliefs. He'd acted

atrociously following those beliefs, but he could be counted on to follow certain actions.

Ian pondered Riken's nature for a moment before continuing. "Collette confronted Riken to give time for the people she'd freed from the labor camp to escape. From what I could see, she shattered his kneecap with a single kick." Ian couldn't help chuckling. "I didn't think someone could be so severely injured with a kick, but I overheard another member of her party remark she is unusually strong."

Ian observed Crem's expression as best he could while they walked, watching as the man considered his words. Despite their short acquaintance, Ian recognized the moment the former guard realized the queen was stronger than she should be.

"It's because she grew up with us," Crem said. "She grew into it around me and the others, and it just became something Collette could do. We never viewed it as something unusual." Crem shook his head. "Dear Mother, the things you miss when it's right in front of your face."

Ian kept his mouth shut. If the people of Quenall could so easily miss Queen Collette's strength, then they could easily miss more obvious questions, like her parentage.

The two continued to walk until they reached a cave covered by a well-hidden guard to either handle an intruder or run inside to warn the others. Crem gave the man a complicated hand signal, and the two were allowed to pass.

A walk of a few minutes on unstable ground led to a big open cavern shored up by large wooden beams. Ian would bet good money the cave and the connecting ones had been used for smuggling at some point in the past. It was what he would have used it for at least.

On one side of the room sat an attractive blonde woman, mending garments with a deft hand. On the other side, standing over a table covered in maps and small figures, stood one of the largest men Ian had ever seen. His broad shoulders, dark skin, and long black braids with gray threaded throughout created an imposing figure. Ian recognized the man immediately as Sunny Howle, and he quickly pushed down the urge to ask the man to bed.

"Diana, Howle, I have more news and a new friend."

Diana had already looked up when she'd heard footsteps, and though her brows were raised in surprise by the presence of a stranger, her expression remained friendly. "What news does your friend bring?"

Ian watched as Crem held up the letter. "A handwritten letter from Whyldon giving us confirmation they are alive and well and headed to the Nereid kingdom." The former commander practically glowed with joy.

Ian turned to look back at Howle as he snorted. "We already knew she was alive, but it's good ta have confirmation." Howle gave Ian a cautious once over, his eyes not lingering anywhere interesting which caused Ian to internally curse. He'd have no luck there.

Diana put her sewing aside, rose, walked over to Crem, and plucked the letter from his hand. Her eyes widened in excitement at the familiar scrawl. "Whyldon's confirmation provides necessary proof."

"Are ya thinkin' of printin' the letter and sendin' it around town?" Howle asked jokingly.

"There are those who will want to see proof since Rhoslyn and Riken have pushed their way forward," Diana reminded Howle.

Ian considered the benefit of such a move even as he observed Crem roll his eyes and drop a kiss on Diana's forehead.

"The letter also mentions Ian is here to help with other matters," Crem said in a casual drawl, and Ian found three sets of eyes on him, "but he doesn't clarify how."

Ian gave the three his most charming smile. "I'm here to help you rescue Sara Whyldon."

Diana's mood shifted to something much less hopeful. "Whyldon's sister? What's happened to her?"

"She is a resident of the palace's prison. Arrested for treason before I met up with the queen."

Diana bit her lip. "Security over the prison was increased after Queen Collette escaped." She looked to Crem. "Do you think they expect her to come mounting a rescue?"

Crem looked thoughtfully over to Howle before shaking his head. "There are some who will advise Rhoslyn of Collette's intention to return, if only because of her connection to Whyldon. Rhoslyn, on the other hand, might be one of the few people to never have underestimated Collette. Naïve and idealistic Rhoslyn may believe Collette to be, but she would know Collette wouldn't risk her kingdom for one person."

"Riken isn't nearly as perceptive," Diana pointed out, "based on what Agnes reports."

"Riken is a man with status, power, and a home base where everyone thinks he's right and rarely disagrees with him. He may have known Collette was trained to fight, but with the way he was raised, in his mind, Collette was never going to be a match for him," Ian said thoughtfully. "Outside of Wildrun, the majority of people on my side of the mountain don't agree with Riken's ideals. Inside Wildrun, however, well, Lord Riken has never faced a reality check quite like our queen before."

"One would have thought he would be more wary of her since she banished him from Quenall originally," Howle muttered.

"Thank you for the lecture," Diana said, brow raised as she surveyed Ian. "None of what you said addresses that the now emasculated and humiliated Lord Riken again resides in the palace with a chip on his shoulder about what happened. He can sway Rhoslyn to act foolishly, no matter how cunning she might otherwise be."

"Sorry," Ian said with a slight blush of embarrassment as he realized yes, what she said truly did go over his head.

A nod from the blonde acknowledged the apology, and Diana continued, "To the point, Riken likely hasn't learned his lesson."

Ian felt Crem nudge him as if to say, "it happens."

"No, he hasn't, but with his own man assaulting Rhoslyn, she might question his judgment enough to not listen to him," Crem said.

"What?" Ian asked in confusion, causing Howle to laugh.

"How about we sit down, have a drink, and trade stories? You can tell us how you ran into Whyldon and our queen, and we'll let you in on the shit show in Quenall."

# Chapter Four

Collette blinked, waking slowly. The luxurious bedding, nicer than anything she'd encountered since fleeing Quenall, tempted her to ignore the source of her consciousness, but she knew she could not. She'd been exhausted the night before, a combination of her ongoing fight against insomnia and travel, but now she was awake enough to take in the room.

At one end was the large bed with a vanity and wardrobe. Closer to a set of double doors sat a small round table with two chairs. A side table with a pitcher of water and a bowl of fruit stood near the bed. She recalled other rooms through the set of double doors, though Collette didn't know if the earthy tones of the bedchamber flowed into the space.

After brushing her dark hair from her face, Collette stretched out an arm across cream sheets, finding the space next to her empty but still warm. A low murmur of voices sounded from the door on the other side of the spacious room. A slight turn of her head, and Collette spotted Larent leaning against the doorframe talking to another person.

## Chapter Four

"So, instead of sleeping, you decided to spend last night roaming the island and are now freaked out by the plant life?" Larent asked.

"I am not freaked out. I'm just concerned," replied a soft feminine voice.

"You are," Larent contradicted playfully, "because some of the plants glowed, and one tried to eat you."

"It did not try to eat me,"' Nawalya insisted. "It moved and a vine wrapped around my wrist unexpectedly."

"So, you killed the poor innocent plant. It just wanted to love you, Nawalya."

"Larent!" Nawalya protested firmly, though the word ended in a whine.

Collette smiled at Larent's warm chuckle. "I would have freaked out, too. Don't worry, though. I'll tell Freckles in case you murdered some rare or holy plant so there isn't an incident. Maybe go get some sleep, though?"

"I should, but I may explore more. The island is beautiful."

"And new," Larent said. "I may have to check out the glowing plants come nightfall."

Nawalya replied, her voice too low for Collette to catch, but whatever she said had Larent laughing.

"Go have fun, and try to avoid killing more plants, okay?" With a shake of his head, Larent closed the door and strolled back to the bed, footsteps soft against coral tile. He smiled softly upon catching her awake. "Hey, Freckles. I hope we didn't wake you."

"Neither one of you was exactly being quiet," she pointed out.

"Sorry," he said, climbing into bed. "I had meant to keep it down."

"So, laughing loudly was keeping it down?" she teased as he settled beside her. She reached up and ran her fingers through his russet hair a few times.

"Apparently," he joked. Laying on his back, Larent got comfortable before reaching out for Collette, and as always, she moved to cuddle with him. "Nawalya got spooked by a plant. I couldn't not laugh."

"The elf woman who helped me take on a prison camp full of elves and Nereid was truly afraid of a plant?"

Larent chuckled. "Yup. She was sitting by one of the many, many ponds and fountains, and a glowing plant wrapped around her wrist. It startled her so badly she ripped it up by its roots. She then tried to replant it, but…" Larent trailed off as laughter shook his frame, though he forced himself to stop as she settled against him.

"I suspect she's never been somewhere so different from Coralia before," Collette said, an observation more than a question. "Which surprises me given how much Arian tells me the three of you have traveled."

"We have traveled a lot, but the Nereid islands are probably the most unique of places we've been." He yawned as he lazily ran his fingers through her hair.

"Sometimes I think the lot of you spent more time fucking around than anything else."

"Arian would deny the accusation to his dying breath. Besides, we weren't fucking around with the man-eating plant. We realized our mistake when Nawalya was almost swallowed whole."

"I believe about half of your stories," Collette replied, head now resting on Larent's chest. She sighed, content as she listened to the steady beat of his heart.

"Which half?" Larent asked.

"I'll let you figure it out."

Larent laughed. "Okay, fine. It didn't nearly swallow her. The plant did have strangling vines, and we knew about them beforehand. We just almost got caught," he admitted. "Mostly because Nawalya and I were fucking around, and Arian was upset enough at us he wasn't paying attention."

"See? I am not the only one who makes dangerous choices."

"I've never claimed you were."

"Yeah," Collette agreed, casting her eyes toward Larent's face, "but Arian is still very unhappy with my choices."

"It's how he shows love. The angrier or more protective he gets, the more he loves you. Which means you're his favorite person."

"Obviously. He's my brother. I'm also certain he'd lock me in a room somewhere and leave me there if he could get away with it."

"Oh yeah, he would. Shit, he'd push you in a broom closet and hope you couldn't escape if he was desperate."

Collette gave a quick laugh. "He would, which means next time I decide I need to go on an adventure, I should include him." She would have at the camp had Arian been closer.

"Or make sure there are no closets nearby if he happens to overhear you making plans to adventure."

"Oh, I plan on adventuring much more in life," Collette assured him. "But first, I think I must rise and get ready. Aphros has much he wishes to discuss with me today."

"Or we could say in bed and see how soundproof the walls are?"

Collette laughed. "We will have time to test that later."

Larent rolled them over so he was on top of Collette, his weight held up by his arms. "But where's the fun in waiting? I think hearing you scream this early in the morning would be a fun way to wake everyone else up for their day."

"You would," Collette said, reaching up to cup the back of his neck with her hand, her fingers playing with the ends of his russet hair. "We do not have the time for a long, lazy morning."

Larent gave her a sharp, mischievous grin. "We have time for a little fun though, don't we?"

Collette met his mischievous grin with her own. "Very brief fun."

Larent bent down to kiss Collette, nipping at her lower lip. "So, three rounds only. I can manage that."

When Collette emerged from her rooms later, every inch of her spoke to her position as Coralian queen. Although her hair still brushed the tops of her shoulders, the front strands had been pulled back and secured with twinkling jeweled pins while the rest fell in gentle waves.

She'd also been provided with clothing beyond what she'd traveled with, and her dress, a pale rosy pink accented in silver, practically floated around her. Nothing she wore compared to the heavier, richer materials of Quenall high fashion, but the elegant, slimmer silhouette suited her well.

Larent stepped out of the room next to her, dressed just as smartly, his russet hair mostly tamed. Collette gave him an approving nod, finding him quite handsome, though she always did. With a viable option to regain her throne, Collette now had to prepare for political and military maneuvers. They hadn't really talked about what role he wanted, if any, as she reestablished her rightful place, but he had wanted to join the discussion between her and Aphros.

"Thank you for letting me come with," Larent said, his usually confident smile doing nothing to hide his nervousness.

"Of course," Collette said with a reassuring smile. "I want you to be involved to whatever extent you want."

"I can't promise I won't embarrass myself, but I'll do my best. I mean, how much does politics differ from spy work?"

Collette chuckled. "Politics are often a mix of stealth and cunning," she agreed. "Just know, I love you for who you are, no matter what."

"Honestly, I plan to see where I fit best and go from there. Shit, if I can manage not to embarrass either of us, I'll call it a win."

"You won't," she insisted, and she waved as Whyldon appeared, his increasingly silver-streaked brown hair pulled back from his face. His relaxed expression showed an ease Whyldon had not worn at any point on the road, and his shined boots, dark breeches, and wrinkle-free shirt and jacket made him look every bit the royal advisor.

"Well, you cleaned up well," Collette complimented.

"As did you," Whyldon shot back with a grin, his blue eyes twinkling. "I'd almost forgotten you could."

"Oh, you know, I try," Collette shot back. She might have continued their banter, but light footsteps sounded in the hallway, and her attention was drawn to the ginger hair of Ceto.

"A glorious morning to you," the Nereid said, beaming brightly. She looked Collette over, her smile growing ever brighter. "You look so lovely. The color suits you."

"Thank you," Collette said, amused as always by Ceto's excitement. The woman practically vibrated whenever she and Collette occupied the same space.

Ceto clapped her hands together, as though to designate a beginning to more official proceedings. "Aphros asked me to escort you to breakfast," she explained. "Of course, your whole party is welcome if you would like. From there, he would like to discuss the process of Marking."

"Of course," Collette agreed.

Ceto motioned the group to follow, and as they traveled down the corridor, Nawalya joined Larent on his left, and

Collette shot her an amused look as she recalled the conversation with Larent. The lithe elf didn't quite blush, but it was close.

"Did Arian and Thomas sleep in?" Collette asked Nawalya.

"Not at all," Arian said as he stepped out of the room he and Thomas had been assigned. "We had a busy morning." Arian's mussed blond hair and Thomas adjusting his shirt told the others just what they were busy with.

"I had a similar morning," Collette pointed out. "I was on time."

Arian raised an eyebrow. "Then we must assume shifters do not have the same stamina as elves."

Laughter bubbled up at the response. Arian may still harbor ill feelings about the prison camp situation, but given his quip was so quick and affectionate, she knew his lingering anger would eventually fade. "I have no complaints, I assure you."

"Good," Arian replied. "I would hate to have to give Larent pointers."

Larent cackled in response.

"I would like to hear your pointers considering you don't like women," Nawalya said with a raised eyebrow and an evil little smirk.

"I don't know," Thomas interjected, ignoring Whyldon's amused, but audible sigh. "Some of the mechanics are similar."

Larent had to stop walking and lean against a wall for support he was laughing so hard.

Nawalya just stared at Thomas for a moment. "No. Fucking a man and fucking a woman is only similar in so much as a dick goes into a hole."

"How does that differ from what I said?" Thomas asked her. Despite his rumpled shirt, the fletcher's pale blond hair was smoothed back, and the ink stains on his fingers had lessened.

"You'd never know this was a royal party on its way to have talks with another monarch," Whyldon observed mildly.

"Be glad Jayden is not here," Ceto said after a small giggle. "He is worse. I should know after traveling with him for months."

Arian looked at Thomas with a slight grin. "Did you not say Ambassador Drake was the height of respectability when you met him in Quenall?"

"He was," Thomas replied. "In Quenall."

Jayden had been much more relaxed since Collette had been reacquainted with him, though she could understand the change. He wasn't surrounded by people who thought ill of him or wanted to harm him. He had the luxury of relaxing and enjoying himself.

Larent collected himself and went back to Collette's side. "You will never have a dull day with us around."

"I've learned as much since meeting you," Collette assured him.

The party made their way to the dining hall, smaller than the one at Gadleigh Palace but brightly lit and warm. The walls were the same sandy white color, and here and there, rich tapestries of coral, peach, and blues hung. Collette was shown to her seat by Ceto, and the others were invited to take the other available places.

Larent took the seat on Collette's right, and he reached over to take her hand under the table. She was uncertain if his motives were supportive or nervous, but she squeezed his hand all the same.

A handful of Nereid appeared, uniformed in red and blues, and they placed trays of food along the table. Ceto insisted everyone help themselves as wine was poured, and they began eating.

"Does anyone know where Tolan and Rion are, or did they sleep in?" Arian asked curiously as he helped himself to a pinkish fruit.

"They are on the training grounds. Rion appeared to be beating Tolan half to death," Nawalya responded.

"Did Tolan piss him off, or is Tolan still avoiding everyone?" Thomas asked.

Nawalya made a thoughtful face as she put a few pieces of what looked to be crab meat mixed with brightly colored vegetables on her plate. "From what little of their conversation I could overhear, Rion was teaching Tolan to be better than his past. Using the training to wear out Tolan's anger."

Collette caught Arian and Larent exchanging a thoughtful look, but neither commented. "They'll need to eat at some point," she pointed out.

"Indeed," Aphros said as he entered the dining hall. His wavy hair was slick with water, and it looked darker while drenched. "Sorry for my lateness. I went for a swim and got drawn into a debate." The Nereid king dropped into a chair and began to fill his plate while a servant filled his chalice with sweet red wine.

"Was it at least amusing?" Ceto asked him.

"Do you find lobster mating habits amusing?" Aphros asked with a grin.

Jayden slipped into the hall and took a seat near Thomas and Arian, much to Arian's displeasure if the look he shot Jayden was any indication. Jayden's answering grin and narrowed golden eyes made it clear he enjoyed the blond elf's ire. Once comfortable, he said, "It depends on the lobsters, I think. The large ones cause a lot of havoc when mating season arrives. The smaller ones are boring."

"How do the larger ones cause chaos?" Larent asked.

"They are bigger than any of us, and they like to mate in the growing fields," Jayden replied, causing Larent's brows to crease.

Chapter Four

"The tales say most of the giant lobsters died out," Whyldon added after sipping from his glass.

"Most have," Ceto confirmed. "But a handful of the giants are enough to be a pain."

"And we've been doing what we can to help them repopulate, but sometimes I wonder if it's worth the effort," Jayden remarked.

"It's not," Ceto said flatly. "And you know it."

"You, my dear, are mostly upset because they ruined your entire garden during last season's mating." Jayden looked over at Collette. "Ceto grows the most beautiful of our underwater flowers."

Ceto did not address Jayden, instead looking to Aphros. "Can we remove him from your court? He is aggravating."

"I would," Aphros said with a shrug. "But our guests seem to like him. Most of them, anyway."

Larent and Nawalya laughed while Arian just pressed his lips together to hold back a grin.

Jayden, on the other hand, winked at Ceto. "You love me."

"I'm waiting for you to make a point," Ceto shot back.

"She's so vicious in showing her love or overly enthusiastic." Jayden shot Ceto a smirk.

Collette watched the two exchange a series of rude expressions and gestures but said nothing as she ate. The easy banter and obvious affection helped contribute to the much more optimistic position she held now in the Nereid kingdom.

"Would you two like to fight it out?" Aphros asked. "I did have some things I would love to discuss with Queen Collette, but a show before talks would likely entertain."

Jayden immediately sat back in his seat, away from Ceto and Aphros. "No, thank you. I will not enter the ring unless I am on the same side as Ceto."

"Afraid she would kick your ass?" Larent asked, interested.

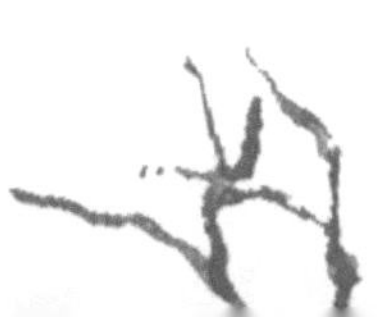

"She would," Jayden said. "Our society is matriarchal by nature. Our women are all fighters, and Ceto is one of the best. Not to say men don't fight, but our women are always better." He raised a glass to Ceto, who returned the gesture.

"I would like to see," Collette said, and Ceto's smile grew.

"I'd be happy to do a demonstration or even spar with you," she immediately volunteered.

Larent quickly grabbed his cup and took a drink, unable to hide his smile from Collette. Nawalya's similar reaction was rather telling.

"I would like to watch. I have rarely seen a Nereid fight," Arian said.

"It would be beneficial, I think, for all parties," Whyldon added, his blue eyes cast down at his drink, but his amusement still sat clearly on his face.

"Sure," Collette easily agreed. "I think it would be nice to have some difficult opponents." Riken had not been, after all.

Nawalya gave Collette a thoughtful look. "If you would like more sparring partners, I would be happy to join in. After all, tossing Arian bodily from a house doesn't count as sparring."

Arian speared another piece of unknown fruit. "We will be here a while, I think. It would be best to stay in shape and practice."

"I doubt you'd convince Collette to remain inactive," Whyldon said with a soft chuckle.

"And practically speaking, we know gathering here with Fythias due in the next few weeks will lead to battle. Getting everyone in fighting shape is for the best," Aphros pointed out. "We'll all have different disciplines and forms of combat."

"We will," Collette agreed. "And given who we will go to war against, I think we're starting in better condition." There were agreements all around, though Nawalya's feral grin indicated she was the most excited person at the table.

"What should we anticipate when it comes to the army Coralia will present?" Aphros asked. "Azmarin's army is well disciplined and large. They will present a challenge."

Whyldon replied. "It will depend on who joins Rhoslyn and Riken's ranks. Riken's soldiers have, traditionally, been well disciplined. The Almeidas have not."

"No matter what they cobble together, it's going to be small units from various noble estates with different levels of skill and order," Collette added.

"Could they attempt to force enlistment on the regular towns folk?" Jayden asked.

"It's possible, but higher numbers require more money, resources, and the like," Whyldon pointed out. "They may decide numbers aren't worth it."

"Let us hope you're right. I would hate to kill those being forced into a war they don't want," Jayden said solemnly.

"You are being idealistic, cousin," Aphros pointed out over his chalice. "Almost every soldier you ever encounter on a battlefield ultimately does not want to be there." He took a sip and waved away the subject as though it mattered little.

Turning his eyes to Collette, Aphros smiled. "Have you given thought to the Marking?"

She nodded. "I have, and I would be honored to accept it."

"Wonderful!" Aphros declared. "After you have finished eating, we will go chat with the priestess about the process. If she agrees, Ceto has requested the honor of giving the Mark, assuming you find her involvement acceptable."

"Yesterday you mentioned Marking having cultural significance for acts of service?" Larent made a face as he tried to remember exactly what was said. "What exactly is a Marking, and how often do people not a part of your culture earn one?"

"Marking is what it sounds like," Ceto said. "It can be tattoo or scarification, depending on what the recipient requests and what the priestess deems prudent."

Aphros nodded in agreement. "And we have offered the honor to many non-Nereid, including Coralians."

"You mentioned seeing a priestess. Are there religious connotations with Marking?" Arian asked. Larent sat straighter in his chair as if he suddenly remembered something important.

"There are, but a recipient does not have to hold the same beliefs," Aphros said.

Arian nodded, eyes sliding to Larent as the other man relaxed back in his chair. "I admit to not knowing much about the Nereid as a whole. Is your priestess open to answering questions, or is there someone else I should speak to?"

"I think it would depend on the questions, would it not?" Aphros asked.

Arian nodded. "Very true."

"You are welcome to join us with the priestess," Aphros offered.

Arian looked at Collette. "Only if you do not mind."

"I do not," Collette confirmed.

Arian gave a small, pleased smile.

"It's not like she would tell her brother no," Larent joked, and Arian discreetly flipped him off.

Aphros chuckled. "Let's eat, and we can then go about the business of Marking."

# Chapter Five

The Nereid temple stood at the most northern part of the island, made of a similar sandy white stone as the central palace. The building appeared taller than any other, and the gold trim along the edges of the roof sparkled, inviting all to come forth. Elevated by six distinguishable layers of heavy stone, the temple entrance was accented by four decorative white and gold columns holding up the coral triangular roof. The space directly behind the columns served as an open-air meeting place with larger rooms in the back secured by a heavy gold door.

Several Nereid women walked along the open-air space, some attending chores and others chatting. Their faint scales glittered under the sunlight. "This is the temple of Galene, the sea goddess," Aphros said to Collette as they ascended the stone stairs leading up to the temple. Arian, Nawalya, Whyldon, Larent, and Thomas followed behind them. As always, Arian, Whyldon, and Larent remained as close as possible without offense while Nawalya and Thomas gave Collette and the Nereid king more space.

Aphros gestured to the women within the space. "These women are newly ordained or working to become ordained. You can tell by the colors of their garments. Pink for training. Blue for the newly ordained. The high priestess wears purple."

No woman present wore a shade of purple, and Collette assumed the high priestess, should she be present, would be the one to discuss Marking. "Is she here?" she asked as the group made it to the top of the stairs.

"She will be in the inner temple," Aphros explained.

Aphros quietly spoke with one of the younger priestesses, and she ran to the inner temple, the door creaking open as she approached and closing once she disappeared into the chamber. While they waited, Aphros gave a brief tour of the open-air room, discussing architectural features and histories of certain places and items and introducing priestesses who were more established in their role.

Now and then, Collette's gaze went to Arian, who was silent and stoic as always, though his eyes shone with inquisitive thoughts she knew he wished to ask. When their eyes met, she gave him a knowing smile, though her attention returned to Aphros.

"The door here is made from orichalcum," the Nereid king explained. "It is one of the strongest materials in the world. We felt it necessary to provide those serving in the temple with sufficient safety should the need to hide arise."

Collette took a few steps toward the door, taking in the tiny, intricate engraving along the top and bottom. Another step closer, and the door opened, slow and heavy.

The corners of Aphros's lips turned up, though he did not speak for several seconds. "I believe you've been invited in."

Arian studied the doors. "They are magically sealed?" he asked, his brow creased.

"Very astute," Aphros replied, seemingly impressed.

"Thank you." Arian moved to take a closer look. "How did they know to unlock for Collette?"

"Well, usually, only Mers can unlock them," Aphros replied.

Whyldon's blue eyes glanced at Collette before turning to Aphros. "Are you suggesting…" he began.

"I do not know," Aphros said, bemused. "Queen Collette has not informed me of her lineage, but the unlocked door does suggest certain things."

Arian looked hard at the doors, then at Collette, eyes narrowed in thought. "That would make sense," he said.

"The Nereid are exceptionally strong," Aphros replied, smiling at Collette. "My cousin informs me you are as well."

"I am," she confirmed.

"And your presence unlocked the door," Aphros added. "I think you might consider the possibility."

"Do the Nereid keep track of genealogy?" Arian asked, the gleam in his eyes one Collette didn't recognize.

"We do," Aphros confirmed.

"May I have permission to go through them?" he asked Aphros.

"If you wish to spend your time in such a way, I have no complaints. For now, we should see the priestess."

Arian nodded, and he whispered something to Whyldon that Collette could not hear. Whyldon gave a decisive nod she recognized, but Collette decided she would ask later. For now, she proceeded into the inner temple at the insistence of Aphros, the king just behind her while the others followed. Once inside, Collette heard the heavy door slowly close.

Beautiful lanterns hung along the wall, silver and ornate and meticulously crafted. The inner temple was well lit as a result, and the creamy walls were covered in tiny depictions of what she assumed was the goddess Aphros had mentioned before.

"These are the stories of Galene," Aphros volunteered as she looked at them. Arian joined Collette in studying the pictures. Intricate and swirled, the designs beautifully depicted the goddess as a child and later in what looked to be wedding attire. Near the corner of the wall, she saw a depiction of the goddess in armor, blood-stained and battle-worn, but standing victoriously.

"The goddess has faced many different trials," a husky, warm voice said from behind the group. Collette turned to see an elegant woman with dark skin and long black and gray curls which fell to her waist. The tall woman drew closer, and a purple glitter of her scales shone brightly when she passed the lantern light, complimenting her lilac robes.

"Aurae," Aphros said, lowering his head to her, "it is good to see you," he said. He motioned to Collette. "Our visitor, the true ruler of Coralia, Queen Collette."

Aurae smiled at Collette, her head tilted ever so slightly to the left. "You are so young," she said in the same deep, warm voice. "How is it such a young woman must carry so much weight on her shoulders?" As she spoke the words, her hands rested on the sides of Collette's upper arms, though the gesture seemed motivated by comfort and concern rather than something more malicious. "Such burdens should not fall on you."

"I have been lucky to have the support from my friends," Collette replied, and Aurae's bright gold gaze turned to those who had accompanied her to the temple.

"You have seen the queen safely to our kingdom. You must be wonderful friends indeed." Slowly, Aurae's gaze took in each of the companions, Thomas first, followed by Larent, Nawalya, Arian, then Whyldon. Her eyes lingered there, and her head leaned in the other direction, scrutinizing him even if her pleasant demeanor did not change.

She looked back to Aphros. "May I inquire as to your visit?"

"Indeed," Aphros confirmed. "Ceto and Jayden have individually recommended Queen Collette for Marking for her acts of courage and sacrifice."

"I see," Aurae replied, seemingly unsurprised despite Collette's Coralian affiliation. "Marking is one of our highest honors, and it creates an indelible spiritual and physical link to the Nereid. Knowing Ceto and Jayden as I do, I cannot doubt the sincerity in their nominations." She smiled at Collette. "As you have approached willingly, I cannot doubt your own willingness to be here. How about your friends? Do they support the weight of your acceptance?"

Larent, who'd been unusually quiet during the interaction, simply nodded, as did Nawalya and Arian.

Thomas, who remained near Arian, chose to speak. "How is the Marking done?" he asked.

"A design is chosen, usually something representative of the person receiving the honor. Then a location on the person's body is designated. Using a needle and ink, the design is permanently placed on the body." Aurae smiled again. "You have, no doubt, seen others with similar Markings."

Arian and Larent traded a look, and Larent couldn't help the growing grin on his face. "I've seen them before, though I'm pretty sure I wasn't supposed to."

Whyldon raised an eyebrow at the exchange. "Lord Barris has them," he said. "Starting on his neck and traveling down."

"He does," Aurae confirmed with a nod. "He has served the Nereid well, and his Markings demonstrate as much."

Larent nodded. "After discussions of Marking arose, I realized the tattoos I saw on him were the Markings."

Aurae confirmed his connections with a nod. "So, Queen Collette, are you consenting to the Markings, knowing they will forever connect our two worlds?"

Collette nodded. "Given everything, I cannot turn down such an honor."

Aurae brought her hands together. "Wonderful. We shall arrange it."

"Ceto has requested permission to be the one to perform the Marking," Aphros added, his expression full of humor. "I believe she is excited for the opportunity."

"Then she shall be invited to oversee the ritual, assuming there are no objections," Aurae replied. To Collette, she added, "Ceto is quite gifted. You will be pleased with her work."

"I look forward to it," Collette replied. She knew Ceto was quite fond of her, and nothing would be done poorly by her hand.

"Then we shall proceed with the ritual this evening," Aurae determined.

"Can we all attend, or is this private between Collette, Ceto, and yourself?" Nawalya asked.

"The process is highly intimate, but we will honor the wishes of Queen Collette," Aurae replied.

"If you just wish for them to be there," Nawalya said, motioning to Larent, Whyldon, and Arian, "I am fine with that."

"I think I would like to follow whatever the usual protocol is," Collette decided. While she understood her companions may not appreciate her decision, it seemed the most respectful of their hosts.

Other than Arian, who Collette suspected wanted to never have her alone in the presence of someone outside of their collective group, no one else looked offended. Even then, a nudge from Larent had Arian's expression changing into something more neutral. "We respect your decision," he said.

"I do think Arian will want to be close by, all the same," Collette amended, adding the compromise to make the elf happy.

## Chapter Five

"Of course," Aurae replied. "There are many parts of the temple he might explore while Ceto works. If you are amenable to entertaining yourself, Arian."

"I am more than amenable," Arian replied, though Collette suspected he would never be far off.

"Then my brother will accompany me," Collette said simply.

The honorable title she'd bestowed on Arian brought a surprised but all the more genuine smile to Aurea's face. She nodded. "Of course."

Arian's expression remained stoic, though Collette could see the corners of his lips turn up ever so slightly.

"Sounds like a plan," Larent spoke up as he came to stand next to Collette before placing a soft kiss on her cheek.

"Wonderful," Aurae said. "Please feel free to continue looking around the temple. Many of the priestesses would be delighted to answer questions. For now, I will need to seek out Ceto."

The group dismissed, Aurae headed farther back into the inner temple, disappearing behind another door. No doubt, there would be much to learn during their time in the Nereid kingdom.

Larent threw an arm around Collette, pulling her a little closer. "Anything you want to see?" he asked. Collette noted Thomas being given the Arian equivalent some feet away while Whyldon and Aphros entered quiet conversation.

"I think we just explore until we grow weary of it," she replied.

# Chapter Six

Rion took in a deep breath, cracking his knuckles as he watched the sun slowly rise in the sky. Despite retiring from the Queen's Guard years ago, he'd never fallen away from his habit of rising early. Granted, he rarely had complaints about early mornings. After leaving the guard, early mornings had often provided him with the most access to the furs he sold. It also allowed him to travel better and plan out his day more productively.

Now in the Nereid kingdom, he was able to enjoy the beautiful morning. Although Rion was no stranger to Mers and other non-human groups, he'd never been somewhere like the Nereid kingdom. Although much of it told him he'd not want to live there, he couldn't deny the peace of the waves crashing against the stone-filled beaches, the climate, and the plentiful delicious food.

The Nereid were also more welcoming than Rion thought any Coralian had a right to expect. His accommodations had almost tempted him to sleep in, and every person he spoke with smiled with such genuine pleasantness. Things seemed almost too wonderful here, even with the promise of a coming war.

He stretched again and took a seat on one of the larger stones just out of reach of the sea foam, his tall stature making the seat almost unaccommodating for him. He'd gone for a morning walk, a couple of pastries in hand, when he'd run into Tolan. They'd practiced sparring for a bit as Tolan looked in need of a distraction. From Rion's perspective, the former gladiator's lack of progress in re-ingratiating himself with Queen Collette and the rest of the party boded poorly for his already dampened spirits. Then again, he didn't think the other man had made much of an effort.

Rion scratched at his gingery beard before opening his pack and removing the remaining pastry. "Do you ever plan on something other than moping?" he asked, looking over to Tolan who still stood, dark eyes gazing out at the sea.

Tolan laughed and shook his head, nearly black wavy hair swaying with each movement. "I tried to talk to Collette one evening when we were on the ship. It was late, and I thought the others were asleep. I approached and tried apologizing. She looked me dead in the eye, then looked above us and told Arian to throw me overboard if I ever spoke to her again. I decided it was best to wait to approach her."

Nothing about the story seemed false or even exaggerated. Once Joss lost her temper, she remained angry, even when she kept the anger beneath the surface. "She can't have you thrown overboard anymore," Rion pointed out, managing to avoid laughing for now. Besides, he knew he couldn't say much. Collette seemed to like him as much as she ever had, but being around her, knowing nothing had changed, always felt a little bittersweet.

"That's why I'm looking for an opportunity to approach her. I know I can't do it when Larent is around, and I just don't feel comfortable doing it in front of the Nereids, let alone their king," Tolan admitted.

Rion chuckled before taking a bite of the pastry. He couldn't quite identify the flavor, though the sweet heat reminded him of cinnamon and fruit. He licked his lips after swallowing and watched as a white and gray bird landed near, hoping for him to drop a piece of his breakfast. "We're in the Nereid kingdom. Can't exactly escape them," he reminded Tolan. "Do you want me to talk to her?"

The responding tilt of Tolan's head told Rion he was considering the offer. "No. I need to handle things myself. I just don't want to get yelled at, scolded, or ignored by her in front of their king in case my cousin wants me in any meeting chambers with them."

"She's not going to behave so poorly in front of King Aphros," Rion replied, deciding to give the bird the remnants of his pastry. He tossed it, and the morsel didn't even make it to the ground before the bird snatched it up and took off. "And you're cousin to Alaoin. You have some leverage there," he told the former arena fighter.

"I'm not worried about her as much as myself. Collette would never embarrass herself in front of another royal, not unless I acted out first. Even then, she would still handle me with grace. I don't trust myself not to say something stupid if she brushes me off." Tolan watched the ocean waves for a moment before turning to finally look at Rion. "I know I need to speak with her, but I also know I need to be smart about how I approach a discussion."

"You need to do something," Rion retorted. He glanced back in the direction of the Nereid palace, knowing increased activity would have followed the rising sun. "You will more than likely be involved in discussions, given the role you played with Fythias."

"I was hoping I could talk to her today, though it may not work out the way I'd like," Tolan admitted, his mouth twisting into an unpleasant grimace.

"If she continues to ignore you, I will intervene," Rion said, not because he thought Tolan was owed forgiveness, but because it was what would ultimately be best for Collette. "I think even Whyldon is beginning to pity you. Clearly, an intervention is needed."

Tolan let out a huff of air, the idea of Whyldon pitying him not sitting well. "Okay, I can agree to your suggestion." He looked away from Rion again. "This place is beautiful, but I don't think I'd want to live here."

"I was thinking the same thing," Rion agreed. "The beaches and ocean are nice, but I will always prefer a dense forest."

"For me, it's being landlocked. I enjoy having the freedom to go where I wish." Tolan ran a hand through his dark locks. "The Nereid ability to change forms, though, makes me see the appeal."

"They've good protection, both in location and magical gifts," Rion pointed out. "Besides, they know when ships approach long before the ship can cause any damage."

"You know, I thought Nereid had tails like others Mers." He laughed. "It's stupid to think Nereids have lived with us for so long, and we know so little about them. We just group them in with the other Mers. It's a wonder they put up with us at all."

Rion chuckled and nodded. "I think we lost a lot of what we knew about a great many things when Sargarus was on the throne. By the Mother, I don't even think humans with magic still know how to fully use their powers."

"There were rumors Sargarus burned books about other races and religions. I never investigated it though—didn't care enough to. I rather regret that now." Tolan gave Rion a wry grin.

Rion narrowed his brow. "If he did, it was well after I joined the guard, and Joss never mentioned it. In the days after Sargarus died, she was quite intent on figuring out exactly what measures he'd taken about a variety of atrocities." He motioned back toward the palace. "As you see, she became enraged over the treatment of Nereid."

"Enraged is an understatement," Tolan said wryly. "Honestly, Sargarus committed so many atrocities and claimed so many others, it's difficult to know what's real. Even being allowed here speaks to all Collette has done to atone. So many would have never forgiven us for any of it." He shook his head, sighing. "I should go see if Collette is free." The reluctance in his voice did not hide the determination in his eyes.

"You should," Rion agreed. "She's smart, even with the hurt you caused. She knows it's better to move forward with civility."

"It is," Tolan agreed. "I'm going to try finding her. Thank you for sparring with me earlier."

"You needed the distraction," Rion replied with a shrug.

"I did but still—thank you."

Rion nodded. "Of course. Good luck."

Tolan nodded his head once in farewell and walked briskly back to the castle.

# Chapter Seven

Tolan spent the rest of the day keeping track of Collette. As he'd suspected, the queen kept a busy schedule, first at the temple followed by a tour of the gardens and city with Ceto as her guide. He kept a close watch, looking for any opportunity to approach his former love, all the while learning about the people and place.

By evening, the others had wandered off, even Larent who'd been sent away with a kiss and a laugh before her appointment at the temple. Tolan grew hopeful at finally finding time to talk, and he approached her, careful to make enough noise she'd hear him coming.

Collette sat on a bench, ankles crossed in front of her, her carob hair hanging in front of her face as she looked down. A pang formed in his chest as he remembered lazy mornings, running his fingers through those locks. He'd accepted he would never again have the opportunity.

She glanced up, hearing his steps, and her initial reaction told him she'd been waiting for someone. The slight frown which appeared upon seeing him more than informed Tolan she was no happier seeing him now than she had been since his return. "Yes?" she asked him.

Tolan almost faltered for a moment, his first instinct to turn around and go, but he marshaled his courage and took the next step forward. "If you have a moment, I was hoping we could talk."

"What do you want to talk about?" she asked him. Collette uncrossed her ankles and sat up straighter. She didn't sound angry, but she spoke with a tired disinterest—which was somehow worse.

"I would like to know what I can do, other than offer a sincere apology for the hurt I've caused you. I want to make things, if not right, then better between us," Tolan said, even as he internally winced at his wording.

Collette looked down again, and Tolan struggled to stay silent. Knowing her as he did, he knew she was struggling with what she was willing to say and show him. Another sign of how distant they now were.

"I don't know what you want me to say, Tolan. I have tried, very hard, to be fair to you. To treat you civilly. To not beat the shit out of you when every part of me thinks you deserve it."

"I'm hoping we can work past everything, because if you think threatening to have Arian throw me overboard for approaching you is civil, then we do need to at least move forward before my cousin arrives," Tolan pointed out.

She shrugged. "Given what Arian wishes to do to you, I thought my plan was kinder." She sighed and finally looked at him, her brown eyes focused in a way they had not since he'd left. "What you did was shitty."

Tolan closed his eyes for a moment. He could picture what Arian wanted to do and decided he would need to talk to the other elf before Arian decided to enact one of his plans.

Opening his eyes, he looked at Collette. "Shitty is too subtle a word for what I did."

"Perhaps," Collette agreed. She shifted on the bench, crossing her legs into a more comfortable position. She was fidgeting. She never fidgeted. "What exactly did I do, or not do, to make you feel like leaving in the middle of the night without a word was such a good idea?"

Tolan opened his mouth to answer with a quick denial, one she wouldn't accept and Rion had advised him against. Instead, he took a moment to find what he hoped were the right words.

"I left because of me. I let my insecurities get the best of me. I allowed the words of others to affect how I saw myself, my self-worth, and my worth to you."

"You give a very rehearsed answer," Collette replied.

"Not rehearsed, just thought out." Tolan did his best to keep eye contact with Collette as he went on. "Rion doesn't accept bullshit. He says me blaming anyone but myself and my faults for leaving is bullshit, and he's right. I can blame Larent, Arian, or the circumstances, but at the end of the day, I could have ignored it all or made a smarter decision. I just didn't."

"When Rion left me, he had the balls to tell me why," Collette replied.

Tolan nodded, hating how much he had contributed to the substantial losses Collette suffered. "I know," he said quietly. "He's explained his reasons and how he handled walking away compared to the choices I made from insecurity and jealousy."

Collette let out a sigh. "Do you know why it was so easy to get close to Larent?"

"Why?" Tolan asked, resisting the urge to cross his arms. He didn't particularly want to hear why Larent had become her confidante, but if she wanted to take the conversation there, he would follow her lead.

"He just let me breathe," Collette replied.

"And I didn't?" Tolan asked, realizing too late how Collette had meant her words.

"Not since we left Quenall, no," Collette said. She leaned forward, resting her elbows on her thighs, her hands clasped together. "Everyone had all of these expectations of me when we left. I was supposed to remain strong and stoic as I rallied an unbeatable force for some. Others thought I was going to fall apart and need my hand held while I was pulled through the countryside. I never seemed to be doing what everyone else expected of me, no matter what I did, and unfortunately, you were the most obvious with your displeasure." She shook her head. "And I just kept trying to make you happy, despite everything else falling apart around me."

Tolan took in her words, mentally reviewing his actions, trying to see it from her point of view. At the time, he felt he'd been supportive, especially at the beginning, despite his petty and stupid interactions with Larent. Given the context of her experience, he could see where he had come off as pushy and upset at her. "I meant to be supportive, not suffocating," he explained. "My displeasure was not at you but more Larent for what I saw as stealing your time. I felt you were going to him for comfort instead of me. But it was more he just let you be."

She nodded. "As I said, Larent just let me breathe and exist without expectation or obligation. I could just relax and feel what I was feeling. I needed the time and space to work through things. I still do."

Tolan couldn't help his retort. "Sometimes the people in charge don't get the time they wish. They just have to deal with the immediate problems and sort their feelings later, especially when people's lives are on the line." He regretted the words immediately.

Collette stared at him for a long moment, her lips together, but otherwise her expression was mostly neutral. "Perhaps it's a good thing you left before if you think I don't deserve to be able to take care of myself while also doing everything I can to help my people. Maybe you're too self-absorbed to comprehend this, but I cannot fight for anything if I am not in the right mental and physical state to take on those burdens. Expecting me to be perfect or able to face anything under any circumstance is beyond ridiculous."

"I don't expect you to be perfect, but I had been hoping—" Tolan's words stopped short as he felt a knife against his back.

"Finish your thought, and I will remove your kidneys," Arian growled from behind him.

"Arian," Collette said, a gentle warning, or perhaps request, for the elf to stand down.

Arian obeyed, though he did not put away his weapon to retreat very far. Tolan knew he was testing his patience.

Collette unfolded her legs, rose from the bench, and approached Tolan and Arian, though she left about a foot of space "I shouldn't have to spell out what I have been through. In one day, I was overthrown, subjected to arrest to save the life of another person, and I lost my brother who marched down to the castle prison to mock me for the arrest. All of this happened before we even left Quenall. I mourn the loss of my brother to this day because there is no recovering what Zephraim and I once shared. I grieve the lost lives which resulted from my overthrow."

She paused and took a deep breath, as though trying to will herself into a more tranquil mindset. "Then I find myself on the road with three virtual strangers and two people I love more than anything, none of whom I want to get hurt because of me. I get to decide if we march over the mountains as winter approaches, condemning us to the high probability of freezing to death, or going into Azmarin where I know I have angered the reigning monarch by breaking our betrothal. While there, I

get subjected to subtle and not-so-subtle digs about the decision while I try to stroke your ego to the point of letting you assault me in a way I would have never allowed before and figure out the next steps. Then at the end of it, I'm subjected to a tirade about the ownership King Brath believes he has over me, all the while knowing if I were less physically capable, he'd have violated me before anyone got in the room."

She crossed her arms in a protective stance and let out a laugh as she shook her head. "Failure in Azmarin meant we had to figure out where we were staying for the winter. Then while we are on the road, you abandon me without a word. So, not only do I still get to march forward, trying to figure out how I'm supposed to fight for my kingdom, I also have to determine how to keep myself just moving, and that's before I nearly bled to death. Since then, we've all been forced to openly admit I have no birthright to the throne I'm fighting for because my actual father is a farmer from Galel. I'm also not fully human, which adds to the obviousness of my lack of connection to Sargarus. You brought Rion with you when you came back, which just reminds me of more loss over my inability to be perfect for someone else. I don't want the fucking job of queen to begin with, and you expect me to be okay? To be perfect?"

She shook her head again, letting her arms fall back to her sides. "I am not okay, Tolan. I have not been okay since before I left Quenall, but I will say this. When it comes down to it, I have made the best choices I could in every situation. I got arrested so Jayden could escape. I put up with Brath because it was the safest option we had at the time. I got punched in the fucking mouth by Riken so the prisoners in the labor camp had the opportunity to escape. I have stepped up and made the right choice, as a queen, when it has mattered. So, I am not getting the time I wish I could have. I *am* dealing with the immediate problems we face, and it's still not good enough for you."

# Chapter Seven

Tolan stared at Collette, letting her words settle in his mind. He wanted to formulate an appropriate response, but somehow, he knew he'd have to ruminate on her experiences and perspectives before he said something appropriate. Arian must have realized he would offer nothing substantive because he felt the press of the knife against his back once again.

"Nod your head and leave. If you truly want to apologize and put yourself as an acquaintance instead of a nuisance we are forced to deal with, you may consult with Rion and make an appointment to speak with our queen."

Collette shook her head. "It doesn't matter, Arian. I fail to live up to whatever standard Tolan has decided on."

"I doubt any of us do," Arian growled out, pulling his dagger back and pushing Tolan away.

Tolan caught himself, straightening his posture, and turned to object. He hadn't meant to imply expected perfection, but he realized he'd demonstrated the expectation all the same. Still, he kept his thoughts to himself when he caught Arian's expression. "I'm sorry. This isn't how I wanted the conversation to go. I'll see you later." Tolan didn't give either time to respond. Instead, he abruptly turned around and retreated.

Tolan sat down hard on the stone bench, burying his head in his hands. Every time he tried to approach Collette, he said the wrong thing, did the wrong thing. She wasn't taking what he said the wrong way, but he wasn't expressing himself correctly or even looking at the situation the way he should be. No, he always focused on himself and how he had been hurting when he left, all the while implying his decision had been her fault when it very much wasn't.

Tolan sat there, wallowing in his failures, when he felt someone take a seat next to him. He dropped his hands, expecting to see Rion next to him. Instead, he saw Larent.

The russet-haired man didn't look at him, didn't acknowledge Tolan gaping at him. Instead, they sat there in silence for several minutes, Larent not once looking at him before finally breaking the silence.

"You run when things start to get too complicated, too messy, too much, because you don't know how to handle it. It's a pattern. You've done it to me and Collette. You may have done it to someone else before us." Larent shrugged as if the answer didn't really matter. "You need to start by acknowledging your tendency to run and keep the realization in mind next time you talk to Collette. You should also be honest and admit you considered hitting the road well before we ever left Quenall."

"I didn't—" Tolan insisted.

"You did," Larent replied evenly. "When you realized how complicated her life was growing, you know you questioned the wisdom in sticking around. You can't convince me otherwise." Larent finally looked at Tolan. "Admit to her, and yourself, she's not the reason you fled. Her actions and her choices are not at fault. You are a fucking coward who never learned to deal with his feelings and emotions, and you've spent your entire life running from one thing to the next. I'm not making a judgment here—just stating facts."

He shrugged again and continued, "Obviously, you intended to come back this time, but you still ran. I'm not sure if she's even convinced you planned on returning. The good news from Fythias might have all been a coincidence. She actually hasn't shared all of her thoughts with me just yet. Either way, you should have stood strong beside her and supported her because you loved her and trusted her judgment. If you can admit as much to Collette, maybe you can start working toward friend-ship again."

Tolan once more felt his mouth drop open before anger started rising to the surface. How dare Larent sit there and tell him how he felt? How dare he assume he knew Tolan well enough to throw out such assumptions? As quickly as the anger rose, it dissipated. He slumped forward again. Larent was right. Over the years, Tolan had broken off from the group numerous times, the latest driven by jealousy and insecurity.

"Why?" Tolan finally asked.

"Why what?" Larent raised an eyebrow.

"Why are you helping me?"

"Because helping you will, in the long run, help Collette. Every time you approach her, she gets hurt, and I'm not okay with it. She holds the weight of possibility on her shoulders when it comes to you. The weight of what could have been, of why you left, of why she wasn't good enough for you. I remember holding the very same weight when you left me, and it ate me from the inside out for a very long time. If I can take the burden from her shoulders, I will. Don't get me wrong. I don't like you, even if I've forgiven you for what happened between us. I do love her, though. So…" Larent shrugged and stood. "Just take my advice and stop being stupid."

His opinion voiced, Larent strolled away, not letting Tolan say anything else.

# Chapter Eight

Collette watched Tolan leave, half wondering what he might have said without Arian's intervention. Part of her was thankful Arian had been nearby. She knew he was unhappy with Tolan's choices, though he'd avoided doing any real damage to the other man since his return. Still, she had a nagging suspicion she and Tolan were going to circle one another in a state of uncertainty until they had a real discussion.

Letting out a breath, she looked at Arian. "Did you lock Thomas in your room for the evening?" she asked, deferring to happier and more humorous topics.

"I considered it if only to keep him out of Jayden's path. However, Nawalya has taken to hovering around the corridor to our room, so I thought it best I give her no reason to break the lock," Arian explained.

Collette gave him a weak smile. "Thomas has eyes for you alone, no matter what Jayden says or does. I think you have nothing to worry about."

"I know I do not, but it has been fun to mildly frighten Jayden," Arian informed her before stopping and looking

Collette over. "I will offer this freely one time. Would you like a hug?"

"I would," Collette confirmed. She knew she must appear absolutely defeated after the discussion with Tolan for Arian to make the offer, but she wasn't going to worry about pulling herself together just yet.

Arian's lips twisted into a knowing smile as he opened his arms to her. Collette did not hesitate to walk into his embrace, and she hugged him back, thankful beyond reason she had people who unselfishly cared about and for her in moments when she felt lowest.

Arian wrapped her tightly in his arms, holding Collette without making her feel trapped or caged in, his chin resting on her shoulder as he pulled her close. She remained for several long moments, only pulling away when she felt as though Arian had reached his limits of toleration. "Thank you," she said. "I needed that after Tolan's bullshit."

"I thought you might." In an uncharacteristic move, Arian nudged her shoulder. "It will not happen again."

The gesture brought out a smile, small though it was. "Is he completely selfish or just stupid? I genuinely can't tell anymore."

"Stupid," Arian answered after a few moments. "Stupid with a lot of self-doubt and self-loathing mixed in for good measure. It is a bad combination all around."

"He needs to get his shit together, either way," Collette said. "And I need to stop worrying about him."

"It is okay to worry about him. It is a habit for you and will take time to break. There is nothing wrong with it," Arian told Collette as they began walking toward the temple.

"Perhaps," she reluctantly agreed. "Perhaps it would be more accurate to say I shouldn't have to worry about him pointing out his perception of my failures every time he decides to speak to me."

"I do not think he possessed such intentions, though I do not honestly know what his intentions actually were."

Collette shrugged, looking at the careful path leading to the temple. High lanterns flickered on as the sun set beneath the horizon. A pinkish cast fell across the path, once again reminding her of the beauty of the island. "Either way, I have a Marking to face and little time to focus on him."

Arian looked over at Collette as they walked, his expression mostly relaxed except for the set of his jaw. "The little research I have been able to do today tells me Marking can be uncomfortable or even painful, but they have a numbing solution made from one of their underwater plants should you need it. I also read some find the Marking process calming," Arian explained, his eyes alight with interest.

"Are we going to have to leave you and Thomas here once everything is settled?" Collette asked, lightly teasing him. Arian's interest held no surprise. He'd voiced a desire to learn more since arriving, and he'd taken the opportunity. She could hardly blame him.

"Not at all, but I may try and convince him to visit."

"I don't think Thomas will take much convincing. He'd follow you anywhere and do anything as long as he got to be with you," Collette replied.

"I still think it foolish at times, but then, I feel the same," Arian admitted.

As they reached the bottom of the temple, Collette drew to a stop. "You realize Thomas put himself in danger well before he ever met you, right?"

"Do not remind me," Arian said as he looked up at the temple. "Sometimes I worry he has no sense of self-preservation."

"He's smart, and he managed to survive the overthrow long enough to meet up with us after we left Azmarin," Collette reminded Arian. "He's able to handle himself long enough to get away from the most pressing danger."

"I know. I know he is capable, intelligent, kind, and he will use his words to get out of any situation he can." Arian pressed his lips together in genuine worry for several long minutes before continuing. "When we first met, however, some of the guards had him cornered and were going to teach him a lesson for speaking against you." He rolled his eyes, letting Collette know how much he loathed the tale. "Thomas decided to taunt them."

"I believe I've heard the story," Collette said, nodding in understanding. "But as someone who recently allowed another person to assault me for very good reasons, I can understand him choosing to mouth off over the alternatives."

"I understand why he did it, even if I did not at the time. I was just as unhappy then as I was when I saw Riken hit you. Just because it is the best thing you could have done at the moment, the smartest thing you could have done, does not mean I have to like it."

"I have a feeling there will be many things you don't like in the coming weeks," she replied. She honestly felt the same. War would inevitably arise, and people she cared about would step onto the battlefield without the promise of survival.

"You could probably get away with locking Thomas away."

Arian shook his head. "No, I do not think I could. He would view it as a lack of trust, both in his ability to keep himself safe and his personal choices."

"Then continue to exercise the good judgment I know you possess," Collette advised. "And now, it is time to be Marked." They began the climb up the steps leading to the open-air room, the pale stone shimmering beneath the darkening sky.

"I was able to look through a few of the genealogy books with the help of the librarian, and I believe I found some information you would be interested in," Arian said.

"Oh?" Collette asked.

"It looks as if your mother's family did visit the Nereid some generations back, and they went home with more family members than they arrived with. I can show you the books when we have more time if you want to confirm my finding," Arian offered.

"I do want to look, but not because I doubt you," Collette replied, looking back up at the temple with some curiosity.

"Nervous?" he asked Collette as they ascended the steps.

She considered the question, surveying her feelings, and nervousness didn't seem to belong. "No. Not really. I think I'm still surprised to hear the Nereid think I'm worthy of something they find to be a high honor."

"Why?" Arian asked, his voice growing softer as they got closer to the top. "You have put yourself in danger twice to save their people and your own."

"I did, but those actions don't wipe away the harm they suffered at the hands of Sargarus."

"They do not. Nothing can, but you are trying. You are making efforts to improve lives, and those efforts are meaningful," Arian pointed out.

"Doing the right thing shouldn't warrant honor just because other people fail in kindness," Collette replied. The top of the steps led them back into the open-air room of the temple, though fewer people wandered about, making for a more serene visit than earlier.

"From my reading today, kindness, service to others, and self-sacrifice for unselfish reasons are some of the highest tenets of their belief system and what they strive for as a culture," Arian said. "So, for them, it makes sense."

"Still…" Collette replied, only to be interrupted when Ceto emerged from the inner temple, her bright hair bouncing as she sprinted over to them.

"You're here!" She beamed.

"I am," Collette replied, her excitement rising with Ceto's. "Arian came with me as promised."

"Wonderful. You can observe if you would like," Ceto said, and she linked arms with Collette to lead her into the inner temple. Arian followed behind, silent as he had been earlier in the day. Ceto led the two to another room farther inside the hidden temple, this one pale green and furnished with a cushioned bench. Next to it was a wooden table topped with a pot of an inky black substance, a bottle of something like lotion, and a long, hollow needle.

"You will be there while we do the Marking," Ceto explained. "After we discuss the design and placement, you will get comfortable." She went to the table and picked up the bottle of lotion. "We will put a solution on your skin to help with the discomfort." She put the bottle down and picked up the needle. "And obviously, here is the Marking tool."

Arian took a seat in the corner, out of the way but close enough to observe while Ceto continued explaining the process. It seemed simple enough, though time-consuming and painful, but Collette had suspected as much.

"Will the priestess be joining us?" Collette asked.

Ceto shook her head. "No. I have been allowed to perform the act, both practical and ceremonial. It will just be the three of us. If you are okay with just us."

"I don't see a reason to not be," Collette replied. She took a breath. "So, what does the Marking look like?" she asked.

"Well, the design requires your input. Your Marking technically represents two different acts and nominations. So, you are entitled to two separate Marks." Ceto's smile brightened.

"Some who are being honored with multiple Marks at the same time will combine them into something larger."

"Then let's make it a larger design," Collette decided. Of course, the decision led to another choice. "What would the design be?"

"Good question," Ceto replied, her smile dropping as a more thoughtful expression rose on her features. "Both nominations for Marking involved the Nereid people, so perhaps waves should be present. Waves also serve as an important symbol for our people."

"In what way?" Arian asked.

"Oh, many," Ceto said. She leaned against the bench, her hands moving as she spoke. "Strength, of course. Waves have the ability to conquer. To change worlds. But they can inspire peace and transformation." She smiled, her cheeks flushing, though she concealed her expression by looking down. "I do believe waves represent you well."

Collette nodded. "Then waves," she easily agreed.

"Great," Ceto said, clapping her hands together. "I also think something more should be added. Perhaps something floral."

"I trust you will do something beautiful and meaningful," Collette assured her. "You just tell me what you would like me to do."

"Hmm…" Ceto said as she stood again. "What about your back? The process will be a little more uncomfortable, but I think you would like it."

"Then let's get started," Collette replied.

"Of course," Ceto agreed. She patted the bench. "You'll need to remove your shirt and lay face down on the bench. I'll take care of everything else."

"Okay," Collette said. She glanced at Arian. "If you're staying in here, close your eyes," she directed, although she knew she didn't have to request as much from Arian. She pulled out the tails of her shirt from her trousers, both of which she'd changed into earlier in the afternoon for comfort. After unlacing the top, she pulled it from her body, handing it to Ceto who silently reached for it, her eyes lingering on the long scars on her side left by Larent's claws. Collette then got comfortable on the bench, lying with her back exposed as she had been instructed.

"Oh," Ceto observed as she picked up a bottle from the table. "You have some scarring on your shoulder."

"Yes," Collette replied. "From a riding crop."

"Who would do—" Ceto began.

"Sargarus," Collette replied. "After I refused to enter a betrothal. I have a matching scar on my forearm." Collette could not see Ceto's expression, but she felt a brief pause in her movements, a pause corresponding with the low growl issuing from Arian. No doubt he was displeased with the information.

"Would you like me to cover it?" Ceto asked.

Collette didn't immediately know how to answer. A part of her knew there was no covering the past. The scar would exist regardless of the Marking. Another part of her wished to create as much possible distance between herself and the man she would never again call her father. "Yes," she said, finally deciding.

"Okay," Ceto agreed, and she began rubbing a cold, silky substance onto Collette's skin. Her skin tingled momentarily, and Collette realized it was the numbing cream. The bottle clinked dully on the table when Ceto put it down. Collette turned her head, watching with interest as the Nereid woman prepared the hollowed needle. By the time it pressed into her skin, the numbing balm rendered the process almost painless.

# Chapter Nine

Barris sprinted through the castle, keeping an eye out for guards as he went. He hated the idea of leaving, of abandoning the city to the whims of Rhoslyn and Riken, especially when he could contribute. He could spy for Crem and the reinvigorated movement. He could help dismantle the current reign and bring Collette back to power.

Admittedly, Zephraim's melancholy since Rhoslyn's self-appointed rule also had Barris hesitant to leave. Zephraim remained as a figurehead, though he was forced to comply with any order Rhoslyn gave under pain of torture or worse. Zephraim's situation continued deteriorating once Riken returned. The false queen did nothing to hide her relationship with the returned lord, giving mere lip service to the charade of her marriage.

Zephraim dutifully stayed within the boundaries placed on him, or rather, he played up his intention to do as much. Barris could not help but note how he'd dialed back his drinking, how he carefully observed and agreed without doing any actual support. Barris found hope in the subtle change, which was why, instead of leaving the moment Lynessea's brother had appeared

# Chapter Nine

with intel of the Coralian intention to attack the Nereid, he went looking for Zephraim.

Searching the palace took longer than he liked, and Barris was forced to ask Gisela if she had any idea where Zephraim might be. "The library, I think," she said in a quiet, almost childish voice. The poor girl's half-elf status left her looking stressed and tired if the dark circles under her eyes were any indication. Barris had no doubt she was the recipient of criticism and cruelty.

"Thank you," he said genuinely. He would intervene on her behalf as soon as he could.

After ascending several flights of stairs, Barris soon found Zephraim tucked away in a far corner of the large library hidden almost out of sight. Zephraim looked up as Barris approached, the sound of his footsteps alerting him.

Barris gave the king a warm smile, an expression he was sometimes told negated the effects of his dark hair, piercings, and tattoos. He knew the other man could see his smile was laced with strain and slight exhaustion. "Hello, Your Majesty."

The returned smile was briefer and every bit as strained and reserved. "Do I need to bother with the title anymore?"

Barris motioned to the soft tall reading chair close to Zephraim's, and he sat when he was given silent permission. "While your ascension to the throne may have been through less than ideal means, you are more our king than Rhoslyn is our queen."

"I believe the actual queen has been confirmed alive," Zephraim pointed out, leaning back in his chair, his lean frame all the more evident for the movement. "And coming for all of our heads if you hear Riken tell it."

Barris couldn't help the vindictive smile. "I wish Collette had just killed him," Barris confessed, using words he'd only ever uttered to Lynessea.

Zephraim shook his head, rose gold curls swaying. "Collette is many things, but a killer is not one of them, even when it is Riken."

"True, but whatever her reason, we now have two monsters to contend with instead of one." Barris flashed Zephraim a curious look. "If you could leave Quenall, would you?"

"Perhaps," Zephraim said with a shrug. "But we both know I cannot. Not yet."

"Tell me what you're hoping to accomplish by staying?" Barris asked.

"I'm still a figurehead, even with Rhoslyn's silent take-over," Zephraim said plainly. "Her preference for violence and Riken's extremism won't win them support. In the meantime, I hope to mitigate whatever damage I can."

Barris nodded. Zephraim's reasoning made sense because regardless of what Rhoslyn and Riken thought, Riken's guards couldn't force everyone to accept their rule. His growing army was a different matter. Barris studied Zephraim before responding, noting the lines bracketing his eyes and mouth.

Barris sighed, a decision made. As much as he knew Lynessea would hate him, he found himself asking, "Would you like help?"

"What sort of help are you offering?" Zephraim asked, sitting back in his chair and surveying Barris.

"Whatever you need," Barris said, leaning forward and resting his arms on his knees. "A safe place to plan. People to aid you or help keep you safe." He offered the king a genuine smile. "A friend, someone to further buffer you against Rhoslyn and Riken."

Zephraim took some time to answer, his fingertips tapping on the chair arm in random patterns with no discernible rhythm. "If my sister truly plans on returning, I intend to keep things from further breaking down as best I can. Help with keeping Quenall from falling completely will be needed."

Barris leaned closer and looked around, making sure they were still alone. It would be a shame to get arrested now. "I have people who would be willing to help. Spies. Fighters. Friends. Whatever you think you need."

Zephraim looked over at Barris. "What do you have going on?"

"A little of this. A little of that. A lot of treason." He gave Zephraim a bright grin. "It might be best to show you. If you're willing to trust me."

Zephraim let out a breath and nodded. "I might as well. My instincts have proven incorrect up until now. How much worse could it get?"

Barris answered honestly. "Much worse, but what's life without a little risk?" Standing, he offered Zephraim a hand, which the king took.

They left the library, only for Lynessea to join them less than a hundred feet down the corridor. Barris's wife could hardly hide, even in the shadows. She had the vivid gold eyes of the Nereid, and her hair, though mostly black, also held the purple and teal of her shimmering scales. Those scales were further emphasized by her olive skin. She raised her eyebrows after looking at Zephraim. "Do I wish to know?" she asked him sweetly.

"No," Barris said, his joyful expression remaining solid as they walked.

"I've been told to trust him while he shows me the treasonous things he's done," Zephraim explained.

Lynessea took a deep breath and gave Barris an incredulous look before laughing. "They are going to have collective heart attacks."

When the trio arrived at the main hall entrance leading to the bridge into the city, they were thankfully alone. Glancing at Zephraim for a moment, Lynessea gave a delicate shrug before reaching for Barris's hands. "You will earn another tattoo if your plans work out, you know."

Barris rolled his eyes. "I'm not doing anything worthy of one."

"You are bringing someone back to the light," she argued.

Barris shook his head and, leaning down, touched his forehead to hers. "I won't be able to go back with you."

"I know, and I will leave two of my brothers to act as your support, but I must go. I have to warn Aphros."

Barris nodded. "With you goes my heart."

"With you stays my hope," Lynessea replied. They closed their eyes for a second before Barris released her hands and Lynessea was gone. Turning to Zephraim, Barris gave him a sad smile. "Let's go meet my friends."

"Let's," Zephraim agreed, giving the other man a sympathetic smile.

Barris led Zephraim from the castle, pausing as the gate came into view. Pairs of guards stood, marking measured distances along the exit and out onto the bridge. "Think they will ask any questions?"

"As long as they don't think I'm acting against Rhoslyn, they don't pay me much attention."

Barris nodded, finding the lack of concern shown by Rhoslyn interesting. As they passed the first pair of guards, he began a lively discussion which promised a night of merriment. "Which tavern is your favorite?"

Zephraim maintained a practice air of calm indifference, though he smiled as though anticipating a great evening. "I've too many favorites to count," he replied. "Wrenn and I used to frequent one tavern near the outskirts of the city. It always promised a good evening."

Good. A fond mention of Rhoslyn's brother was good. "Well then, I guess we will make merry at all the taverns in town." Barris nodded at the next set of guards, giving them a bright smile which was quickly returned.

They went over the bridge leading into the city, away from the guards without looking back. "You know, they basically pay me no attention these days," Zephraim said quietly after they'd put some distance behind them.

"Truly? I would have thought they would keep a closer eye on you so you didn't cause trouble."

"They think I'm stupid," Zephraim said with a shrug. "I'm not. I've never been."

"I've never considered you stupid," Barris said, but he continued after carefully choosing his words. "I have been surprised by some of your actions over the last year."

Zephraim nodded, not arguing the point. "Looking back, I am as well," he agreed. "Turning my back on Collette, even in my anger and grief... it's unforgivable."

"It's not, but you'll have some work to do." Barris gave Zephraim a wry look. "I doubt there's anything you've done you can't come back from with repentance and good deed. Collette is the forgiving type. Or she was."

"She won't be. Not for my sins," Zephraim said. "Still, I'm not seeking atonement. I'm interested in preventing further damage."

"And I can help you, I hope." As Barris led them farther through town and closer to the caves, he spotted a familiar form heading in the same direction. He wasn't sure at first, but once she lowered the hood of her cloak, there was no mistaking Diana Hawke. "Mistress Hawke!" he called out to get her attention.

Diana looked over her shoulder to Barris, a smile forming as she saw him, though she paused as she spotted Zephraim.

"Lord Barris," she said in a jovial tone. She nodded, giving a small bow to Zephraim. "Your Majesty."

"How serendipitous! I am taking our king to see our friends. Maybe you can head down first and let them know so we don't have any misunderstandings?" Barris suggested as he offered Diana his arm.

Diana gave him a dubious look but shrugged and took the offered arm. "I make no promises on my ability to smooth things over."

"Just let them know I'm bringing him, and I will be displeased with negative reactions." He gave Zephraim an apologetic smile as they walked the rest of the way. Once they reached the hidden entrance, Barris released Diana's arm. "Shall we say five minutes, or would it be best to wait for you to come back?"

"I would wager you're better off waiting," Diana replied.

Barris nodded and let Diana head off into the caves. "So, any questions?" he asked Zephraim as if he wasn't putting lives at risk with his current actions.

Zephraim shook his head. "Without getting specific, I think I can safely put together the gist of what has been going on here. Like I said, I'm not stupid."

"Fair enough," Barris said. "While we wait, you should know Crem didn't kill Lord Elrick," Barris confessed. He chose to not confess he was the actual culprit. Not yet.

"I know," Zephraim replied.

"When did you figure it out?" Barris asked.

"I never thought it very likely he would kill Elrick. Commander Hawke has always been a practical man. Someone who wanted to do as much as he could to bring my sister back on the throne wasn't going to put himself in jail." He shrugged. "Besides, it's not as though everyone believed the circulating story. Elrick disliked many people."

# Chapter Nine

"I have never understood why he hated me. His dislike didn't bother me until he put his hands on my wife." Barris sighed, letting the statement stand on its own.

"I remember you telling me about their encounter," Zephraim replied. "I cannot blame your anger."

"I feel horrible for allowing Crem to take the blame, but they were after him anyway, especially after saving all those people."

Zephraim nodded. "Had he not been pinned with Elrick's death, something else would arise to blame him for. I think Rhoslyn and Riken planned to remove anyone who supported Collette in any meaningful way."

"Very true," Barris agreed. He'd observed the same thing in their actions. "I'm fortunate. She thinks I'm an idiot, and he thinks I'm just like him. I have no idea why."

"Your wife and her family have acted as servants when they have been spotted with you," Zephraim suggested. "Riken would see you living under what he views as the natural order of things."

"So why does Rhoslyn see me as an idiot? I'm not an especially good actor." Barris's question was laced with laughter because he knew the constant beaming smile he wore did much to maintain his reputation.

"Rhoslyn thinks little of men as we've recently been informed."

"Well, except for one." Noise down the tunnel drew Barris's attention. Diana soon reemerged, looking cautious, though optimistic. "How'd they take it?"

"You're invited to bring him down, but I can't promise Howle won't point a sword the entire time," Diana said, crossing her arms.

Barris laughed. "Sounds like Howle." He turned to Zephraim. "You remember Howle, yes?" A nod of confirmation, and Barris was content to move forward. "Diana, if you

would please lead the way, and Zephraim can follow after me." The formation would be the safest for Zephraim, especially if Howle became overzealous.

"Come on, then," Diana replied, and she went back into the caves.

As Barris walked slowly behind Diana, he fingered one of the small, slender knives on his person. He prayed to the Goddess he did not have to use it on one of his allies to protect Zephraim. He nodded to the guard as they passed, noting the tense shoulder and how the young man wouldn't look at them.

Upon entering the main cavern, Barris was only slightly surprised to find only Crem and Howle, the latter of whom did, in fact, have his sword out.

"Well met," Barris said jovially. He joined the others at the makeshift table and took a seat before motioning for Zephraim to take the seat on his left, away from Howle.

"I think ya should save the optimism for after he explains why he's suddenly had a change of heart," Howle said, practically spitting at Zephraim.

"I agree," Crem added. "After everything..." His words trailed off, and the former commander held his hands out.

"You both know he was already having doubts," Diana interjected calmly. "He does have things he should account for, but there's been no sudden change."

Crem nodded, and even though it was obvious Howle didn't want to, he set his sword aside while keeping it within arm's reach.

"We've been hearing rumors about the things your bitch has been doing," Howle said to Zephraim, ignoring the face Barris made at the vulgar words.

"You ought to know they are not rumors, given where both of you currently stand," Zephraim replied.

"We would like to know what your final straw was, given how much has happened," Crem redirected.

"The confirmation of her intent to rule alongside Riken, knowing their extremism was my determining factor," Zephraim replied without excuse or apology. "But I have disliked the way they've handled things for some time."

"And yet, ya allowed them to reopen the labor camps and enslave people until yar lady no longer showed ya affection," Howle bit out.

"Howle!" Crem admonished the larger man.

Zephraim surveyed Howle with a blank expression. "You are mistaken in what I allowed for and what happened," Zephraim said. "I never approved of slavery, and the conditions I agreed to for labor camps were no different than what has traditionally been allowed in our country and elsewhere. People who were found guilty of severe crimes would be sentenced for a specified time, then be set free. I approved of nothing like what Riken implemented."

Howle cackled at Zephraim's answer. "I worked for yar father for a long time. Yes, originally the camps were set up for those found guilty of horrendous crimes. But yar father used them ta hold regular people who did nothin' more than ask questions and those he didn't care for. Ya had to have known Riken would overstep. He worshiped yar father."

"You're not helping, Howle," Diana interjected. "Allowing the camps wasn't the best move, but you cannot hold him accountable for what you deem his intentions. Only for what happened, and how he's willing to help fix the problems we are now faced with." Her lips pressed together, her stern approach to the problem evident in her stance. "It is not in anyone's best interest to pick fights right now."

"Alright, alright." Howle eyed Zephraim. "Yar lucky ta have her on yar side. She's a good woman."

"She is," Zephraim agreed with a nod.

Crem looked down at his hands, then back up at Zephraim. "As Howle's now done with his bit, do you have any questions for us? Anything you want to know?"

"I would like to know what he thinks of Riken slaughtering a village of elves in the name of his kingdom?" Ian asked as he stepped out of one of the alcoves. Barris wasn't quite sure how he'd missed the innkeeper, but then, he'd been too focused on Howle.

"I've heard the rumors but no confirmation," Zephraim admitted. "I have never supported the slaughter of any people, especially when no reason can justify it. If the rumor is true, then those people need aid and justice."

"Your sister gave the survivors their freedom. Lord Riken decided to take a handful of adults and all the children to the camps and burn the rest alive. Aid is being given to the survivors by Pontus Bay," Ian informed Zephraim.

"Lynessea told me as much," Barris confirmed. "But surely more can be done and will need doing over time."

"It will," Zephraim replied, quiet but firm. "Before the overthrow, Collette had been providing different types of aid to people who had been massacred decades prior. It will take generations before some groups can even begin to recover."

"If they ever can," Diana added. "Your desire to assist shows some understanding of the deep level of pain so many have suffered. We must prevent more, and we have to return Queen Collette to her rightful place."

"We also have to make sure her reign is secure. She cannot have the Crobáns and Almeidas of the world in her court," Zephraim replied.

"Considerin' how many nobles have died since this one took the throne, one would think if we sowed more discontent, the whole corrupt lot would take itself out," Howle said.

Crem's eyes narrowed in thought. "How many nobles have died since you took the throne?" he asked Zephraim directly. "I can only think of six with Lady Elrick dead."

"Death isn't unheard of with nobility. Not at least in the last several decades," Zephraim replied. Many died under Sargarus, though fewer had died under Collette. "But, yes. I'd say six confirmed."

"I'm surprised only six have died," Barris said as he contemplated the situation. "I don't think we can currently do anything about the nobility, not unless we can appeal to those who are more neutral in their standing. Given how many live outside of Quenall, reaching out to them would only put Zephraim in danger."

"Attention should be focused on rallying the common people, at least for now," Ian interrupted. "The nobility are important, and their armies will be needed. For now, though, the people of Coralia hold more collective power."

"You've been rallying people in Galel," Diana said to Ian. "What is happening in Branlin and Myrefall?"

Crem looked over at the map. "I haven't heard anything from Branlin, though I haven't really asked. The rumors out of Myrefall say the political leanings are a mixed bag with some people supporting the new rulers and others not." He looked over to Zephraim to see if the king knew more.

"Branlin has been mostly silent, though the prevailing theory suggests they follow Galel's example. I think they have a decent relationship with the Nereid people, so their behavior follows expectations. Myrefall has traditionally followed the path of Quenall," Zephraim added.

Barris eyed the group. "It will take a little while, but I can send out a letter asking about Branlin's relationship with the Nereids. See what other news I can gather. The rest of you will have to figure out Myrefall. I have no contacts there."

"We know a few people who moved on to positions in Myrefall after Sargarus died," Diana said. "I'd hesitate to speak with them, though. Who knows where their loyalties lie."

Crem brought a hand up and rubbed the bridge of his nose. "I can reach out to some people in Branlin as well. It's been a while, but they might write back."

Barris noted Crem's reluctance, deciding to wait until a later time to ask.

"Then we have a start," Diana said, despite the amount of work before them. "For now, what do we need Zephraim doing while maintaining his current position of being ignored?"

Barris looked at Zephraim, studying the other man for a moment. "Exactly what he's been doing. Rhoslyn can't keep him out of most of her meetings, and she especially can't keep him from the council meetings. If you're alright with it, you could listen, watch, and report anything of use or interest."

"He could also get us a list of guards and guard rotations for the prison. We are going to have to handle the issue of a certain prisoner sooner rather than later," Ian pointed out.

Barris nodded, knowing Sara Whyldon remained locked up within the palace walls.

"I won't be able to ask for the rota outright," Zephraim replied. "But I will do what I can to work over the hurdle."

"Don't put yourself in too much danger," Crem said, surprising Barris. Diana put a hand on Crem's shoulder, squeezing it in what appeared to be approval. She genuinely liked Zephraim.

"I won't," Zephraim replied, his own eyes wide. "There are those in the palace who can get information on my behalf without alerting Rhoslyn and Riken."

"Use them if you can, but be careful. As idealistic as it sounds, I don't want anyone hurt. If you can't safely get information, we'll figure something else out," Crem said with a decisive nod, though he reached up and put his hand on top of Diana's.

Howle gave a soft, almost caustic, laugh. "Losin' people will come soon enough. Crem's right. Let's try ta limit the number of casualties for as long as we can. Besides, yar useful."

"I will keep it in mind," Zephraim promised.

"Good," Diana said, and she looked to Barris. "You two need to go get spotted in a tavern somewhere before going back to the palace."

Barris gave Zephraim a sheepish grin. "You'll get to do most of the drinking. I'm not allowed more than two a night." Barris stood and offered Zephraim a hand up. When both men were on their feet, Barris gave a silent wave to the others, and they headed back toward the cave entrance.

# Chapter Ten

Rhoslyn stretched, her limbs curling slightly, then straightening as she relaxed. She made no effort to leave the bed, deciding she was in no rush to leave the comfortable warmth. Her cinnamon hair pooled around her, contrasting brightly against the pale sheets and her fair skin. She turned her gaze to the right, green eyes taking in the handsome features of Riken.

Despite her initial anger upon his return, she could not deny missing him. His failures in Galel aside, Riken still represented the best Coralia had to offer in men. Handsome and clever, he matched her wit and drive, and his absence had been felt. Even now, after he'd been in reach for weeks, she still craved him, feeling half-starved for his affections from his stay in Galel.

"You continue to please," she observed.

"I live to please you," Riken responded easily, reaching out a hand to stroke her delicate jaw. "I would forfeit my life rather than displease you ever again."

She believed his words, despite how much Riken had lost in his confrontation with Collette. Riken was many things, but he was never truly deceitful, especially with her. "I know," she replied.

"The Mother has blessed me in so many ways, but none more than when she made you." Riken leaned over and kissed her gently, his movement careful of his bad leg, she noted. He was always careful with it and would likely have to be for the rest of his life.

"Are you certain there is nothing more to be done by a healer?" she asked when the kiss broke.

Riken shook his head. "The last two healers are at a loss at how a simple kick from someone Collette's size caused so much damage. They considered rebreaking the knee and starting over with treatment, but they don't have much hope it will work." Riken sighed and settled back, obviously discouraged by his new reality. "One of their assistants asked if Collette was simply strong enough to cause an injury, rather than the working theory of getting an exceptionally lucky shot. Both masters threw him out of the room for it." Riken let out a soft huff of air. "There's another healer I can speak with, but so far they've all said the same thing."

"If you think it is worth pursuing, then speak to the healer. If not, focus on moving forward," Rhoslyn suggested.

"Cadan wants me to keep trying, but I am ready to move past my injury. I can live with the pain. I can work through it. I would rather move forward with your plans for our kingdom, with you." Riken's eyes shined with sincerity. Resigning from further pursuit would leave him with a limp and in pain, but he'd emphasized, time and again, his view on the importance of their plans.

"I think we can focus on our plans, but we shall keep watch for possible relief," Rhoslyn replied. She shifted to her side so they could talk and so Riken had to put in less physical effort. "We've gained so much ground in righting Coralia, in removing ridiculous barriers. However, when an opportunity arises to better your current state of health, you should take it."

"Then I will keep my eyes and ears open for any opportunities. I will say, though I agree with almost everything King Sargarus did during his rule, I do wish he had kept the magic healers alive. They would have been useful in healing my knee if nothing else," Riken replied with a laugh. "What plans do you have for the day?" His hand moved to stroke her side in gentle, barely there touches.

"Azmarin wants to negotiate an alliance," Rhoslyn shared, her mind wandering to the light touches rather than her work. "They've reports of movement out of Fythias."

"Good. I was worried we would have to remind them who their allies were in the wake of their king's death. It's a good sign they're pulling their kingdom together so quickly." Riken let his hand trail down to her stomach. "What movements are they reporting?" he asked, his voice laced with concern.

"Nothing concrete as of the last report," Rhoslyn replied, her eyes briefly dipping down to his hand and back up. "But there are rumors they may send an army to the Nereid-occupied islands."

"We may need to move up any plans to take the Nereid kingdom then, especially with *her* there," Riken said, his voice becoming firmer, even as his touch remained gentle.

"We have to solidify things with Azmarin first," Rhoslyn insisted. "Especially when we know we'll get pushback from those along the eastern coast. Barris won't be happy, to start."

"Barris will be fine with it in the end. He may be kind to his servants, but he wants what's best for the kingdom as well. I'll talk to him and prepare him for what will inevitably come. You are right, though. We should wait and make sure we have more support behind us for such a push," Riken conceded.

Rhoslyn nodded, happy he had been swayed into seeing her viewpoint. War would come, as it always did, but she was optimistic. "With any luck, Fythias will give away their intentions, and our people will want to strike before they do."

"Should we release the news of Fythias' movement? Maybe if we get ahead of them, we can control the narrative better. Fear always helps to bolster the numbers in an army," Riken said as his hand moved lower down her stomach.

"If we can be discreet about it, I think it would be more effective," Rhoslyn replied. "What do you think?"

"I think I can send some people out to spread rumors at the local taverns. It should help start the process."

Rhoslyn smiled and kissed him. "Then you have a task to oversee."

"What is your plan with Whyldon's sister?" Riken asked as his hand slipped down between Rhoslyn's legs.

Rhoslyn closed her eyes, her mind now entirely focused on something other than politics and strategy. She took a breath, trying to right herself a bit. "She needs to be questioned."

"Should I send Cadan to do so, or do you have someone else in mind? You should know Cadan is very good at getting information." Riken's tone could almost be taken as smug, though Rhoslyn wasn't too concerned.

"Whatever you think will yield the best results," she breathed.

"Cadan would be the best option then." Riken slipped two fingers inside of her, causing her to gasp. "How did your meetings with the lords go yesterday?" he asked casually.

"I don't want to talk about lords and meetings right now," Rhoslyn replied as one of her hands curled into the bedding.

"Are you sure? There is so much to go over, after all."

She let out a breathy laugh. "I don't want to talk about your soldiers, or my prisoners, or some fat lord sweating in the spring sunlight while your fingers are buried in me, Riken."

"Well then, we can talk business later." Riken moved closer, kissing Rhoslyn. "Let us enjoy our morning."

# Chapter Eleven

Nawalya waited at the end of the corridor with an impatience she didn't often feel for Arian to leave his and Thomas's shared room. She knew she could just go and talk to Thomas now, but she really did not want to discuss her questions with Arian around. After many conversations about allowing her to figure out her own problems, she didn't think anything would be helped by asking for help in front of Arian.

She'd apologized to Whyldon before leaving Barcomb Mill, but beyond occasional civil, though stilted, discussions about their mission, they were no closer to friendship. Nawalya knew she needed to approach Whyldon first because she had been the one to screw everything up.

Finally, after what felt like forever, the door to Arian and Thomas's room opened and Arian emerged with Thomas following him to the doorframe. They exchanged a cute temporary goodbye, something Nawalya found hilarious as she never thought she'd consider anything involving Arian cute. Knowing it was a possibility Arian could have forgotten something, though unlikely, and return, she waited another fifteen minutes before finally approaching and knocking on the bedroom door.

# Chapter Eleven

The movement inside the room informed her Thomas had risen to answer, and when the door opened, the ink stains on his fingers told her he'd been writing. "Hi Nawalya," Thomas greeted.

"Hello Thomas," Nawalya replied, her voice firmer than she intended to hide her nervousness.

"What can I help you with?" he asked. "Unless you're looking for Arian. He's already left."

"I was hoping to talk to you. I need some advice," Nawalya said with a small grimace. Perhaps she'd been mistaken in coming to see Thomas.

"Then come in, and I'll try to give you advice," Thomas said. He stepped out of the door frame so Nawalya could pass.

Nawalya took a steadying breath as she entered the room. "Thank you. I know you're busy." She motioned to his ink-stained fingers.

"I usually am," Thomas replied as he closed the door behind them. He strolled back into the room, taking a seat in one of the cozy chairs by the desk. "What sort of advice did you need?"

Nawalya's lips twisted, and she looked away from Thomas for a moment. "I don't know how to become friends with Whyldon." Her statement didn't encompass half of what she wanted to talk about concerning Whyldon, but it seemed like a good start.

"The two of you barely speak," Thomas replied, surveying Nawalya. "I believe speaking to be a crucial part of friendship."

"I don't—" Nawalya took a deep breath. "I don't know where to start," she admitted.

Thomas nodded, then looked across the room, staring at no discernible point, an action Nawalya observed in Thomas when he felt thoughtful or contemplative. "There are two possibilities, I think," he finally said.

"What would those be?" she asked, trying to sound neither too impatient nor too hopeful.

"You either be direct about wanting to establish a friendly relationship, or you start engaging him more frequently as the opportunity presents itself."

Nawalya blinked, finding the provided options far too simple. Still, Thomas was intelligent, so she forced herself to consider the suggestions. "He would more than likely appreciate the direct approach."

"Whyldon is a direct person," Thomas acknowledged. "Honestly, though, he's not exactly intimidating until he puts his mind to it. And given intentions on both sides to see Collette back on the throne, you should be in communication."

"We are talking when necessary," Nawalya admitted. "I would like it to be more often. I apologized at Sara's, but I don't feel like it was enough."

"His anger was fresher then," Thomas said. He offered her a reassuring smile. "Whyldon is a practical man, though. He will understand the necessity of becoming friends again."

Nawalya made a face again. "I don't want him to talk to me out of necessity, but I think I must take what I can get." She flexed her hands lest she ball them into fists. "Anything else I should take into consideration?" she asked softly.

Thomas crossed his legs, settling his hands on his knee. "I think part of your problem is your desire to skip over the toughest parts of reconciliation." His words might have been harsh, but nothing about his tone or the genuine affection on his face suggested anything unkind.

"Doesn't everyone?" Nawalya asked, though she wasn't truly looking for an answer.

"People do, but I think you've let your hesitation fester out of the desire to avoid conflict. The necessity of friendship may not be ideal, but it is better than nothing. And necessity can turn into something more."

What "more" meant, Nawalya wasn't sure. She could just barely admit to herself she wasn't sure what she wanted or could reasonably expect. "I will try and go from there."

"At least you have something resembling a plan now," Thomas pointed out. "You started with less."

She did, and even with the lingering uncertainty, she would leave Thomas and Arian's space with some direction. "Thank you, Thomas. I will let you get back to your writing." Nawalya gave him a small smile and moved toward the door.

"I fear Arian may take my ink and pen away before long," Thomas said with a chuckle. "It shall be an interesting few moments when it happens."

Nawalya paused as she reached the door and laughed. "Kiss him if he tries. The few times I've seen you kiss him, even just on the cheek, it seems to give him pause."

"Well, of course. I will use whatever tools I have at my disposal," Thomas said.

The smile grew on Nawalya's face. "I am sure you do not need me to tell you that you are the only weapon you need against Arian, but I will wish you luck anyway."

"Thank you," Thomas said. He rose from the table, leaving behind his writing supplies, and crossed the room to Nawalya. When he spoke, no hesitation or nervousness showed. "I know it must be hard, being so closely knit to the things we've been dealing with and knowing the distance remains between yourself and Whyldon."

"It has not been easy, but I just keep moving forward." She shrugged because it wasn't like she had a choice. Well, she did, but Nawalya wasn't going to walk away. The mission was so much larger than her.

"I think moving forward is often the best choice, even if it is difficult."

Nawalya nodded mutely, his words only confirming what she'd been thinking for weeks now.

"You have friends and support," Thomas reminded her gently. "Every single one of us is struggling with something. We're all getting through those struggles because we have people we can rely on."

Nawalya blinked. "What are you struggling with? Other than Arian?"

"Arian, I assure you, has never been a struggle," Thomas replied with a gentle laugh. "And for those things counting as struggle… Well, I'll keep those to myself for now."

Nawalya nodded. She understood. However, she was now faced with an understanding of how much of a stranger Thomas still was to her. She would need to rectify the state of their relationship.

"I suppose I will see you later, then?" Thomas asked.

"If you're not busy, yes," Nawalya replied. "Good luck with Arian." She slipped out the door, no closer to knowing what to say to Whyldon but having a better idea of where to start.

# Chapter Twelve

Fythian ships appeared on the horizon early the next morning, prompting Aphros, Collette, and their collective entourages to gather to greet the newly arrived royal. Mere weeks had passed since Collette's ship docked in the harbor, though she'd been kept so busy, her time in the Nereid Kingdom felt like hours.

"What should I know?" she asked Aphros as figures in the distance descended a gangplank. They would be the royal party, and the soldiers on other ships would disembark from their ships over the next several hours.

"Nothing you would not already know," Aphros replied. "When you were arrested, Fythias made no official decrees, and they have not recognized Zephraim as the Coralian king. Your position remains validated by the decision."

"A benefit," Collette replied.

"More than a benefit," Aphros said. "Two kingdoms officially backing you will hopefully bring more support."

Collette nodded. Although the challenges of the coming battles couldn't be escaped, they would, she thought, be heavily favorable to her ultimate goals.

She turned her attention back toward the Fythian royal party, identifying the man leading the groups as King Alaoin.

Alaoin bore no resemblance to Tolan beyond deeply tanned skin, surprising Collette. *Cousins*, she thought, *must surely share some resemblance*. The Fythian king was leaner, and as he drew closer, she took in his heavily hooded blue eyes, giving him an appearance of perpetual exhaustion. His hair, a golden blonde, was shaggy and arranged messily, as though intentional. Even his warm smile spoke of a casualness not usually displayed by royalty within official meetings. Collette found herself liking the king.

To his right was a slight-framed woman who looked like she might be approaching her forties. Her long hair curled gently around her face, the light caramel tresses accented by sparse strands of silver which twinkled here and there under the afternoon sun. Her rich green eyes, noticeable even from a distance, spoke of wisdom and humor.

Flanking them from behind was the tallest elf Collette ever laid eyes on. Though lean, his broad shoulders, accentuated by a length of black curly hair, and his height created a formidable presence in a group thus far filled with humor.

"I didn't know you guys could grow so large," said Larent from behind her. The following equally soft grunt told Collette Arian had an opinion about Larent's observation. A quick side glance confirmed her suspicion as Larent massaged his stomach.

Collette looked back to the approaching party, noting another man catching up to the large elf. Smaller in stature, his pointed ears confirmed he was a much more average-sized elf. His coloring, the same caramel hair and eyes a darker shade of green, suggested he was, perhaps, a half-elf. He held what looked to be a ledger in one hand and a quill in the other, poised to take notes. Her lips quirked up as she took in the permanently ink-stained fingertips. She would always associate ink with her meeting with Thomas.

"Welcome," Aphros said jovially as he held out his arms in a welcoming gesture. "It is so good to see you again, my friend." Alaoin and Aphros embraced before Aphros turned to Collette. "May I introduce the queen of Coralia?" he said.

"Oh my, you are stunning," King Alaoin said as he slid up to Collette. "I have heard tales of your beauty, but they did you no justice. Sabine," he addressed the woman behind him, "I'm not engaged to be married anymore, right? I did manage to chase off the last woman, didn't I?"

"Your Majesty, you've managed to chase off your last seven suitors," replied the enormous elf from behind the woman called Sabine. The corners of his lips turned up as Sabine's green eyes glanced up at him.

"Wonderful," Alaoin replied, clapping his hands together as he took in the group with mischievous eyes.

Alaoin turned his head to the smaller elf. "Éric, can you add courting the Queen of Coralia to my schedule while we're here please?" he said sweetly, as if asking for tea or something less important.

Éric looked up from his book, giving the king a rather unimpressed look. "Of course, Your Majesty." He waited until Alaoin turned back to Collette to roll his eyes.

"I am afraid I am not available to be courted, but I would like to get to know you all the same," Collette replied.

"Ah, how unfortunate," Alaoin said with a dramatic sigh. "In any case, I shall be polite and make introductions." With a flourish, Alaoin motioned to the woman. "This is the Duchesse Vassetre, Sabine. She is the High Minister and Advisor in my court."

The woman known as Sabine inclined her head in a respectful bow, and when she lifted her head, the full weight of her piercing, vibrant eyes was not lost on Collette.

"It is a pleasure, Your Majesty. Our king has often spoken of his eagerness to meet you," Sabine said in a warm, confident voice.

"Though, where he gets his information, we truly aren't sure," said the large elf.

Alaoin looked up at him with a large grin. "The mountain is Faron, Sabine's husband, and a general hardship to be around."

"You wound me," Faron deadpanned.

"A pleasure to meet you all," Collette acknowledged, managing to suppress an amused chuckle. She motioned to Whyldon, who joined her side upon the acknowledgment. "Allow me to introduce John Whyldon. He serves as the captain of my guard and my top advisor."

"A pleasure," Alaoin replied, nodding to Whyldon with genuine respect. "Faron was Sabine's personal guard before they married. He also aided in reorganizing and training her guards as well as my own. I wouldn't have leadership for the troops, let alone strategy, if not for him. From the looks of you, I'd say Queen Collette received similar advice and training as well," Alaoin said with a grin as he offered Whyldon a hand.

Whyldon took the offered hand. "Indeed," he confirmed. "Her Majesty made for a great student. Teaching her, passing on my knowledge and skills, was one of my great honors."

Alaoin's smile somehow grew wider. "I'm glad to hear as much. I think, if you're amicable, I would like for you and Faron to meet up to talk troops and plans of action. In the bigger meetings, smaller details can get lost in the shuffle. When you have time, of course," Alaoin said with a slight shrug.

"His Majesty is concerned over reports of our movements reaching Azmarin," Sabine explained.

"And if Azmarin knows of your movements, Coralia soon will," Collette summarized.

"Precisely," Sabine confirmed.

"I haven't been a very good neighbor to Azmarin. They like to keep an eye on us because of it." Alaoin's gesture encompassed their group. Éric, meanwhile, continued scribbling notes in his book.

"I believe Azmarin has found many neighbors lacking these last few years," Collette replied.

Alaoin's expression grew thoughtful. "When you're back on the throne, they will no longer have strong allies." He turned to the smaller man. "Make a note. When the matter of Coralia is settled, we should discuss integrating Azmarin into our kingdom." He turned back to Collette with a charming smile. "I'll give you half of their kingdom. We could call it a wedding present." The charming, boyish smile couldn't mask the otherwise shrewd glint in his eyes.

Behind him, Faron's brows knitted together while from behind Collette, she heard Larent. "Did they just decide to invade Azmarin?"

"Yes," Arian replied, his voice firm.

"I'm not opposed to dealing with Azmarin," Collette replied. "First, we must deal with the imposters on my throne."

Alaoin's eyes narrowed at the mention of Zephraim. "Oh yes, we will definitely be removing him." The king stepped closer to Collette, barely keeping out of her personal space. "I am sorry for everything you've been through." His chin moved in the direction where Tolan stood toward the back of the group, and Alaoin's voice lowered for Collette's ears only. "I am especially sorry for the action of my idiot cousin."

His eyes were full of compassion, not pity, and Collette had to wonder what Tolan had told the other man. Before she

could inquire, Alaoin stepped back and asked, "Who else is with us today?"

Collette's delayed response only lasted a couple of seconds. She hadn't expected the compassion from Alaoin or the overt recognition of Tolan's betrayal. Still, she pulled herself together quickly enough, and she turned toward her people. "I have introduced Whyldon, of course," she began, then gestured to Thomas. "Thomas Fletcher, one of my advisors and favorite critic. Next to him is Arian Tal'Dela. He's quite a gifted healer amongst other titles." She then motioned to Nawalya, whom she introduced. "A skilled fighter and strategist. Perhaps when Faron and Whyldon talk, she might be included." She introduced Rion next and briefly relayed Alaoin's acquaintance with Tolan. Larent was saved for last. "Larent Leassitor," she said, "and the reason I am terribly afraid we cannot marry."

Alaoin nodded warmly to each person, though he sensually eyed Larent up and down. The lecherous grin on his face spoke volumes of his intended comment, but he flinched as a hand went to his lower back. His head snapped to Éric who blinked innocently at him. Alaoin gave him a look then turned back to Larent and Collette. "It is a pleasure to meet you. I just realized I forgot to introduce my right hand Éric."

Collette nodded to the young man, amused by the silent dynamic between servant and king. She pondered the depth and true meaning, knowing it would likely remain a mystery.

Éric bowed his head to Collette. "Pleasure," he said, his voice smooth and deeper than his slight frame would indicate. Collette had the impression he didn't speak much.

"Don't mind Éric. He's a stick in the mud," Alaoin said as he offered his arm to both Collette and Larent. "I know my group could use a few hours to freshen up, but otherwise, what are our plans for the evening?"

# Chapter Twelve

"I thought we could meet for a general exchange of information," Aphros spoke up as the group began their walk back toward the palace. "And a dinner to continue talks."

Alaoin gave Collette and Larent a warm bright smile as they took his offered arms. "That sounds brilliant. I can't wait."

# Chapter Thirteen

"I think the meeting and the introductions went well," Whyldon said, taking a chair across from Collette. They sat by a window in the queen's provided suite, a pitcher of chilled wine placed on the table between them. Whyldon lifted it and filled the goblets with the pinkish liquid, handing the first over to Collette before pouring some for himself. "Alaoin likes you quite a lot."

"He seems to," Collette agreed, not yet sipping her drink. "And he's shrewd. I gather people underestimate his intellect."

Whyldon nodded, taking a drink and thinking back over introductions. He often found himself thankful for the opportunity to silently observe during political game-playing. Alaoin was indeed a shrewd man who used his sleepy looks and easy charm to work his way into positions where he could flex his might. The elegant woman and giant elf who supported him held surprises Whyldon had not yet worked out, but he found himself thankful to be on Alaoin's side.

"I think he's used to being viewed in a certain light," Whyldon agreed. "Seeing beyond his façade impressed him."

# Chapter Thirteen

Collette laughed and shrugged. "I am impressive. He thinks I am quite kind in allowing Tolan to remain with our group. I have to agree." She drank from her cup and rested her head against the back of her chair for a moment, eyes closed as the sun caressed her skin.

Whyldon hated his inability to give her a peaceful life or at least something more personally rewarding. Her life would never truly be her own. He pondered the remnants of his glass then looked back at his daughter.

"Collette," he began, using her name in a rare moment. The only time he'd done so, especially after she'd been crowned, had been during those long-ago hunting trips. He missed those days and wondered if they would ever be in a place for them again.

"Yes, Whyldon?" she asked him, her eyes open again, though she'd not moved.

"Given the connection between Alaoin and Tolan, when are you planning to reestablish something friendlier with him?" He had no reason to name the "him" he referenced. Collette's raised brow demonstrated the instant connection.

A dismissive noise escaped Collette's throat. "He made his choice," she replied before taking a much healthier gulp of her wine. "I have made mine. He can disappear in the middle of the night again for all I care."

"I fear you would care very much, and I say as much knowing how every time he speaks to you, he manages to dig himself into a deeper hole," Whyldon contradicted, and it was not often he did this where Collette was concerned. "And you are letting your anger and hurt over many hardships these past months influence how you handle his return. He did return, after all."

"I am rightfully angry with him for the choices he made," Collette argued, her tone a little harder now, though her posture

and gaze remained as they had been. "He should have had nothing to return from."

"And I do not dispute the point," Whyldon replied. "He seems ashamed of how he chose to leave, but he returned. All the same, he returned."

"Because he thought I was dead."

Whyldon shook his head, the loose brown locks brushing against his shoulders. "Not entirely. He also returned because he'd secured aid. Rumors of your death just hurried him along."

"I knew you felt sorry for him," Collette said with another, more bitter laugh. "Rion does, too."

"I can't speak for Rion," Whyldon said. He rose to his feet, grabbed the pitcher, and refilled Collette's glass. "But I can say I think there are no excuses for what Tolan did, regardless of intent. I fully agree with you. However—"

"Of course," Collette interrupted.

"However, he came back with support, and he's stayed. He deserves some credit."

"He chose to stay knowing how angry I am," Collette retorted, her free hand slapping the chair arm. "He does not have to remain with us if my indifference is such a trial."

Whyldon sighed and resumed his seat. "Politically speaking, you are the person he aligns with most. You champion for the people, even those who suffered long before your father reigned. You have done much to alleviate suffering in the land. Despite everything, he wants to make sure you are able to continue with the work you have done."

Collette didn't respond at first, her gaze focused on some random point beyond his chair, and Whyldon was happy to sit in the silence. Too many people needed the noise and action to feel comfortable.

When she decided to reply, it was prefaced by a huff of air. "He still blames me for his choice."

"Does he?" Whyldon asked.

"I think he does, at least partially. If I'm being fair, he's not especially gifted in explaining his actual meaning when I do allow him to approach me."

"Do you give him grace, knowing he's not good at expressing his true meaning?" Whyldon asked.

"I try, at first," Collette replied defensively. "But it becomes increasingly difficult."

"I'm sure it does," Whyldon sympathized. "But eventually, either he figures out how to speak to you, or you will have to accept his limitations and move forward."

Collette nodded, but her uncertain expression told Whyldon she would consider the conversation for a while longer before acting. Another sip of wine, and she asked, "Does our talk mean you will resume something friendlier with Nawalya?"

"Nawalya and I are on better terms than you and Tolan," Whyldon said, his gaze intent on his wine.

"True, but those terms are hardly friendly."

"Nawalya likes to avoid anything that centers herself in conflict," Whyldon replied. He'd given the matter of his former lover quite a bit of thought over the weeks since their relationship had abruptly ended once news of the vision reached him. He understood her fear, and as he'd quietly observed her interactions with Arian and Larent, he'd grown to see she'd often avoided the consequences of her actions. To her credit, he saw her trying to change.

"Most people do if they can help it," Collette said.

"You don't," Whyldon countered. "You plunge forward despite danger and wisdom, but what you, I, or most people would do isn't the point. She's got to decide if she wants to continue avoiding me because it's easier. Longing looks do not soften me."

"Fair enough," Collette replied. She drained her cup and placed it by the pitcher. "Aphros, Alaoin, and I have a dinner meeting. Do you plan on dining with the others?"

"I had intended to," Whyldon replied, scratching the side of his chin. He needed a shave. "I'm interested in speaking with Faron."

"He seems like a knowledgeable man and likely a powerhouse in battle," Collette observed. "He's insanely in love with Sabine."

"One would hope a husband is in love with his wife," Whyldon said with a laugh. "What makes you say as much?"

Collette's eyes went to the ceiling, her lips moving ever so slightly as she formulated an explanation. "He moves with her," she said, her lips pressed together as if irritated by her response. "It's as though every gesture, every single breath, pulls some invisible string, forcing him to do the same."

Whyldon had not given the elf and his wife enough attention to notice, but he had something to look for later. "Perhaps it is because she's human," he guessed.

"Perhaps," Collette replied. "And she already looks older than he, though his eyes speak of decades more life than she could ever dream of having."

"A sad thought, but living without the person you love will always be a harsh existence." Whyldon knew part of him would never move on from the loss of Adorra. He drained his cup and set it aside. "Since you have more meetings this evening, I will let you have some peace," he decided.

"Thank you," Collette replied, giving him a tired smile. "Perhaps we shall soon see progress."

"I hope so." Whyldon rose from his chair. Instead of bowing, he gave her a warm smile. Then, he left the room to rejoin the others.

Nawalya had spent her limited free time since her conversation with Thomas not exactly stalking Whyldon, but close enough. She'd made sure to stay out of his line of sight and hopefully far enough away to avoid Whyldon knowing her actions. The Guard Captain had surprised her before, though.

She wanted to approach him, to say hi, or even start a conversation. Something easy, something mundane, and she could see where such a conversation went from there. It should be easy, simple, and yet she was nervous in a way she never was.

Still, as the afternoon went on, she knew she had to approach him now or lose her nerve and possibly even her chance. So when Whyldon emerged from Collette's room alone, walking down the corridor, she took her chance and quickly fell in step beside him. "Hello," she said, her voice even softer than usual, and she internally cursed herself.

Whyldon's pace did not alter, despite Nawalya half expecting it. He glanced her way, blue eyes meeting her own for the briefest of moments. "Hello," he returned.

Nawalya tried to think of something to say, something funny or meaningful. She instead found herself just walking with Whyldon in silence for several moments before asking awkwardly, "What do you think of King Alaoin?"

"I think I'm more than happy he is on Collette's side," Whyldon replied, and though his response was brief, it did not feel dismissive.

Nawalya thought carefully over how to build on the conversation, her fingers picking at others in nervousness. She decided to just say the first thing that popped into her mind. "I have never seen an elf so large in my life."

Her words did bring Whyldon to a brief pause, chuckling all the while. "He is quite tall," he agreed. "And his wife and son's much smaller statures only emphasize how much."

Nawalya nodded. "I'm surprised Éric isn't taller with such a sizable father."

"He resembles his mother more than his father," Whyldon said.

"I have to wonder if they have any other children, and if so, who they may take after," Nawalya pondered. She enjoyed the easy banter and the walk. She just hoped she could keep the conversation going, though Whyldon seemed willing enough to go along with her plan.

"You could always ask," he suggested. "I doubt they'd be offended by polite inquiry."

"I may after they settle in." Nawalya's mind drew a blank on how to keep the conversation going.

"You'll have plenty of opportunity," Whyldon said, thankfully. "I'm not sure which one might be the safer approach."

Nawalya kept the sigh of relief to herself, thankful for his willingness to continue their conversation. "I want to say Sabine, but I don't think she's the right choice."

"Why not?"

"As we have more than learned from Collette, appearances can be deceiving. Sabine could be the more dangerous of the two and not appreciate questions about her children."

"Fair enough," Whyldon said as they made their way toward the dining hall. The castle was much smaller than Gadleigh Palace, which meant moving from one location to the next took very little time.

Nawalya let the silence stand as they walked before finally deciding to share something she'd kept with her for months. "I had a vision, only once, of the Nereid kingdom under attack. They were losing. I had already decided to help save the Nereid, but being here and seeing this place for myself has helped strengthen my resolve." She knew it was a risk, talking about her vision, but confiding in Whyldon felt right.

"Only once is a good thing, yes?" Whyldon asked, his tone hesitant and perhaps curious. He stopped and turned to face her. His blue eyes were serious but not unkind. "Didn't you tell me your visions must repeat for you to take them more seriously?"

"It's extremely rare for a vision I've had only once to come true," Nawalya explained, though her words hesitated on her tongue. She wasn't used to talking about her visions with people who weren't Arian or Larent. "We've also changed much since I had the vision. For starters, none of us were there."

"What do you want to do with the information?" Whyldon asked.

"I don't know," she admitted. "Having not had the vision again could mean everything is dependent on the choices we make going forward, as it should be. There is also the chance the information gets to the wrong people. If I say anything, the vision could become true anyway because people put too much stock in visions. Convincing soldiers to fight when they think they've already lost would be near impossible."

Whyldon nodded, folding his arms as he thought. "Then I think we need to speak with our group at the very least. Not everyone is aware, I'm sure."

"Until the other night, I had almost entirely forgotten about the vision, to be honest," she said earnestly. The last thing Nawalya wanted was for Whyldon to think she had kept something else from the group.

"Given everything, I can see how this particular vision got lost. We've been on the run for months."

"Still." Nawalya reached out, placing a hand on Whyldon's arm. "I am sorry," she said sincerely.

Whyldon looked down at the place where her hand rested on his arm. "I know," he said. "I know you are."

Nawalya swallowed. "Can we… Can we try again?" She pressed her lips together, fidgeting for a moment. "I mean as friends. We weren't really friends before everything, but I would like to try."

Hesitation followed the request, and Nawalya bit her lip, worried she'd asked too much.

"I suppose we can try for friends," Whyldon eventually replied, absentmindedly scratching the patch of beard beneath his ear.

Nawalya nodded, making sure to keep her expression calm. Sure, she could be friends with Whyldon. A part of her wanted to be more than friends, but friends could be a good place to start. A good place to possibly build from. She opened her mouth to say something, anything, but found she didn't know what else to say.

Whyldon, thankfully, did. "We should go eat dinner while we have the chance," he suggested. "The others will already be there."

Nawalya wasn't very hungry but nodded all the same. "Of course."

# Chapter Fourteen

arent leaned back against the blanket and looked up at the stars, the sound of the water splashing surrounding them. As much as he had loved Barcomb Mill and their time at his grandparents' house, he found the Nereid kingdom incredibly peaceful. The ocean sounds and scents might have been enough to create the preferable atmosphere, but everything contributed to the soothing calm. Buildings of white and coral blended with the fluffy white clouds in the sky.

His eyes flicked to the left to check in on Collette. She lay next to him, still propped up on her elbows, her shoulder-length hair blowing gently in the salty breeze. He swore that every time he looked her way, she grew more beautiful, and he fell in love more deeply.

Looking back up at the stars, he smiled to himself, pondering the life he'd literally stumbled into. "I think I started falling in love with you the first moment we met," he shared without really knowing why.

Collette looked over to Larent, smiling softly in his direction. "Why do you think so?"

Larent let his eyes roam around the night sky, taking in the stars. "You weren't afraid of me, a stranger who just appeared on your balcony. You were just okay with it."

"True," Collette agreed, finally laying back so she was also looking up. "But then, you didn't appear to have bad intentions, and if you had, I knew I'd put up a nice fight."

"Nah," Larent joked. "You just liked my charming smile. You knew immediately I could be trusted. Admit it: had I been Arian, you'd have drawn a blade."

"I knew Arian," she reminded him. "He was pretending to be one of my guards." She turned her head to look at Larent. "Probably, he'd have apologized a hundred times, turned red, and thrown himself from the balcony before I could react."

Larent laughed. "What about Nawalya? What do you think would have happened if it had been her?"

"Nawalya wouldn't have fallen onto my balcony," Collette replied simply.

Larent made a face. "True. Most days, she shows more common sense than Arian and I. Most days."

Collette turned on her side and moved closer to Larent. "I think I'm just going to be thankful you did end up on my balcony, especially since you've decided you started falling for me at the exact moment we met."

"How could I not?" Larent asked, his question serious and tone fond. "You're the most amazing woman to be born." Larent knew he sounded sappy, but he didn't give a shit. Collette was everything he could ever dream of wanting, and for some unknowable reason, she wanted him.

"You are biased as fuck," she replied, her tone equally as fond.

"True, but I'm not wrong."

Collette gave a soft laugh, and she draped her arm across his waist. The healing Mark, which covered the top of her back and swirled down her shoulders, peeked out one side of her shirt collar. Though the skin had initially been red and irritated, the Marking had mostly healed.

"Your Mark is beautiful, too. How does it feel?" he asked curiously.

"It's not itching as much," Collette replied. "Thankfully."

"And you can't scratch it. Though Ceto would be ready and willing to make any necessary repairs," Larent said. He pulled her closer, careful not to touch the Mark.

"See what happens when I'm nice?" she quietly joked.

"I think you're always nice," Larent countered, pressing his nose against her hair. He knew he was practically addicted to Collette, but he didn't see a way around those feelings or even a reason to.

"How nice am I?" she asked.

"Should I start with not gutting me when I showed up on your balcony and end with everything you did for those prisoners?" Larent asked teasingly.

"Had you been a problem, I would have gutted you," Collette replied. "Or pushed you off the balcony at the very least."

"But you didn't. You gave me a chance, demonstrating kindness in and of itself," he pointed out as he gazed into Collette's eyes. "You're kind, caring, intelligent, and beautiful."

"You're all of those things too, you know," Collette replied, shifting closer still. "And I think you sometimes deny as much, even to yourself."

Larent swore his heart started beating a little faster. "Well, of course I'm beautiful, and I can be smart. You're biased on the kindness part, though," Larent said as he used his free hand to caress her arm before moving to her side.

"You are exceptionally kind," Collette contradicted. "The work you have done, and continue to do, only emphasizes your kindness." She leaned in to kiss him. "And I can name many other examples if you need them."

Larent returned the kiss, unable to help himself. "I'm only a mercenary 'cause it's an excuse to kill bad people," he joked as his hand continued to caress her side. He was close to where the scars from his claws were, and Larent had to push away the intrusive thoughts of how bleak his life would be without her in it, how worthless.

"I recall," she replied. "You were bad-guy hunting when you showed up in Quenall if I recall." She must have noted his distress in finding her scars because she rose and moved to straddle him. "Look at me," she directed.

Larent looked up at Collette, loving the way the stars haloed her as she looked down at him, the way her hair fluttered forward.

"We're not going to worry about things that didn't happen," she said, her voice soft and gentle. "We have now, and everything we can get going forward."

Larent didn't say the words forming in his mind. They did have right now, but she had nearly died. With war on the horizon, their future wasn't guaranteed either. Of course, his stupid brain chose his moment of worry to remind him of their different lifespans. As a magic user, Collette might live longer than a non-magical human, but he was a shifter, and if his Nana wasn't messing with him, she was over five hundred years old. He couldn't imagine having all those years without her. He didn't want all of those years without her. He refused.

Instead of allowing his thoughts to spiral, he reached up and cupped a hand to her cheek. "Tell me something."

"I love you," Collette replied, putting a hand over his own. "So very, very much."

"I love you, Freckles," he replied. Larent found himself wondering if he wanted to ruin the moment so he didn't take her where anyone could walk by and see them or if he would forgo the worry and seek refuge in her embrace. For now, he chose the former option. "So I shouldn't worry about Alaoin?" he teased. "He is quite handsome."

"Oh, so you want some time with Alaoin," she replied with a soft laugh. "Should I let you go find him?"

Larent laughed. "Not without you, I don't, but I think together we would ruin him."

"I think I'd rather ruin you."

Now, he was sufficiently distracted. "Oh, I'd love for you to destroy me," Larent breathed. "But I don't want to accidentally put on a show for anyone."

"Then take me back inside," Collette instructed.

Not needing to be told twice, Larent sat up, had Collette wrap her legs around his waist, and when she had, he stood up, carrying her toward the palace. "Whatever you wish."

# Chapter Fifteen

Alaoin's excitement always meant for long days. Thankfully for Sabine, an invitation from some of the Nereid to go drinking meant an earlier night for the duchesse. After sailing into port earlier in the day, Sabine's desire for downtime outweighed her desire for almost everything else. Upon entering her assigned suite, she practically collapsed at the vanity, not bothering with the mirror as her hands began removing hair pins and undoing braids.

She glanced up as she felt a hand close around one of her wrists, spotting her husband.

"Let me," Faron said, and she let her hands fall to her lap as he continued her work with a gentleness his size suggested should have been impossible.

"I think you enjoy having an excuse," she playfully accused.

"I make no denial," Faron replied with a shrug. "Your hair is beautiful, and I will take every opportunity to run my fingers through it. I think I always will." Sabine felt Faron's lips brush against the top of her head, deeply breathing in her scent.

A soft smile tugged at her lips. She'd long since grown accustomed to Faron's easy transitions between doting affection and something much rougher, both sides absolutely adored and craved by the duchesse. His ability to determine what was appropriate at any given moment made her appreciate her husband all the more. "My hair is a tedious burden," she replied. "But I am glad you enjoy it so much."

"I love your hair almost as much as I love you," he said playfully as he removed the last several pins. Forgoing a comb, for now, Faron ran his fingers through her hair, detangling it as he went. "Next time you declare intentions to cut it off, however…" He let the warning hang in the air.

Sabine could not help her response. "I'm pretty sure I make the threat just to see what you'll do."

Faron's hand balled around her hair near the nape of her neck. He pulled her head back, his hold firm but the motion gentle enough to avoid hurting her. Her eyes lit up with the excitement of possibilities for their evening and grew all the more elated as his free hand found her throat. "Do you wish to play?"

Ever so tempted, Sabine had to admit she was far too exhausted to enjoy the promise of her husband's actions and words. "Hands to yourself, for now, my love."

Faron's hand slipped from Sabine's neck immediately. However, he leaned in for a quick kiss before releasing the grip on her hair and going back to running his fingers through it. "Now you know what I might do," he teased, his voice warm and playful. He reached for a brush, now tending to her hair with the sort of discipline it required. "What do you think of the young queen and her group?"

"Before or after they stopped gaping at you?" Sabine asked in amusement.

Faron chuckled. "After so many years, you would think I'd be used to those reactions."

"At least you were welcomed in upon arrival," Sabine pointed out. She stifled a yawn. "I hear you have trouble with such things."

"I'm just an intimidating person," he said dryly. Neither of them could forget how her guards had almost refused to allow Faron onto Sabine's estate when he first arrived in Fythias for his job years ago.

She nodded with a small laugh, though it faded as she considered Faron's original question. "I almost feel sorry for Queen Collette. She's young and looks much younger than she is. And so world-weary. Her struggles are evident even if she doesn't speak of them."

"She must be in her mid-twenties," Faron replied. "I believe it was her birth announcement you tossed away the first week I worked for you."

"I probably did," Sabine agreed. "We were not exactly friendly with Coralia then. We might not have been now, but I'm pleased Alaoin decided to offer his support. She was improving things. She needs her power back."

"As am I," Faron agreed as he ran the brush through her hair. He snorted after a pause. "If he doesn't stop flirting with Queen Collette, I'm certain Éric might truly stab our king with his quill."

Sabine nodded. They'd agreed to avoid discussions in too much detail of their son's feelings for the king, though Sabine was well aware of her husband's feelings on the matter. "You'd help him bury the body if it came to it," Sabine said. "Alaoin is such a good king, but he is often ignorant of certain things."

"I would," Faron replied without hesitation. "I do not care if we practically raised Alaoin. If our son ever needed help, I would be there." Faron set the brush aside with a sigh. "Éric needs to tell Alaoin how he feels."

"He does," Sabine agreed. "But we cannot force him to act until he is ready."

"I know," Faron agreed. He walked around to look at Sabine face-to-face. "Would you like me to braid your hair, or do you want to leave it down?"

"Leave it down," Sabine decided. As thick and heavy as her hair was, she needed relief from any particular style lest she wake up with a headache.

Faron nodded and helped Sabine rise to her feet. He motioned for her to turn around so he could undo the laces on her dress. "I think the next few weeks are going to be interesting. I worry battle will come sooner than we think."

"It will, especially if Coralia knows of Alaoin's movements," Sabine replied, removing her jewelry, except for the delicate ring on her finger, while Faron unlaced her.

"I thought we removed the spies from the palace, but we were not thorough enough." Faron's hands paused on Sabine's laces. "Have we received word from Avana?"

Sabine shook her head. "We were on a ship for over a week, and we've received no news since arriving."

"I was expecting a letter to beat us here, letting us know if the girls had burnt down the kingdom yet." Faron's hands resumed undoing their laces. "Why Alaoin thought putting the girls in charge while we were here was a good idea, I do not understand."

"Amélie would have come with us had she not been assigned a task," Sabine replied. "And where Amélie goes, Elyna would follow. Besides, I genuinely think Alaoin wants to see how far he can push things before one of you slaughters him."

"I'm not the one he has to worry about. Éric on the other hand…" Faron trailed off. "Besides, the girls are worse than Alaoin could ever be. More ruthless too. We will be lucky if any of the nobles who've been giving Alaoin trouble are still alive when we get home."

"And if they aren't, we shall contend with it when the time comes," Sabine replied with a laugh. "Our girls may look like me, but they inherited your impatience and temper."

"And my skill with a sword, though we could have done without Avana teaching them about poisons and such." Faron snorted, and Sabine knew he was thinking about how their oldest daughter had used the threat of poisoned drink to scare away her last three suitors.

The laces of her gown undone, Faron helped Sabine out of the dress. While he put it away, she sat down again and undid the ribbons holding her stockings around her thighs.

The dress put away, Faron came back and leaned against the bedpost. "Would you like me to help?" he asked, his voice deeper than before.

Sabine withdrew her hands from the ribbon. "Of course."

Faron dropped to his knees in front of Sabine and slowly dragged the first stocking down her leg. Keeping eye contact with her, he leaned forward and placed a kiss on her inner thigh just above her knee. He then moved to the other stocking, repeating the same actions. "Anything else I can help you remove?"

Her exhaustion was still present, but Sabine had never quite figured out how to make herself reject her husband's passes, no matter how subtle they were. "I believe I am still mostly covered," she replied. "How do you plan on resolving the issue?"

Faron laughed and kissed her left thigh once more. "By stripping you nude, cuddling you until you fall asleep, and in a few hours, waking you up by devouring what is mine." He let his fingers brush up her leg and closer to her center.

"How appealing," Sabine replied. "You should get started. I am quite exhausted."

Faron kissed her thigh once more and stood, pulling Sabine up with him. He slowly unlaced the ties on her chemise then helped her out of the thin garment, laying kisses on her shoulders, upper arms, and anywhere else in easy reach. "Lay down and get comfortable while I undress."

She pulled him in for another gentle kiss, her bare breasts pressed against his shirt. When she released him, she followed the order, drawing back the rich covers of their bed and crawling in.

Faron nodded and gave Sabine a pleased smile before quickly stripping down and putting away his clothes. He knew she appreciated his stature and naked body with as much enthusiasm as he had for hers. He joined her in bed, wrapping his arms around her body, an embrace which always left her feeling wanted and safe. "Sleep. I know when to wake you."

She did not argue, closing her eyes instead. "Goodnight, my love."

# Chapter Sixteen

Larent looked around the corridor leading out from the spacious meeting room. After his lazy evening with Collette, sleep evaded Larent as he pondered the very real fact he would outlive Collette. With war approaching, Larent didn't deny the possibility either one of them could get hurt or die, even if the thought of Collette in any state other than perfect and happy felt repugnant.

Assuming they made it through the war, she would eventually die, and he could possibly face centuries without her. Without her laugh and smile. Without her eyes narrowing and accusing him of treason. Without having access to admire the dusting of freckles across her nose and cheeks. Such possibilities left his chest hurting with near physical pain.

He liked to think he was a strong man, even if he wasn't always the cleverest or most practical. People lost their partners, their loves, every day, and they managed to carry on with their lives, sadder perhaps, but forward-moving. Larent didn't think such an existence would be possible for him.

Plagued with the terror of eventually facing a world without Collette, Larent realized someone currently residing in the palace must feel the same. He first thought to seek out Arian and discuss how he felt, knowing Thomas would likely die before the elf did. Bringing up the possibility with Arian, who was exceedingly fragile when it came to Thomas, seemed a bad idea, and Larent pushed the thought aside.

Then, he realized that Faron, the giant elf, might understand his worries. Larent hadn't spoken with Faron before, although the elf had been in frequent communication with Collette, Whyldon, and Arian. From what he understood, Faron was a decent person, even if he did come across as gruff and sardonic. Larent also recognized Faron's bone-deep affection for Sabine, which suggested he could likely get some helpful advice if Faron consented to a chat.

As the doors to the meeting room opened, Larent quickly made a decision. Alaoin approached, his arm looped with Collette's as they wandered to the door leading outside. She smiled, waving a few fingers in his direction, then turned back to the Fythian king. Larent was perfectly happy to let them pass. He had a mission, self-imposed though it was.

There was no missing Faron as he exited the meeting room, his son and wife beside him, though both bid their farewells to the man for reasons Larent didn't catch. He used the opportunity to approach Faron, feeling as though he kept his expression and body language, if not relaxed, then neutral.

"Hi," he said, noting Faron's raised eyebrow. Not the worst response. "I was, uh, hoping to ask you a few questions. You know, assuming you don't mind."

Faron didn't answer at first. Instead, he stood there quietly staring at Larent, who never felt more judged in his entire life. Whatever Faron thought of him, Larent just hoped he wasn't found lacking.

Finally, after an eternity, Faron nodded. "You are the shifter who's in a relationship with Queen Collette, correct?" Faron motioned for Larent to follow him.

"Yes," Larent answered. "How did you know I'm a shifter?"

"I have working eyes," Faron replied.

"Oh," Larent replied. He didn't know how he felt about the answer because as far as he was aware, nothing about him had been very wolfy since he'd attacked Collette. He followed Faron for several steps, debating how he wanted to begin. "So, I had questions about your wife," he said, then winced since his words could be taken poorly.

"My wife?" Faron repeated, dark brows raised again. "What about Sabine?"

"Well, not Sabine specifically," Larent amended. "More… She looks at least ten years older than you, but I know she's not. You're an elf. You're older…" He sighed, the words not forming correctly on his tongue.

"Ah," Faron said, his tone suddenly understanding. "You want to know how I manage, don't you? Being in a relationship with a human, knowing I will likely outlive her by a century."

"Lady, yes. I have no doubts about my relationship with Collette or how much I love her. I just—she was injured badly several months back, and now with war approaching, I'm thinking about the very real possibility of separation."

"Most humans do not live even one hundred years," Faron summarized. "From the stories I've been told, shifters can live for centuries. You had to know you would inevitably walk this world alone." Faron led them outside, and they quickly found a bench overlooking one of the many courtyards where members of the Coralian, Fythian, and Nereid parties mingled together, enjoying an elegant picnic.

Faron leaned forward, resting his elbows on his knees, and steepled his fingers together. "What you are asking does not have an easy answer. The truth is, I struggled with the question for quite some time. Sabine's mortality was the main reason I spent so much time unwilling to admit my love for her or to recognize the returned love she had for me."

Faron's gaze, even now locked on the woman he'd married, grew distant. "I almost lost her twice, once to my foolish insistence we could not love one another."

"And the second time?" Larent asked.

"The second time she nearly died from poison," Faron said, his voice quiet and rough.

Larent let the words linger in the air, feeling as though Faron needed a minute to pull back from what had to have been some of the worst moments of his life. The elf eventually shook his head and continued.

"After I admitted how much I loved Sabine, the worry did not leave me. Even now, her mortality sits with me, a little ball of fear living in the back of our minds about the limited time we share." Faron sighed and looked at Larent. "Eventually, I realized I could continue to worry, or I could enjoy every moment I have with her until she takes her last breath." Faron gave Larent a quick, sad smile, and his gaze returned to Sabine.

"Did you ever consider—" Larent asked, then stopped himself mid-sentence, not sure how best to continue.

"Are you asking if I considered making what some would say is the most romantic gesture I could make by ending my own life when she dies?" Faron asked.

Larent nodded mutely.

Faron, to Larent's relief, laughed. "Of course, but as Sabine has reminded me, my self-imposed death would be no grand romantic gesture. At its core, it would be the most selfish act I could make, especially knowing my death would leave our children without parents." Faron gave a small, quiet laugh. "I

assume, if you and Queen Collette had children, she'd feel the same way."

Larent grimaced. "I don't think Collette wants children. At least, she does not want them now. She's got a kingdom to win back and settle." And only the Lady would know how long the task might take. "And to be honest, I don't know if I want to create more potential shifters. The world is too dangerous for so many as it is."

"Opinions might change," Faron replied. "I recall not wanting children until I met Sabine." A wide grin spread across his face. "I'm lucky she gave me three."

"You have three kids?" Larent asked, brows raised in surprise.

"Yes. Éric and two girls. They're terrors, both of them," Faron deadpanned. "Alaoin left them in charge while we're here."

Larent caught the way Faron said the last part. He would mention what he'd learned to Collette if only to watch her laugh.

"So your advice is to just be happy with the time I have with her?" Larent asked, bringing the conversation back to the original point with a raised eyebrow.

"Yes, and stop worrying as much as possible. Cherish the time you have, whether it's a day or another fifty years." Faron gave Larent a sad but understanding smile and clapped the shifter on the back. "Easier said than done, I know."

His gaze turned forward as Sabine joined them, her expression playfully annoyed. "You have sat brooding here long enough. Come join us."

"I wasn't brooding. I was making a friend." He gestured to Larent but stood anyway.

Larent gave a cheerful wave to Sabine and stood as well. "Hi."

"Hello," Sabine replied, turning her vivid eyes toward him. "You are Queen Collette's paramour, are you not?"

# Chapter Sixteen

Larent nodded. "Yes, I am." He found he liked the way Sabine said paramour. It sounded better, more serious than suitor or lover.

"I thought so," Sabine replied. "I see it in the way she looks at you."

"If she looks at me even close to how I look at her, I will die a lucky man," Larent said earnestly.

"I think she counts herself as the lucky one," Sabine replied. She turned her gaze to Faron. "Do you plan on keeping me waiting, my love?"

"Never," Faron said, then leaned forward and whispered something into Sabine's ear that Larent couldn't catch thanks to having such a tight lock on his wolf. "You two have fun. I'm going to find Collette." He knew where she was, having watched her with Alaoin and Aphros in the distance, and Larent wanted nothing more than to join her.

# Chapter Seventeen

The thundering clap of a hand meeting face reverberated across the stone dungeon. No sound escaped Sara Whyldon's lips even as the metallic taste of blood filled her mouth. She lifted her head, tossing the gray-streaked carob hair out of her face, and met the eyes of a young brunette guard with the dullest expression she'd ever witnessed. Without breaking eye contact, she spit out a mouthful of blood. The new stain made no difference in the filthy chamber and would soon dry and brown, matching other spots of old blood on the walls and floor.

Another blow, this one harder and delivered by a lanky man with greasy blond hair, landed against the same cheek, whipping her head to the side. Still, she made no sound. Sara knew her limits. She knew the two young guards charged with torturing some sort of useful information out of her would fail, but others might not. The pain, uncomfortable as it was, as damaging as it could potentially be, didn't even tempt her. The ropes binding her to the chair placed in the middle of the stone floor of the room caused her more grief.

# Chapter Seventeen

A deep sigh came from the door to the room, and Cadan stepped forward. He looked over Sara with deep gray eyes before turning to the two guards he assigned to her. "I should have appointed a veteran," he muttered as he approached the group, his shadow made greater by the blazing fire on the far side of the room.

Reaching out, Cadan took Sara by the chin, his grip harsh and unyielding. His close proximity allowed Sara to see slivers of silver in his otherwise dark hair. "You need to stop focusing on her face or at least her cheeks. Slapping causes little damage and less pain. And if you don't know what you're doing, you might break her jaw, and she won't be able to answer questions." His casual, practically bored tone suggested he fancied himself a great philosopher.

He released her chin and rubbed his hands together before hitting Sara with his not-inconsiderable strength right below her ribs. All the air in her body seemed to vanish, and Sara gasped, both from pain and a need to breathe, but even still, she refused to give in. She refused to speak.

Cadan watched her reaction, nodding as if he'd known the outcome of his blow. "She does not want to answer," he explained to the younger guards. "To cry out. To give us anything. Such behavior is normal for most prisoners we see. Which means, for the moment, our goal is not to make her answer any questions but to see where her threshold for pain lies." He hit her again, this time on the left side, ignoring Sara's gasps for breath. "At which point, she will ask for it to stop, beg even. Once she begs, we draw the pain out further." He swung twice more, hitting her in quick succession in the same spots.

When Sara gave no more of a response, the blond guard spoke up. "How can she beg if she can't breathe?"

"String her up," Cadan ordered. The two men approached Sara carefully, one taking a firm grasp on her arms while the

other undid the rope. Once it was off, Sara's hands were secured above by rusted chains.

Cadan picked up a multi-tailed flail and held it out for the guard. "Since you're so concerned about her breathing. It works best on bare skin." Cadan waited until the younger man took the whip before moving to lean against the wall which would give him the best view. "Remember, she is a traitor to our kingdom, our queen, and our lord. The Mother has no mercy for people like her."

If the young guard had any trepidation about the order, he got over it. Over and over again, the sting of the whip left welts and bleeding cuts in Sara's skin, many she knew she would have to let remain even if she planned on healing her ribs.

Unsatisfied with the progress, the guard was ordered to pass on the whip, and his companion took over, striping her back and shoulders opposite of the marks she already bore. Blood oozed down her back, itchy and smarting. Gasps of breath turned into sounds of distress in the back of her throat, muted by lips which refused to open.

As the whip could not pry her lips apart, Cadan returned to the table, selecting a metal rod. He handed it off to the young guards, who took turns striking at her back and limbs. Nothing broke, and the rod made no cuts, but the bruising felt bone deep. After the first series of blows, Sara gritted her teeth, breathing through the worst of it. She would not betray her family. She would not betray Collette.

Eventually, when the guards grew tired, and Sara was slumped forward in abject pain, the beating ceased. "Sir," said the young guard, "I don't think she's going to speak."

"She's stronger than most," Cadan acknowledged. "Do not be disheartened by her silence. You are doing the work of the Mother, and she will break. Eventually, they all do." He surveyed the work they'd done, satisfied for now.

# Chapter Seventeen

"I do not know what you hope to gain from your silence," he said to her in the same calm informative tone he'd used during his instruction. "You can share what you know, accept your punishment, and the worst will be over."

Sara raised her head, glaring at him, but not speaking. The tear tracks on her face and the blood on her body had not served the intended forced compliance.

Cadan sighed. "She is going to make this very hard on herself." He took in a deep breath, glancing around the mostly empty room and back to Sara. "We shall give you some time to think. The next time we return, our kindness will not be given so generously."

He stepped away, brushing his hands together as if he were the one who had delivered the blows. "Untie her and take her back to her cell."

"What about her clothes?" the blond guard asked. "The back of her dress—"

"Sara Whyldon has chosen treason over her country," Cadan interrupted. "She knew the risks associated with her choice. Sitting in prison with a tattered dress on her back is the least of her worries." Cadan left without further worry, leaving the guards to follow through with his instructions.

Her limbs were freed from their binds, and the two guards wordlessly lifted her by her arms, carrying her out of the room and down a short corridor to the main prison. They weren't exactly gentle in placing her back on the prison floor, but the lanky one looked at her with pity.

"You should think about doing what he wants," he said quietly. "He'll go easier on you."

"You poor thing," Sara replied, her voice rough.

The guards left, and once again, Sara sat in the near-dark silence of the otherwise empty prison cell. She crossed her arms, hands going flat against her torso, and her healing magic

flowed into her middle, healing the bruises which most bothered her. The more visible marks, like the cuts on her back, sadly had to stay.

With a sigh, Sara leaned her head back against the wall and closed her eyes, intent on following her path.

Cadan had taken a moment to clean himself from the dirt and grime prisons always seemed to leave on a person. As he approached the favorite garden of the queen and his lord, he felt he looked appropriate for a meeting with the active Coralia rulers. Black breeches and a deep blue shirt and coat had him feeling dapper, despite their rendezvous not occurring in an office. He supposed he could see the appeal of a private outdoor space. The sun could be inviting, and the fresh air a good change from political scheming.

After stepping into the garden, he approached the couple sitting on a bench, their heads close together as they looked over a book held in the queen's hand. They made a handsome couple, though their relationship wasn't something he was particularly interested in. As he got closer, he realized the two were deep in their conversation and hadn't heard him approach. Taking a deep breath, he cleared his throat and waited for them to turn to face him.

Rhoslyn's eyes slid from the book pages first, clearly perturbed by the disruption, but not reproachful. "Yes, Cadan?"

Riken said nothing, just raised a displeased eyebrow.

Cadan bowed low, and when he stood, he kept his eyes down in reverence. "I came to report on Sara Whyldon. She is proving to be much more resilient than originally thought. I fear making her talk will take longer than expected. I apologize for the news, and I will double down if you think it wise."

"We knew she would be," Rhoslyn said with a sigh. She closed the book and rested her small, pale hands on the cover. "Her stubbornness suggests she knows quite a bit."

Cadan watched Riken lean forward, resting his elbows just above his knees as he thought over what might be best. Riken's father had mastered the art of interrogation, and Cadan well remembered the ease with which he drew information from prisoners.

"Keep trying your normal tactics. If after a few days you haven't gotten any results, come see us again, and we will discuss the next steps." Riken's eyes narrowed.

Cadan immediately knew what the next steps might include. For a moment, he felt sorry for Sara, but she was working against the designs of the Mother. If they had to break every bone in her body, well, Sara Whyldon would be responsible for her own choices. They were guilt-free. "Of course, my lord." His eyes went to Rhoslyn. "Is there anything you need me to do, my queen?"

"Yes," Rhoslyn replied in a soft voice. Cadan thought he was finally starting to recognize the meanings of her different tones. The queen had not yet reached annoyance over Sara. "How has Zephraim behaved today? No problems detected?"

"No, our people report he has been keeping mostly to himself, either in his office or the library. His only consistent visitor has been Lord Barris and only for a short period." Cadan might have been worried had Barris not struck him as incredibly naïve, and perhaps a little stupid.

"Good," Rhoslyn replied. "Perhaps he is happier without having the burden of decision-making to contend with." She ran a hand along a strand of her hair as she spoke, a move to tantalize Riken, no doubt. "As long as he behaves, do not bother him."

"Of course, my queen. I will make sure to report any changes of behavior your guards see." He took a moment to contemplate his next question and decided to risk it. "If he decides to have another night on the town with Barris, should I send guards with him, just in case?"

"Not unless you see a reason to," Rhoslyn replied without consulting Riken. Cadan wondered if his lord remained out of her good graces still. "Barris is his little friend, and neither has the drive or intelligence to intentionally cause any harm. However, I do know how conniving members of the court can be. Should you note someone else joining their little gang, then might be the time to reevaluate."

Riken nodded his agreement with Rhoslyn but added nothing. "As my queen commands."

"Indeed," Rhoslyn replied. "Thank you for the information, Cadan. I know you will figure out how to crack Sara Whyldon."

"I have a few ideas." Cadan bowed low. "Have a good day, my queen. My lord."

"Oh, and Cadan," Rhoslyn said as the man moved to leave the queen and lord alone.

He paused in his steps, turning back to face them. "Yes, my queen?"

"We know Fythias has set off for the Nereid kingdom. We will need you in the war room later."

"Of course," Cadan turned and continued on his way, his mouth set in a grim line. The news of Fythias joining the Nereid, and therefore Collette, was not good, but Fythias had long since abandoned the Mother. He could only confirm the Mother would have abandoned them.

# Chapter Eighteen

"I heard back from my contacts in Branlin. They are rejecting the new laws and refusing to allow the Merscale trade. The few merchants who were for reinstating it have vanished, apparently. No one knows what happened to them. So Branlin stands strong, and the letter clearly states they support Collette. Word from Myrefall is scarce, but from all appearances, they have fallen in line and are even sending troops to aid in the upcoming invasion of the Nereid Kingdom."

Diana scowled as she listened to the conversation between her husband and Howle. Casual and seemingly unconcerned with more local matters, Diana thought them in need of a reminder. She approached and slammed her flat palm down on the table, disrupting the papers and strategically placed figurines. Raised brows and startled jumps from the unsuspecting men did nothing to deter her. "When do you plan on doing something about Sara Whyldon?" she demanded. Weeks had passed since the older woman's arrest, and the latest intel from the palace indicated her status as prisoner had changed to torture victim.

Crem eyed Diana wearily but otherwise gave no other reaction. "As soon as we have more information and a viable plan which doesn't end in all our deaths. Unless you would like to be a widow sooner rather than later?"

Diana raised an unimpressed eyebrow at her husband. "Given the number of reckless things I've seen you do, I think you'd figure out how to live through it," Diana replied. "They started torturing her at daybreak, according to Agnes. How long do you think she's going to survive?"

"We have to wait until one of our people can get access to the new guard rotation. Riken's man has been adding more guards, switching things up, trying to avoid a repeat of an important prisoner escaping. I want to get her out, and I want to do it as soon as possible, but we must be smart," Crem tried to explain as calmly as possible, but even the calmest of voices did nothing to obscure the prominent stress lines around his mouth and eyes.

"Diana, we have ta go about a rescue the right way," Howle said, coming to stand behind Crem, a hand placed on the man's shoulders. "If we don't and they capture, let's say Crem, what do ya think they'll do ta him? Ta any of us here?"

"Do you remember why I left the palace, Howle?" Diana asked, her lips pursed in great displeasure. She hated being condescended to, and there was no mistaking the intent in Howle's words. "I'm more than aware of the dangers from inside the palace walls. Sara will be as well, and she's not in a position to defend herself from the danger as I was."

Crem stood and pushed Howle back before he could respond, silently telling Howle to shut up. "You got yourself out in time," Crem said to Diana. "If I could, I would go in right now and get her out. I'm just not entirely sure how we could go in and successfully retrieve her." He lowered his voice as he rested his head against hers. "I'm almost positive we are going to lose people."

Diana sighed. "I know any plan is going to be dangerous," Diana replied, but she couldn't get the image of Sara, bloodied and beaten and constantly under threat of death or worse, out of her head. "I'm just afraid if she is there any longer, a rescue will soon become pointless. People can only survive so much."

Crem sighed and pulled away, though he nodded in acknowledgment.

"Well then, we'll just go out tonight, bust in, and hope all turns out well," Howle growled as he approached her.

"Don't be stupid," Diana snapped at Howle. "You need a viable plan, but I am not wrong. There is no telling how they've treated her so far, and we know they've escalated as of this morning. They are not going to stop. Something has to be done, and you don't get to use me emphasizing as much as my endorsement for the lot of you to run for your death."

Howle brought up a dark, calloused hand, three fingers sticking up. He stood, his face inches from her own, as he wildly gesticulated. "We've had three different plans, and each one of them all had ta be scrapped because we got new information, or we had ta go save someone else before they were tossed in prison. Ya've been here. Ya should know. Yar not the only one frustrated."

Howle went to say more, but Crem got between them. "We are not about to start fighting amongst ourselves," he said, his ire mostly directed toward Howle. "Go check on Ian and cool off," Crem ordered.

Howle just shook his head. "Oh, come off it," he said, but he turned and marched off, obedient as always.

Diana's lips pressed together as she watched Howle walk off, and her temper flared. "I apologize if I seem critical or judgmental," she said to her husband. "I am neither. I know you

are stressed. I know you carry a large burden. I'm not diminishing any of what you are dealing with."

"I know. I understood your points and your urgency," Cream said tiredly. "I have no idea what's crawled up Howle's ass. Maybe I need to send him to see some of the escorts in the warehouse district," Crem joked lamely. He sighed. "You have every right to be concerned about Sara. I'm worried about Sara, especially now."

"They think she knows something, and they're probably right. If her arrest was a means to get Queen Collette's attention, they would've been louder about it. They haven't, which tells me they are going to go as far as they have to in order to get the information they want."

Crem nodded. "The tentative plan we've been working on was to try to get in tomorrow night, rotation changes or not," Crem confided.

"What about using Zephraim?" Diana asked. "It's only a matter of time before they come for him, and the risk grows every day. We can get him and Sara out in one move."

"That's what I'm hoping to do. Barris is supposed to be arranging it. I wanted to keep Zephraim out of the important parts for as long as possible, but as of this morning, it became impossible." Crem sighed. He still didn't trust Zephraim. Not really.

"He is a good man who has done bad things," Diana gently reminded him. She approached Crem, cupping his face in her hands. "He wants to atone. To make things right."

"I know, it's just—" Crem gathered his thoughts. "He's sent us good intel, helped us to save people in this city. However, he has proven he was willing to overthrow his sister for that horrific woman play-acting as queen. What if Rhoslyn were to decide she wants him instead of Riken? Where are we then?"

# Chapter Eighteen

"He is not blinded to her charms anymore. Nor the grief of Lord Veitel's death," Diana said. "He was manipulated by a woman he thought loved him. The consequences just happened to be substantial with him, but he's hardly the only man who ever fell victim to those exact circumstances."

"I find it hard to trust him is all. I know I need to move past my reservations, but it is so very hard." Crem ran a hand through his short-cropped hair. "I will send a note to Barris, and we will go from there. My aim is tomorrow night. I would go tonight if I could, knowing the things they are more than likely doing to her, but unless Zephraim thinks he can walk her out or has another plan, I just don't see how."

"He is still king, technically," Diana pointed out. "He could demand an audience with a traitor."

Crem made a thoughtful noise, his eyes moving away from Diana as he considered the possibility. "I may not trust him, but I'm not sure I wish to put him in so much danger. However..." He trailed off as he considered another possibility. "I think I need to talk to Barris right now."

Rhoslyn brought the wine to her lips, consuming the sweet plum-colored liquid with a delicacy only a true lady of the court could master. Even as queen, she thought the skill served her well, a reminder of the little show she could put on while otherwise ruling without kindness or mercy. They all could watch as she primped and preened, waiting for her allowances, her go-ahead. Those who displeased her would summarily suffer, and none, not even her favored Riken, could escape her wrath once earned.

"So, we know Fythias sailed to the Nereids," she said as she set the goblet on the table before placing her hand on her lap.

"And we know Collette sailed there as well a few weeks ago. It seems to me they've declared their intentions for war."

Riken rested his elbows on the table, steepling his fingers, his eyes on Rhoslyn.

Across from him sat a grim-faced Cadan. Cadan looked down at his bowl of stew, spoon moving through the liquid without an effort to gather enough to eat.

"I don't see how we can interpret it any other way, not with that joke of a king on board," Riken said.

"Alaoin is a fool," Rhoslyn said in agreement. "He's somehow tricked others into ignoring his eccentricities in favor of propping up his aims." She picked up her wine again and drank, only continuing with a temporarily quenched thirst. "Granted, he's a skilled tactician. I wouldn't deny his talents. It serves no one to pretend otherwise."

"If I'm correct, he's made it as far thanks to his skills and the aid of his advisor. Duchesse Safron, I think her name is. Thirty years ago, everything suggested Fythias would crumble, and Azmarin would annex them into the empire," Riken mused. "I remember my father would talk about it at length and what it would mean for Coralia."

"My queen," Cadan interjected, "I know you said Azmarin is eager to help us per their last letter, but would an offer to help them take Fythias, when everything is more settled here, help to strengthen our alliance even more?" Cadan asked before finally moving to eat some of the food placed before him.

"I should think it would," Rhoslyn replied. "Their king is newly appointed, so I'm hesitant to make too many promises too quickly."

"Not with them unable to make good on any promises they may make during this time," Riken said in agreement. "Do we have any information on the new king?"

# Chapter Eighteen

"Mallan Hialti has branded himself regent rather than king," Rhoslyn said, listing off facts she could recall. "And he is angry over what Collette did to their prior king Brath." She gave a delicate snort of a laugh. "I will give Collette this. Brath was an idiot. I'd have killed him as well."

Riken gave a small chuckle, nodding his head in agreement with Rhoslyn.

"Do we know why he's named himself regent instead of king?" Cadan asked.

"Appearances, I would guess," Rhoslyn said, her shoulders rising and falling in the shallowest of shrugs. "In my personal experience, one cannot simply snatch what they want. Slow methodical retrieval is always the wise move."

Cadan nodded, and Rhoslyn smiled at the reminder of his loyalty.

A door from the kitchen opened, and Gisella walked in, carrying a tray of pork. She carefully placed it on the table, an act she'd repeated again and again since she'd begun working in the palace.

"Are you not going to serve us?" Rhoslyn asked, her voice calm. She cast her eyes upward, glaring at the young half-elf.

"I did not—" Gisella began, only to cry out when Rhoslyn backhanded her.

"Do as you're told," Rhoslyn commanded.

"Disobey an order from your queen again, and I will personally correct your lacking habits," Riken said with a sneer.

"Stupid elf," Cadan muttered.

The mark of Rhoslyn's hand shined bright red as Gisela tearfully served the meat around the table. Even when she finished, Rhoslyn refused to dismiss the girl.

"Your mother works in the palace, does she not?" Rhoslyn asked. "I believe Lord Elrick favored her."

139

"She does, Your Majesty," Gisella confirmed in a quiet, fearful voice.

"And did she not instruct you on expectations?"

"She did, Your Majesty. As did Mistress Hawke."

Riken's hand visibly tightened on his fork, as if it took everything in him not to lash out at the girl for even mentioning Diana Hawke.

"Both women have poorly guided you," Rhoslyn said. "I suggest figuring out how to do your job before serving at my table again." She waved her fingers to the side. "You may go."

Riken looked down at the food haphazardly piled on his plate. "That girl has been employed far too long to be so sloppy. She knows better. Maybe you should consider firing those taught their jobs under a traitor and start all over again. Collette may have been satisfied with subpar service, but you deserve the world."

"I could," Rhoslyn said, "but I am nothing if not benevolent. The last thing one wants to do is fire others for having earned a wage under a terrible leader, but she should know how to do her job by now." Rhoslyn picked up her fork. "I shall have her let go come morning. We wouldn't want to send the young thing out into the night, after all."

"You show such kindness with your decision," Riken said with a soft smile to Rhoslyn.

Cadan, on the other hand, had a thoughtful look cross his face. "She said she worked directly with Diana Hawke, the woman who had tried to make friends with the king?"

"She did claim to be taught by Diana," Rhoslyn confirmed.

Cadan's head tilted slightly to the left, his eyes taking a faraway glint as he considered something.

"What are you thinking, Cadan? You can speak freely here," Riken said.

Chapter Eighteen

Cadan raised an eyebrow, causing the other man to flush slightly in shame.

"I am wondering if our queen wouldn't mind me having a long talk with the girl after she is let go. She might have overheard something about the location of Cremisius Hawke's rebellion or other such information without realizing it."

Rhoslyn sat back in her seat, considering the idea. She thought it unlikely Gisella knew anything, and Rhoslyn was aware they needed to act with great caution. They could not afford to be viewed as cruel or violent. The criticisms of Sargarus had been valid. He'd gone too far, and Rhoslyn felt it prudent to exercise restraint.

"Do not treat her like a prisoner," Rhoslyn replied. "Do not cross what you are legally allowed to do. We don't want the staff slitting our throats in our beds."

"Of course, my queen," Cadan said with a firm nod.

"Have there been any updates on the search for Cremisius Hawke?" Riken asked Cadan, causing the other man's lips to curl upward in a small snarl before he schooled his features.

"No, but his little group intervened and prevented a lawful interrogation of prisoners from Stanlow." He breathed out deeply and turned to the queen. "There was no way they should have known about those prisoners, nor the shipment they sabotaged the week prior. I fear someone might be feeding them information."

"Well, we knew we have a leak," Rhoslyn replied. "The problem is finding out who."

"We could try setting a trap?" Riken said with a raised eyebrow at Rhoslyn. "And not one like that idiot Elrick tried to do."

"See, you are mistaken," Rhoslyn countered after she took a bite of her dinner. "Elrick's plan was not terrible. The men we are trying to extinguish are simply good at what they do. We cannot afford to underestimate them."

Riken thought about that for a moment. "Very true. Hawke wouldn't have been guard commander if he wasn't good at the job. I may be less than charitable to Lord Elrick. Due to other circumstances," Riken admitted.

"Then you must learn to do better," Rhoslyn said. "The last thing we need is another overthrow thanks to simple matters we can correct." She took another bite of her food. "No worries. I know we will sort it all out."

# Chapter Nineteen

Cadan sprinted to ensure he met King Zephraim at the entrance to the prison. He could never consent to allow the king to meet with Sara Whyldon alone, but there was no way to deny the man of his demands. Cadan had not had time to run the request through Rhoslyn, so when he arrived, breathless and suspicious, he determined he'd stay alert. Running a hand through his hair before wiping the sweat from his brow, he approached the king, bowing and rising. "King Zephraim, I have been informed you wish to see the prisoner?"

The king stood with a younger guard, finely dressed, with his red-gold curls perfectly styled. He looked much the way Cadan always saw him. Perhaps even less stressed than usual. "Yes," Zephraim said, his eyes barely glancing in Cadan's direction. "I hear you have someone who conspired with my dear sister, and you've failed to get information."

Cadan motioned for the guard to step aside, which they did promptly, leaving Cadan alone with the king. "We tried simply questioning her before yesterday. Now we are trying a harsher method. I'm not concerned about silence. She will break eventually."

"As long as she's been here, you'd think more would have been accomplished," Zephraim replied. "We know she's been in the presence of the traitor, correct?"

"Yes, but we don't know how—" Cadan paused, hearing a strange squeaking noise behind them as they approached the entrance to the prison. He turned to look, but a hand on his arm from Zephraim, paired with an unimpressed raised eyebrow told him the king was displeased.

Cadan's training surfaced, and his attention turned fully to Zephraim as they resumed their walk. "We don't know how long she was there or who, other than John Whyldon, might have been with her."

"The letters from Azmarin indicated she has a handful of supporters with her," Zephraim stated. "And we have their names. You have truly gotten no new information for Her Majesty?"

"We have nothing at the moment to report, no. She was resistant to the methods we applied yesterday. I have been keeping Her Majesty up to date." Cadan tried to swallow the shame of not having broken the woman already.

Zephraim let out a frustrated sigh and pinched the bridge of his nose. "How ridiculous. How hard can it possibly be to get an old lady to talk?"

Cadan schooled his features and bit back his caustic response. "Well, since we are here, I am sure you will find out for yourself." King or not, Cadan didn't appreciate the jabs, but he would voice his displeasure later. Cadan moved to lean against the wall closest to the cell doors, only for Zephraim to point to a spot farther back as if Cadan was a servant to be pushed around. Another raised brow from Zephraim had Cadan grumbling as he took a few more steps back.

Seemingly satisfied, Zephraim approached the cell doors, looking at the whole setup with a distaste frequently seen in the aristocracy. They hated to dirty their hands.

# Chapter Nineteen

"Sara Whyldon?" Zephraim asked, his distaste for the dirty, bloodied woman even more pronounced than the filthy state of the prison.

"What?" the woman responded, voice strained.

Cadan pressed his lips in displeasure and settled in to take note of every word that passed between the two to report to his queen and lord when this mess was over and done.

"What?" Zephraim repeated with a flabbergasted laugh. "Is that how you speak to your king?"

"Show me a king," Sara replied.

Cadan may not have respect for Zephraim, but he was still king. He cleared his throat in warning to Sara, mentally marking the insult.

"You are quite feisty," Zephraim said, his response not sneering or petulant as Cadan had expected. "My sister must have loved you."

Sara smirked at the king, confirmation enough for Cadan. Zephraim's response indicated he thought the same.

"And how is Collette? I hear she's made quite a mess of things everywhere she's stepped foot."

"I'd be wary of the rumors, especially if you think them true," Sara replied.

"Why do you say so?" Zephraim asked in sleepy amusement.

"Because she's coming here, if you trust the rumors," Sara replied with a shrug, though she winced with the effort. "And I doubt she'd have very many nice feelings about the lot of you."

Cadan held in a snort, knowing Collette would come, and she would ultimately lose.

"If my sister had any sense, she'd stay away. She cannot win. Not against what faces her here. If she could, she'd not have been arrested in the first place."

"Given how the guards here talk, I think her arrest had more to do with your desire to taste between your whore's creamy legs than what the actual queen can or can't do," Sara taunted.

Zephraim growled. "Open the cell."

Cadan stood there dumbly for a moment before quickly moving to the cell. "I am more than happy to suitably punish her for the insult." Cadan unlocked the cell door and went to go inside.

"Wait your turn," Zephraim demanded once the door was unlocked. He stepped inside, stalking to Sara like she was prey.

Cadan made a displeased noise but did as he was told. He closed the door behind the king, just in case Sara somehow got the upper hand in whatever was about to happen. Still, he decided it might be best to step away when there was a sudden sharp pain at his temple and the world went black.

Zephraim turned around to see three men of various builds on the other side of the cell, one holding Cadan's unconscious body, slowly lowering the man to the floor. A second man held the object used to knock the man out, the hilt of a dagger. The third stood a ways back, acting as a lookout. The three each wore the uniform of a guard. They would pass inspection at first glance, but a closer look would reveal ill-fitting garments and flashes of gold eyes and glittering skin.

"Thank the Spirits," Zephraim said to himself then looked up to the three guilty Nereid. "He sent a guard in search of Riken and Rhoslyn. You won't have much time."

"The guard is one of Crem's new recruits. He was going to try and give us as much time as possible, but I assume we have another ten minutes at most." The Nereid's dark hair had a sheen of purple to it, and his bright gold eyes kept darting around the room.

The second Nereid stepped forward and opened the door. "Can you run, my lady?"

Sara rose to her feet, a little shaky at first. "I'll be fine to run," she replied. She took seconds to press her hands against her most obvious wounds.

Zephraim watched in amazement as they disappeared, and as Sara stepped into the light from the cell, he practically stumbled back. Sara Whyldon could have been Collette's mother. He tore his gray eyes away from the woman, choosing to ignore what he now knew to be true. "Did Gisella make it out of the palace?" he asked, looking to the closest Nereid. "Agnes said she got out but was shaken."

"Yes, Barris was able to escort her out without any eyes on them," the Nereid replied while the other handed Sara a clean hooded cloak and gave her instructions for how they were getting out. "I'm going to have to knock you out," the Nereid said.

Zephraim almost missed the small twisting of the man's lips. "Do it," Zephraim encouraged.

"I'd say I'm sorry but—" the Nereid said, then Zephraim knew no more.

# Chapter Twenty

Crem paced back and forth, footsteps echoing through the cave as they waited for the Nereids to arrive with Sara Whyldon. His anxiety level was unwarranted, and Crem realized as much, but so much could go wrong. He also worried about depending on Zephraim for the mission. He wanted to trust the man, but he'd placed his hope on Zephraim before, only to have it crushed with the overthrow and the subsequent problems.

Silently, he cursed the inability to see the sky from the cave interior. Tracking time, and everything else, came less easily in hiding. And with a bounty on his head, Crem knew he could not leave the safety of their headquarters.

Turning on his heels, he went and sat next to Diana who had decided the best revenge on Howle would be to trounce him thoroughly at cards. Her irritation with Howle grew more pronounced in her expression any time she came in contact with him, and Crem thought if they not been waiting for news, she might have continued to ignore the old soldier.

# Chapter Twenty

"We should hear something soon," Diana said without turning her gaze from her cards. She tucked her wavy blonde hair behind her ear, then let the hand go to Crem's knee.

"We should," he agreed, appreciating the contact even though it was barely a distraction. He took a deep breath. "The plan was easy, but—"

"The easy ones tend ta be the ones ta go wrong," Howle finished, throwing a card down on the table as he waited for Diana to beat it.

Crem marveled how they were playing Nightgrace without saying a word to the other. The game normally included a lot more bluffing and insults, but Diana had pointedly avoided speaking to Howle since their confrontation. He sighed, knowing he'd have to intervene if they didn't warm to each other soon.

Diana studied her hand, then carefully selected a card and slammed it down on the table, a winning play for the current round.

Crem listened as Howle huffed out a breath and pushed the winnings to Diana before gathering up the cards and shuffling them. "Want to join, Crem?"

"No, I don't have the nerve for it right now. The two of you would drain me dry."

"We'd know if something had gone wrong by now," Diana reminded her husband as she gathered up cards to shuffle. "Bad news travels faster than good."

Crem nodded, deciding to focus on the game. His eyes kept glancing toward the cavern entrance, though he tried to remain positive. Diana trounced Howle twice more before a noise caught his attention and in walked Queen Collette. Crem stood, his chair toppling over from the effort, causing the woman to pause beside her Nereid escort.

"Your Majesty?" Crem asked, confused. The woman was covered in blood and filth, no doubt, but he was much mistaken if the woman accompanying the Nereid was the queen. She had the same carob hair as the queen. The same large eyes. The same pale complexion. The poor lighting obscured some of her features, but Crem suspected he'd see a spattering of freckles across her nose and cheeks were she closer.

"I'm afraid you're looking for someone about thirty years younger," the woman responded. As she approached, he started to notice the differences. She was indeed older and a little taller than the queen. Gray streaks highlighted her hair, and her eyes, though large and round, were the same blue as Whyldon's and slightly more narrowed. Though certainly not Collette, she looked as though she could be her mother.

Howle swore while Crem just stood there dumbly. "Sara Whyldon?" he finally asked.

Sara nodded, and she gave a small chuckle. "I see John was quite secretive during his time in Quenall."

"Clearly," Diana said as she rose to join the men. She blinked, pushing aside her surprise. "Please, come sit. You've suffered so much."

Crem and Howle moved almost at once. Crem pulled out a chair and motioned for her to sit while Howle went over to check on the Nereid and make sure everything went well. "Are you hungry?" Crem asked Sara.

"I'm well," Sara insisted with much more strength than any in the room anticipated. "I was able to heal many of my injuries while imprisoned," she explained as though it were the most natural thing in the world. "Not all of them. I did not wish to raise an alarm or suspicion."

"Heal your injuries?" Crem said in slight awe. He'd heard of those types of powers before, but it had been so long since there were magic users in Quenall, let alone magic healers.

"Of course," Sara replied with a shrug.

"Whyldon did keep secrets," Diana mused with a soft laugh.

"Apparently," Crem muttered. "Are you sure you don't need anything?" he asked again, only for Ian to come out of one of the side tunnels with a tray filled with a steaming pot of tea, a large bottle of what looked like rum or bourbon, and several mugs.

"Sara is self-sufficient. She doesn't like people fussing over her," Ian said as he placed the tray on the table. "Hi, Sara. You're looking better than I hoped."

Sara gave Ian a tired smile. "I'll take your words as a compliment," she said as she picked up one of the bottles, removing the cork and handing it over to be poured. "Thankfully, a couple of boys were tasked with most of what happened."

Ian side-eyed the Nereid men who were talking with Howle. "We're just glad you're safe. Tea or spirits?"

"Spirits, please," Crem said, sitting down heavily as his reality shifted.

Diana resumed her prior seat, her demeanor less overwhelmed than her husband's. She leaned forward, resting her elbows on the table. "Have you seen Her Majesty?" she asked.

"Of course," Sara replied. "She was well, last I saw her, which I am grateful for. She'd been badly injured when she arrived in Barcomb Mill."

Crem snapped out of his stupor. "Can you give us more details on what happened? Whyldon sent a letter with Ian, but it didn't contain a lot of information."

"She nearly died from what John told me. She was attacked and almost bled to death. It took her a long time to recover, and she's got some nasty scars from the encounter."

Crem shook his head. Even knowing Sargarus wasn't her father, Collette was the rightful queen. She loved her people and had put her life on the line defending what she felt was right.

She deserved her throne, and Coralia would be lost without her had she passed from injury. "I'm glad she's okay." Crem became distracted when the Nereid took their leave.

Howle rejoined the group. "According ta them, things went really well. One of them might have taken a bit of pleasure out of knocking Zephraim out." Howled turned to fully face Sara, taking her in, in full. "Sorry ta say, but I don't think we can let ya leave until everything is over, and we most certainly can't let ya be seen."

"I don't believe I asked for your permission," Sara replied in a snarky quip which sounded too much like her niece. "I didn't trade one prison for another, after all."

Laughter bubbled from Diana, who had to rest her forehead on her arms until the initial fit left her.

"Howle, maybe you should quit while you're ahead when it comes to the women in our group," Crem said.

Howle just rolled his eyes.

"What you should have done was ask Sara if she was alright going into hiding," Ian popped off, patting Howle on the shoulder.

"And naturally, I am much more inclined to do as asked. We're lucky the people I dealt with in the prison did not have a personal acquaintance with our queen. No unwanted connections were made." Sara thanked Ian as he poured her a drink, and she took a healthy gulp.

"Even Zephraim?" Crem asked, certain if he had made the connection so quickly, Zephraim should have as well.

"He is on your side now, is he not?" Sara asked.

"Zephraim is, but his desire to thwart Rhoslyn and Riken doesn't mean he wouldn't use your connection to Collette to claim the throne. Granted, I'm not sure Zephraim even wants the throne," Crem admitted.

"He doesn't, and dwelling on the throne as though it is some end goal for him is a disservice to all," Diana said plainly. "What he wants has nothing to do with power and title."

"Sorry, I just can't dismiss it out of hand, how her connection to the Whyldons could be used against her. Even with Zephraim not wanting the throne." Crem gave Diana an apologetic look.

"You can refocus the worry on someone more likely to try and seize power," Diana said simply.

Crem nodded. "What do you want to do?" he asked Sara.

Sara drank from her mug, her expression thoughtful as though weighing options or perhaps contemplating what she wanted to share. "I think there is wisdom in staying here for now," she replied. "She is coming eventually, and those fools in the castle fail to understand how small Quenall is compared to the rest of Coralia. She has the support she needs and more."

"Collette didn't realize how much support she had until she ran into my group and saved a bunch of people from a labor camp." Ian pitched in.

The reminder had Diana scowling. "I can't blame her for doubting her popularity or the devotion from the people. She was treated abominably for so long by the asshole nobles."

"By the Mother, she was. I don't think there was a moment during her reign they weren't trying to undermine her," Crem said, knowing none of them could express the depth of Collette's experience and treatment. He had been there for it. They never respected Collette the way they should have. "There aren't many nobles left, and there will be even less once she is back on the throne. I hope she replaces any who even looked at her wrong when she takes over."

"She probably will," Sara replied. "And I have an idea of who she will surround herself with."

Ian gave Sara a knowing grin.

"I assume you mean the people she's traveling with?" Crem asked.

"Yes, indeed. She is very fond of the members of her group. You should know most of them, I would suspect."

Diana smiled. "I'm glad to hear it. She will be more openly and enthusiastically supported this time. Let's get you something to eat, and you can tell us anything we need to know."

Sara consented, and Crem sat back, thankful for the success of the evening and the promise of substantial progress.

# Chapter Twenty-One

"Already planning another war, and we've barely started this one," Sabine remarked as she sat down across the table from Alaoin. Her long, light caramel hair was pinned up above her shoulders, and a new purple bruise sat in prominent view on her collarbone.

"Of course," Alaoin said with a chuckle. He had his legs draped over the arm of his chair, a goblet of wine in reach and a bowl of fruit in his lap. "Azmarin has been a problem and will continue to be a problem even after we get the imposters off the Coralian throne. You are the one who said it is to everyone's benefit to clean the empire out and start fresh." He grinned at Sabine. "See? I am a good listener."

Faron gave Alaoin a look Sabine referred to as "exasperated parent." "We've also told you to take on one problem at a time."

Éric pointed his quill at his father. "That you think he listens or retains what either of you say reflects poorly on the two of you after all these years."

"Hey!" Alaoin exclaimed. "I am your king. Some respect for my position, please."

"Do some of the work of king rather than having me do it for you," Sabine suggested with a smirk, causing Alaoin to roll his eyes.

"Yes, Mother," he replied.

"It bothers me when you call her that," Éric said under his breath.

Faron laughed. "He does some of the work. Some."

Sabine reached over to pat her son's hand. "Alaoin has very few refined manners."

"I live with him. I'm aware of his manners."

"I am right here," Alaoin said, pointing to himself. "And I am your king."

"As you've said," Sabine dismissed. "Which takes us back to your plan to go after Azmarin. How do you see it playing out?"

Alaoin shrugged. "We get Coralia back for Collette, then we turn toward Azmarin. Mallan isn't much of a leader from what I hear. I doubt they have the needed organization to lend real help to Coralia right now."

Éric reached into his satchel and pulled out a book. Flipping through it, he landed on the page he needed and quickly scanned it. "Your spies report unrest over Mallan's management. Now would be a good time to take Azmarin, especially if Mallan is stupid enough to send the majority of the army to Coralia to help in this fight."

"And do we have enough troops to go after Azmarin and help the Nereids and Queen Collette?" Alaoin asked. "I did promise my cousin I would help her, and I've no doubt she's going to be an excellent ally."

Faron glanced at Éric's notebook for a moment. "She'll help. She needs Azmarin handled as much as we do. Moreso, I think."

"But can she help now? I doubt it," Alaoin said. "We're going to have to wait until things with the Nereid are settled at least."

Éric put the book down. "I think help from either side will be difficult to determine until we know how the first battle shakes out. I believe we have the bigger army, and the Nereid have as much love for Azmarin as we do. I think we will have to hope one of us kills Mallan on the field if he bothers to fight, and the unrest in Azmarin lasts long enough for us to take advantage of it."

"What do you mean 'one of us'? You aren't getting near the battlefield," Faron growled at his son who just waved it off.

Sabine's gaze traveled to her husband, and even when their eyes met, she said nothing.

"Mother is the only one who needs to stay off the battle-field. I'm capable with a sword," Éric said offhandedly when Faron went to say something else. "You can't keep me from fighting, Father."

"What if I give Sabine a sword?" Alaoin broke in, perhaps to cut through the tension between father and son. "You could have a nice little family line on the battlefield."

"Mother isn't fighting," Éric said.

At the same time, Faron growled, "Sabine isn't stepping foot on the battlefield." Both men looked at Sabine and echoed each other. "Unless she wants to be."

"Trust me," Sabine said with a shake of her head. "I've no desire to be on a battlefield, and not just because it would prove a great distraction to you both."

"He's going to be distracted enough as it is," Faron said, his head motioning toward Éric.

"Father, shut up."

Alaoin laughed as he sat up, his feet going to the floor. "The three of you provide excellent entertainment. Elyna and Amélie will be sorry to have missed the show."

"They'll be more upset about missing the battle." Faron rolled his eyes.

From Éric's position in the corner, Sabine noted her son playing with his quill, something he only did when nervous. Again, her gaze met Faron's, and she nodded in silent communication. "They will," Sabine agreed. She rose from her seat. "Éric, come with me. I have a matter I wish to discuss."

Éric glanced at Sabine before picking up his bag and hoisting it over his shoulder. He winced a bit as the weight settled, and Sabine was half-tempted to tell him to unpack the thing. "Coming, Mother. Alaoin, don't piss off my father."

"How would I manage such a thing?" Alaoin asked, feigning insult.

"You know your father," Sabine said to Éric, her voice teasing. "Alaoin will glance at him, and Faron will decide it was a slight."

Éric turned back to glare at the two as if they were younger than he before following Sabine out of the room.

The two strolled down various corridors in silence. Sabine knew her son well, and giving space and silence often helped him articulate what he wanted or needed. "So you've decided to fight?" she prompted after several comfortable minutes of silence.

"Yes," he admitted without apology or excuse. "I know Alaoin is skilled with a sword, but the fool has been so busy with everything else, I can't remember the last time he picked one up to practice." Éric's face stayed calm, but his voice gave away how stressed the idea of Alaoin being out of practice made him.

Sabine nodded. "Obviously, you have my support in following the path you've taken. Just keep in mind you won't be able to guarantee staying close to Alaoin."

"I know, but I can't leave him out there without support." Éric ran a hand across his face, ignoring the ink he smeared across his skin. "If the fool gets himself killed..." He paused and shook his head.

"I know, sweetheart," Sabine said quietly. "I know. Every time your father has gone off to fight, I cannot do anything until he is back and safe. Which is why I ask you to be as careful as you possibly can. You have a very sizable piece of my heart, my son."

"I'll try," Éric promised, though Sabine knew he'd sacrifice himself to save Alaoin and not just because Alaoin was their king.

"Have you considered asking Alaoin if he would like to train with Queen Collette?" Sabine asked after a moment. "She is well disciplined. You could spin it as a need to strengthen our odds by ensuring a cohesive fighting strategy."

"I can try," Éric conceded. "He refuses to train with Father, so getting him to practice with Queen Collette may be my best option."

"He likes Queen Collette, and he wants an alliance with her. I think he will listen," Sabine said. "I'm also certain she will come across as much less harsh than Faron can be."

"As long as he can be appropriate. We know he isn't serious when he flirts, but she may not." Éric's nose crinkled in anger, his unhappiness with Alaoin's flirtation toward the queen evident.

Sabine stopped them, and she reached out, placing a hand on his arm. "You could always speak with him, you know. Alaoin isn't the most perceptive."

"He's not interested in me, Mother. Trust me." Éric gave her a tight smile. "I tried once, years ago at one of your parties. The spirits we imbued made confessing seem like a good idea. Alaoin nicely shut me down by pretending to have not heard me. He decided to talk about one of the ladies he was considering bedding that night. So no, I will not be trying again."

Sabine sighed. "Did you know your father once declared he did not love me?"

Éric's eyes scanned Sabine's face for a moment before shaking his head. "No, the two of you always make it sound like you fell in love at first glance." Éric made a dismissive noise as if he hadn't been in love with Alaoin his entire life.

"In many ways we did, but your father, being your father, did not immediately recognize what he felt, and there were some hurt feelings in the interim before things were sorted."

"How did you fix it?"

"Well, I tried to carry on with my duties, though my hurt was not as well concealed as I might have liked. He spoke with our family about his action, and ultimately, we just decided to be very honest with one another about how we felt and what we wanted. One of the things your father had to contend with was not just how he felt but also the acceptance of my feeling the same way."

"Your story sounds overly complicated and exactly like something you and Father would do," Éric said. "If I ever decide to try again with Alaoin, I will aim for something easier."

"Alaoin isn't as vexing as your father, thankfully. You should have a little more self-awareness from him."

"You present your own opinion. I feel it is wrong, but we can disagree."

Sabine laughed. "You should ask your father about the time I fired him," she suggested. "You might change your mind."

"If you fired Father, he must have done something truly horrendous. Considering the antics the two of you get up to, I'm afraid to ask him."

Sabine laughed again. There was no hiding the voracious appetite she and her husband shared for one another. The bruise on her collarbone indicated as much. "It was the night we met Avana, actually. We were still behaving at the time."

# Chapter Twenty-one

Éric tilted his head to the side, squinting his eyes in thought. "Ah, when he paraded you around the chateau naked in front of everyone because he was 'worried about your safety'?"

"In his very slight defense, I was not entirely naked," Sabine replied. "But your version is close enough to the truth."

"But naked enough," Éric said sarcastically. "Aunt Avana loved to tell the story… with embellishments."

Sabine snorted and nodded. "I've heard some of her versions. They are quite amusing if nothing else." She put an arm around her son. "Do you truly never plan on bringing up your feelings with Alaoin?"

Éric shook his head. "I tried once, and he brushed me off. I don't know if my heart could handle another rejection. We both know if he was to marry anyone, it would be one of the girls. He likes feral, pretty things like them."

"He might not," Sabine pointed out. "And he might just be clueless about what you feel. Wanting to protect your heart is a valid desire, but I'd hate for you to lose out on great happiness out of fear."

"I will take your advice into consideration, Mother," Éric said. He brought them to a halt and placed a kiss on Sabine's cheek. "I think I will go find Queen Collette and inquire if she's alright with Alaoin joining her training session."

Sabine knew Éric was removing himself from the discussion. "Of course, darling. We'll get Alaoin out there to practice if she'd agreed for him to join."

Éric nodded. "I will let you know." He quickly made an escape, leaving Sabine to return to Alaoin and Faron on her own.

# Chapter Twenty-Two

"So," Jayden drawled as the door to the meeting room emptied, leaving him and Ceto alone. He'd wanted to tease her for weeks, and after spending several long hours watching her lean toward the queen, he couldn't help himself. "When are you going to tell Queen Collette you want to ride her until waves overtake the world?"

Ceto raised an eyebrow, her bright gold eyes glancing up at him from her seat. "You should know better, Jayden," she said as she gathered her parchment. "A woman like Queen Collette requires a much gentler and thorough touch."

Jayden couldn't help but laugh at her response. "You have put some thought into a theoretical opportunity." Teasing Ceto had become one of his favorite pastimes, and he would take any presented opportunity. "What about Larent? Have you planned for him as well?"

Ceto rose from her seat, her arms filled with the notes she'd taken. "As nice as I'm sure he is, he doesn't do anything for me."

"Mmm," Jayden said with a nod. "You have made yourself a problem if you're not interested in both. They seem very attached."

"Which is why I anticipate nothing happening."

"You could always inquire about his feelings on voyeurism." Jayden tapped his chin with his index finger. "In fact, I'll ask for you." Jayden gave her a devilish smile and turned to the door.

Ceto waved him off, clearly not the least bit threatened or embarrassed by her feelings. "I hope you have fun," she said, chuckling. "She's likely figured out you're nothing like your ambassador persona, and she knows I'm not."

"You think so?" Jayden asked. He thought back to the very serious demeanor he had put on while in Quenall, a demeanor he'd needed to maintain for his protection. "I believe the entire kingdom thought Nereids had no sense of humor by the time I fled." His people could often be reserved but only with outsiders and only when necessary.

"She is as intelligent as she is lovely," Ceto pointed out. "And Aphros believes she is one of us, at least in part. Just be sure to let Aphros know she is about to be insulted."

"Why? It will provide me with much more entertainment to find out about the same time Collette pulls all of her support after you send me to make inquiries about your desire to have her for a night." He dodged a quill Ceto tossed his way.

"I am not sending you," Ceto retorted. "I'm simply not stopping you."

"Which is why I can get away with saying you sent me." Jayden shrugged and gave her a wink as he strode out the door. "I'll have your answer in an hour."

Jayden stood outside the door for a moment, looking to see which direction Collette might have gone with Larent. Thankfully, they hadn't wandered very far as he spotted them just down the corridor. He jogged over to the couple. "Hello! May I have a moment of your time?"

Collette pulled away from Larent where she'd pressed him against the wall. "Sure," she agreed, not looking at all like she wanted to.

"So, my cousin arrived in the underwater city about an hour ago. It appears she may have run into a shark while coming in from Quenall. She should be surfacing soon, and I believe you will want to meet her. But before you do—" Jayden gave Collette a mischievous look. "Can you look back at Ceto like we are talking about her please?" Jayden smiled at Larent as he burst out laughing.

"Are we harassing her?" Collette asked. "I'd like to know why I'm being asked to be mean."

"We aren't being mean. We are just giving Ceto a hard time," Jayden insisted. "She does similar things to me all the time."

"We are being a little mean," Larent corrected. "You told her you were going to tell Collette, didn't you?"

"I might have, yes."

"Was I not supposed to know?" Collette asked though the three grew quiet as Ceto walked past them.

"I figured you did," Larent said after Ceto's figure disappeared.

Jayden found himself slightly envious of the smile the shifter gave Collette as if everything good came from her. He supposed for Larent, it did.

"I wasn't sure. You don't give much away."

"Years of training," Collette explained. She pointed up at Larent. "One of the very few people who can see beyond it."

Larent just shrugged which just made Jayden laugh.

"Well, your skill is a boon." He started forward, motioning for them to follow.

"And where are we following you?" Collette asked as she took Larent's hand.

"I'm hoping my cousin is in Aphros's office. So I thought we should start there," Jayden responded. "Since she's coming from Quenall, I'm hopeful she'll have news. Maybe you would like to be there."

"I would, yes," Collette confirmed.

Jayden nodded. "I thought as much." They walked quickly, making small talk as they went. When they reached Aphros's office, Jayden knocked and was granted entrance. He held the door open for Collette and Larent to enter first, then followed behind them.

Lynessea stood on the opposite side of Aphros's desk. She was average height with long black hair streaked with indigo and sea green. Her scales, blending into her olive skin, reflected a similar color. She wore a light dress with no shoes, which told Jayden she'd been in a hurry to get to Aphros.

"Cousin, I'm glad you arrived safely. Well, mostly safe," Jayden said, and Lynessea held her arms open, embracing Jayden warmly when he stepped closer.

Pulling back, Jayden made a face as he realized his shirt was now damp thanks to her hair. He shrugged it off and motioned to Lynessea. "Queen Collette, consort Larent, may I introduce my cousin, Lady Lynessea?"

Lynessea's gold eyes went wide, but she quickly turned and bowed to them. "It is a pleasure to meet you both."

"It's a pleasure to meet you as well," Collette replied, her smile warm. "I understand you came from Quenall?"

"I did," Lynessea replied. "The city is much as I'm sure you expect it to be."

Aphros grinned as Jayden made the introductions. "Ceto stopped by a few minutes ago, cousin. We shall have to talk, I think," he whispered.

"I thought she might, which is why I brought the queen," Jayden replied. He turned to the women. "I thought the

introductions prudent since I am certain we will all be spending more time together should Barris survive." Jayden flinched when Lynessea hit him.

Dawning comprehension crossed Collette's face. "You're his wife," she guessed.

Lynessea looked away from Collette for a moment, and Jayden was reminded how much she hated being in the spotlight. "Yes, I am."

"He plays the fool quite well," Collette said.

"He isn't always playing," Lynessea said, punching Jayden once more before stepping toward Collette, her discomfort seemingly ebbing. "It is nice to formally meet you."

"You as well," Collette replied. "Tell me, if you and Aphros are both cousins to Jayden, what is your relationship with each other?"

"He is my brother, though few outside of our people know of the connection," Lynessea said.

Jayden was surprised she hadn't side-stepped the question as was often the case.

"I can see a need to keep it silent," Collette said.

"Especially since I live in Coralia," Lynessea quipped.

Jayden caught the implications right away and almost nudged Lynessea for it. "Didn't you say you had news?" he asked as Aphros motioned for Collette to take a seat.

"Yes, I was just going over the details with Aphros, but I am happy to start over if His Majesty doesn't mind?" Lynessea looked over at the king.

"By all means," Aphros said with a wave of his hand. "It concerns Coralia, so Collette should be involved." Without prompting, the king rose to his feet and went to the table holding his collection of liquor. He began pouring glasses for everyone, passing them out a couple at a time.

# Chapter  Twenty-two

Jayden watched Lynessea take a deep breath, her eyes dropping to Aphros's desk as they took on a faraway quality. He'd noticed his cousin's habit appeared when she needed to get her thoughts together.

"Lord Riken returned to Quenall with the majority of his soldiers. His knee is apparently shattered in what they are calling a vicious attack from the Outlaw Queen who wrongfully freed a large group of dangerous criminals from a labor camp." Lynessea let the news settle. "Rhoslyn was extremely upset with him, to the point of making him kneel on his injured knee and explain exactly what went wrong. Or at least, that is what we were told." She looked around to see if there were any questions.

"Rhoslyn's actions and the spin they've put on the story sound about like what I expected," Collette said, pausing to thank Aphros for the drink he pushed into her hand. "Do you think they feel panicked or secure?"

Lynessea thought for a moment. "Considering the same night they started discussing plans to attack us here and take your head with or without Azmarin's help, I would say laughably secure."

"Should we be expecting Barris to show up with soldiers?" Jayden asked, his mind racing on how many ships Barris might bring and where to put his men.

"No, my husband has decided to stay in Quenall." Lynessea's tone told everyone how unhappy she was with the decision.

"You said as much," Aphros said after taking his seat again. "But you haven't fully explained his choice."

Jayden saw Lynessea's eyes slide to Collette and braced himself for whatever news she was about to deliver.

"To help Crem, Zephraim, and the rest of the rebellion against Rhoslyn and Riken."

Collette's jaw literally dropped open in surprise. "Zephraim?" she said in utter disbelief.

"Yes…" Lynessea drawled, ignoring the look of shock on the faces of everyone present.

"Why would he be helping Zephraim?" Collette asked, managing to avoid sounding completely accusatory. "A great deal of what happened to me and to Coralia rests on his shoulders."

"Barris would tell you Zephraim regrets his choices and is trying to make up for the damage he's done, partly due to Zephraim considering pardoning you. I honestly don't know other than he has said he is against Rhoslyn and Riken's more radical politics. It took a lot for him to reinstate the Merscale trade."

"It shouldn't have been reinstated at all," Collette said, shaking her head. "I cannot believe anyone would trust the little rat ever again."

"Barris and Diana saw something in him these last few months. It made them decide to give him a chance," Lynessea replied.

Collette shook her head again. "They should be wary in their dealings with him, no matter how contrite he claims to be now."

"I have warned Barris of your point, and he quoted our beliefs against me," Lynessea said with an eye roll.

"Of course he did," Jayden breathed.

"Perhaps we get Queen Collette's warning back to Barris, and we hope he is wise enough to see through possible trickery," Aphros suggested. "I'm sure we don't know the depth of harm his actions have truly caused, but if he has truly turned and wishes to atone, he can be quite valuable."

"Barris has taken him to where Crem and his people are. If they are smart, they will have used him to handle a few issues. I am hoping we'll have a letter from him soon, but I am happy to write to him as well," Lynessea replied.

Collette's gaze shot to Larent, starting a brief silent conversation between them before she faced Lynessea and nodded. "Whatever you think wisest," she said.

Jayden caught the look between the two. "Is there more you think we should add to the letter?"

Collette looked back at Larent. "Do you want to share?"

Larent stared at Collette for a moment, and Jayden felt his anxiety grow at the weight of the look.

Larent turned back to the group with a sharp animalistic smile. "I can't currently access any of my shifter abilities because if I do, I'm likely to murder Collette thanks to Zephraim using blood magic on me." He confessed in such a casual way, it took a moment for the words to sink in before both Lynessea and Jayden started cursing.

"Zephraim used the blood magic sometime over the winter, which is when I was injured and the rumors of my death began circulating," Collette explained after Aphros had silenced the room. "If Zephraim has changed since then, maybe he's not playing a long con. But like I've said, I wouldn't trust him."

"I will write to Barris right away," Lynessea said. She only looked at Aphros long enough for him to nod for her to go before leaving the room.

"I think you're going to need to give us the whole story," Jayden said, leaning against Aphros's desk.

*My dearest Barris,*

*Collette has let us know Zephraim used blood magic to try and kill her. I won't tell you what to do or how to handle this information. But please, please be careful.*

*All my love,*
*Lynessea*

# Chapter Twenty-Three

Darkness surrounded her from all sides, boxing Nawalya in, suffocating her with feelings of dread and deep anxiety. She tried to breathe through it, tried to keep herself grounded through the techniques she had learned throughout the years as well as Sara's teaching. Yet, a familiar arrow appeared in the darkness. A normal arrow with no markings or anything special about it, twirling slowly in the air.

Nawalya's anxiety grew, followed by a low-grade sense of horror, ripping her training from her, almost dropping her to her knees. She fought back as best as she could, forcing her body forward, a hand on the rough coral walls as she blindly made her way to where she thought Collette would be.

She hated feeling like she had no control, like her visions would always possess the ability to consume her at any given moment, but Nawalya was more surprised it hadn't happened sooner. Stress had always made her visions worse, more unpredictable. Just like being in Quenall had been extremely stressful, so was being here, preparing for war.

The worst part was the difference in her current vision. Nawalya was used to seeing the possible lives of those around her, the possible future in front of her. But since Whyldon learned about her vision of Collette's possible death, all she'd seen was an arrow in the darkness. It had been rare in the beginning, but lately, she couldn't go a night without seeing the arrow. Sleep became her most hated enemy, leaving her anxious and desperate. The arrow had to mean something. Using the hand on the wall to guide her, Nawalya continued forward, continued toward help.

Collette did not find her, even though she had been Nawalya's intended target. "What's wrong?" Whyldon's voice spoke through the vision's mental fog. She hadn't heard him approach, or perhaps she had stumbled on him.

Nawalya's breath caught at the sound of Whyldon's voice. She turned her head in the direction she thought he was, fighting back against her vision with renewed force, trying to shake free. She reached out to him. "Vision," she called out.

She felt Whyldon's arm go around her shoulders, gently guiding her away from the wall. "Come on," he said gently. "Just trust me. I'll get you somewhere safe."

Nawalya nodded. She'd always trusted Whyldon. Even when he'd been mad at her, Nawalya knew he wouldn't hurt her. He was the voice she'd heard her whole life, and even now, he was a safe harbor. Wrapping an arm around Whyldon, she let him guide her.

She wasn't sure how much time passed between Whyldon finding her and him helping her settle into a chair in one of the rooms given for their use by Aphros, but Whyldon remained close and attentive as the effects of her vision began to wane.

Nawalya closed her eyes as the darkness faded, and she felt herself drawing away from the vision. Slowly, the horror and bone-deep anxiety left her body, leaving her feeling drained and sluggish. Leaning her head back against the cushion of the

chair, she slowly opened her eyes, allowing them to adjust to the light of the room. "Thank you," she said softly.

"Of course," Whyldon said. He stayed respectfully to himself, but his willingness to stay by her side while she went through the vision spoke volumes. "Should I get the others, or do you need some time?"

Nawalya didn't want to be alone. She wanted to crawl into Whyldon's lap and have him hold her until she felt better. As her desire wasn't an option, she said, "Go get the others, please."

Whyldon nodded, though he waited with her several more minutes before leaving the room. Alone again, Nawalya buried her head in her hands as she pulled herself together, pushing Whyldon from her mind and focusing on what she knew an arrow could mean.

The door opened minutes later, and three distinct sets of footsteps sounded across the room. Nawalya looked up and spotted Collette, Larent, and Whyldon entering the room.

Nawalya gave a small tired wave as she sat back in the chair once more. A hand landed on her shoulder, and she knew right away it was Larent.

"You okay, Waya?"

"No, but I will be," she replied softly.

"Anything we can get you?" Collette offered.

"Water, please."

Whyldon moved to pour water for Nawalya from a pitcher. The Nereid tended to put fruit or flowers into their water, lightly flavoring the drink, and when the chalice was handed over to Nawalya, tiny delicate petals floated on the surface.

"Thank you," Nawalya said. She admired the petals for a moment before taking a sip. The edible petals provided a light floral flavor she'd never experienced before. "I saw the arrow again. It caught me by surprise. I was in the hallway, and my vision was suddenly gone, leaving nothing but darkness, anxiety, and horror before it was just there." Nawalya looked up at Collette. She had made sure the woman was informed of her vision. Had done her damnedest to keep her promise. "It's been every night over the past week, but today was the first time I've been awake and not meditating."

"The arrow obviously means something," Collette said gently. "Any possible ideas of what? It's a symbol, especially in the middle of war escalation."

"There is nothing special about the arrow. It could be something Thomas made for all I..." Nawalya trailed off as it occurred to her the arrow could represent Thomas.

Larent cursed. "Arian is going to lock him in a room and never let him out." He turned to the door. "I'll go get Arian and Thomas."

"You might as well get Rion and Tolan, too," Collette said, looking over to Larent. "We need to discuss the arrow and the meeting we just left."

"Alright, be right back," Larent said and jogged out of the room.

Whyldon took one of the seats while Collette stayed close beside Nawalya. "It doesn't necessarily mean anything about Thomas," she said gently. "Arrows have many meanings, and your vision doesn't sound very clear."

"Arian is going to assume, though," Whyldon said with a sigh.

"Arrows mean so many possible things, but with Thomas being a fletcher, Arian is not going to respond well." Nawalya took another sip of her water. "Thomas is capable though. He won't let Arian do anything drastic."

"He won't tolerate it, anyway," Whyldon said in agreement.

The door opened, admitting Larent with Arian, Thomas, Tolan, and Rion. Nawalya knew the moment Arian realized she'd had a vision.

A curse spewed from his lips, and he turned as if to rush from the room, only to stop himself and turn back around to face her. "Would you like me to get you a potion?" Arian asked.

"Yes, please. I'm feeling rather weak." Nawalya pressed her lips together. "But not until after we've talked, please."

Everyone else settled for the moment, Nawalya's condition making it clear they were there to discuss her latest vision. "I saw the arrow again. It appeared with a strong feeling of anxiety and the added bonus of horror. It's just a plain arrow. I don't know anything else."

"Arrows," Thomas spoke first. "They could mean moving forward. Or pointing to something. Arrows are highly symbolic for many."

"Yes, but the feelings behind a vision are often just as important. I do not think the anxiety and horror suggests moving forward," Arian pointed out.

Nawalya was not happy with how Arian looked at Thomas as it confirmed her and Whyldon's fears. "The vision feels like a bad omen, but I don't think it involves Thomas." Her gaze shifted from Arian to the fletcher. "Unless you're suddenly making a magic arrow or doing something we should know about?" Nawalya joked as she tried to break the tension in the room.

Larent laughed. "Imagine what fire arrows could do."

"People already use those without the need for magic," Rion pointed out.

"They do," Thomas confirmed. "And there are no magical arrows to be associated with me, regardless."

"So what are other possibilities, then?" Whyldon asked. "Since we just can't assume the vision focuses on Thomas."

"It could mean the battle won't go in our favor. Or heavy losses. Have you had the dream about the Nereids being murdered while Aphros is forced to watch since leaving Quenall?"

Tolan asked, referencing their conversation in the tavern months upon months ago.

"No. I only had the vision once. I think enough has changed since then," Nawalya replied.

"So what do we do since the vision could mean anything?" Rion asked, rubbing his bearded chin in thought.

"We normally just keep an eye out for anything unusual when things aren't clear," Larent said with a shrug.

"I don't think there is anything else we could actively do without more information," Collette agreed. "Even if we were relatively certain the vision was about Thomas, a foreboding arrow doesn't tell us much of anything."

"I wish I'd seen more, but even when I meditate, I can't move past the arrow."

"It is affecting your sleep, correct?" Arian asked, and she nodded. "Would you like a sleep potion?"

"Yes, but with the dreams coming every night, it may not be best." Nawalya didn't say she feared being unable to rouse herself from the vision if she drank the potion.

"You need sleep, especially with everything else approaching," Collette said. "If someone needs to be with you so you can get some, it can be arranged."

"I'll do it," Larent and Arian said at the same time.

"If you don't mind?" Larent asked Collette.

Arian looked at Thomas, and Nawalya noticed his eyebrow raised as if questioning Thomas as well. Nawalya still didn't like the look in Arian's eyes though.

"You're free to do as you like," Thomas said to Arian. "As am I."

Nawalya watched as Arian's lips formed a flat line. She decided she might need to grab more blankets for the next few nights. "If I have another vision, or should the arrow reappear, I'll let you all know."

"Thank you, Nawalya," Collette said, offering her a thankful but sympathetic look.

"Whyldon said you and Larent had news," Rion prompted.

Larent chuckled. "You could say that." Larent motioned for Collette to go ahead.

Nawalya found herself sitting up straighter at the dangerous look in his eyes.

Collette began the explanation without ceremony. "Cremisius Hawke has led something of a rebellion in Quenall, and Lord Barris is acting as part of the rebellion. He is married to Aphros's sister and Jayden's cousin. She arrived earlier today, and she reports Zephraim's participation in said rebellion."

"What?" Whyldon demanded, sitting up straighter. "Why are they trusting him? Don't they know how dangerous he is?"

"I doubt it," Collette said with a sigh. "But they seem to trust him all the same."

"Zephraim must have done something to earn the commander's trust. Cremisius Hawke is not a stupid man," Arian said.

"He's not," Rion confirmed. "Spirits, he was always the most difficult to deal with of the guard leadership. He's not prone to just believing someone because they want to be believed."

"So Zephraim must have done something fairly convincing," Tolan added.

"I know he used blood magic on Larent to try to kill me," Collette said, her views clearly less optimistic than the others. "How do you go from using the darkest of magic to being worthy of trust?"

"People do surprising things all the time," Nawalya said. "But I wouldn't be surprised if he's kept his dirty little secret to himself."

"I'm hopeful Zephraim is genuine in his attempts to help the others, if only for their sakes," Whyldon added with a sigh.

"Either way, if Aphros and his people know, Crem and anyone else he works for will soon know as well."

"Think about the ways they could use him if he is being genuine," Arian said thoughtfully.

Larent fondly rolled his eyes. "Arian's thinking Zephraim could be used to poison Rhoslyn. I'm calling it now."

Arian shot Larent a rude gesture, proving his point.

"I refuse to entertain the notion of Zephraim having changed," Collette said, her hand cutting through the air as though to wave away even the remotest of possibilities. "He might very well be unhappy in the chaos he created for himself, but his being unhappy doesn't change everything he did."

"It does not," Arian agreed as Larent nodded.

"Good, so let's not dream over how helpful a benevolent Zephraim could be. He'd just as soon poison one of us if he thought it beneficial," Collette said.

"Not if we slit his throat first," Tolan muttered as Arian gave an affirmative huff.

Collette gave a tired laugh. "See? We're on the same page again." She rolled her shoulders, obviously annoyed by the discussions surrounding Zephraim. "I'm going to rest before dinner," she announced. "If the lot of you vote Zephraim into the group while I'm gone, I'm starting a new group." Joke given, she exited the room, closing the door behind her.

There was a small chuckle from several people in the room, and Arian took the moment of levity to approach Nawalya. "Potions to deal with the aftermath of the vision, but nothing for sleep, correct?" he confirmed as the others started rising to leave.

"Yes, please."



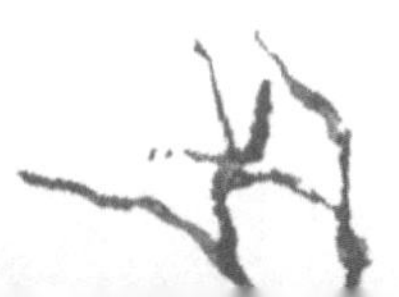

# Chapter Twenty-Four

Arian walked from the meeting room at an even pace, his fists balled at his sides. He needed to get to his and Thomas's room to retrieve the potion for Nawalya. She needed more than something to rejuvenate her. She needed sleep, but she'd made her stance on a sleeping potion known, and he wasn't going to argue the point with her.

Besides, he had other, more important things on his mind. Things like the unknown arrow. As he caught up with Thomas, who'd left the room a few minutes before he had, he grasped the other man by his upper arm, pulling him down the corridor.

Thankfully, Thomas did not resist or even look surprised. He followed happily enough. "What are you doing?" he asked.

Arian said nothing, just continued to pull Thomas along with him, not trusting himself to speak out in the open. Even balled into a fist, Arian's free hand silently shook. His mind conjured too many potential atrocities, too many potential losses for him to behave rationally. He pushed the intrusive thoughts from his mind until they were in their room.

# Chapter Twenty-four

Once they were alone and able to shut out the world, Arian crowded Thomas against the door, their bodies pressed together. "You will not step foot on any battlefield."

Thomas did not reply at first, and his expression remained mostly kind. "I have no intention of fighting if that is your worry, Arian." He nudged the elf away from him without the action turning forceful. "But I am not Larent, and I will not cheerfully take orders."

Arian refused to move, instead resting his head in the crook of Thomas's neck. "What if the arrow is about you?" he breathed against Thomas, his hands moving to rest on Thomas's hips.

"What if it is?" Thomas replied. "Ordering me around isn't going to resolve things, Arian. And we don't know if it's even about me to begin with."

"What if it is?" Arian repeated. "Losing you is not acceptable." His hands tightened on Thomas's hips as he tried to convey, badly, the worry which had settled into his chest over the past twenty minutes. Thomas had become so important to him in such a short amount of time, and nothing in the world could convince him to take on any avoidable risk.

"Arian, we are about to go to war. We are going to lose people. The likelihood of everyone in our group surviving is minimal. I know you are aware of as much."

"What if I only care if you survive?" The words were out of Arian's mouth before he could consider what he was saying.

Thomas sighed and wrapped his arms around Arian, holding him close. "You care about the fate of many more people than me alone," he said. "I will do what I can to stay safe, but you cannot order me around."

Arian took a stuttering breath against Thomas's neck. "Please, please stay off the battlefield. Stay somewhere safe." He buried his face farther into Thomas's neck and said the next words in a soft whisper. "I love you." His hands flexed on

Thomas's hips before he wrapped them fully around Thomas. His breathing caught once more at the contact. "I love you," he repeated, louder this time, more for himself than Thomas.

"I love you," Thomas said, the words echoing through Arian.

Arian pulled back enough to gently kiss Thomas before resting his forehead on the other man's.

"Collette wishes me present during the first battle," Thomas quietly reminded Arian. "I will tell her no if it is what would make you most at ease, but I think I will be far enough back from the action, I should be among the safest on the island."

"I need you safe, but if you want to be there," Arian closed his eyes, willing some easy answer to come to him, "I will not stop you." And he meant that, no matter how much it pained him.

"Okay," Thomas replied, his voice calm and soothing. "We'll figure something out. In the meantime, you should get the potion to Nawalya. She looked pale."

Arian wanted to say Nawalya could wait. Everything outside of their room could wait. All he wanted to do was be there, in the moment, with Thomas. He might have had he not promised to return to Nawalya, a promise he now regretted.

He forced himself to take a step back. Closing his eyes, Arian wrestled himself back under control and moved to his pack. "I apologize," he said.

"I know," Thomas said as he crossed the room and took a seat at the desk chair near where Arian worked. "And I understand. I know there are so many factors we have no control over. It's easy to panic."

"Which is why Nawalya is the one who ensures our plans go the way they should or enacts the new plans. I tend to start stabbing people when things do not go my way," Arian said, only half-joking as he pulled the potion from his pack.

"I think I've heard something about your tendencies," Thomas replied.

"Larent does enjoy going on about them," Arian responded and, without thinking about it too much, leaned down and kissed Thomas once more. "I will be right back."

"Looking forward to it," Thomas replied.

Arian stepped out into the hallway, his head down as he considered the vision and the upcoming war from every angle. He also considered how he and Thomas would spend their evening, knowing there was nothing they could do without more information. He stumbled back as he smacked right into another person not five feet from the door.

"Hey there, Chuckles," Larent said, grabbing Arian's shoulders so he wouldn't hit the ground. "You alright?"

Arian looked up at Larent. For a moment, he considered shrugging him off, but he knew the shifter didn't deserve poor treatment. Opening his mouth, Arian intended to tell Larent he was fine, but what came out of his mouth was something completely different. "I am aware you volunteered to stay with Nawalya tonight. Is that still your plan?"

"Yeah. I mean, I'm going to check with Collette to make sure she's good with it, but yeah."

"Good." He shoved the potion bottle at Larent. "I am staying with Thomas, then. You can take Nawalya the potion and let her know. Come by my room later. I will leave the sleep potion outside. Do not knock on my door." Arian made sure Larent had a firm grip on the bottle before turning on his heels and going back to his room. He almost missed Larent's parting cheer.

"Go get some, Chuckles."

Arian rolled his eyes, but he forgot about Larent as he reentered the room he shared with Thomas. "I am yours for the night, if you will have me."

Thomas grinned. "Then come here."

The shadows flickered across the wall as the fire blazed comfortingly from the hearth. She was alone for the evening, a first in a period so long she couldn't truly remember the last time she'd had a bed to herself. It had to be back in Quenall.

Knowing she wouldn't be able to sleep, she'd opted to forgo her bedroom and sat in the same common room the group had shared earlier in the day to discuss Nawalya's vision. She'd settled into a comfortable chair near the fire, silently and peacefully enjoying the passing minutes.

Collette wasn't sure how much time had passed in comfortable silence when a soft knock was heard at the door. "Yes?" she called without making any other effort.

"May we come in?" asked Rion from the other side.

"It's supposed to be a shared space," she called back, totally at ease in her position and unsurprised Rion would seek her out. As happy as she'd been to reunite with him at Barcomb Mill, they hadn't had much time to talk. She suspected he was partially avoiding her, but Collette didn't want to make such accusations.

Rion walked into the room, followed by another pair of footsteps. Collette opened her eyes and spotted Tolan, though she wasn't surprised to see him. Rion seemed to like Tolan, although Tolan's discomfort was palpable if his determination to not meet her eyes was any indication.

"You two are up late," she said as she settled back in her chair.

"And you're not?" Rion asked.

"I'm the queen. I'm allowed."

Rion rolled his eyes. "You're also the biggest pain in my ass."

"And yet, you got around to running at my beck and call."

Tolan laughed at the comment but quickly tried to hide it behind his hand.

Collette was in a good enough mood to invite both men to join her, so she motioned toward the open chairs. "I repeat, you're both up late."

"I couldn't sleep, so I went to see if Rion was up. He decided we should see if you were up and wanted company," Tolan said as he took a chair opposite Collette. Rion took one closer.

"We knew you wouldn't be asleep," Rion explained. "You quit sleeping the moment you became queen."

"Well, it is a rather difficult job," Collette said with a laugh.

"Oh I know," Rion assured her. He glanced around the room, and his face brightened as he spotted a decanter and glasses on a table in the corner of the room. He rose from his chair and went to pour drinks. "Don't worry, Joss. One day soon, you'll be back on hunting trips and enjoying yourself."

Tolan nodded in agreement with Rion, even if his face showed some worry, but there was a lot to worry about. "That's something worth toasting to."

Collette decided to be generous. "A long hunt would be glorious," she said as she accepted a glass from Rion. The next was given to Tolan. "We once took a trip down to Myrefall, hunting elk I think."

"Are you talking about the trip where I was robbed by the barmaid?" Rion asked.

"Yes, and Crem had to lend you money until you were next paid." Collette laughed, only gaining enough self-control to take a quick drink.

Tolan sat back in his seat and took a drink, a small smile on his face. Collette noted, with some interest, Tolan's eyes lingering on Rion as much as her as they chatted.

"Crem walked around broke from women and gambling half the time before he married," Rion pointed out. "It didn't hurt him."

Tolan chuckled. "I always saw him as so put together."

"No," Collette insisted. "He's always been good at his job, and he's a good person, but Diana is the reason he cleaned up so much."

"I can see her cleaning him up. I just have a hard time picturing Cremisius Hawke as a skirt-chasing gambler," Tolan mused.

"Whyldon knows all the good stories," Collette said. "I was only there for some of it."

"She doesn't tell you she was the one Crem would lose his money to," Rion said after taking a hefty gulp from his glass. "Joss is excellent at cards."

"We played a few rounds, and she usually wiped the floor with me. So, I can see it," Tolan assured Rion.

"Challenging me to cards was always foolish on Crem's part," she said with a shrug. Rion got up to pour more drinks.

"I think anyone challenging you to cards is foolish. Though Arian was always rather good."

"And how much money have you lost to Arian to have such knowledge?" Collette teased.

"Four good jobs worth, so about three months of kitchen work," Tolan said, pausing to presumably add the sum.

The confession made Collette giggle, and she had to hold her glass out to prevent sloshing the liquid on her. "Now I need to ask Arian to play cards—and to hear his version of winning your money." She didn't know why she found Tolan's confession so funny. Laughing felt good, especially when she spent so much of her time feeling the creeping tensions of battle.

"Imagine Arian putting his battle tactics to cards, then add how good he is at hiding his emotions. It's a bad combination, especially since half the time he's bluffing."

"Good story," Rion said, chuckling as well. "But is he truly a good player, or are your skills poor?"

"I'm good enough to make more than enough to move from town to town comfortably and always have a roof over my head, even when funds run dry. Arian is good enough to ensure the entire group is well taken care of. I think Collette could beat him, though."

"Well, when Arian is not occupied with certain fletchers, we shall have to arrange a game to see how things go," Collette replied. She moved to take the bottle from Rion and topped off each of their glasses once more.

Rion gently grabbed her wrist with one hand and removed the bottle from her with the other. "Get your own," he joked.

Tolan took another drink. "I think it will be a long time before he's unoccupied with Thomas." He leaned back again and watched as Collette lightly punched Rion in the arm and wrenched the bottle back from him.

"I'm only going to share with Tolan now," she taunted as she resumed her seat.

Tolan looked at his glass then downed the drink before putting the newly empty glass on the table. "Guess I need a refill then."

Collette grinned and leaned forward to pour. Her mischievous gaze met Tolan's for a brief moment before moving on to Rion. Finding some levity in a shared moment with Tolan for the first time since his return was nice.

Tolan returned the grin before turning to Rion, a teasing glint in his eye. "Looks like you're cut off for the night."

"The fuck I am," Rion said with a chuckle. "They have taverns on the island, and I have money. They'll serve me."

"You'd leave our company to drink alone in a tavern?" Tolan asked with a raised eyebrow.

"Of course not," Rion said. "I'd invite you both."

"Going out could be fun," Collette decided. It certainly appealed more than her empty bed.

Tolan tilted his head to the side and looked up at the ceiling. "I feel like I should say that's a bad idea, but fuck it. I'm filled with those so let's go." He gave Collette a wry grin.

Collette grinned back. "I guess we're going out."

# Chapter Twenty-Five

Tolan leaned against the bar, looking around as he waited for drinks. The tavern Rion had picked was very different from what he was used to. Open-air and decorated with a light color palette, the tavern provided a warm and welcoming atmosphere. A couple of fire pits sat in the back at opposite ends of the bar. Some tables were spaced around the rest of the tavern, wooden and metal, but they looked light enough to move around as groups gathered.

On the sides of the building were built-in cranks attached to hangings which could close off the space from poor weather. Tolan wondered how often the hangings had to be used as there had not been poor weather since their arrival.

Noise from the left drew his attention back to his group, now including Alaoin, Ceto, and Jayden whom they'd picked up on the way out of the palace. He couldn't hear what was going on, but it was obvious Collette was giving Alaoin shit about something.

The bartender came over with a tray of drinks in a variety of colors, and Tolan took it with a warm thanks, heading back to their table.

"So Arian is your 'brother'?" Alaoin asked, brows raised in skepticism.

Tolan sat the tray of drinks down, passing some out while others were grabbed by their intended recipient.

"Yes," Collette replied.

"But he's an elf," Alaoin said.

"Correct."

"And you don't share parents?" Alaoin asked.

"Nope."

"It's not difficult to understand," Jayden said with a grin. "You and Éric have the same relationship, do you not? Or do you not see him as a brother?"

Tolan couldn't help but chuckle, realizing Jayden was fishing for gossip. Who knew the Nereid had it in him? Jayden had been anything but humorous and playful when in Quenall, but now in his own space, his infectious laughter followed wherever the ambassador went.

"You know perfectly well they aren't brotherly," Ceto said, falling into a seat beside Collette, her delicate fingers wrapped around a glass of a deep red liquid. "Éric likes to poke Alaoin a bit too much."

Jayden shot Ceto an amused look before he turned back to Tolan with a grin and grabbed his drink. "Families poke at each other. Friends do too. I was just trying to make a comparison."

Tolan rolled his eyes and pushed the tray of remaining drinks to the center of the table.

"Yeah, but are those pokes hints for non-familial pokes?" Collette asked, creating chaos for no discernable reason other than her own amusement. Tolan was reminded of a long-ago meeting in a tavern.

"I don't know." Jayden turned back to Alaoin, his grin broad and teasing. "What types of pokes do you think they represent?" Jayden asked.

Tolan couldn't help but laugh.

"Jayden is more sober than us, yet I think he's going to cause more problems," Tolan said softly to Rion and Collette.

"He's a troublemaker," Rion said with a hardy laugh.

"Yes, he is," Tolan agreed, ignoring the way his smile wanted to grow at Rion's attention. He turned to Collette. "How long until Ceto makes him stop, you think?"

"I think Ceto will probably fuel his little fire," Collette said after plucking one of the new drinks from the tray. "We should all be on her side. She's devious."

Tolan laughed. He could see Ceto's potential for deviousness, but he was also concerned about the extent of Ceto's deviousness. He looked back up to Alaoin as his cousin started to answer Jayden's question.

"I think you need to get a hobby if you're busy conjuring up possibilities of any pokes concerning me," Alaoin replied with a cheeky grin.

Jayden and Ceto exchanged looks, then the redhead passed some coins to Jayden. Tolan wondered if they had bet regarding Alaoin and the potential feelings surrounding Éric.

"I think I can name a person or two who wouldn't mind poking you," Jayden said smoothly to cover up the momentary pause.

"Would one of them happen to be you, Ambassador Drake?" Collette asked, a pointed sarcasm on the title before bursting out in laughter.

Jayden laughed with Collette. "No. No offense to Alaoin or the others here, but while I will, on occasion, poke men like Alaoin, my tastes run more toward those like Thomas and Éric."

"Your interest in Thomas has been noted by my brother," she replied.

"And I have been sufficiently warned off. I would never come between a happy couple, but watching Arian get upset has

been fun. However, Thomas requested I stop so I've decided not to flirt with him anymore."

Jayden turned back to Alaoin. "Is Éric unattached?" Jayden flinched, and a satisfied look from Ceto suggested some subtle retaliation on her part for the question.

Alaoin bought himself time by drinking deeply from his mug. "He might be," he answered.

"Well, I know what I'm doing tomorrow," Jayden said as he took a sip from his drink.

Tolan had to hide his laugh in his drink.

"Jayden, I need you to explain something to me," Collette said.

"Yes?" Jayden asked.

"Why are you such a fucking liar, Mr. Ambassador?" she asked, causing Ceto to start cackling.

Jayden's smile didn't fade, but it did become slightly sharper, his eyes brighter like he couldn't wait to see where Collette's accusation would lead. "How am I a liar, Your Majesty?"

"You show up in my fucking kingdom with the biggest stick up your ass, treating me like I was a tyrant, and suddenly, once you're out of Quenall, your real personality shows up."

Jayden chuckled. "Oh, that."

Ceto laughed so hard she nearly fell out of her seat. "He's—" she began and had to pause as laughter erupted. "He's certain people won't find out what he's like when he plays ambassador."

"Because I'm sure you showed up to meet him asking if he needed his balls emptied or a fucking drink, Joss," Rion said, renewing Ceto's laughter.

Tolan choked on his drink. Still coughing, he glanced at his cousin and saw Alaoin having the same problem.

"It might have made things more interesting. However, the only person I met, outside of Thomas, who I'd have considered was your brother. Even then, I would have needed to be quite drunk, and he would have needed to be gagged," Jayden said.

"I'm not claiming him," Collette said with a shrug. "But he does like a certain kind of man. You might have been lucky."

"We'll never know," Jayden said. He grinned at Alaoin again. "What type of man does Éric like, or does he not like men?"

"Are these not questions best directed at your intended target?" Alaoin asked, his expression less amused now.

Jayden's expression suggested he knew he was in dangerous waters and gave absolutely zero shits about it. "I could and I will, but I thought some insider information might be helpful before diving in."

Tolan glanced at Collette, catching her devious smile, so different from the ones he was used to seeing in Quenall. He had to look away before his thoughts became improper.

"Be nice," Ceto said to Jayden. "Aphros will have Lynessea take you out for making Fythias back out."

"Oh I wouldn't back out," Alaoin said with a shrug. "But punishing Jayden could be interesting."

"Ooo. How are we punishing Jayden?" Ceto said, perking up.

"I would also like to know. Depending on the punishment, I might enjoy it," Jayden said.

Tolan's eyes grew wide. He shared a glance with Rion and Collette before waving one of the barmaids over to order more drinks. He would have headed back to the bar, but he truly didn't want to miss anything.

"Good question," Ceto said. She leaned closer to Collette so their shoulders were touching, and Ceto put a hand on Collette's forearm. "What sort of punishment would be best, do you think?"

"Hmmm," Collette replied. "Something painful, maybe."

"I don't know," Ceto replied. "I think he likes pain."

"I'm not opposed to pain, but it does have to be consensual. It's no fun if both parties aren't enjoying it." Jayden winked at Collette.

"Punishments aren't supposed to be fun, Jayden," Ceto replied.

"At least not this kind," Collette added.

"Never stopped me before. It's also not my fault Aphros has handed off my punishments to other like-minded people." Jayden made a thoughtful noise. "I think he often forgets to assign them to Ceto or someone similar because he has so much on his plate."

Tolan shook his head as he tried to figure out how the conversation got so off track. He thanked the barmaid who arrived with another tray of drinks. He relieved her of the heavy tray and happily put it down on the table. He pulled out some coins and paid her to make sure their drinks stayed full for the rest of the night so he didn't have to keep waving someone over.

"Smart man," Rion commented as he helped himself to another.

Tolan waved off the praise and grabbed his drink before anyone else could, noting that Alaoin practically downed his in one go. He wondered for a moment if he should be concerned.

Jayden once more opened his mouth. "Collette, how have you avoided marriage? We all know how Alaoin has managed, but what about you?"

"Well, the first marriage I avoided by having the old king croak, becoming queen, then saying no," Collette explained. She motioned to Rion. "I was with him for a bit. Then him," she pointed to Tolan. "And now, I'm with Larent, and I've been busy not dying." She explained the brief history of her love life with such a casual tone, she might very well have been discussing the weather.

If Jayden was taken aback by the information, he did not show it, nor did Ceto. Alaoin, on the other hand, had to quickly hide his reaction behind his mug. Tolan did the same thing.

# Chapter Twenty-five

He wasn't able to see Rion's reaction, and he wasn't sure he wanted to.

"So, is marrying Larent on the table, or are you free for other advances?" Jayden jumped in once more, glaring at Ceto. Apparently wherever she'd pinched him the second time was more sensitive.

"I do plan on marrying Larent, yes," Collette confirmed simply.

"Good for you," Alaoin said, genuine for once. "You should hold onto someone who looks at you the way Larent does."

"He does worship the ground you walk on," Jayden added.

Tolan had to take another drink to not make a face or comment because Jayden and Alaoin were right. Larent loved Collette fully and fiercely.

"How did you meet? I assume it was before the overthrow started, but I don't remember seeing him at the palace."

"He was working at the palace, and he quite literally fell onto my balcony," she replied.

"Unintentionally?" Alaoin asked with a grin.

"Indeed," Collette confirmed.

Rion reached for another drink which Tolan slid closer to him with a quick, pained smile as he listened to Collette. "How did he even end up there? I've seen the layout."

"Jumping out of a window from what I understand," Collette replied as she brushed some hair from her fair. "The angles didn't quite add up to me, but Larent manages surprising things, sometimes."

"He's a shifter. I don't think the same rules apply to him," Tolan pointed out. He'd seen the man do amazing feats some elves couldn't pull off thanks to his ability. Tolan wondered how hard it was on Larent not to have access to his powers and the skills shifting granted him. Instead of pondering long, however, he drowned the question with more alcohol.

"Sabine had an uncle who was a shifter, so she'd probably known better than I, but I was under the impression the skills only worked when in a non-human state," Alaoin spoke up.

"Larent can tap into his wolf so he can access its powers even when fully human. He can even just shift parts of his body. His grandparents taught him how to do it. They are rather up there in age if his Nana is to be believed," Tolan explained as he searched his memory for the things he had learned the few times he'd been to the Leassitor household and the years spent in Larent's company.

"Interesting," Alaoin said. "I shall have to see what Sabine remembers of her uncle."

"Not much is known about shifters anymore. It's sad as there are so few left in the world," Jayden said thoughtfully before downing his drink. "Alright, who wants to play a drinking game?"

"Spirits, please," Rion easily agreed.

"Alright." Jayden exchanged a look with Ceto, prompting Tolan to stay quiet for now. "Ceto will get the drinks, and I'll explain the rules." Ceto hopped out of her seat and sprinted back to the bar.

While they waited, Jayden, instead of explaining the rules, baited Alaoin once more about Éric, drawing Rion into the conversation somehow. Tolan, seeing the soft smile on Collette's face and relaxed set to her shoulders, decided to try starting a conversation. He leaned over. "Hey," he said, his voice soft enough to not draw Rion's attention.

"Hey," Collette replied.

Whatever he meant to say was lost as the next words tumbled out of his mouth, unable to stop themselves. "I'm sorry for everything."

Collette gave him a soft smile, and she reached out to place a hand on his forearm. "I know. It's okay."

Tolan shook his head. "It's not okay at all. What I did to you was wrong, and I will never be able to make it up to you. But I'm sorry, and I am so grateful you have Larent," Tolan admitted, no matter how much it hurt.

"Let's try to be friends, then," Collette suggested. "I think friends are better than whatever the fuck you call we've been doing for the past few months."

"I'd like that, a lot." It was more than he deserved or hoped for. Tolan opened his mouth to say something else, only for Ceto to almost crash into the table in her excitement. How she didn't spill the drinks Tolan would never know.

"Drinking game time," Ceto sang out.

Several rounds later, everyone at the table appeared red-faced and glassy-eyed. Alaoin told a story of questionable truthfulness. "I once dueled a duke for another's hand in marriage. I won, of course, but benevolently, I did not insist they honor the agreement."

"Bullshit," Ceto called out.

"It is not!" Alaoin insisted. "I am many things, but dishonest is not one of them."

Tolan found himself laughing. "No, I agree with Ceto. It's bullshit, or you'd be married."

Alaoin turned to Collette, who was so drunk she was laughing at just about everything. "Do you see how they doubt me? Have my hand and let us flee their nonsense."

"She is one of us," Ceto interjected. "She's not going to want to go with you."

"I know! You should duel over her hand," Jayden announced.

Tolan had a suspicion he was still the most sober one there.

Ceto stood up in her seat, a feat since she was quite unsteady. Alaoin did the same. "Do not worry, dear Collette. I will win against Ceto, and we shall be the most formidable royal couple the world has ever seen," the king declared.

Tolan couldn't help the laughter bubbling up out of him. He might have fallen over had Rion not put a steadying hand on his shoulder. "Someone's going to get hurt," he said, his words slurring slightly.

"Looks like," Rion agreed with a chuckle.

The actual duel ended rather quickly as Ceto did fall out of her chair and Alaoin tripped in his efforts to help her up. Rion chose to put an end to the evening. He stood and gently grabbed Collette by the forearm, helping her to her feet. "Come on, then," he said to her. "Tolan, you good to help me with her?"

Tolan glanced at Jayden to see if he would need help with Alaoin and Ceto only to find the other man laughing so hard he was tilting sideways.

"I have these two. You go on," he said between laughs.

Tolan just nodded, turning back to Rion. "Let's get her back to her rooms," he said, standing only to have the world tilt to the left slightly. Straightening himself, Tolan let out a small chuckle. "Guess I had a bit more than I thought."

"Guess you did," Rion said. "I can carry her if you're not steady enough."

Tolan tested his balance. "That might be for the best."

Rion nodded. "Alright Joss. I know your ass can't walk back, so I'm lifting you."

"Fuck you," Collette said without a drop of malice in her voice.

"You have," he assured her with a laugh. Soon, Collette was in his arms, and they made their trek back to the palace.

Tolan followed alongside Rion, cursing when they stepped outside to see light slowly peek over the horizon. He hadn't thought they'd been drinking for so long. With a huff of laughter, he continued, figuring they could drop Collette off before heading to their rooms.

# Chapter Twenty-five

The palace seemed quiet and relatively empty as they strolled inside, and Tolan vaguely recalled early hours for kitchen work. No doubt, back in Quenall in the days before the overthrow, he'd have been yawning as he joined Diana.

Tolan could admit to himself he missed Diana and Crem, their morning arguments and the warmth that always seemed to fill the kitchen, but that time was over. He had more important things to focus on now.

As they got closer to Collette's room, they saw another person approaching from the other direction.

"Oh, looks like you three had fun tonight," a sleepy-looking Larent called out as he jogged to reach them.

Tolan heard more than saw the fond sigh he gave when he saw Collette curled up in Rion's arms.

"I believe this is yours," Rion said, handing Collette over to Larent. "She had quite a bit of fun as you can tell."

"I'm glad she did. She needed it." Larent gave the now softly snoring queen a look so full of love it made Tolan's chest ache. "Thanks for taking her out. You two have a good night," Larent said before he disappeared with her into their room.

Rion yawned. "A bitter pill, isn't it?" he commented.

Tolan nodded. He still loved Collette, and he imagined he always would. He just knew Larent loved her better. "He loves her, every part of her."

"He does," Rion agreed. "And he makes her happy. She deserves that."

"She does, more than anything." Tolan knew that, unlike him or Rion, Larent would never run, never leave her. She was in the best possible hands she could be in. The acknowledgment hurt, but he would be okay with it, somehow. Rion had managed as much.

Catching himself as the world tried to tilt on him again, Tolan changed the subject. "I'm slightly more sober, but we drank a lot."

"We did," Rion acknowledged. "I'm going to get a few hours of sleep. You should do the same."

"Yes, of course," Tolan replied. "Sleep well."

"Same to you," Rion said, and without waiting for a response, he turned to head to his room.

Tolan watched Rion go, thoughts swirling in his head but unable to come into focus. He turned the other direction and went to his room.

# Chapter Twenty-Six

"Freckles, sweetheart, it's time to wake up," a soft voice called to Collette from her drink-induced slumber. She felt something, a hand perhaps, running through her hair and a warm body pressed against her. "I know you don't want to, but it's time to wake up, love." The voice stayed soft and low, and lips brushed against the side of her head. "I have water, and the curtains are closed."

A sound of protest rumbled in Collette's throat, though the effort didn't bother her nearly as much as she had expected it to. As consciousness slowly inched its way into her mind, she realized Larent was the one trying to rouse her. Instead of responding verbally, she turned over and snuggled against him.

Larent wrapped his arms around Collette, pulled her close, and brushed another kiss across her forehead. "Morning Freckles, or I should say afternoon?"

"Whichever," Collette mumbled against him.

Larent laughed softly. "Arian is bringing his hangover potion which should help. Did you have fun last night?"

"Mmhmm," she replied softly. "Throw something at him if he starts lecturing."

"He already promised he wouldn't. Besides, he looks like he didn't sleep all night. He has no room to complain. Though, when you're more awake, you might want to give him shit for the marks Thomas left all over his neck. Sister privilege and all." Larent brought up a hand to brush away hair from her face.

She gave the briefest of laughs and stopped when it made her head throb. "Good for him."

"I swear Thomas mauled him last night. I did not know the fletcher had it in him." Larent sounded both amused and a tad bit terrified.

"Thomas can be aggressive when needed," Collette reminded Larent. She never forgot how he used to stand outside her palace and criticize her.

"I guess I didn't realize how aggressive." A knock sounded at the door. "Can I get up, or should I invite him in?"

"Whichever," she said, repeating her earlier words without relinquishing her hold on him.

Larent laughed before calling out for Arian to come in, though he kept his voice low. Collette heard the door open but no footsteps after.

"Thanks. I'll make sure she drinks it," Larent said.

"Ceto and Alaoin joined Collette at some point last night. All meetings have been canceled. She can sleep if she wishes. Just…" Arian trailed off.

Collette could picture the look he was giving Larent.

"I will make sure she drinks it. Go get mauled by Thomas some more," Larent replied with a laugh. Silence followed until the door opened and closed once more. "Need help sitting up?"

Collette shook her head as much as she could. Letting Larent go, she shifted back enough so she could sit up without hitting him with some part of her body. She groaned when she was upright and put her hands on either side of her aching head.

Larent wrapped an arm around Collette, helping to keep her upright. "Let me know when you're ready."

She nodded and focused on slow breaths for a few moments, willing her body to cooperate with her. Eventually, when she didn't think her skull was actually going to burst open, she nodded again. "I'm ready." With Larent's help, she was able to slowly drink the entire potion. Thankfully, the flavor was light, making the consumption all the easier.

"It should kick in shortly," Larent said.

"I hope so," Collette replied.

Larent cuddled up to Collette. Just holding her close, quietly letting his warmth soak into her. She took advantage of their positions to rest her head on his shoulder. She could acknowledge the effectiveness of the potion, though it worked more slowly than she liked. "How was Nawalya last night?"

"Not terrible. She had one incident where I had to wake her up, and she settled pretty quickly afterward."

Collette nodded, glad to hear Nawalya got what sounded like a decent night's sleep.

"Sounds like you decided sleep was for the weak, however?"

"It wasn't a straightforward decision," Collette said. "Same effect, though."

Larent laughed. "So tell me about it."

"Rion poured drinks. Rion tried to steal drinks. I stole them back, so he decided we were going to a tavern. We picked up company on the way out."

Larent laughed. "Did you have a good time?"

"I did," she replied. "Tolan has developed feelings for Rion, I think." She could feel Larent start next to her.

"Really?"

"Yeah," she confirmed. "Tolan kept shooting these longing glances in Rion's direction. Ceto asked me how long the attraction had been going on. I said I didn't know."

"I'm going to assume Rion knows. Is he even into men?" Larent asked.

She shrugged. "Maybe. I didn't see reciprocation of the feelings, but Rion isn't as expressive."

Larent was silent for a few minutes. "I can't see how they would work. I mean, Rion doesn't put up with his shit, and he knows Tolan has tons of issues. Maybe it could work, or maybe Rion could just fuck the issues out of Tolan and walk away. I don't know."

"You are very invested," she observed, amused despite feeling terrible.

"It's just not something I was expecting. It's almost like realizing Thomas is a vampire from the look of Arian's neck."

"There may not be much to it. Tolan might have a little crush which he quickly moves on from."

"Very true." Larent kissed her cheek. "Feeling any better?"

"A little bit. Pretty sure my head won't explode anymore."

"Exploding heads would be a horrible way to die," Larent said fondly before pressing his mouth against her hair. "So, how many times did Alaoin propose? And did Ceto make a pass at you at least once?"

"Alaoin and Ceto got into a fake duel for my hand, actually," Collette said with a tired laugh.

Larent started laughing. "Did you tell them you have to marry me first, and they are battling for the place of second consort?"

She smiled at the thought. "I'm thinking I'm only going to marry you if it's all the same to you."

"Well, you know I'm perfectly fine with that. I just figure they should know they will only ever take second place in your heart."

"And not even a close second," Collette said. "Besides, I'm relatively certain Alaoin's secretary would assassinate me if I gave serious consideration to anything resembling a proposal. Or he'd have his gigantic father do it."

"Yeah. Éric is so painfully in love with Alaoin, I've been debating locking them in a pantry together. Then I remember his father is the largest elf I have ever seen."

"Are we pretending you are more subtle with your feelings?" she asked, glancing up at him.

"Not at all. It makes me wonder if Alaoin truly hasn't noticed how Éric feels, or is his refusal to acknowledge the obvious a gentle letdown?" Larent asked.

"I think he knows, and I think he's afraid."

"Why?" Larent mused.

The answer seemed obvious to Collette, but she was in a position where she had to consider some of the same questions Alaoin would. "A person in Alaoin's position has to think about how his position impacts and informs relationships with people around them. They risk their loved ones in forming those associations. The possible losses."

"Yeah, but from what I've gathered, Éric's mother is the most powerful woman in the kingdom, second only to Alaoin, and I question how much day-to-day he attends to. Éric grew up in the court. I think Alaoin would be less concerned about being with Éric than you should be where I'm concerned." Collette could feel Larent smile. "And I gathered all of that information from watching them, not from breaking into their rooms. You should be proud."

"I generally am quite proud of you. You're perceptive, intelligent, and quick on your feet," Collette said. "And so many other wonderful things."

"Thanks," he murmured against her temple. "You're pretty wonderful yourself. You're exceptional, Freckles."

"And did you know that before or after you stumbled onto my balcony?"

"Before. Definitely before. It was just confirmed the moment you didn't push me off or scream for the guards."

"I scream around you plenty."

"Yeah, but your screaming is very, very different."

"True," she said. She sighed, content and measurably feeling better. "I missed you last night."

"I missed you too," Larent replied, and he kissed her hair again. "I'm sorry I wasn't here."

"You don't have anything to apologize for. You have people and priorities outside of me."

Larent shook his head. "I should have waited and talked to you first before volunteering to watch over Nawalya. You have so much on your shoulders, and I have to remember to put you and us first."

Larent and Arian had spent years caring for Nawalya when she'd needed it, and in prior conversations, Larent had admitted to a lot of enabling bad habits over the years. Collette knew they were all trying to move past those times, but she didn't expect them to just abandon one another, either.

"You're always free to go wherever you think you're most needed at any moment," Collette said. "I'm not going to be selfish enough to tell you not to do something you want to do. Nawalya and Arian are family. We take care of our family."

Larent gave a soft chuckle. "What did I ever do to deserve you?" He turned her head to give her a soft sweet kiss. "Now, tell me who won so I can challenge them at dinner tonight."

"Ceto," Collette replied. "I'm pretty sure she could take all of us down if she wanted."

Larent made a thoughtful noise. "She can take me, but I'm still gonna challenge her."

"More sleep first," Collette insisted.

Larent laughed. "Sounds like a plan," he said as they settled back in the sheets.

# Chapter Twenty-Seven

Mallan Hialti arrived in the Coralian court, flanked by a series of underlings who might have been lords or servants. They were all finely dressed in silks and wool and gold, but Mallan's finery stood out amongst the rest. Though the man styled himself regent rather than king, his body language, attire, and overall demeanor spoke of someone who'd gained a great deal of power and respect in a short period. His dark black trousers, rich blue overcoat, and sparkling silver buttons more than substituted for the Azmarin crown. He held his chin high and he refused to meet the eyes of those he considered beneath him.

Somehow, Rhoslyn doubted he would last long without showing at least the façade of humility.

She was in the open hall where centuries of Coralian rulers met with visitors and the public. Instead of meeting the Azmarin party at their point of arrival, Rhoslyn deemed it prudent to solidify her position as queen by having someone of lesser rank come to her. She sat on a dais, the deep green velvet of her dress highlighting her hair and eyes. She'd opted to wear one of the smaller tiaras. Dotted in pearls and emeralds, it spoke of restrained and modest power. Anytime she wore the headdress, she couldn't help but think how much better it suited her compared to Collette. The surrounding stone walls, decorated with lush tapestries and beautiful ancient portraits, spoke of her high position.

Pausing in front of Rhoslyn, Mallan lowered his head in the shallowest of bows. Up close, he reminded her of Wrenn. Handsome and broad, even his brown hair and eyes reminded her of her deceased brother. Of course, the disinterested gaze and the signs of lingering drink from the evening before did nothing to dissuade her of his equal uselessness.

"Your Majesty," Mallan greeted as he rose. "You are lovelier than anticipated. I was ill-prepared for your beauty."

"Let us hope you have even higher compliments for my intelligence once we have had the opportunity to discuss the matter of the Nereid and Collette," Rhoslyn said.

"I am certain we have much to say when it comes to the fallen queen," Mallan replied, his tone almost casual. "Though you have suffered more at her hands than we have, from what I understand."

"You are correct," Rhoslyn replied with a nod. "Three short years left us with much to correct, but with the matter of the reigning monarchs settled, we are hopeful."

"As you should be. I understand you have surrounded your-self with good people. People who are happy to do what is nec-essary to right the wrongs." Mallan glanced at Riken, then his eyes fell on Cadan. Neither man held any sign of being part of her rule, and thus, his gaze didn't linger.

"I have," Rhoslyn confirmed. "Lord Riken and his men have been truly inspirational for the court. Riken's vision of Coralia embraces all the good from prior reigns while correcting those areas in most need."

"And what of King Zephraim?" asked Mallan, his bored expression fixing on Rhoslyn. "I do not see him here. Surely he has thoughts or at least a desire to greet guests who have traveled far to aid Coralia."

"King Zephraim was recently attacked by the supporters of the former queen. He is indisposed at the moment, but we are hopeful of his full recovery," Rhoslyn replied.

"How terrible," Mallan exclaimed, going so far as to dramatically place a hand against his chest. "I do wish him well."

"I shall pass the message along," Rhoslyn assured him. "Now, did you want to get settled, or should we adjourn to the meeting room?"

"I think we should like to get started, if it is all the same," Mallan determined. "We have much to discuss before we set out for the Nereid islands, and we should prepare to move out soon, given how much of a head start Fythias has on us."

"I agree," Rhoslyn said. She rose to her feet and stepped down from the dais, Riken and Cadan following behind her. She joined Mallan at his side and beckoned him to follow.

They strolled from the open hall and down the corridor, the war room their intended destination. The slight clack of Riken's walking stick drew attention amongst the muffled footsteps of their two parties. "What's happened to your friend there?" he asked, motioning toward the limping Riken.

"Lord Riken suffered an unfortunate encounter with Collette," Rhoslyn said, her tone icy on the last syllable. "She plays dirty."

"Why hasn't he been to a proper healer?" Mallan asked. "We have a glorious talent in our party. All she has to do is lay hands on him, and he'll be good as new."

"She uses magic?" Rhoslyn asked, a part of her doubting Riken would agree to the arrangement.

"She does," Mallan replied. "I know magic is often looked upon with deserved skepticism, but I think it serves us well to know when it can be put to good use." He looked over to

Riken. "Would you like to see my healer about your limp? No need for a young man in his prime to limp around when he doesn't have to."

Riken's eyes met Rhoslyn's, and she could see the concern. The doubt. None of the nobles who'd supported Sargarus had liked magic users and had passed on to their children a deep fear of the harm a magic user could cause. Especially a magical healer. "I do think Riken was joking the other day about wishing we had a magical healer around. I'm sure he would be open to speaking with your healer."

"I'd be happy to," Riken said with a small smile.

"Wonderful," Mallan said. "I shall make introductions later today. For now, let's chat."

Riken limped his way to the liquor cabinet and grabbed his best spirits and two glasses. Cadan had been restless for weeks now, and the restlessness had grown worse since the meeting with Azmarin's regent. Riken had a feeling he knew why Cadan was on edge, and discussing his apprehension would require them to consume liquid fortification. Riken could not, would not dismiss what Cadan had to say out of hand. He'd done so too often as of late and repeated casual dismissal had cost him greatly.

Mallan claimed his healer could fix Riken's knee, and though Rhoslyn had encouraged him to see the healer, Riken had been left to make the final decision. The thought of magic touching him sent a shiver through him. The Mother had granted humans access to magic through her sacrifice, but so many undeserving had also been granted use. Evil—no—wicked uses of magic had led to so much terror in the world, and good leaders like Sargarus had done what they could to limit it in Coralia. Still, if

Rhoslyn thought it best for him to use magic to heal, he would. He had to make up for his spectacular failures.

For now, he would need to field Cadan's concerns. Setting down the glasses, he began to pour. He motioned for Cadan to talk.

"I wish to bring Zephraim in for questioning," Cadan admitted, causing Riken to completely miss the glass and spill liquor everywhere. Riken spun as best as he could to face his second oldest friend.

"What?"

"I wish to bring Zephraim in for questioning," Cadan said, his face straight and serious.

"But why and for what reason?" Riken demanded.

"Something doesn't feel right about how Sara Whyldon escaped the prison, and Zephraim is the only true outlier. I have no proof, however. I wish to speak with Her Majesty." Riken let out a breath.

"Of course, you can talk to her. By the Mother, I thought you were going to complain about me seeing a magic user, not an escaped prisoner."

"Do not doubt my unhappiness about possible exposure to magic, but if it can heal your leg, we must consider it. You'll be needed on the battlefield more than I. If I am right, I'll need to stay here to keep the queen safe, though I would rather be out there fighting with you."

"My plan was for you to come with me, to fight on the battlefield in my stead, a vexing thought since I was injured." Riken steadied his hand and finished pouring, then held out a glass for Cadan. "It would be stupid for me to not meet with the healer, and I have been stupid enough recently."

"Not stupid, my lord. Just overconfident," Cadan said.

Riken didn't miss the twist of the other man's lips. "We will pretend you're right." Riken sighed. "I'll see when Rhoslyn is free, and we will see what we can do to put your plan into action."

# Chapter Twenty-Eight

Crem held back a wince as his fist connected with Howle's jaw, the larger man staggering back at the unexpected blow. Movement from the other side of the room let Crem know Ian and Sara had decided to flee.

"The fuck?" Howle exclaimed as he righted himself.

"I don't know what's going on with you, but once again, you're disrespecting my wife, and I will not have it," Crem said, shaking out his hand. He always forgot how much punching someone in the face could hurt. "I get you're stressed, but you could go to the warehouse district and resolve your stress. Go spend a few hours there, and come back when you're in a better mood."

"I'd rather fuck the two of you than some stranger in an ally," Howle bit out, causing Crem to take a step back. Yes, the three of them joked, but Crem's gut screamed the other man wasn't playing around.

Diana watched Crem's response, though her expression gave none of her thoughts away. "You know, being a pain in the ass isn't the best way to get Crem to sleep with you."

"It works well enough for ya," Howle said with a wink. "Besides, Crem isn't the only one I'd be interested in sleeping with."

"It's still not the way to go about things and can't be the only reason you've been an ass lately," Crem shot back.

"Lately?" Diana quipped.

"Okay. More of an ass," Crem said.

"Still, you pose a valid question," Diana said, looking back to Howle. "You've been more cantankerous than usual."

Crem watched Howle closely as the other man sat on one of the barrels instead of his normal chair near Diana.

"I'm just stressed," Howle said.

"Bullshit," Crem spat. "We're all stressed, but you're the only one taking it out on Diana, and you're refusing to talk about it." Crem looked at Diana for help.

Diana shrugged. "Howle knows what his problem is. He doesn't want to talk about it, and he can make whatever choice he wants. He's not going to continue talking down to me, though."

Howle ran through his long, locked hair. "I'm sorry. I've been an ass. I'll work on it. Everythin' we've been dealing with just has me in knots. I feel like we are reactin' and not actin', and it makes me itch. Not controllin' the situation is when yar most likely ta lose people, and I don't like the idea of losin' either of ya," Howle explained, not looking at either of them.

Crem shot Diana another look. There was more going on. Taking a step forward, Crem reached out to touch Howle's shoulder with his newly bruised hand. "We're going to make it. All of us."

Diana nodded. "No one has discovered our base yet. Crem hasn't left in weeks, and he's the one of us with a bounty on his head."

"Neither of ya can make that promise." Howle stood and rubbed his sore jaw.

Crem didn't regret hitting Howle for disrespecting Diana again, but at the same time, he was starting to understand how much worry the other man bore.

"No one can guarantee what is going to happen even under the best of circumstances," Diana said before Howle could make a retreat. "You can choose to make the most of the time you have at the moment, or you can choose to pick fights with me, which probably won't work out in your favor."

"Fightin' with ya may be the stupider option, but it's the safer option," Howle said. "I am goin' to get a drink."

Crem tried to get Howle to stop, but the larger man just shouldered past him, traveling farther into the cavern. "I am so confused right now," Crem admitted to Diana.

"His confession wasn't one I anticipated ever hearing," Diana agreed, crossing her arms.

"I don't think he meant to." Crem brought up a hand and scratched at the back of his head.

"Probably not," Diana agreed. "But we can deal with the confession later. He did have a good point about being reactive rather than proactive."

"He did, which is one of the reasons he's been picking fights with you. He wants the same thing, and yet..." Crem looked toward one of the other tunnels. Shit, he'd always thought Howle was just screwing around when he flirted with them. "We will have to see what we can change, I guess."

"We could always ask Barris to step up his watch," Diana said. "And Zephraim has more than done his part. Unless we have someone in the room with Rhoslyn and Riken, I don't know what else we could do."

"With Gisela leaving the castle, we are severely down on spies. I won't ask Agnes to spy. Rhoslyn doesn't trust her,

anyway." Crem thought about their options. "I could have the soldiers we've slipped into the guard start to mingle with the Azmarin soldiers. Maybe they can gather more information. I'll also talk to Barris and see what else we can do."

Diana approached Crem and put her arms around him. "We are all doing the best we can," she assured him.

"We are," Crem acknowledged, holding Diana close. "What do we do about Howle?"

"I don't know," she replied. "Do you want to do something about what he said?"

"I have no idea what to do. I always thought he was joking—never once did I consider he was being serious."

Diana chuckled. "Then you should think about what you want to do, if anything. Howle is a good person deep down, and he would understand if nothing came of his confession. I'd not begrudge you if you want to try things out with him. I can appreciate the appeal of a soldier."

"I wouldn't do anything without you there and involved, but I have honestly never considered it." Crem shook his head, amazed at her easy acceptance. "I will take time to consider it and if this is even a good time to act on his feelings."

"You should figure out what you want beyond anything else," Diana said.

"I already have what I want," Crem said before pulling Diana into a kiss. "This is about what we want and what's best for us."

"For some foolish reason, all I've ever wanted was you," Diana insisted, then kissed Crem again. "Everything else is negotiable for me."

Crem laughed. "And here I was hoping you'd have the answer."

"Well, I cannot do everything, Crem," Diana responded in a playful tone. "Growing your child and arguing with Howle is a lot of work, you know."

Crem opened his mouth to reply only for Diana's words to truly sink in. "Say that again?" His voice was firm, harsher than he meant it.

"New tone," Diana directed.

"Sorry, sorry. I just—" Crem swallowed. "Did you say you're pregnant?"

Diana nodded. "I did. Just a couple of months as best as I can tell."

Crem blinked several times as he let the information process before calling out. "Hey, Ian! How do you feel about getting Diana and Sara out of Quenall as soon as possible?"

"Hey now," Diana said, shoving her husband back. "I've already told you. I leave when you do."

"I guess we are leaving Howle and Barris in charge, then."

She crossed her arms in response and obstinance settled on her face. "I know you better than that. You haven't wanted to leave before now."

"You weren't pregnant before." Crem held up his hands to fend off the very real possibility Diana would hit him. "I know you can take care of yourself. I know you're a capable woman, but for The Mother's sake, if Collette shows up with an army, Quenall is the last place I want you."

"You're really going to try sending me away?" Diana asked him.

"No, because I would be with you," Crem argued.

"And I just don't see you walking away. Not really."

"I think if we made it out of the city, I could keep going," Crem admitted lamely. He wanted Diana out of the city, away from the possibility of battle, and yet he doubted his ability to follow.

"And I know you're lying to yourself," Diana said. She heaved an exasperated sigh. "You figure yourself out, and you prepare yourself for the repercussions if you end up deciding you're going to send me away."

Defeated, Crem took her hand and pulled her close, resting his forehead against hers. "I won't send you away. You are strong and capable, and I wouldn't diminish you just because you're pregnant."

"And how much of your declaration is motivated by my ultimatum?"

"A little, but really, I can't force you to leave. It's hypocritical of me to try, especially when you've already made your stance clear."

"Good," Diana said. She sighed again but more softly. "I know you are worried, but I still have more freedom than you. And I've always done the right thing when trouble comes my way."

"I know, and I trust you to take care of yourself. Sorry for trying to make you leave again."

"I know," she replied, echoing his words. "If I didn't love you, I might have punched you by now. I still might if you keep it up."

# Chapter Twenty-Nine

Riken sat down in the chair, stripped to foundation garments, his eyes never leaving the healer as she examined his knee. Her closeness made him uncomfortable, as did her gentle touches as she examined his knee. Thankfully, Cadan was also there, and even if his presence hadn't been sufficient, Rhoslyn had made it clear she needed him in top shape. He'd already disappointed her enough. So, he gritted his teeth and let the woman do her job.

The woman's mahogany hair sat in a loose bun on top of her head, shifting slightly as she moved throughout the examination. "I'm surprised you can put any weight on your leg," she said, though more to herself.

Riken didn't tell her of the sheer agony it caused him or how he forced himself to move it every day despite the radiating persistent pain. Instead, he sat as still as possible and let her keep working.

The woman sat back on her haunches and looked up at Riken with a pair of piercing blue eyes. "I should be able to heal you completely. You will have to do nothing. I will simply place my hands on and around your knee. Your skin may tingle as my magic flows into you, but you will experience no pain. Do you consent to proceeding?"

Riken said nothing for a moment, his eyes meeting Cadan's and noting his commander's hand had moved closer to his sword. Knowing Cadan would strike her down if anything happened, Riken finally spoke. "Yes, I give consent."

A nod of acknowledgment, and the woman looked back down at Riken's knee. She placed a pale hand on top of his knee and another on the side.

Riken took a deep breath and waited to see what would happen. At first, he felt no difference, no changes, and he wondered if the damage was too much for the supposed healer to fix.

Glancing in Cadan's direction, it seemed as though his guard commander felt the same. Riken was about to say something to the stupid hack of a woman when he felt his knee shift. It wasn't painful, just odd. The longer he sat there with her hands on his knee, the more shifting he felt until it just suddenly stopped.

The healer withdrew her hands from him and stood from the ground. "Stand," she instructed.

Riken took a deep breath but otherwise kept his expression neutral. He pushed his hope down just in case the healing did not work. Standing slowly, Riken was careful of the weight he put on his leg. Slowly, he allowed himself to try, and almost immediately, he realized the pain was gone. He couldn't help but stare at his knee in amazement.

"So?" prompted the woman.

"There's no pain." He looked up at Cadan before striding over to the other man and back.

"Good," the healer said. She didn't look the least bit bothered by Riken's almost total dismissal. "Your knee should behave as though it was never injured. I will inform Regent Mallan of your recovery."

"It does," Riken said as he moved and flexed his leg. "What's your name?" he asked, realizing he should have asked before starting.

"Synophe," the woman replied. "I have served the royal household in Azmarin for some time."

"Thank you," Riken said. He may not trust magic wielders, but she had helped him. He would not be seen as ungrateful.

"Of course," Synophe said with a nod of her head. Without another word, she exited the room.

"I'm off to see Rhoslyn. Healed, I can lead her army against the Nereid." Riken's smile was sharp, and Cadan followed behind him as they went to see the queen. He would make Collette pay and skin every Nereid alive.

They arrived at Rhoslyn's office in less time than it had usually taken Riken since his arrival from Galel. The healed knee gave him excited confidence which continued once admitted into the room. "My queen, I am very pleased to report I am fully healed," Riken announced, a large smile gracing his lips. He only hoped she was as happy as he was.

"Really?" Rhoslyn asked, her bright smile genuine. She rose from her desk and walked to him. "Mallan's healer actually knew what she was doing?"

"Yes, it was very simple and painless." Riken knew he sounded surprised. He'd never imagined a time when he might rely on magic, nor did he think he would ever consider allowing for well-regulated use.

"I'm just pleased you are no longer in pain," Rhoslyn said. Despite Cadan's silent presence, she wrapped her arms around Riken and drew him into a kiss. "A young man like you has no use for a bad knee."

"And neither does a young queen," Riken murmured into the kiss, only for a cleared throat to interrupt their moment. Had it been anyone else but Cadan, Riken would have struck them down where they stood.

"Before things go much further, I would like permission to move forward with our plans to catch the traitor."

Riken turned his head to look at Cadan, whose face was turned away from the two of them.

"What plan?" Rhoslyn asked, her impatience nearly concealed.

"To spread misinformation to certain people who may be working with the resistance and see where Cremisius Hawke and his people show up," Cadan said quickly. "It's a quick and dirty way to discover our traitor, and it will leave very little room for them to claim innocence."

Riken pressed his lips together in similar impatience. "It's not a bad idea."

"It's not," Rhoslyn agreed. "Go implement it so I might catch up with Riken."

"Of course, Your Majesty." Cadan bowed, awkwardly since he wouldn't even look at them, and made a quick exit from the room.

"Where were we?" Riken asked before kissing Rhoslyn again. Riken deepened the kiss and backed Rhoslyn up until she gently hit her desk. Lifting her, he set Rhoslyn on her desk and settled between her legs.

"Tell me of all your plans now you are healed," she encouraged between increasingly heated kisses.

"To set the world at your feet. To do what I can to make up for my past failures," he declared as he hiked up her skirt. She shifted her position ever so slightly, legs widening, allowing him better access. Riken slipped a hand under her skirt and trailed his fingers up her thigh and to her core, his fingers caressing her hot center. "Anything you want, I will do."

# Chapter Twenty-nine

"Right now, I just want you," she said, her voice breathy and distracted.

"Whatever you want," Riken said as he slipped his index finger down and inside Rhoslyn, his thumb continuing to rub the tiny bud. It felt empowering to be able to do this with her again without the pain, without the embarrassment of her constantly needing to be on top. She moaned softly, her breaths coming quicker as he teased and stroked. Riken didn't want to prolong the wait. He yearned to be inside of her, to feel Rhoslyn cling to him. Still, he added a second finger as his thumb continued to rub circles.

Pulling away from her lips, Riken laid kisses upon her jawline and down her neck. She tilted her head back in response, inviting more of his lips caressing her skin. A noise of pleasure left Rhoslyn's lips. Her thighs further parted, and more pleasured moans sounded.

"Don't stop," she demanded.

"I didn't intend to," Riken said into her ear before continuing to kiss down her neck, leaving a trail of love bites until he got to where her neck met her shoulder. Having found one of Rhoslyn's weak spots, Riken knew she wouldn't last much longer. Determined to draw out her pleasure, Riken's fingers continued to pump into her as she grasped onto him. He felt her tighten around his fingers, her moan muffled as she pressed her face against his shoulder.

Using his free hand, Riken loosened his pants, freeing his throbbing cock. He waited until she was coming down from her climax before lining himself up and thrusting into her. "I've missed this," he growled. One hand moved to her hip as Riken set a punishing pace, and he groaned in satisfaction with each thrust. She clung to him, legs going around his hips, encouraging him to go harder and deeper.

Riken's grip on her hip became tighter as he thrust into Rhoslyn harder. "You feel so good."

"So do you," she breathed.

Riken bit down on Rhoslyn's shoulder, an easily covered spot, as his thrusts became erratic. He was close, but he wasn't about to finish before her. He'd left her unsatisfied enough with his actions. She nearly screamed the second time she came, the sound heated and desperate and absolutely delicious to him. Only then did he allow his release, uttering a litany of praises and adoration for her. Even when his body stilled, he remained where he was, holding her close and kissing her once more.

"I love you," she whispered against his lips.

"I love you, too."

"You had better," Rhoslyn replied.

"You act as though my entire world doesn't revolve around you," Riken said with a raised brow.

"Oh I know it does," Rhoslyn replied. "And I could not be a luckier woman for it. Still, it is comforting to verbally acknowledge what we share."

"It is." Riken sighed. "How long until your next meeting?"

"I am done for the day," Rhoslyn replied. "So I am yours."

"Thank the Mother." Riken gently pulled out of Rhoslyn and tucked himself away before moving her skirts down to better cover her legs. "Your evening is now fully booked."

"Let's go enjoy the evening, then."

Riken nodded and helped Rhoslyn to stand. Once both were presentable, he escorted her from the room and into their chambers.

# Chapter Thirty

Collette flexed her feet, making sure her battle boots were properly secured. She'd agreed to some sparring with members of the Fythian party, and she looked forward to seeing just what they could do. Her group planned on being present as well, and though Collette would never argue it, she doubted there was anything anyone could do to prevent Arian from an opportunity to train.

She stood and stretched, looking around her quarters as she stood from the bed. She left the room and strolled down the bright corridor. She'd hoped to catch Larent before going out to the practice field. Even with his playful complaints, she knew he looked forward to training almost as much as she did.

As Collette approached the library, she paused, overhearing familiar voices. As the library was not a private space, she took a detour inside and smiled upon spotting Larent. Seated with him was Sabine, the royal Fythian advisor. "Hello," she greeted.

Sabine replied with an elegant, "Hello." She and Larent were seated at a large round table, one of many in the bright library. Like the rest of the palace, the walls were bright, and accents in corals and blues could be spotted about. Rows of books lined the walls, and additional shelving scattered throughout the space begged visitors to browse the collection.

Larent gave Collette the wide-eyed look of someone caught in the middle of poor behavior, though Collette couldn't imagine what guilt there was to be had in a library. "Hi," he said brightly.

"I somehow think I am supposed to suspect you guilty of something, but I cannot fathom what," Collette said. She walked over to the table, leaning against it so she could look down at Larent. "Has he been misbehaving?" she asked Sabine.

"Not more than I usually observe," the duchesse replied. Collette hadn't had much chance to converse with Sabine outside of formal meetings, and though she did not elaborate on her answer, Collette detected real playfulness in the response.

"Hey, I'm perfectly innocent, as always." Larent even batted his eyes.

Collette laughed. "I think everyone on the island would call bullshit."

"Naw, people who haven't met me would believe me," he claimed.

Collette shook her head.

"I'm not wrong," Larent said.

"You are," Collette replied. "And you're stalling. What were the two of you in here doing?"

"Nothing," Larent said.

Collette knew he was messing with her, and she was happy to play along. "When you have to go sleep in Arian and Thomas's room, do you think you'll get to sleep in the middle?"

Larent laughed. "Oh, no. It will be on the balcony if they even consider it," he replied. He glanced at Sabine who sat watching. "Sabine has been teaching me the finer points of politics, starting with the different cultural norms and traditions."

"Really?" Collette asked. Larent had worried over his knowledge of history and politics, and she found it incredibly sweet for him to have so intentionally made efforts to learn and grow.

"He's a good student," Sabine complimented.

"She's being nice. I'm a horrible student. But I'm trying." Larent gave Sabine a grateful smile.

"You're intelligent and you easily make connections between events and motivations. Not knowing the histories is the only thing you truly lack, and you have been working on it," Sabine insisted.

"Thanks," Larent said. "What are you up to?" he asked Collette.

"I was going to meet some of the others on the training field," Collette explained. "I can leave you here if you prefer."

Larent bit his lip. "You're sparring with Faron today, right?"

She nodded. "He offered. I figure he'll kick my ass, but it's a good opportunity to learn. He'll be stronger than I am, too. It will be a new experience."

Sabine smiled as they discussed Faron. "He's a positive instructor as long as you make an effort," Sabine offered. "If not, he can show some impatience."

Collette nodded. Faron had a natural sternness in his expression, but he'd always been polite and respectful toward Collette's party. He also demonstrated nothing short of worship toward Sabine.

"I think I would like to pause here and go watch her spar with Faron. Maybe some of the others will want to do the same." Larent stood up and started gathering the books to put them away. Sabine did the same.

When their study session was fully cleared away, Larent thanked Sabine and followed her from the library. "I think I need to go get my stuff if I plan to join you," he said thoughtfully.

"Do you want me to go with you, or do you want to catch up?" Collette asked.

"Best to catch up. Otherwise, I might be tempted to distract you." Larent winked. "Wouldn't want you to be late."

"You were quite an excellent distraction last night. And this morning."

"I aim to please, Freckles." He tapped her on the nose and sped off. "I love you!" Larent yelled back before disappearing.

Collette laughed, ever amused by him. She continued on her short quest to reach the training grounds. Unsurprisingly, she was among the first to arrive, though she spotted some unknown Nereid in a distant corner. Unlike the grounds in Quenall, there was no high fence to both protect and conceal those training. She went to examine the available practice weapons, testing out the weight of swords when she heard others approach.

"I am positive Queen Collette could take you in a fight, no question," said Éric's voice as he, Faron, and Alaoin came into view.

Collette noted the amused tilt to Faron's lip as Éric continued. "She has more training and skill from what I've been led to believe. You refused to touch a sword until you were ten."

"I picked up a sword when it was prudent," Alaoin replied. "I am plenty skilled now, thank you."

"You picked up a sword because the girls decided you were an easy target, and you realized if you wanted to remain unharmed, you needed to learn quickly," Faron said, causing Éric to laugh at the reminder.

"Your daughters look like Sabine," Alaoin insisted. "You cannot blame a man for assuming they'd have the same disposition."

"Éric is the only one with a disposition similar to Sabine. The girls take after Avana, a fact you knew beforehand. Lisbeth warned you," Faron replied.

"Hello, Queen Collette!" Éric called out.

"Hello," she replied, smiling at the group. "The three of you seem eager for some training."

"Some more than others," Éric said wryly as he joined Collette by the practice swords.

"Alaoin often finds reasons to avoid sparring practice. He's quite good, but I think he'd be a pacifist if the world allowed it," Faron informed Collette.

"Pacifism is a nice ideal," Alaoin explained with a shrug.

"Certainly, but it's not realistic from my experience," Collette replied.

"I will let the two of you debate that. I am worn out on the subject," Faron said.

"No debate," Collette said with a shrug. "It's good to know how to defend oneself even if you aren't keen on grabbing your sword."

"A fair assessment," Alaoin acknowledged.

Faron and Éric both stopped looking at the training weapons to stare at Alaoin. "You agree when she says it but will fight us. I'm telling Mother. She can lecture you," Éric declared.

"Sabine likes me," Alaoin declared. "Her lectures are sweet."

Éric's lips flattened as he picked two short swords. "We shall see," he said and motioned to Alaoin to choose his sword.

Faron shook his head. "How do you prefer to train?" he asked Collette.

"No real preference. As long as I learn and get good practice, I'm genuinely open to anything."

"Then we shall start with hand-to-hand and move from there." Faron moved to the left of the training area, making sure they had enough space to move around and stay away from where Éric was getting ready to square off against Alaoin. As they walked, Collette couldn't help but watch Alaoin and Éric.

Despite the king's dislike of combat, his solid stance showed his skill.

"Éric should win, though he doesn't know Alaoin has been practicing with the girls." Faron shrugged and motioned Collette to come at him. Faron kept his arms loose at his side and moved his left foot back slightly; otherwise, this could have been any other time she'd seen him, he looked so relaxed.

In a real event, time to contemplate and strategize usually consisted of a couple of seconds, if that. Sparring a new opponent on a practice field afforded another second at most. Knowing he would easily take her down, Collette moved forward with precise, deliberate movements. Faron didn't change his stance, and his eyes followed her every moment as he looked for her tells.

Seeing Faron waiting for her to strike first, she lifted her right hand and swung, the blow soaring through the air toward the giant elf. Faron caught her fist, an eyebrow going up in surprise, but Collette wasn't sure what he was most surprised about: her form or her strength.

Using her momentum against her, he moved to pull Collette forward. Collette managed to wrench her hand out of his grip, though just barely. He was stronger than most she fought with. "It's been a long time since someone managed that," she shared. "Again."

"Alright." He relaxed his stance again and signaled he was ready.

They went through the motions a second time, Collette throwing the first punch once again as he waited for her to. This time when Faron caught her fist, he pulled her forward right away. Catching her off balance, he used her momentum to flip her onto her back. She sat up quickly, eager to continue. "I need to see that again."

Faron nodded. "Swing at me again." Once Collette did, Faron once more caught her hand and pulled her forward. He moved slower through the steps so she was able to see and feel his other hand as he used both to flip her onto the ground, something she'd missed last time with the speed at which he'd put her on the ground.

They went through the exercise several times, Collette's attention now examining various aspects of how Faron approached her attacks. She'd determined if she met someone like Faron in the future, she'd have to outthink and outfight them.

She rose from the ground again as some of her party finally showed up on the field. She dusted her hands off and waved in their direction.

Larent jogged over to her. "Sorry, I ran into the others, and they wanted to come watch." He thumbed back at Nawalya, Whyldon, and Rion.

"No reason they shouldn't," Collette replied. She nodded toward Faron. "He's been kicking my ass. I'm impressed."

"Yeah?" Larent looked over at Faron who watched Éric thrash Alaoin. "Are you learning while he does so?"

"I wouldn't let him put me on the ground so many times if I wasn't getting something out of it," Collette shared. She wouldn't be surprised if she had a few bruises come morning, but mild injuries came with practice.

"I figured, but..." Larent shrugged.

Collette understood how much he hated her getting hurt in any way, so she put an arm around Larent. "I promise I'm well," she whispered to him. They had a few moments while Faron paid attention to a duel between Alaoin and Éric which was monitored by Whyldon.

Larent returned the embrace. "I know, but just in case, I'll grab some cream from Arian, for the spots you can't heal." He

gave her a sweet kiss before breaking away and walking over to Nawalya who was waiting for him with an amused smirk.

She waited for Faron's attention to leave Éric and Alaoin, although Collette didn't blame the giant elf for watching. They were each giving admirable effort, though Alaoin's technique was a bit dirtier than the other man's.

"Éric is a bit too technical, especially when he fights Alaoin," Faron shared, earning a nod from Collette. He shrugged and turned back to Collette. "How would you like to continue?"

She nodded. "I'm up for anything. Are you bored of throwing me to the ground yet?" she asked.

"Not at all. In fact, I can even teach you other throws." Without warning, Faron shot forward, put the lower half of his leg behind Collette's, and pushed hard with one hand. She toppled backward, though he caught her before she could hit the ground.

Collette didn't miss the mischievous twinkle in his eyes, and she laughed as he righted her on her feet. She appreciated the well-concealed humor Faron possessed.

"You can use the move on anyone, no matter their weight or height," Faron told her. "Your strength will be useful with most people on other moves, but this one will work no matter who you're facing." He nodded in Éric and Alaoin's direction. They were going through the same move, and as Éric tripped Alaoin, the king grabbed ahold of Éric's shirt and pulled him down with him.

Éric barely caught himself with his forearms as he landed on top of Alaoin. Collette could see a blush tint Éric's cheeks as he lay flush on the other man, though their attraction hadn't needed as much of an announcement. Nor did the prolonged pause before Éric got up and pulled Alaoin into an overly aggressive headlock.

"Damn," Faron muttered, shaking his head. With an aggravated sigh, he turned to Larent and Nawalya. Larent was holding his own, but Nawalya was dancing circles around him.

"It's a sight to behold, isn't it?" Collette said.

"Yes, it is," Faron replied, watching Larent. "He's still struggling with the weight of the false claws, overbalancing slightly on his left. He's used to them being an actual extension of himself, and he isn't taking into account the new weight."

"You should go help him," Collette suggested.

Faron shook his head. "Not yet. If you watch the way—" He paused as though he couldn't remember Nawalya's name. "You can tell with the way she's moving around Larent, she's teaching him how to better compensate in her way."

Collette watched longer and eventually nodded in agreement. Larent could certainly hold his own against most, but his skill was lacking compared to Nawalya.

"Well. Let's get back to it."

*Dearest Mother,*


*We hope you are well. Of course, we also wish the same for Father and Éric, but we know they both possess less of a self-preservation instinct than you. Still, we know you do your best to keep them from being too difficult.*

*As much as we hope you are well and miss you, we wanted to let you in on important news. We know Mallan has traveled to Coralia. No doubt, his visit to Coralia will formalize a plan of attack on the Nereid kingdom and, surely, a potential threat to Fythias as their ally.*

*We've made the decision to send the remainder of the designated soldiers to you as quickly as possible. We think it prudent to keep enough fighters behind in Fythias in case units from Coralia and Azmarin are dispatched here. I know you will*

*notify Alaoin and the others. We've written Alaoin as well, but you know how quickly he sees to his letters.*
*Stay safe, Mother. We send our love.*

*Yours,*
*Amélie and Elyna*

# Chapter Thirty-One

Larent rubbed the cream between his palms, trying to warm it up a bit before placing his hands on Collette's bare back. Darkening patches of bruising continued to form along her back, just out of reach of her healing touch. He didn't know how well her magic would work when not directly on an injury, and she hadn't attempted to heal the remaining spots which promised to turn nasty shades of purple in the coming hours. When she hissed a little, he couldn't help but lean down, placing a kiss on her shoulders. "I tried to warm it up."

"I know," she said, her head resting on her folded arms as he worked. "It's fine. Just a little cool."

"Did you have fun with Faron?" Larent asked as he put more cream on his hands, once more trying to warm it up before applying it to a nasty bruise just above her hip she hadn't dealt with. He thought she'd enjoyed herself quite a lot during training, despite the bruises. Every time he'd managed to look her way, she'd been actively engaged with Faron, laughing, nodding, and otherwise applying his careful instruction.

"He teaches differently than Whyldon," she'd explained as they walked back to the palace. Larent assumed different was not better since she'd hardly critique her father. His work with Whyldon in Barcomb Mill had proved more than sufficient.

"I learned a lot from him," she replied. "And I like his sense of humor. He reminds me of Arian."

"Same, though his humor is a bit less biting, I think. Maybe." Larent couldn't help but laugh. "You would like someone who reminded you of Arian."

"I would," she agreed. "I love Arian."

"I know you do, Freckles," Larent assured her. "What did you think of Éric and Alaoin?"

Collette gave a contemplative sigh. "I fully expected Éric to bolt from the grounds after he fell on top of Alaoin. Their attraction is so obvious to everyone else. I wonder why they haven't acted on it yet."

"I don't know. Though, I wonder if they don't know the other is interested. It seems the most likely explanation. Unless there is a rejection or something in the past we don't know about." Larent's eyes narrowed as he considered the possibility. Just as their group shared a plethora of complicated and inter-secting histories, so would those from Fythias.

"True," Collette agreed. "Faron reacted to their antics as though there is some unspoken tension there."

"They were basically raised together. I would be surprised if there wasn't some unspoken tension." Larent applied the last of the cream, then carefully climbed onto the bed and strad-dled Collette's hips before starting to massage her lower back, careful of the bruises.

Collette said nothing as his hands slowly worked down her back. Despite the numerous remaining injuries, she gave no indication of any pain or discomfort from his movements. Her shoulders slumped forward as she further relaxed, contorting the indelible ink, now fully healed.

"Your Marking is beautiful." He leaned down and kissed her shoulder once more as his hands massaged up her back, working out all the kinks.

"Is it?" she asked, her voice low and content. "I think you find most things about me beautiful."

"I do, but I think the wave design fits you. It looks almost alive. Does it still hurt?"

"No," she replied. "Honestly, sometimes I forget it's there."

Larent thought over her reply. He could see it. If the swirling design of her Mark didn't itch or hurt, it would become just another part of her, especially if she couldn't see it. "I wonder if you could get others?" He started massaging Collette's shoulders, laying a kiss on the back of her neck.

"I suppose if I earned more and they were offered," she suggested.

Larent laugh. "I know we are about to go to war, but let's try and avoid death-defying stunts to get more, just in case." Larent started to massage Collette's neck, then down her arms.

"It's not as though I seek out those moments," Collette argued with a light laugh. "I just make decisions as needed."

"The most exciting decisions," Larent said teasingly as he moved his hands from her arms to her sides, gently running his fingertips across her skin in a way he knew was ticklish.

She laughed and squirmed away from his touch. "Stop," she said.

Larent made a thoughtful noise and stopped for a moment, pulling his hands away just for enough time to make Collette think he was actually going to stop before he declared, "No!" He dove in to tickle her more.

"Stop," Collette said, moving enough to physically dislodge his current stance.

Larent laughed as he was moved. "Okay. Okay. Sorry! I couldn't help it." He lay down next to Collette and opened his arms.

Collette sat up and grabbed her shirt, pulling it back on before she settled in Larent's arms.

"Ahh," Larent said with a grin. "And here I was hoping to enjoy the view." He kissed the top of her head.

"Not after tickling me, you don't."

Larent laughed again. "I can accept your punishment. Besides, with those bruises, asking you to sit on my face should probably wait a day or two."

She gently shoved him, her amusement evident in the way her lips curved up. "Remind me why I love you again?"

"Because I'm uniquely talented in giving you pleasure and cuddles. Better than anyone else ever." Larent nodded sagely. "Or because I make you laugh. I'll let you pick."

"Yeah, those things contribute," she agreed. "How did you enjoy practicing with Nawalya? Feeling battle-ready?"

"It was fun. Hard but fun. She helped me work on a balance issue I didn't realize I had. She also promised next session she wouldn't go easy on me, so I may need help with my own bruising." The claws didn't replace his wolf, but he felt more confident now than he had since he'd been subjected to the blood magic spell.

"I'm happy to help you with bruising," Collette promised him.

"Thanks, Freckles." He had no doubt she would do anything for him, just as he would do anything for her. Her willingness to give without concern for herself extended to him, probably more than what she'd give others. He took comfort in knowing he would never put her in a situation where she had to choose him, in whatever capacity, over herself.

As time passed, Larent heard her breathing start to slow as Collette grew more comfortable. He had been about to ask her if she wanted to head out for food, but it seemed like a nap was now on the agenda, and really, he couldn't complain.

# Chapter Thirty-Two

Faron walked into the rooms Aphros had given him and Sabine. Once the door was shut, he took a moment to stretch out his back, letting out a low groan when something in the middle popped. "I thought I had a few more years until my joints started hurting," he jokingly complained to Sabine.

His wife sat at an oak desk located in a corner of the front-most room. She had no quill or ink out, which meant she'd only just begun reading whatever she'd received. "Didn't you choose to spend the afternoon tossing around Queen Collette?" she asked without looking up.

"I did," Faron allowed as he strode across the room to kiss Sabine. "Someone must be willing to give the queen a challenge. I also would have missed the awkwardness between our son and king." Spirits, he was getting so tired of those two.

"I think you'd have preferred to miss Alaoin and Éric dancing around their feelings," Sabine said. She set the letter aside. "So, is Queen Collette a decent fighter, or have her people allowed her to think she is?"

"She is quite skilled. It's obvious she's been training since she was young. However, she's never fought in a battle before.

Small fights, yes, but nothing like what's coming. The battle will be the true test, and I believe she will hold her own quite well." Faron paused as he considered his next words. "She is very, very strong. More so than a human should be."

Sabine nodded. "I've heard rumors about her strength since we arrived. Aphros believes she may be part Nereid."

Faron had been so focused on planning, training, and watching over Alaoin, he had missed that piece of information. "If he believes it, there must be a reason for it."

"I assume so. You said yourself she was far stronger than a human should be, and most Merpeople are stronger than humans."

"So are some elves, and there are other races who left this corner of our world ages ago whose blood could run through her veins. Nereid sounds right, however, and is most likely." Faron eyed Sabine. He knew he would get in trouble if he did what he was considering, but it might be worth it. First, though, he walked to the washroom and started the overly large tub, checking the temperature before going back to where Sabine sat.

She extended the letter she'd been reading to Faron. He accepted it despite the knot forming in his gut. Letters always seemed ominous to him. Thankfully, the letter he possessed held nothing more than an update on the Azmarin forces and the girls' response. He didn't know what he would have done if they had caught another spy or taken care of another pushy noble, though Sabine often handled court-related news. "It seems they are handling leadership better than I expected," he said, handing the letter back. "No one's dead and nothing's on fire."

"People frequently underestimate their abilities because they are so outgoing and bombastic," Sabine pointed out. She pointed at him, a playful smile on her face. "You should know better."

Faron met her amused gaze. "They lit Avana on fire when they were seven. No one knows how, not even Avana, and she was there. Despite Alaoin having a very capable spymaster, the girls are frequently the ones who catch the spies. I do not put anything past them."

"I am aware," Sabine replied. "I have been present in their lives, after all."

"And yet, you were the one to suggest they be left in charge." He winked at Sabine. Faron leaned forward, placing his mouth near her ear only for their bedroom door to suddenly open, allowing Alaoin and Éric entry. The two were arguing, which told him his plans for the evening were a bust.

"King or not, you are expected to knock before entering my quarters," Sabine interjected, putting a stop to the argument.

"My apologies, Sabine," Alaoin said. "Your son is impossible, though."

"I'm impossible? By the spirits, you never listen!" Éric exclaimed.

Faron knew their intrusion was due to something either very serious or something exceedingly stupid. Éric never yelled, and his hair was disheveled. Faron left to turn off the water in the washroom, returning as quickly as possible.

"Will the two of you please act your age and explain what the problem is?" Sabine said, her tone parental in a way it hadn't been in quite a few years.

Éric straightened up immediately, running a hand through his hair to fix it. He then motioned to Alaoin to go on, something Faron felt the other man wouldn't do given the set of his jaw.

When neither of the younger men replied, Sabine rose from her seat. "I'm not putting up with the two of you acting like children," she declared. "We're on the brink of war, the rest of the Fythian soldiers allocated for the upcoming battle are enroute to the islands as we speak, and you two want to behave like children. I did not tolerate this behavior when you were teenagers. What makes you think I will now?"

Faron moved to stand behind Sabine, showing both men he would support any decision she made. He made a point to stare Éric down until his son finally explained what was going on.

"I was trying to convince Alaoin that a decision he was about to make was not the best decision, despite what local culture might say."

"What decision was that?" Faron asked before Alaoin could say anything.

"Skinny dipping with some of the Nereids may not have been in our best interest right now."

"Really?" Sabine replied, her lips flattening into the most unimpressed expression she could muster. "You two came in here, unprompted and without permission, over whether or not Alaoin should go skinny dipping?"

"Sabine," Alaoin began, only for Sabine to hold up her hand.

"I do not want to hear anymore."

Faron opened his mouth to support Sabine and tell them they would be training with him before the sun rose the next day when Éric cut in.

"I was on my way to speak with you when I found him with the Nereids in question." He held out a letter for his mother. From the writing on the front, Faron knew it was from the girls. "I assume you got your own but just in case."

"We did," Sabine confirmed. "Mallan has traveled to Coralia; thus, we have more soldiers coming here."

"Why did I not get a letter?" Alaoin asked,

"They said you did," Sabine replied.

"It's your letter. I found it in the trash—unopened," Éric said, his voice so similar to Sabine's in tone and inflection when she was truly upset, Faron struggled to keep in his laughter.

"You've seen the nonsense they send me because they think it's funny," Alaoin grumbled. "They act like I am not their king."

"Perhaps you should strive to be kinglier more often," Sabine suggested. "None of us expect you to do nothing but rule, but you have treated much of our stay here as a holiday rather than a serious matter."

Alaoin started to roll his eyes but thought better of it after catching Faron's gaze on him. He sighed and nodded. "Of course, you are right, Sabine."

"Tomorrow, both of you will meet me for training in the early morning." Faron gave them a minute to ponder what he meant by early. "Expect me before first light. Now get out."

He watched both men for their responses. Éric decided to keep his mouth shut, but Alaoin looked like he wanted to dig himself a larger hole.

"Don't," Sabine warned the king before he spoke. "Go enjoy the rest of your evening and rest up. You will need it."

Alaoin left, unhappy with the dressing down he'd been given. Éric followed quickly behind.

Faron made sure the door was locked before turning back to his wife. "Would you like to take a warm bath with me?" he asked before something else could come up.

"To start, yes," Sabine said.

"I like the sounds of that." Faron moved behind Sabine and began to undress her. As he did, he noticed the tilt of her head. "What are you thinking about so very hard, my wife?"

"Perhaps having a conversation about some things with Queen Collette and Larent."

Faron closed his eyes and held in a sigh, even as his hands continued to remove her clothes. If there was one conversation he did not want to have with anyone else, it was the one Sabine hinted at. He knew, deep down, they should talk to Collette and Larent, but not now, not yet. So Faron began to litter Sabine's shoulder with kisses, nipping every third kiss. "Later. For now, let us enjoy each other."



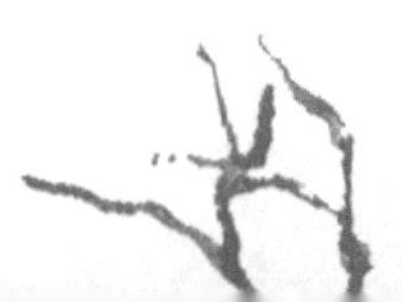

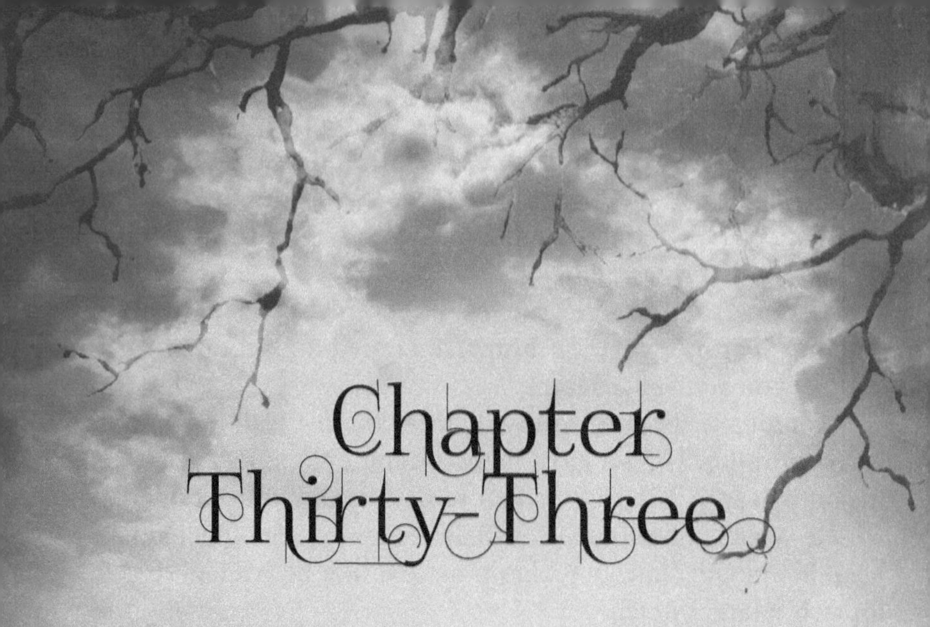

# Chapter Thirty-Three

*My Dearest Lynessea,*

*I am glad for your letter about Zephraim, even if it held the worst of news. I will talk to him, and we will go from there. I thought it best, in wake of your news, to write to you, requesting you please let Her Majesty know Zephraim is the reason Sara Whyldon has been freed from prison and is safe with Cremisius Hawke. I miss you every day, my waves.*

*Be safe,*
*Barris*

Barris didn't slam his hand on Zephraim's desk, but it was close. Tension radiated from the Golden Lord in waves, putting Zephraim on edge before he noticed the parchment under the hand on his desk.

"Zephraim, I need you to explain this to me, please. I'm not accusing you of anything. I haven't shown anyone else, but I need you to explain these accusations."

Without having to look at the letter before him, Zephraim already knew the contents. There could only be one thing to inspire Barris's ire. He folded his hands on the desk in front of him. "I am guilty of the accusation," he quietly confessed, "and I have no justification."

Barris let out a harsh breath, an underreaction to what Zephraim had expected. "Okay, but why blood magic?"

"At the time, I'd probably have said she deserved it for trying to challenge me, to remove me from my seat. For trying to take what was mine. Now... now I know I was petty and jealous and supremely dangerous."

Barris nodded, no longer looking at him, leaving Zephraim believing what little support he had was now gone. It was the least of what Zephraim deserved.

After several silent, agonizing minutes, Barris spoke. "That you can admit how you truly feel and the mistakes you made is a good start. I'm not happy about what you've done, but knowing what happened puts a few things into perspective. Especially the sadness lurking behind your eyes, your mentions of seeing her face. You believed you killed Collette, and you felt guilty for your actions, didn't you?" Barris moved from around the desk, closer to Zephraim.

"I did," Zephraim replied with a nod. "Not at first but very soon after. I couldn't escape the horror of what I had done. And even with her having survived..." His words trailed off, and Zephraim closed his eyes.

Barris studied Zephraim closely, crouching down so they were at eye level. "What did you mean by 'take what's yours'? What else is there for her to take other than her throne back?"

Zephraim remained silent for several long beats. "Larent," he said quietly. "I never had any deep feelings for him. It just felt like a personal dig for her to be in Azmarin, claiming

marriage. She'd been romantically attached to another in her party, so her claiming of him felt motivated."

"You and he were together?" Barris asked carefully.

"In a casual sense, yes."

"So, you felt betrayed. When did you use blood magic? What else was going on?" Barris kept eye contact with Zephraim, making it obvious he wanted to understand.

"Everything, really. Riken was passively challenging me at every turn. The manipulations from Rhoslyn were becoming more apparent." He sighed and shook his head. "I truly felt as though everything I was doing was being challenged or questioned, and I just … snapped."

Barris looked down at the floor, a hand absentmindedly coming up to rest on Zephraim's knee in comfort. "You had other options, Zephraim. I understand you were angry and hurt, but what you've confessed to is a lot." Barris looked back up at the other man. "I won't tell anyone else. Not Crem, not the others if you don't want me to. I believe you're sincere in your regret. I need to believe you are sincere in your regret." Barris gave a small huff.

"It is a lot," Zephraim easily acknowledged. "And it's unforgivable using blood magic. Let alone on my sister." He took a breath. "I'll leave it up to you to share or not. The others already don't trust me."

"I don't know if I want to share this with them," Barris admitted. "But eventually, they should know."

"I'm fairly certain Collette will take care of me in a rather permanent manner when she shows up," Zephraim said as if the matter was simply a factual observation. "They will certainly know then."

Barris closed his eyes again and set his jaw. "No, she won't."

"You are more optimistic than I."

# Chapter Thirty-three

"I'm more optimistic than most people." Barris laughed. "Right now, however, I fully believe you were sent by the Goddess to test my faith. She instructs that so as long as someone is willing to repent, we are to help them. You're willing. Therefore, if needed, I'll spirit you away to Pontus Bay, and Collette will never have to know."

"You've never been on the receiving end of my sister's temper," Zephraim said with a quiet laugh.

"No, I have not, but I will weather the storm when it comes." He squeezed Zephraim's knee before moving to stand. "I won't abandon you."

"You're a good person, you know?" Zephraim asked. He'd spent his life around people who wouldn't hesitate to backstab or do any other number of things to get what they wanted. He'd done as much to Collette.

"Not really," Barris denied easily. "I mean, for all you know, I'm only acting as I am to help save the Nereid."

"You could try to help the Nereid without helping me," Zephraim pointed out.

"Okay yes." Barris smiled down at Zephraim and held out a hand. "Would you like to go get dinner? I'm starving and do not want to be in the castle any longer."

Zephraim looked at the offered hand, then took it. "Getting out of the castle sounds nice."

Barris gave Zephraim a bright smile and pulled him to his feet. "Then let's go." As they walked by the fireplace, Barris tossed Lynessea's letter into the orange flames, not bothering to watch it burn.

# Chapter Thirty-Four

Riken paced from one corner of his room to the other, agitation vibrating through him in a way he rarely felt. "You are positive it's Zephraim?" he demanded once more of Cadan.

"More so than anything," the other man, lounging against the wall near the door, replied.

"Then you must deal with him while I'm gone, even if it's just to throw him in the fucking prison." Riken spun on his heels to face Cadan head-on. "I left Rhoslyn in the hands of another I trusted, and he assaulted her. I know where your desires lay, so I do not worry about repeated offenses. However, if Rhoslyn comes to any harm, I will take your head myself. You *will* keep her safe."

Cadan raised an unimpressed eyebrow as he pushed himself off the wall. "I will ensure her safety, my lord, even if I have to die to do it," Cadan promised.

Riken knew he would follow through. He took a deep breath before grabbing his family sword from where it rested in its scabbard against the wall. Securing it with practiced hands, he looked at Cadan once more. "Then let us go meet Mallan and our queen."

Cadan opened the door. and the two made their way quickly to the main hall where the royals waited. Thankfully, Mallan appeared to have just arrived as well.

"Ah, that is what I like to see. A proper walk for a man. I see my healer treated you well," Mallan commented with an overly pleased grin.

"Your healer is quite the amazing woman," Riken conceded. He once more had to push away the thought of what it would take to convince the woman to come work for them instead, which caused him to wonder how many other magic users worked for Mallan. His face, however, remained open and pleasant.

"She is, indeed. We are lucky to have her on our side, no doubt," Mallan agreed.

"Have who?" Rhoslyn asked as she joined the two men. Her cinnamon hair, pulled up into an elegant twist which rested on the nape of her neck, was accented by a tiara with glittering white and green gems. She'd look lovely no matter what, but Riken appreciated the complimentary colors as they brightened her green eyes.

"My healer," Mallan replied. "We are both so pleased over the help she supplied Riken."

"Ah," she said. "I was pleased as well."

"I will miss your radiant presence." Riken couldn't help the soft smile he gave Rhoslyn before turning back to Mallan who gave them a thoughtful look.

"You are quite lucky to have such an inspirational queen," Mallan said with an oh-so-charming smile. "No doubt the Coralian army will secure an easy victory for her."

"You flatter," Rhoslyn said with a gentle chuckle. "You make a good regent for Azmarin. I am certain you will find yourself seated permanently before long."



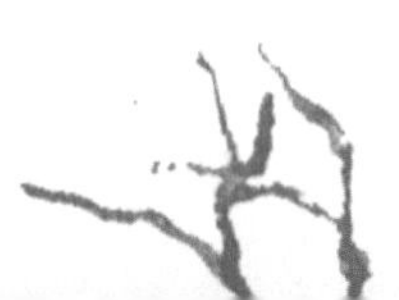

Mallan bowed his head as though the thought had never occurred to him. "Perhaps I shall find myself so lucky."

Riken had to fight to keep the pleasant expression on his face. Something about Mallan screamed untrustworthy. He hoped they didn't have to deal with the man, though adding Azmarin to Coralia wouldn't be the worst thing to happen. "Will you see us off, Your Majesty? I am sure the troops would love to see you before they go."

"I planned on it," Rhoslyn confirmed.

Riken had known as much as they had discussed it the night before, but there was still a façade to uphold. "I will miss you," Riken couldn't help but say into Rhoslyn's ear, his voice barely a whisper. She nodded but voiced no response. She was not in a position, and Riken understood.

They proceeded from the palace out to the grounds where stacks of supplies were being loaded into wagons which would be transported with the army. Soldiers were scattered about, helping with loading, cleaning weapons, and otherwise waiting to be officially sent off. Riken took it all in proudly. Deep in his soul, he knew the Mother would bless them in their endeavor. After all, she hadn't sacrificed herself just to give humans magic, to place those humans above all other races and those who weren't faithful would fall before those who were.

"They should be ready to move out within the hour," Mallan guessed after taking in the scene.

"I think so," Rhoslyn agreed. "We have more supplies and men already waiting at the city's edge. Riken will have additional men as you close in on the coast of Galel. You should have more than enough to take on the Nereid."

"And Fythias, considering the reports say Alaoin didn't even take half his forces with him," Riken agreed. He knew they would be well on their way before any news of Coralia forces leaving could reach the Nereid, let alone Fythias.

"Then I suggest you take your leave and win the first of many glorious victories in my name," Rhoslyn declared.

"It would be my honor," Riken said, squeezing her hand before releasing her arm. Stepping away, he bowed low to Rhoslyn before shooting Cadan a look full of meaning.

Mallan offered Rhoslyn a shallower bow. "I shall accompany you to the edge of the city where my local troops wait. We shall rendezvous with the rest once we are over the mountains."

"I look forward to meeting the rest of your troops. I've heard many tales of the armies of Azmarin," Riken said as he made eye contact with Rhoslyn. He wished he could kiss her, but there were still appearances to keep up, for now. The longing look from Rhoslyn proved she felt the same way.

"I have been honored with the opportunity to see what they can do," Mallan said, drawing Riken's attention away from his queen. He smiled as though he had not a care in the world or any clue what a nuisance he was. "I look forward to showing you the might of Azmarin, Riken."

Riken wished the man would shut up and let him have another moment with his love, but he knew the moment wasn't to be. Not if they wanted to make good time today. "Would you like to say anything to the remaining soldiers?" Riken asked Rhoslyn.

"I think so," Rhoslyn said, glancing out at the soldiers who continued to work. "Gather their attention for me." Her hands rested leisurely on the front of her dark skirt. She looked every bit the chaste, demure young queen.

Riken moved a few steps away from Rhoslyn. He raised his voice to a yell. "Soldiers! Our queen wishes to address you!" Once he had their attention, he bowed once more to Rhoslyn.

Rhoslyn gave him a nod of thanks and took a step forward. "Gentlemen!" she began. "I know you are aware of the sacred duty I have entrusted to you. The Outlaw Queen has established herself in the Nereid Islands, and she has tricked Fythias into joining her. She plans on attacking. On undoing all of our hard work. We cannot let her succeed."

A cheer issued from the crowd, and Rhoslyn presented them with a modest smile. "I know you are up to the task," she continued as the crowd quieted. "I know you wish to preserve the wonders of Coralia and to uphold the values instilled in following the Mother."

Riken turned so he could watch the crowd devour Rhoslyn's words as she worked her magic. She was stunning, and her words came so easily, as if she had been born—no—made by the hand of the Mother to be their queen.

"Go forth and win this battle for me. For you. For Coralia," Rhoslyn finished, earning more cheers. She stepped back and looked at Mallan and Riken. "I wish you all the luck," she expressed to both men. "Riken, would you be so kind as to escort me inside before you leave?"

"Of course, Your Majesty." Taking the few steps needed to stand by her side, Riken once more offered Rhoslyn his arm and escorted her inside, leaving the cheers behind them as they entered. Once they were behind closed secured doors, Rhoslyn took hold of Riken's shirt and pushed him against the door before kissing him.

Having known she would want a private goodbye, Riken found himself temporarily taken aback by the physicality of her actions. He quickly got over it. Placing both hands on her hips, he pulled her flush against him as he returned her kiss. She kissed him fervently, as though she might never get the opportunity again. Her hands smoothed up his arms and over his shoulders.

Riken deepened the kiss, his tongue meeting hers. If he thought for a moment he could get away with it, he would have switched their positions and taken her against the door. Rhoslyn must have wanted the same because she broke the kiss, relinquished her hold on him, and took a step back. "Do not get hurt."

"I will come back in one piece. I swear it."

"Good. Hopefully, she will get killed or maimed in the battle, and we won't have to worry about her. If not, break her." Rhoslyn's decisive words left no room for interpretation or argument.

"It will be my pleasure, my love," Riken growled and kissed Rhoslyn once more. He truly did not want to leave her.

"Good," she repeated before kissing Riken desperately. Eventually, she settled. "You need to leave, I know."

"I don't want to go. Last time I left…" Riken didn't finish the sentence. There was no need to rehash what had happened. "I know you can take care of yourself, but if Zephraim, Cadan, or anyone even looks at you wrong, promise me you'll gut them."

"You know I will," Rhoslyn said.

Riken nodded, and before he could prolong their goodbye, he pulled away from Rhoslyn after one last kiss. "I will win for you and be back as quickly as I can."

"We shall celebrate upon your return," she replied, smiling up at him. "Now go before I decide you cannot."

Riken nodded and didn't quite flee but almost. He opened the door and joined the army, taking one last look back before he vanished into the crowd.

# Chapter Thirty-Five

Sitting on the rug in his bedroom, back against the footboard of his bed, Barris looked up at the stone ceiling in contemplation. He wasn't drunk, but he was buzzed enough to be slightly bolder in his questions than normal. Turning his head, Barris looked at the man sitting next to him. "I've been wondering—" He paused to get his questions properly formed. "Did you truly believe Collette killed Wrenn?" he asked Zephraim.

"I did," Zephraim admitted with a nod, red gold curls swaying. His hair was in dire need of a cut. "She'd always disliked Wrenn, and once she became queen, she'd not made an effort to conceal it. When he and Rhoslyn arrived for the tournament, things escalated. He wasn't living up to his responsibilities on his estate, and he was mouthing off to her when she chastised him. Then he blew up at her in the middle of a corridor for everyone to hear. Next thing anyone knows, he's dead. It seemed probable at the time, and after denying my marriage to Rhoslyn, I was in a mind to believe the story."

Barris had never spent much time around Wrenn. The man had been an obnoxious drunkard and womanizer who cared little for those outside his circle of people. Barris had witnessed the disrespect Wrenn casually threw Collette's way throughout the years.

"Wrenn was disrespectful to Collette. I think it got worse when she became queen. I remember him telling others Sargarus should have beaten her more growing up." Barris looked at Zephraim. "But murder? No, she never would have done that. Do you think you were more inclined to believe it because she said no to your marriage?"

"I think I was angry about her denying the marriage, but I think it was one of many things which culminated in my participation to remove her from the throne."

Barris nodded. "And how do you feel about Rhoslyn now?" Barris asked as he nudged Zephraim.

Zephraim gave a brief laugh. "I think I feel sorry for her, truly."

"Why?"

"Because many of her choices were made in the name of self-preservation. Eventually, those choices will come back on her, and the world is exceptionally cruel to women compared to men," Zephraim said.

"True, though Lynessea would argue society allows the poor treatment of its women. I do question how Riken fits into her plans for self-preservation. In all honesty, I believe she would have been better off staying loyal to you."

"She loves Riken or experiences something close to it," Zephraim guessed. "She'd not tolerate his consistent blundering of opportunity otherwise."

"I think it will be Collette who gets them. I could be wrong, but I don't think so." Barris looked over at Zephraim. "Would you take them out if you had the chance?"

"Possibly, but I am not certain I have the constitution to kill anyone."

"Truly?" Barris asked, surprised. His expression grew thoughtful. "Not all of us are made for it, and I hope you never have to." Barris nudged Zephraim gently again.

"I think many more find themselves in the position to make the decision, though," Zephraim replied with a sigh. "I think, should it come down to it, I could if needed."

"Again I hope you never need to, but with everything going on…" Barris shrugged.

"With everything going on, there is no hope of a peaceful resolution," Zephraim said bluntly. "I think we all know it, especially when my wife and Riken seem determined to burn down anything resembling dissent."

"Oh, all of this will end in bloodshed," Barris said with certainty. "I was just saying maybe you'll be one of the lucky ones who never has to know what it feels like when someone's life blood spills out of them and onto you."

"I somehow doubt it," Zephraim said.

Barris shrugged. "I would say it's getting late, and I should head back to my rooms. I realize we are in my room, however, and I assume you are in no hurry to head back to yours." Barris looked over at one of the tables on the far-left wall holding several full bottles. "So, would you like another drink or something else?"

"I can let you have your evening if you want it," Zephraim replied. "I think I might get something to soak up the alcohol."

"I don't wish to be alone yet if you don't mind my company for a little while longer."

"I don't mind," Zephraim assured him. He gave a slight grin. "It's not like I have a kingdom to run."

"Did you enjoy being king, even a little?" Barris asked. He stood, offering his hand to Zephraim, who accepted. He accidentally pulled Zephraim closer than he meant to. They paused, though briefly, as Zephraim's chest nearly fell against Barris, but Zephraim righted himself and stepped away.

"You ask a lot of questions," Zephraim continued.

"I've been told it's part of my charm, though some do find it annoying as well apparently."

"It's not annoying," Zephraim replied. They quietly walked from Barris's rooms and into the corridor. "It's just interesting, as I said."

They were halfway to the kitchen when Barris heard voices coming from a door left ajar. He thought nothing of it at first until Zephraim placed a hand on his shoulder, stopping him as something caught Zephraim's attention.

"Cadan," Zephraim shared in a barely audible whisper.

Barris tilted his head to listen. Nodding to Zephraim, the two men moved closer to the door to listen in.

"After the breakout of Sara Whyldon, we've determined the prison is no longer secure. Tomorrow night, we will be removing the remaining prisoners to a well-fortified labor camp in Myrefall. The wagons will load a few hours past nightfall to not attract attention." A silent murmuring from the other guards sounded, though Barris couldn't quite catch what the soldiers said.

Cadan continued, "I want twenty-two guards on these wagons. There should be enough men to hold off any surprises. If there are no questions, I expect a list of guards come morning, and for those guards to be ready to go before nightfall."

Barris heard the acknowledgement and footsteps headed in their direction.

Grabbing Zephraim by the arm, he dragged him away as quickly as possible, hoping neither of them were spotted when Cadan opened the door a few moments later. They hid in a corner behind a door as the men filed out, and they waited long after the footsteps had subsided.

Barris sighed. "Well, that's good information to have."

"It is," Zephraim agreed, his gray eyes looking off in the direction where the men had exited. "It also feels convenient."

Barris nodded in agreement. "Cadan has been very careful with information. Why would he suddenly be so careless?"

"I don't think he would be, but now we must figure out how we want to handle the situation. If we were just lucky and stumbled upon plan-making, there are people to help. If we are being set up, there's an entirely different problem to overcome."

"Let's head down to the kitchen, grab some food, and retreat to my room to talk this over. If we can't come up with anything, we can take it to Crem and see what he says."

Zephraim nodded, and he led Barris to the kitchens to grab some food.

# Chapter Thirty-Six

Cadan growled softly, watching from his place in the shadows as Cremisius Hawke and his men swarmed the wagons holding prisoners of no worth to the kingdom. Hawke's presence had been the expected outcome, though Cadan hated the truth of Zephraim's betrayal and the heartache it would cause Rhoslyn.

The wagons had moved beyond the part of the city where he had felt Crem would attack without incident, and Cadan had felt a small ember of hope build in his chest. His hope was dashed just out of sight of the palace gates. Cremisius Hawke had appeared as if he was some hero of legend here to save the haggard and beaten-down people of Quenall.

Now Cadan just watched, six of his men behind him, while the soldiers he'd assigned to the wagons followed his orders to the letter. They put up enough of a fight to make their presence seem legitimate but not enough to get themselves killed. Two of his men died anyway, men who obviously shouldn't have been on the mission, upsetting Cadan deeply. He would ensure someone would pay for it.

Watching any further would just upset him more, so Cadan turned on his heel and signaled for his men to follow him back to the palace. The walk back felt like it took seconds, and before long Cadan found himself standing in the dining room waiting patiently for Queen Rhoslyn to acknowledge him.

Rhoslyn's brows rose at Cadan's appearance, though she took a sip from her goblet before acknowledging him. "Yes?"

"Cremisius Hawke and his men attacked the wagons," Cadan knew Rhoslyn would understand and he watched her face for her reaction.

"Are you certain no one other than Zephraim heard the plan?" Rhoslyn asked carefully as she put her cup on the table.

"I didn't see anyone else in the hallway with him," Cadan replied. "Could there have been? Possibly, but I didn't see anyone, and no one else passed by the room."

"Then if you are certain, you know what to do."

"Would you like to accompany me and issue the order?" Cadan asked. He knew he could handle Zephraim on his own, but he thought the sentence might have more meaning coming from Rhoslyn.

Rhoslyn leaned back in her seat, hands resting on the arms. "I don't think he is deserving of my presence."

"He is not, Your Majesty," Cadan confirmed before making a swift exit from the dining room.

The men he'd had with him earlier waited where he had left them, standing at perfect attention. He could not have been prouder of them. "Men, you will accompany me to finish the unsavory task of arresting King Zephraim for treason."

The six were some of his best recruits, so none of them questioned the order out loud, even if he could read the confusion in their eyes. Ignoring it, he headed up the stairs, content when he heard them following behind.

# Chapter Thirty-six

Cadan counted the steps as they went up to the library on the third floor where he had noted Zephraim had started taking his dinner. He was not disappointed when a passing servant confirmed the location of the soon-to-be ex-king.

Reaching the library, Cadan stopped outside to take a deep breath. Only then did he enter at a measured pace, heading for the back of the library. Seeing Zephraim seated there alone, he felt another weight leave his chest at the knowledge he would not have to contend with Lord Barris whom Cadan thought might protest what was about to happen quite loudly.

A part of Cadan wanted to knock the book from Zephraim's hand to forcibly remove him from the chair and humble the king, taking a small revenge for the men who had needlessly died tonight. Cadan was a professional, so instead, he cleared his throat, catching Zephraim's attention and letting him put his book down.

Zephraim didn't speak, though his gray eyes met Cadan's darker ones in a silent defiance Cadan used as confirmation of Zephraim's deeds.

Cadan didn't try to hide the satisfied smirk crossing his lips as the next words left his mouth. "Zephraim Villot, you are under arrest for treason. Will you come quietly?" The threat of what would happen should he decide not to was clear as Cadan let his hand move to the long sword strapped to his side.

Still, Zephraim continued to look unimpressed, as though Cadan's words and actions meant nothing. "Tell me, how does a king commit treason against himself? I think the last time the lot of you concocted this kind of story, accusations of murder and Merscale trade were at the forefront."

Cadan gave Zephraim a pitying look. The man really believed he could talk his way out of his arrest by bringing up his sister. Motioning the guards forward, he said, "By order of Queen Rhoslyn, you will be confined to your rooms, unless

escorted by two guards, at all times. Visitors must be approved by the queen, myself, or Lord Riken upon his return. Should you be found in violation of these rules, you will be thrown in the dungeon or executed immediately." Two of the guards took hold of Zephraim and forced him from the chair.

Infuriatingly, Zephraim still did not behave with the alarm an arrest should have warranted. He simply allowed the soldiers to act. Cadan proceeded, refusing to be deterred by Zephraim's arrogance. "Your crimes are conspiring against Her Majesty with the rebel Cremisius Hawke, which I have proof of." Cadan paused to meet Zephraim's eyes. "If it were up to me, you would be cut down where you stand. Good men were killed tonight because you told Cremisius Hawke about those wagons. Be grateful Her Majesty is merciful."

"I think you'll find she is not," Zephraim replied. "Of course, I refer to our actual queen. When she arrives, I think none of us will live long enough to suffer as we truly deserve."

A surge of anger flooded Cadan, but he knew Zephraim was baiting him. Instead of acting on the rage, Cadan did an about-face and started from the library, the two soldiers holding onto Zephraim, tightening their grips as they followed. The other four soldiers took position around them in case Zephraim tried to fight.

"I wouldn't worry about the false queen for much longer. Riken and Mallan will handle her and the Nereids," Cadan said with all the confidence of a man who knew how life should and would be going forward. "Worry more for yourself. Rest assured no one else will care what becomes of you."

"Of that, I have little doubt."

When they arrived at Zephraim's room, Cadan opened the door and the guards pushed him inside. "You were a worthless person before, spending your time moping and drinking instead of doing anything of note with your life. You were just as useless and weak as a king. Take heart you will at least be remembered as the man who overthrew Queen Collette and helped put a strong leader on Coralia's throne."

Zephraim righted himself, turning back to look at Cadan. "The fact you think any of you will hold power much longer continues to astonish, truly. Rest well in your unfounded confidence."

Cadan couldn't help the laugh that left him at Zephraim's words, the naivety of them. "Do you have any questions about the terms of your sentence?"

Zephraim finally grinned, mocking and condescending in a way Cadan had not expected. "Have a good night, Cadan," he said and approached the door before closing it in Cadan's face.

# Chapter Thirty-Seven

Zephraim settled in the armchair close to his fire, not at all perturbed by the encounter with Cadan. He'd known it was a matter of time before Rhoslyn and her minions took some official stance against him, and he'd been wary of the plot concerning Crem. House arrest, which was the only way he could think to refer to his current state, wasn't exactly a terrible condition. His rooms were large and comfortable, and he doubted anyone in the palace could count on their positions remaining intact for very long.

He leaned back in his plush chair, contemplating what he would do in the long term. He smiled as he considered the frustration he'd seen in Cadan's face. The man had wanted Zephraim to argue, to fight, to somehow rebel against the treatment. Zephraim hadn't given him the desired ammunition, and he wouldn't going forward.

A knock sounded at Zephraim's window, concealed by closed curtains, pulling him from his thoughts. He contemplated ignoring the sound, but curiosity won out, and Zephraim rose from his chair. He leisurely walked to his window and threw back the curtains.

On the other side waited Barris, crouched on the edge of the window ledge. "Hello," he said with a wave and a bright smile, though Zephraim could read the worry and anger in his eyes. "May I come in?"

News spread quickly, it seemed. Unlatching the lock, Zephraim wordlessly opened the windows for Barris and stood back so he could safely navigate his way in.

Barris entered cautiously, careful not to slip on the ledge. Once grounded, he turned to face Zephraim, placing both hands on his shoulders. "Are you alright?" Barris asked, concerned.

Zephraim nodded. "Cadan tried to conduct things with rationality and peace all the while trying to goad me into resistance. I did not give him the satisfaction."

"Goddess, he is such an asshole. I'm glad he wasn't able to get a rise out of you." Barris released Zephraim and looked around. "So what do we need to pack up?"

"What do you mean?" Zephraim asked him seriously. "You know I cannot leave. Not when they will have a renewed interest in getting hands on Crem and the others."

"But you're not safe here," Barris said in confusion, stepping close to Zephraim once more. "Zephraim, they will kill you or try to, at least." The steel blooming in Barris's eyes told Zephraim the other man's offer of protection would include fighting the entire palace if he had to.

"I signed my own death warrant when I turned on Collette," Zephraim said, his tone level. "We both know I'm right. The only lingering question is who will deliver the final blow. If my staying put helps to keep others safer for a little longer, then it's what I have to do. It's the least I owe."

"There's no guarantee staying here will keep them safe. Cadan will have already sent soldiers out to look for Crem's people, and when they don't find them, it will only be a matter of time before Cadan convinces Rhoslyn that torturing you will be the best way to find them." Barris gave Zephraim a soft smile. "I already told you Collette will not harm you. No one will harm you. I won't let them." Barris spoke with such conviction, as if standing up for Zephraim, protecting him, meant as much as protecting the kingdom did.

Zephraim couldn't help but smile. "You have been a good friend when I have not deserved it, you know."

"I'm trying to be," Barris replied easily. "Though if you would agree to come with me, I would be thrilled," Barris tried once more.

"And what would you do with me?" Zephraim asked.

Barris swallowed hard at the question before he responded. "I would get you out of the city. It wouldn't be safe for you here. I would take you home."

"You know I'm not likely to be safe anywhere in Coralia?" Zephraim said. "Which puts you in danger if I agree."

"I'm already in danger," Barris argued. "Eventually, they will figure out where my loyalties truly lie. Someone with even the smallest knowledge of the Nereids will figure out the meaning of my tattoos. At some point, I would have been forced to flee or be arrested. So why not go now?"

Zephraim sighed, acknowledging the good points Barris made. Finally, he nodded. "Okay."

Barris relaxed at his concession, but he immediately turned serious. "Gather up what you think we need, then we can go. I hope you're not afraid of heights."

"You underestimate me," Zephraim said with a soft laugh. Still, he did as instructed, and soon, the two were on their way.

Barris and Zephraim arrived at the hideout less than an hour later thanks to incredible luck sneaking out of the castle grounds.

He couldn't help but wonder if Queen Collette had a similarly easy time during her well-debated escape, but Barris had other things to worry about.

As they entered the cavern, Crem's raised voice greeted them as he talked to the men who had accompanied him on the rescue mission tonight. "Those soldiers you killed didn't need to die tonight. They barely put up a fight. All you've done is put us even more at risk by surely angering Cadan."

"We were already at risk," argued a younger man, his chin held up in stubborn defiance.

"We were," Ian agreed in a quieter, but no less annoyed, voice. "But I think we're all aware they will use what happened tonight in defense of any action they take against us."

"You mean like arresting Zephraim on charges of treason so he and I must now leave Quenall before he faces immediate execution?" Barris called out as they entered.

Crem's face paled at the news, and he silently dismissed the men he'd been talking with. Only Howle remained by Crem.

Ian glanced at Barris and Zephraim, who stood partially obscured by the lord. "It looks like you got him out of the castle," he commented, "but we knew it was only a matter of time before they made up some excuse to go after him."

"Yes, but Cadan contends only Zephraim overheard the plan the lot of you reacted to tonight. Somehow, they missed my presence the night we overheard." Barris made a face and tried to banish the guilt from his voice. Guilt which had been eating at him since the news of Zephraim's arrest and the reasons behind it had started circling the castle.

"You're set on going with him?" Crem asked.

Barris nodded. "They'll put two and two together after this. I'm the person he's most seen with after all."

"How do you plan on getting out of the city without being spotted?" Ian asked, crossing his arms. "I'm not saying it's impossible, but the second they realize he's missing, they are going to send the guard out."

"I assumed we'd leave now, and I was hoping you might help us," Barris said.

Howle finally spoke. "It's not a bad idea. There isn't much for ya ta do here, and ya were saying the resistance on the other side of the mountain would need ya," Howle reminded Ian.

"How can I help, then?" Ian asked, turning back to Barris.

"I'm not as familiar with the area between here and Pontus Bay as I wish I was. I was hoping you were."

Ian nodded. "I am very familiar with most of Coralia. I can get you back to Galel and onto the coast."

"Thank you so much. I'm more than happy to pay for anything you need and any lodging we stay at on the way," Barris offered as he realized Sara and Diana had been sitting off to the side, watching the whole thing play out. "I know you can't go back home," he said, addressing Sara, "but you are welcome to join us if you wish to head back over the mountain."

"If we are about to be truly hunted down, it might be best if you went with them," Crem added. "But it's your choice."

"I'll go with you," Sara easily decided. "I never much cared for Quenall. No one in my family did." She looked squarely at Zephraim. "Including my niece."

Zephraim nodded in agreement but said nothing.

Barris eyed Sara once again. He would never get over her resemblance to the queen. "We don't have to worry about the others in my party. The moment we heard of Zephraim's arrest, I sent them to the Nereid kingdom." It had been a small fight as none of Lynessea's brothers had wanted to leave him alone, but in the end, reasonable heads prevailed.

"Then we should leave as soon as possible. The more distance we put between ourselves and the palace, the better," Ian said.

"I think we're as ready as we can be," Barris said, looking at Zephraim for confirmation. Zephraim nodded.

"I'll pack some things for Sara," Diana volunteered. "It will take only a matter of minutes."

Barris nodded to Diana in thanks, prompting Diana to disappear from the main cavern. He turned to Zephraim. "Are you alright with all this?" he asked quietly.

"I suppose," Zephraim said just as quietly.

"Anything I can do to try and make this easier?" Barris asked.

"No, I think this is a much better outcome than I deserve," Zephraim replied.

"No, you deserve to be free and not imprisoned in your own home by a false bitch queen with delusions of grandeur and a love of violence and death," Barris insisted.

"You are far too kind. I created the situation for myself."

"He's right. He did, but I'm more interested in when the two of ya got so close," Howle said from where he was across the room. His head tilted forward about how close Barris was standing to Zephraim while Crem wore a puzzled expression.

Instead of taking a step back or being embarrassed, Barris stayed where he was. "I'm not sure our relationship is any of your business. Zephraim may have had a hand in creating the mess we are in, but Rhoslyn is the true culprit. Zephraim has been trying to make up for his actions. His attempts at atonement are enough for me."

"Me as well," Diana said as she returned, holding a travel pack out for Sara.

Barris motioned to Diana as if her word was law.

Diana approached Zephraim and hugged him. "You are a good person who got wrapped up in a horrible situation," she said before releasing him. She turned her gaze to Barris. "Keep him safe."

"With my life," Barris told Diana seriously.

"Good," Diana replied. "You four should be on your way, then. If the guards are out looking, I'd hate for any of you to get caught."

"Thank you, all of you, for everything." He looked at Crem, Howle, and Diana. "We will see you again when all this is over. In one life or another." Barris bowed deeply to them.

"You shall see us again," Diana predicted. "We have much to accomplish, and I think our queen will need us all."

"Most certainly," Barris agreed. He and Zephraim left the cave first, giving Ian and Sara privacy to say their own good-byes. "That went well. Soon, Quenall will be behind us, and you'll be safe," Barris said to Zephraim once they were a decent way out of earshot.

Zephraim nodded, his gray eyes cast ahead of them. "As you have said. I hope you are right."

"The Goddess will see our way through," Barris said, truly believing his words.

# Chapter Thirty-Eight

The evening wore on, and Rhoslyn had settled in her quarters as she went through the motions of readying for bed. She'd exchanged her rich gown and jewelry for a thicker shift and robe. Although she frequently wore her hair at least partially down, the cinnamon sheet hung loose without ornament or curl. Even alone, she was conscious of the picture of virtue and sincerity she reflected.

She lounged on a chaise near her fireplace as she read, though every so often, she'd glance toward her desk where a sealed letter sat, waiting to be sent to Riken. She'd spent quite a bit of the evening composing the story of Zephraim's betrayal and arrest, a jubilant account which would ultimately end in his execution. As an apathetic fool, Zephraim lacked harm. As someone willing to topple what she and Riken worked so hard to achieve, he was a danger, and she'd have no more prisoners escaping from the palace. She just had to strike at the opportune time.

Knocks sounded at her door as she turned the page of her book. With an annoyed sigh, Rhoslyn set the book aside, slid her feet into her silk slippers, and rose. The only reason she didn't ignore the disturbance was the later hour. Unexpected late visits usually indicated a problem of some sort. She tightened the belt on her robe as she crossed the room, making sure she would remain covered. When she made it to the door, she gave herself a once-over before opening it.

Cadan stood in her doorway, his head bowed and his eyes lowered. She knew right away he came to deliver bad tidings. "What has happened?" Rhoslyn asked, alarmed by Cadan's demeanor.

"Zephraim has escaped, and Lord Barris is missing. It appears they escaped from his bedroom window. I already have guards searching the grounds and the city." Cadan let out a harsh breath before taking a knee. "I should have posted a guard inside Zephraim's room. This is the second time a prisoner has escaped on my watch. I will accept any punishment you deem fit."

Rhoslyn stared blankly at Cadan, somehow unable to fully comprehend, or even believe, just how they'd managed to lose Zephraim after the victory of arresting him. The color drained from her face as worry lines creased her forehead.

She forced herself to take a calming breath, though admittedly it was not very effective. Zephraim escaping as he did presented numerous problems, and neither she nor Cadan had the time to fall apart with worry. "Get up. Now is not the time to grovel. Even under arrest, he served a purpose. Go find him."

Cadan rose, his somber expression slowly transitioning to something infinitely more serious. "Of course, Your Majesty. I will tear the city apart to find him and the rebels."

"You must," Rhoslyn insisted. "There are those who would come after us without Zephraim here pretending to be king." Only the Mother knew what would happen if he joined up with Collette. "If you cannot find him, I will hold a meeting with the council, no matter how late. Tell them he was caught in a treacherous act and fled when confronted. It will buy us some time while we figure out our next steps."

Cadan nodded, his face set in grim determination. "I will accompany you to the meeting if it needs to be held."

"Good. In the meantime, we also need to consider putting an end to the underground maneuvers of Cremisius Hawke's rebellion. They got to Zephraim somehow. He's never been proactive enough to be of use to anyone in the past."

"I believe you are right, Your Majesty. There was a change, and it happened quickly."

Rhoslyn sighed and nodded. Perhaps the way she and Riken had treated him, the unkind indifference they gave him, motivated him enough to actively work against them. She could think of nothing else. "Please," she instructed. "Just go find him."

"It will be done," Cadan promised. With another deep bow, he left to find the former king.

Rhoslyn shut the door behind him, locking it as she thought. She could sway whomever she needed, but the process would need a delicate touch. With a sigh, she walked over to the desk where the letter she'd written Riken waited to be sent. She picked it up and tossed it in the fire.

# Chapter Thirty-Nine

A long meeting with Aphros and Alaoin left Collette eager for relaxation. Although she did not have the same freedom to explore the island as some of the others had, she appreciated the opportunities the island provided to find relaxation. Leaving the palace, Collette soon found herself in one of the many surrounding gardens.

The bright, warm weather resulted in numerous, colorful blooms on many of the flowering plants. Long green vines crept up trees and trellises, and random stones created various paths throughout, though none were perfectly manicured or maintained in the way one might expect from palace gardens.

She wandered the gardens, following paths at random and enjoying the solitude. As always, the company of her loved ones left her appreciative, but the coming war poked at her with increasing frequency. Having a few moments alone, she contemplated strategy, meaning, and how she might deal with any close losses. There would be close losses.

She turned as the path she was on took a sharp right, and Collette wasn't sure what she had walked into as the scene before her provided no hints. She realized she had been paying so little attention to her surroundings because certainly the noise from the scene before her should have reached her before the sight did.

Larent muttered curses as he leaned against a vine-covered pillar, his foot lifted from the ground and his boot badly scuffed. A few feet from Larent, Nawalya stood stock still, her hands covering her face, though she peeked out between her lithe fingers. Behind the two stood the most unbelievable sight. Arian had his face buried in Thomas's shoulder, the stance barely muffling the deep, whole-body laugh leaving the usually stoic elf's mouth.

"Oh, thank the spirits, Freckles," Larent exclaimed in a pained voice. "I need your help or a fucking miracle." His words had Nawalya more fully covering her face and Arian laughing harder.

A smile threatened to bloom, but Collette kept the response suppressed. "A part of me feels like I should walk away and pretend I saw nothing," Collette replied, though she still approached, somewhat slowly.

"You should run away," Arian managed through his laughter.

"Shut your mouth, Chuckles. You've been no help." Larent's tone was mostly good-humored, but Collette detected a slight bite in his words. No doubt, the unknown injury to his foot held blame. "Spirits, I think my foot is broken," he hissed after he tried to flex the injured body part.

"I am so sorry," Nawalya groaned, her words muffled by her hands.

"Okay, Arian has issued a warning," Collette replied. "Explanations or I follow his advice."

"I was trying to teach Nawalya how to dance," Larent said.

"Trying and failing," Thomas quipped, and he had to put both arms around Arian to prevent him from falling over from his hysterical laughter.

"Alaoin is the one who suggested we have a bit of fun after dinner," Larent said. "And Nawalya said she didn't know how to dance." He glanced over at Nawalya. "I don't understand how you can be such a graceful fighter and dance poorly enough to break bones."

Nawalya issued an even more muffled sound which Collette assumed was an apology.

"You already knew Nawalya couldn't dance, and you still offered." Arian no longer laughed, but his words came out breathless and rough.

"I was trying to help," Larent replied as he attempted to put weight on his foot.

Collette shook her head. "Larent, sit down and remove your boot," she directed with a sigh.

Larent did as instructed, sinking against the pillar. He removed his boot, wincing slightly. Collette knelt beside him, taking in the dark purple bruising already forming. She didn't know if Nawalya had managed to break his foot, but she'd caused enough damage for more than a little pain.

"What exactly were you doing to cause so much damage?" she asked, glancing back at the female elf.

"I stomped on his foot. Twice," Nawalya said, letting her hands leave her mouth. "The move is very similar to a fighting maneuver," she quickly defended.

"Except you weren't fighting," Thomas mused, earning himself a rude gesture in response.

Deciding she had more than her fill of explanation, Collette pressed three fingers to Larent's skin, the space growing warmer as her magic healed him.

Larent gave her a warm, loving smile as the pain faded. "Thanks, Freckles." As soon as she was done, Larent gently pulled her to him and kissed her. "Now, do you want to help me out with something else?" he whispered against her lips.

"Sure."

"Thank you," he said in a near-worshipful tone. He kissed her again before rising and pulling her back to her feet as well. He glanced back at Nawalya. "Pay attention," he directed, earning a nod in response.

Attention back to Collette, he extended a hand. "Freckles, can I have this dance?"

Collette smiled, amused by Larent, though she nodded as she accepted his hand. "Of course."

Larent bowed, and once he rose, he approached Collette, placing a hand on her waist while the other gently took her other hand. "We are going to do a simple step," he called back to Nawalya. "Watch Collette's movements." He turned a warm smile on for Collette. "Ready?"

"Well, you did just call me 'Collette,'" she replied with a teasing grin. "I don't know if I should help you further."

Larent chuckled and leaned in, whispering in Collette's ear. "Am I only allowed to call you by your name when we make love, then?"

"There are elves present," Arian called out only for Nawalya to shush him.

Collette laughed. "Perhaps."

Larent pulled back from her ear. "Maybe we'll test that later." They began the easy steps of the dance, their bodies swaying together gently as their feet moved. Every so often, he'd glance back at Nawalya, but Larent otherwise kept his gaze on Collette.

"Are you enjoying yourself?" she asked.

"You are in my arms, and most of my family is present. What else could I ask for?" Larent said softly.

"A balcony to fall onto?" she asked.

"Didn't I already do that?" he asked.

"You did," Collette confirmed. "And I only have one complaint."

"What's your complaint, Freckles?"

"Once we're back, you won't need to pretend to accidentally appear in my spaces. You'd be more than welcome."

"I'd fall on balconies for you, regardless. I'll just make the moments sweet or for special occasions," Larent suggested.

"Or when he does something wrong and has to make up for it," Arian called out.

"Or what he said," Larent replied.

"And what sort of thing do you think you could do to make me mad?" she asked.

"Being thoughtless or stupid comes to mind," Larent said. "But I'm sure I'll do something to upset you at some point. It will be an accident, but it might happen."

"I think we can safely assume we'll make each other mad at some point," Collette agreed.

Larent shook his head. "There's nothing you could do to make me angry with you. Worried, anxious, mildly frustrated maybe. But not angry."

"I anticipate spending my life with you, you know. I feel like you'll at least get close."

"I doubt it. That would be like Arian getting mad at Thomas. It will never happen. Though, I anticipate Thomas getting mad quite often."

"Do you anticipate me being angry with you quite often, then?" she asked.

"I anticipate the possibility. I've been known to be quite vexing." Larent's smile grew, and Collette knew he was about to do something. "This you don't do," he called to Nawalya before he spun Collette out, then back to himself, ending in a dip.

A surprised yelp left her mouth, but Collette ended up laughing almost as quickly. Larent, inevitably, was always

# Chapter Thirty-nine

Larent. Their moment of levity came to an end as Ceto sprinted into their area of the garden.

"We've received news!" she declared as she shook her ginger hair from her face. "Coralian ships have been spotted. The Depth Guard reports less than a day's distance."

Arian pulled away from Thomas, kissing him on the cheek before striding to Ceto. "I'll see you in the meeting room." He took off, his pace more than a jog, Nawalya following closely behind.

"Thank the Lady the rest of the troops from Fythias arrived yesterday," Larent said, his tone light, though worry shone in his eyes.

"Let's go," Collette said, and she, Larent, Ceto, and Thomas began the trek back to the palace.

# Chapter Forty

A muscle in Aphros's jaw twitched as he took a seat at the table, Queen Collette and King Alaoin on either side of him. They'd all known war would come, and they were lucky to have advance notice. The number of potential fighters presented a daunting challenge, though the Nereid king felt like numbers and skill would ultimately fall on their side.

He took a breath, forcing himself to relax as the large party settled around the table, then ran his hand through his salt and pepper hair. "Who wants to start?" he asked.

Arian looked across the table at Faron, the two men staring each other down for a moment before Faron conceded to Arian with a small wave of his hand. "I doubt they will know the rest of the Fythias army has arrived. I believe it would be prudent to have some of those ships engage with the Coralian ships if only to support your people who would be fighting from underneath the water."

"Support above the water will be useful," Ceto interjected from her seat between Jayden and Lynessea. "We have some weapons which can aid in sinking from beneath, but we run the risk of hurting the wrong people since allied ships will also be present in the harbor."

"How many ships were reported?" Sabine asked from her spot beside Alaoin.

"One hundred or so. Most were Azmarin-style ships, but our people saw them flying Coralian colors," Ceto explained.

"And what does the use of your weapons from beneath entail?" Alaoin asked.

"Some of us can create large waves, for one. We also have magical harpoons," Ceto replied. "They explode upon impact. Highly effective, but again, with allied ships so close, we don't want to rely on them so thoroughly."

"And ships above water will engage in close combat on top of the harpoons. The sailors will hope to sink or board enemy ships. Either way, we will be too close for exploding weapons," Jayden added.

"With one hundred ships, we have to anticipate soldiers making it to land. We need to prepare for multiple types of battle," Faron added.

"We do," Aphros agreed. "We're fortunate in the number of battlements we have. We'll have archers prepared for the front lines of those who make landfall to start."

"What about magic users?" Faron asked,

Aphros didn't miss the way Arian bristled at the question or the way his eyes darted to Thomas.

"Magic users here have distinctly different talents," Collette pointed out. "It seems likely each is better figuring out how their powers can best serve them."

Aphros nodded slowly. "I think I agree. If we had groups of those with the same gifts, more coordination would be needed."

"Where are the non-combatants going to be, and do we have an escape plan for them if things go badly?" Nawalya asked.

"Depends on who wants to be present on the field, doesn't it?" Ceto replied.

Aphros raised an eyebrow. "Those who are not in the battle will remain secured elsewhere on the island. Those who will be there, such as medics, secretaries, and whoever else needs to be present, will be set up in the appropriate tented and platformed areas at the edges of the field."

Nawalya nodded and glanced at Arian, whose unfocused eyes and thinly pressed lips suggested deep thought.

"He's doing the math for how many troops should be on those ships," Larent was heard telling Collette.

"How many fighters will be underwater?" Arian finally asked.

"Thousands," Ceto replied.

"We can estimate about one hundred soldiers per ship, which places their numbers around ten or fifteen thousand," Whyldon spoke up. He glanced up at the ceiling as he rubbed his chin. "We have more people who will be fighting on land."

"We will outnumber them underwater and on land," Aphros said. "I think we do not doubt our victory. We just need to minimize damage on our end as much as possible."

Arian and Faron both nodded in agreement.

"Can Nereids manipulate water if they aren't in the water?" Larent asked, his cheeks reddening with the question.

"Some can, yes," Aphros replied with a nod. "As with all magic, some are more gifted in certain areas than others."

"Would it be better to put a few of them on our ships to help mitigate the deaths there? Maybe their powers could be used to damage or capsize the enemy ships?" Nawalya pondered.

"We already planned on it, but again, we are limited because of the number of Fythian ships in the harbor," Aphros explained. "There is simply no way to keep a majority of the battle on the water."

"There really isn't," Faron added. "While stopping a handful of ships may save lives on land, we need to focus on a few key points—one of them being the majority of the battle is taking place on a sandy beach. Not everyone here has experience fighting on such terrain. The Coralian and Azmarin army surely don't." He looked to Collette for confirmation.

Collette shook her head. "There are coastal areas in both countries, much of which resembles the land here. Fythias isn't entirely coastal, either, which means only the Nereid fighters can claim complete comfort in fighting on the beaches here. Positioning those fighters in strategic positions around the battlefield will be key."

"I've been having our fighters train on the beach when they can, but I admit, the sand will hinder both sides, and strategic placement would help," Faron said, his mouth set into a grim line.

"So we reallocate some of our strongest Nereid fighters on the beach instead of on ships or underwater," Aphros said. He pointed to Jayden. "You among them."

Jayden nodded. "I'm more comfortable fighting on land anyway."

Aphros knew the comment was more for the non-Nereid members, but he was also well aware of Jayden's preferences. "Not all the others can claim the same."

"I'm also happier to fight on land," Lynessea added. "I can talk to the troops. See who would be willing."

"Why don't you go get started so we have a solid group?" Aphros said.

Lynessea rose from her chair, nodded, and left the room without another word.

"Does anyone have a specific place they would like to be? Either with the archers, fighters, or support teams?" Faron asked the group.

"Nawalya should be with the archers," Collette spoke up. "She's good with a bow, and if the line is breached that far in the field, she'd be able to handle herself with a blade."

"I can," Nawalya agreed.

"I'll be with the ground fighters," Larent volunteered. Arian did the same.

"Whyldon, Rion, Tolan, and I will also be on the ground," Collette confirmed. "Thomas will serve in an advisory capacity at the edges of the field, but he will not fight."

Arian frowned at the declaration, but he said nothing.

"Alaoin and I will be fighting on the ground. Éric will be—" Faron was cut off.

"I will also be fighting with the ground troops," Éric said.

Alaoin nodded in agreement. "My soldiers will be dispersed among the ships and the grounds with us. Their leadership has already given assignments."

"Are there any questions? Anything else we need to talk about, or should we spend the evening with our loved ones while the troops prepare for what is to come?" Faron asked.

"I think we will dismiss for now and regroup come morning," Aphros said with a definitive nod.

More nods went around the table before everyone stood and started to leave. Most were quiet as they went, except for Larent who was already trying to bring everyone's mood up as they left.

"We are as ready for this as we can be," Jayden said to Ceto and Aphros when they were alone again.

"We are," Aphros agreed. "And we knew the fight would eventually arrive. I say we go drink for now."

"I think a drink is a great idea," Jayden agreed before turning to Ceto. "You're in charge of making sure I don't get too drunk."

"I'll try to remember my mission once I'm drunk," Ceto replied, and she nodded toward the door, encouraging the men to follow.

"Then I guess Aphros must be the responsible one, or we are all screwed," said Jayden.

"You two can argue," Aphros said as he passed both. "I'm getting some rum."

# Chapter Forty-One

Arian sat on the stone bench, enjoying the coolness that seeped into his body. Nawalya was next to him, enjoying the silence as they waited, their knees pressed against one another. Arian had invited Thomas to come, but he had said Arian should take the time he needed with them, just in case.

"I was able to secure a bottle and glasses," Larent announced as he stepped into the garden, disturbing the peace, though Arian didn't mind. Looking at Larent, Arian couldn't help but smile at how honestly happy Larent looked, truly happy. The bottle in his hand looked rather expensive, as did the glasses.

"Do we want to know where you snagged that?" Nawalya asked.

"Nope, but don't worry. I asked first. It would be rude to steal from our hosts," Larent replied.

Arian shook his head as Larent took a seat on the grass in front of them. He watched as Larent uncorked the bottle and poured more than was needed.

Nawalya leaned down and grabbed a glass for the two of them, handing off the red sparkling goblet to him and keeping the blue one for herself. Larent had the green one. The three sat in silence for a moment, and Arian didn't need to glance at either of them to know their eyes were shut as they prayed to their respective deities, something he'd given up long ago.

Closing his eyes, Arian waited for them to finish, not opening them again until felt Nawalya move. Only then did Arian raise his glass, and they followed.

"To the Lady. May she watch over us in the coming battle," Larent started.

"To the Spirits who guide our steps and help our aim stay true," Nawalya followed.

"To our skills and our blades. May they never fail us," Arian added, and the three drank from their glasses. Arian found the taste of the wine a perfect balance of fruit and floral.

Once done, Larent stood and gathered the glasses. "You two be safe out there," he said.

"You as well," Nawalya said, standing. She nudged Arian with her foot as if he needed the encouragement.

"How about a group hug?" Larent joked, only to grunt in surprise when Arian pulled him into a hug, and Nawalya quickly joined.

"Neither of you die. I will not stand for it," Arian growled.

"We will be as safe as possible," came Nawalya's answer.

Arian understood. There was no guarantee any of them would live tomorrow.

"You go see your loves. We will meet on the battlefield or the greenfield beyond." Nawalya smiled, then strode off before they could say anything.

"Night, Chuckles. Enjoy Thomas." Larent laughed at Arian's rude gesture before leaving, taking the liquor back to wherever he'd found it.

Standing alone, Arian looked up at the stars, and for the first time in a very long time, he closed his eyes and prayed.

Whyldon stood by the garden reflecting pool, staring absently into its depths without really seeing it. He'd faced many battles in his life, and in many ways, tomorrow would be no different. They would face an enemy dressed in regalia they did not deserve. They would destroy those who betrayed Collette, those who wished to harm the Nereid, and they would continue.

Still, he hated the thought of his daughter facing the kind of brutality that came with a battlefield. He'd done his best to prepare her for the harsh realities of the world, but he recognized there were intrinsic parts of her which would remain soft and easily broken. He just hoped no one found a way to those parts come morning.

Soft footsteps sounded behind Whyldon, and he looked back to see Nawalya stepping into view. Her attention on the plants surrounding him made it obvious she didn't notice him there.

"Can't sleep?" Whyldon called to her before looking back at the reflecting pool.

Nawalya turned to face Whyldon, jumping a little at his question. "No," she answered simply. "What about you?"

"No," Whyldon replied.

"Is that usual for you? Before a battle, I mean?"

Whyldon shook his head. "I've never been in a battle my daughter also fought in."

Nawalya nodded in understanding as she moved closer. "I can see how the worry would make sleep difficult, but you've trained her well. She's also resourceful and very smart. She will make it off that field tomorrow."

"Still, I can't help but think I should have taken her from Quenall when she was still a child." He sighed and shook his head before turning away from the pool. "She'd have been happier, would have suffered less."

"She would have been happier, yes," Nawalya said with utmost certainty, "but the horrors in Coralia would be much worse, and eventually, it would have reached her. I think in any life she would still end up here: leading an army against tyranny."

"True, but then being here would be the result of decisions she made. She could walk away now if she wanted, but she won't. She never had a choice about what her life would be."

"No she wouldn't, but if she ever decided she was done, I can promise you Larent would take her away as quickly as possible," Nawalya told him. She tilted her head to the side. "Why did you never leave with her? I'm sure you could have staged an accident to make it look like you'd both died so you wouldn't have been hunted or something."

"When she was young, it felt as though it would be too dangerous for her," he said simply. "We all know she wants other things for herself. Now, she won't walk away, but I would do something different if given the chance."

"No, she won't. You raised her to be a good and honorable person who wants to help others and make the world a better place."

"I tried," he said simply. "I'm proud of who she's become."

"As you should be. Collette is an amazing person." Nawalya looked down into the reflecting pool. "Larent, Arian, and I have already spoken tonight about tomorrow and such. Have you had time to speak with Collette?"

"I did," he confirmed as he watched a vine creeping along the ground near the pool. "She said she felt confident, and I believe her. Naturally, there is some anxiety as well. I was happy to let her go spend her evening with Larent."

"He will help keep the anxiety at bay and hopefully make sure she's well rested." Nawalya's eyes darted to the vine, narrowing slightly as if the plant had purposely offended her.

"He does take care of her, and he does it without making a whole show of it," Whyldon acknowledged. He couldn't fault her for wanting to be with him, even if he'd had questions and concerns early on.

"You're still not overly fond of Larent, are you?"

"I'm more fond of him now than I have been in the past," Whyldon replied. "He is good for her in ways her past partners have not been."

"Much better than Tolan for certain. I can say nothing about Rion. We have had very little reason to speak to one another outside meetings," Nawalya admitted. "I'm glad Larent's grown on you. He will end up your son-in-law if he gets his way."

"So I've heard," Whyldon said with a chuckle. "They do not hide their intention to marry one day. It is just a matter of when."

"After she's back on her throne, I think. Unless Collette decides otherwise."

"Why do you think she'd wait?"

"I don't know," Nawalya said. "Maybe to be sure she is making the right choice with Larent? Maybe she's just not ready?"

"Perhaps. I just somehow feel like we will see it sooner."

"With our luck, they'll decide to marry while on the battlefield." She laughed at the thought.

"Don't give them ideas," Whyldon said with a chuckle.

"They'll figure it out on their own. The only question is which one will suggest it." Nawalya gave him a warm smile which he returned.

"If I had to wager, it would be Larent."

"True. She is so much more level-headed than he is."

"About certain things, yes."

Nawalya remained contemplative for a moment. "They balance out each other well. Did you know he's been learning politics and diplomacy from Sabine these last few weeks?"

"Collette told me about his efforts. I'm actually impressed by the initiative. It demonstrates quite a lot about him."

"He wants to be better for her. I told him she loves him for him, but she'll appreciate the effort nonetheless." Nawalya looked up at Whyldon, then down at the water once more. "Be careful tomorrow," she said softly.

Whyldon studied her, letting so many unsaid things remain between them for now. "You as well," he said seriously.

"I'll try," she replied. "I should let you try and get some sleep."

"You should try to get sleep as well," Whyldon said.

Nawalya shook her head. "Not tonight. I'll be fine come morning, but sleep with tensions like mine will prove more harmful than not."

"Ah," Whyldon acknowledged. "Then I shall leave you here."

"Have a good night."

"Good night, Nawalya," Whyldon said. He inclined his head once and walked back toward the palace.



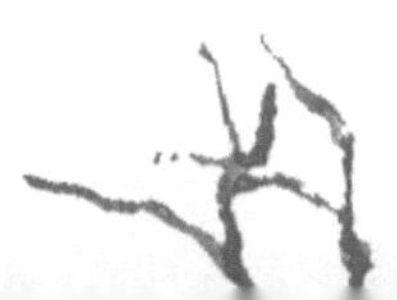

# Chapter Forty-Two

Thomas sat cross-legged on the bed, watching Arian presumably go over unknown lists of things he needed to attend to. The harsh line of tension in the elf's shoulders more than demonstrated his worry, and he moved as though he could deter the risks of tomorrow's fight if he just moved through the mental list of preparations enough times.

"Are you enjoying the view?" Arian asked, looking over his shoulder at Thomas, a small smile gracing his lips.

"I always enjoy getting to look at you," Thomas replied with a returned grin. "You are exceptionally delicious."

Arian blushed and turned back to his pack, pulling out a few more things before setting it aside and walking to where Thomas sat.

When Arian was in reach, Thomas settled his hands on the other man's hips as he looked up at him. "How are you feeling?"

"Calm, determined, terrified in a way I have never been before, knowing you will be on that battlefield with me. Even if you will be far enough away to supposedly be safe," Arian said, bringing up a hand to run through Thomas's hair. "How are you feeling?"

"Surprisingly optimistic," Thomas said after a beat. He knew tomorrow would present untold brutality, but he didn't let it push at his nerves too harshly. "I think things will go our way."

"They will," Arian said with complete certainty. "I'm glad you're optimistic about tomorrow."

"I hate that you're terrified."

Arian looked down, though his fingers continued carding through Thomas's light hair. "In a battle, anything can go wrong. All it takes is the wrong people to decide that the best way to demoralize us is to attack the non-combatants. I have seen it happen before."

"I've heard of it happening before, and I am prepared for if it happens," Thomas reassured him.

"It is horrible when it does, and while I will not ask you not to be out there, a large part of me wishes you were farther away and safe."

"I will not be safe on this island tomorrow, no matter where I may reside," Thomas said.

"I know, and I dislike it, but what am I to do? Steal a ship and force you to go? I would not do that to you even if I thought it would work."

"There is nothing to do but breathe and fight through the hours of battle, and at the end, see that I will be okay."

"You will be. You must. I have lost too much. and I will not lose another member of my family. I will not lose you." Arian bent until their foreheads touched.

"I promise you, I will do everything I possibly can to stay safe. If I see the lines break too closely, I will leave."

"Thank you," Arian whispered.

Thomas nodded, knowing it was the least he could do for his lover. "Now are you coming to bed with me, or are you staying up all night?"

"I am coming to bed. There is no reason to stay up when I can spend my night with you."

"Good. I need to feel you."

"And I, you."

# Chapter Forty-Three

Collette stared up at the ceiling, knowing daybreak would soon rouse the group from sleep. The battlefield awaited them. She looked over at Larent, who had always managed better sleep than she could even dream of, smiling softly at the sight of him. Spirits, if she gained nothing else from these months, he had been worth every second of it. She slid to his side, careful of her movements, then wrapped herself around him.

A soft groan sounded from Larent, more lazy protest than disgruntlement. "Hey," he said softly. "You okay?"

"Mmmhmm," she responded, letting herself enjoy the feeling of his warmth against her. "It's almost morning."

"Almost morning does not mean we have to be awake yet."

"Maybe not you," she whispered fondly. "Go back to sleep."

He groaned sleepily again. "No, if you're up, I'll be up with you."

She wasn't surprised. Larent always seemed to know what she most needed, and he gave it to her if it was in his power. "I have a bad feeling about today," she whispered.

"Bad feelings before battles are normal, especially your first one," he said gently, sounding a little more awake now. "Plans go awry. Something you never expected can arise. It'll be hectic as shit." He sighed, then kissed her temple. "We will make it out, and we will have helped save the Nereid Kingdom and retake your own."

She didn't respond beyond a small nod, her mind racing through everything she knew might happen once Coralian and Azmarin ships reached the island.

"If you want, we can go visit Nawalya," Larent suggested. "Maybe she'll see something."

"We shouldn't bother her," Collette replied. Nawalya didn't deserve to lose whatever sleep she'd found because of Collette's anxiety. "I'm just worried about all of you. I'd hate myself forever if we didn't all walk away from this."

He rose on an elbow so he was looking down at her. "We will make it out," Larent assured Collette as he cupped her cheek. "Even if something happened, you know we all want to be there. For you and the Nereid. We will be fine. The Lady will see us through." Larent's expression grew mischievous. "Want to see how quiet you can be?"

She gave a quiet laugh. "Very subtle," she said. "But sure."

Sometime later, she had to make him stop or else she would be useless in the coming hours. Still, she pulled him up to her, kissing him deeply, tasting herself on his lips. "I think you want me too exhausted for the battlefield," she teased.

"I don't think anyone could keep you away," he replied. He settled beside her on the bed, neither feeling the pull of sleep now. "I think Arian would tie you up and put you somewhere safe if he could. Other than Nawalya, I don't think he's ever cared about someone else like he does you."

"There is a reason I call him my brother," Collette pointed out. "And we all know I have to fight, regardless of what some might want."

"Sometimes, I think he's shocked to have a family again."

"I can't blame him. He and Nawalya lost quite a lot in their lives. It would be hard to even be open to finding a new family."

"They weren't for a long time. I had to grow on them, like mold."

"I hear you do that," she teased. "You were just sort of more important than anything else one day."

"Apparently. How else would I have ended up in your bed?" He snorted when she playfully shoved him. Once settled again, Larent broached another subject. "Think Thomas dragged Arian away from the war table, tied him down, and fucked him 'til he passed out?" Larent chuckled.

"I believe Thomas is good with keeping Arian sane," Collette said after considering it. "And I think we all known Arian needed the distraction. Arian especially."

"I just hope he lets Thomas distract him. I know Aphros appreciated his knowledge of battle strategy and such, but Arian can't do everything."

"He listens to Thomas," Collette pointed out. "And I think Aphros recognizes Arian is no good to anyone if he is too mentally taxed."

"He's a good man: Aphros." Larent sighed, turning his head to look at Collette. "We should get up, get food, and probably find the others, right?"

"We should, but I don't want to face the world yet." Larent was right, of course, and eventually, the demands of the day would force them into action. "They can't start the battle without us, you know." She grinned playfully. "You did wake up very early for some unknown reason."

"Oh yeah," Larent grinned back. "I have no idea why."

"I know. The things you put up with."

"Not put up with. Never put up with."

"Then how would you define it?" Collette asked.

Larent scratched a sideburn. "Enjoying every moment I have with you."

Though his words and tone came across as playful, Collette knew he meant them. Larent's utter devotion to her could never leave her in doubt. Collette moved closer. "You better stay safe today. You haven't even married me yet."

"We could resolve your complaint, you know," Larent replied. "Marriage under the Lady is simple."

"Do you want to get married now?"

"I'd have married you months ago, Collette. Now or later, I will stand by your side."

Collette believed him and had even before he admitted his feelings first developing when they'd met on her balcony. The decision to move forward with marriage, knowing they'd be deprived of an opportunity to celebrate until later, seemed an easy one. "Then let's get married."

Larent grinned, leaned over to kiss her deeply, then jumped out of bed with uncontained excitement. Quickly, the two dressed. "We'll need a few things for the ceremony," Larent shared as he pulled on his boots. "Thankfully, Chuckles has them."

"And what things are needed?" Collette asked, buttoning her shirt.

"You'll see," he said with a mischievous grin.

When they were fully clothed, Larent took her hand and led her from their suite and down the corridors leading to Arian and Thomas's room. Larent knocked, hoping the elf was awake. His grin broadened when a sleepy-looking Arian opened the door.

Arian surveyed them both and nodded. "Took you long enough," he muttered as he vanished back into the room.

When Arian reappeared, he held up small velvet pouch to show Larent. "Do you want your marriage to remain private, or can Thomas come?"

"Bring him," Larent easily decided. "You ready, Freckles?"

"Of course," she replied.

Arian excused himself to fetch Thomas, and when the other man appeared, he looked well-rested and alert.

Larent led the group through the castle and to the main courtyard, past the water gardens, the rock gardens, and several other beautifully designed spaces to a gated-off area. A shake of the door proved it unlocked, and Larent gave a cheer of triumph as he pulled it open.

Collette entered first, taking in the sights and scents of the private garden as much as she still could so early in the day. The sun had not yet risen, though strategically placed lanterns illuminated a stone-strewn walkway. She slowly followed the path, ears picking up on the tinkling of water as she walked.

Turning the corner of a natural hedge strewn with creeping vines, a pond teeming with small gray stones, and a bubbling waterfall came into view. She imagined the space would be quite beautiful come morning.

Larent joined Collette, taking her hand. "Ready?" he asked with a wide grin.

"I've been waiting for you," she replied, earning herself a delighted kiss.

Arian stepped forward, opening the velvet bag where he retrieved a deep purple ribbon which must have been several feet long. "Arms, please," he asked, and when both held them out, he gently wrapped it from her elbow to her wrist. He repeated the action on Larent, though going wrist to elbow. "To represent your love for each other," he explained.

Taking out a sapphire ribbon, Arian wrapped it around their arms the same way. "To represent your commitment to each

other." He then wrapped the fourth ribbon, this a forest green, on top of the other two. "To represent your trust in each other."

The last ribbon he wrapped around their arms was pearl white. "To represent the many years of happiness you will have together." Arian shook the bag once more, and a small black dagger fell out. He held the dagger to where the ribbons held them together. "Once cut, you will wear these ribbons until death separates you. Do you agree to a union under the Lady and the Spirit?"

"I accept the bond until death takes it," Larent said looking directly into Collette's eyes, a soft smile on his lips.

Collette kept her eyes locked on Larent's, knowing this was the best decision she'd made in her life. There was no hesitation, no uncertainty. Just the knowledge she was standing across from the person she wanted to spend the rest of her life with. "I accept the bond until death takes it," she repeated, smiling back at Larent.

Arian cut through the ribbons connecting them, and each set magically twisted into intricate braids around each wrist. "'Til death parts you," Arian intoned. Arian took a step back as Larent practically launched himself at Collette, pulling her close for a deep kiss.

Collette kissed him just as deeply, her arms wrapping around him as though ensuring she could never be separated from Larent. When the kiss broke, she kept her close hold on her new husband, knowing they would hardly have time to celebrate. "I love you," she whispered.

"I love you too," he said, resting his forehead on hers.

"I assume you want to wait to tell everyone else, likely after the battle, so Thomas and I will keep quiet. But if I may—congratulations," Arian said.

Collette gave Arian a genuine smile. "I'm happy it was you who was here to see it."

Arian actually smiled back. "It was my honor," Arian said, bowing his head. "Thomas and I will give you some time." Arian walked back over to Thomas, taking his hand and leading him away, leaving Collette and Larent alone.

Sunlight slowly trickled into the garden, urging them to get on with the intended purpose of the day despite their new union. "Hello, husband," she said, ignoring reality for a few minutes longer.

"Hello, wife," he replied.

"How would you like to spend our limited free time?"

"With you," he said before pulling her against him for another long kiss. "If I wasn't worried someone would stumble upon us, I would say let's have some fun, right here, right now."

"Let's," Collette suggested.

"I don't know. Think you can hold off screaming my name as to not draw attention of the guards or worse, Jayden?" Larent kissed to Collette's jaw, nipping lightly at her skin.

Collette closed her eyes, savoring the feel of his lips and teeth. "It's your fault when I scream, you know."

"Oh, I take full credit." He nipped at her jaw softly once more. "Are you sure you're okay doing this out here?"

"I just want to be with you," Collette replied. "I don't care where."

"Well then, guess we'll just have to keep it down." Larent ran his hands from her hips up her stomach and began to undo the buckles on her vest. As he unfastened each, the fabric fell open a bit more, and she slid it from her shoulders once able.

Larent nuzzled into her neck before biting down softly. His hands began to untuck her shirt. He only pulled away long enough to pull it over her head and toss it somewhere to his left. "You're so beautiful," he whispered, then kissed her again.

As they kissed, she slowly undid the buttons of his shirt, and she groaned softly when he was bare chested. She pressed herself against him, slowly savoring the moment.

Larent let out a soft sigh as he wrapped his arms around her, just holding Collette. His fingers traced nonsensical patters on her skin. "Tell me something," he whispered.

"I love you," she replied first, the response the most honest and obvious one she could give. "I love everything about you. I love every second we've had together."

Larent raised a hand and caressed Collette's cheek as he gazed into her eyes. "You are amazing, wonderful, smart, kind, compassionate. I love everything about you. From the small mole on your right ankle to the dusting of freckles across your cheeks. The Lady created perfection the day she made you."

She drew him into another soft kiss, unable to help herself as his words flowed over her. Larent lowered the hand on her back, finding her hip while the other ghosted along the top of her pants. A soft, needy sound issued from Collette, her lips finally leaving his to travel down his jaw and to his throat, each press of lips against his skin adoring and reverential.

"By the Lady," Larent breathed out. Cupping her breast, his thumb ran across the nipple gently. She gasped and let out a breath, her forehead resting against his shoulder for a moment. Her hands moved to his sides and then to his stomach, fingers trailing down the line of hair which met the top of his trousers. A hand slipped farther down, cupping him through the fabric of his remaining clothes.

Larent's breath hitched, and he barely held back a groan. His thumb flicked her nipple before rolling it between his thumb and index finger. She gasped again, closing her eyes as sparks of pleasure surged through her chest and down to the apex between her legs. Larent repeated the motion while his hands when to her belt and worked to undo it.

"Spirits, I need you," she said, her voice a raggedy whisper.

"I'm already yours," Larent promised. He dropped to his knees, removing her belt and throwing it to the side before lifting her leg to undo the first boot. The other followed, and she watched him work.

"You are," she confirmed, a hand running through his hair. "Always."

Larent smiled up at her as he slowly peeled her trousers down and off, tossing them the same way he had the shirt. He kissed her knee, her thigh, and slowly up to her center. "You might want to grab my shoulders," he said before he titled his head up so he could bury his head between her legs, giving the little bud a lick.

She gasped and did grab onto his shoulders out of sheer need for support. Larent knew all the ways to make her fall apart. The sun would soon rise, and they would be off to the battle, but Larent took his time, lapping at her center with an eagerness and knowledge of what she liked. He coated his index finger with her slickness, then gently pushed it inside of her, pumping in and out in a slow, teasing rhythm. Her grip on his shoulders tightened as her breathing became quicker. Larent added another finger, though he kept up the teasing pace.

"Larent," she breathed out, her tone pleading.

He looked up at her, a teasing grin on his face as his fingers still moved inside Collette. "Yes?"

She took a deep breath through her nose, both frustrated and terribly happy with his teasing all at once. "You know," she replied. "Even if you like committing treason, you know."

Larent laughed. "I love you," he said, before leaning forward once more and sucking her clit back into his mouth, his tongue making circles around it, his fingers picking up their pace.

She titled her head back as Larent's tongue and fingers guided her toward climax, soft moans and cries leaving her

mouth with increasing frequency. She breathed out his name as she drew close, her grip on his shoulders tightening. Her legs trembled as the waves of pleasure overtook her, and though she cried out his name, she was cognizant of being outside, and she just managed to keep her voice down.

"As you wish." Larent stood and quickly stripped himself of his pants and boots, tossing them every which way with little concern. "Come here," he said, his voice husky as he opened his arms for Collette. She did not hesitate to walk into his embrace, kissing him fiercely and tasting herself on his lips. She groaned softly as Larent pulled her flush against him. She could feel his desire, her own renewed with each new kiss.

Pulling away, Larent swept Collette up into his arms and lowered himself to his knees before laying her in the grass and covering her body with his own. "I'm sorry the grass is chilly, but I'll warm you up."

"You always do," she replied as she cupped his cheek, then kissed him.

Larent returned the kiss, his tongue darting out to run across her bottom lip. He braced himself on one forearm while the other hand moved down to her leg. He lifted it to wrap around his hips before he reached between them to guide himself slowly into Collette. She inhaled slowly as she adjusted to him, her hips rising to meet him. An arm went around his broad shoulders as she needed him closer.

Once he completely filled her, he paused, looking down, meeting her gaze. "Please," she repeated.

Larent nodded. He pulled almost all the way out, then slid back in at an agonizingly slow pace. Her moan of pleasure sounded as he filled her again, her fingertips pressed into his skin. "Spirits," she breathed out.

"Oh, I'm definitely not the Spirits," Larent joked breathlessly as he continued his slow pace.

She laughed, though it was disrupted. "Asshole."

"How am I an asshole?" he asked lovingly, the grin on his face speaking volumes about how much fun he was having and how hard it was for him to keep up this desperately slow pace.

"You know exactly how," Collette replied. "You prove it with every long second."

Larent buried his head in the crook of her neck. "You love it," he teased.

"I love you," she replied.

"I love you too, Freckles," Larent whispered, lifting his head to kiss her softly as he finally increased the speed of his thrusts.

The mood of their lovemaking shifted into something infinitely more intimate, and Collette held him all the closer. She didn't care what the rest of the day promised because the only thing she wanted was her husband. Larent must have known what she wanted, and he reached between them to stroke at her center.

"Oh!" she cried out, uncaring of who heard her at this point.

"I thought we didn't want to attract an audience," Larent joked breathlessly as he rubbed her clit, applying just the right amount of pressure, his thrusts deep and sure.

"I'm allowed to enjoy my husband," she managed between quick breaths. She was close, so close.

"I never said you couldn't," he said before he kissed her.

She kissed him desperately, as though the world might burn if he put any space between them. Her second climax roared into existence, shooting through her with an unexpected ferocity. Larent soon followed, leaving them both trembling and breathless. Still, he leaned down and kissed her deeply. Even when it broke, they remained close, their gazes locked in quiet contemplation, both on their early morning choices as well as what the day held for them.

# Chapter Forty-Four

The sun slowly rose, casting a golden hue over the sandy beaches and white and coral buildings of the island. Along the battlefield stood the defiant collective of Nereid, human, and elf, all defending the Nereid kingdom against the Coralian traitors slowly making their way to land. Here on the beaches, three kingdoms would determine one another's fate.

King Alaoin stood by the general's tent, bright silver armor shimmering in the sunlight. Fythian soldiers, sporting coastal shades of blue, flanked the outer edges of the field, serving as a strong line of defense for the Nereid people. The small collection of Coralian and Azmarin ships suggested the combined forces of Collette, Fythias, and the Nereid far outnumbered their enemy, but numbers were only one factor for success.

From along the battlements of the nearby palace and buildings, a line of Nereid stood ready, armed with arrows and blades, ready to pick off successful Coralians and Azmarins who broke the lines farther into the city. Fythian elves stood every few yards along the line of Nereid, their keen vision and hearing a supplement to Nereid might.

Collette marched to join Alaoin, her expression serious but optimistic. "Your soldiers ready?" she asked him. Her armor, a gift from Larent's grandparents, had been modified by some of the Nereid who specialized in metal work to better fit her frame. Magical protections had been imbued in the plates, and she was as battle-ready as possible.

Alaoin nodded, more alert and grim than she'd ever seen him. Holding a helmet under his arm, the king looked ready for the conflict. "Of course," he agreed. "Faron is overseeing the front-line formation. He's got a detailed eye." Collette nodded, and Alaoin cast her a concerned look. "What about your people?"

"Nawalya has joined the archers along the battlements," she explained. "The others are on the field."

"I saw your friend, the tall one with red hair, conversing with Faron. They'll use their size to their advantage."

Aphros stepped out of the general's tent, his armor more blue than silver. Behind him emerged Jayden, Ceto, and Lynessea, all four battle-ready. "The day seems promising," he commented to the other rulers.

"You think so?" Alaoin asked with something akin to his normally laid-back humor. "Think they'll let us stop for tea around mid-morning?"

Collette laughed. "You should ride out and ask once you're sufficiently parched."

A hand went to Collette's arm. "Stay safe out there, and all of us might enjoy a drink after the fight."

"You have a deal," Aphros answered for both. He motioned to Ceto. "She's going underwater to ready those below. Jayden and I will remain on the field with you. They may want our resources, but they will want your head," he gestured to Collette. "So stay alert."

"Now you sound like Arian," she replied.

"He's a good man. You need more of him on your side," Aphros replied. He nodded his head to the other rulers and left the scene with Ceto.

"You should go see your people," Jayden advised Collette. Even in his armor, the scales along his neck sparkled in the sunlight. "It might be some hours before you speak again."

"I will," she promised. "You try to stay safe out there. I got myself arrested for you."

Jayden smiled. "I might remember something about an arrest. It was so long ago." A nod of respect, and the two parted ways.

Collette glanced out to sea as she walked toward Whyldon. The Coralian ships were closer now, perhaps a little less than an hour out. She contemplated what it would feel like to fight against her own people, even though those people were not on her side.

She found Whyldon and Rion standing together, the latter examining his sword as they waited. "Ready for a fight?" she greeted the men brightly.

"Always am," Rion replied, shooting the queen a mischievous look. He nodded his head in the direction of the sea. "If those ships are packed full, we outnumber them by at least a third."

"At least," Collette agreed. "And part of their army will be composed of titled assholes who never lifted a finger in their lives."

"And those will be the ones to take out first," Whyldon said. "The unprepared will be the most desperate and dangerous."

"And I would assume an incentive has been offered to any who can take your head," Arian said as he approached from behind Collette, Larent tailing him. The shifter's eyes were raking across the soldiers then back out to the sea where the ships could barely be seen.

# Chapter Forty-four

"She's smart enough to know that, Chuckles. Freckles will be fine."

"You mean you don't plan to magically fall out of the sky any time I might be in a touch of trouble?" Collette asked Arian. "How unbrotherly of you."

"As hard as we are going to try to stay by your side, in battle, things happen. People get separated," Arian said, his eyes hard. Collette knew he would do whatever he could to stay close.

"I'll tie the two of us together to ensure I don't leave her side," Larent joked as he stepped up beside Collette and wrapped an arm around her. Collette spotted Tolan some feet away, looking uncertain.

"I know people will be separated, Arian. I'm simply questioning your ability to manifest wherever I happen to be."

Whyldon cleared his throat. "I am not suggesting Arian would be successful in an attempt to lock you away somewhere until we're done, but I think you both could expend energies more productively."

Arian made a face, but no verbal retort passed his lips.

"Hey," Collette said. "I promise I will not taunt anyone. I want to walk away from the battle as much as anyone."

"You'd better," Arian muttered.

Larent kissed the top of her head. "You're going to be fine. You've got this."

"Of course I do," she replied. "Just want to reassure my brother."

"I would be better reassured if you were safe in one of the tents with Thomas if only because I know you will taunt someone. You cannot help it. You will enrage someone and they will end you," Arian accused.

"I've enraged you plenty, and I am fine," Collette retorted with a grin. She looked past Arian, seeing Tolan looking their way again. She supposed he wanted to say something. "You can join us," she called out.

She watched Tolan's shoulders tighten before he forced them to relax. Only then did he walk over. "Hello," he greeted.

Arian nodded and Larent waved. "You ready?"

"Can you be ready for something like this?" Tolan asked with a raised eyebrow.

"No," Collette replied, then shrugged. "But then, I have less experience than the rest of you. I might be wrong."

"And I have more experience than you," Whyldon interjected. "Lack of readiness is part of the experience."

"I don't think you can ever be ready for something on this scale," Larent said.

Collette knew he was also slightly nervous, especially as he still couldn't shift to the wolf, and he'd never fought in a battle without the wolf's strength. "We just have to get through the next few hours, and I will personally be angry if any of you have more than a scratch when it's over."

"Even a tiny scratch?" Larent asked.

"They will not touch me," Arian added.

Tolan laughed. "Just be safe, okay? All of you."

"As much as we can," Collette promised, the response much friendlier than anything else she'd said to Tolan in quite some time. She ignored the look Whyldon gave her, as though their talk some time back had finally taken hold.

She stepped forward and took Tolan's hand, giving it a quick squeeze. Their hands fell apart as quickly as they joined, and Tolan smiled before walking away to prepare.

"I am going to walk the front lines once more," Whyldon said soon after. "I will return."

"Of course," Collette agreed. "If something happens before I see you again, keep yourself safe."

Whyldon smiled and nodded. "I still have to get you back on the throne," he said.

"You've done well," Collette replied. She stepped forward and put her arms around him as well. "You've been the best father you could be. Just make sure you walk away from the battle."

Whyldon did not reply. He simply hugged her back, and when it ended, Whyldon stepped back. "Make me proud," he said, and he stepped away.

"Do you want a hug as well?" Collette asked Arian, turning to him.

"I do not," Arian replied, the corners of his lips twitching up despite his decline. He, too, excused himself, promising to shortly return. Collette wasn't surprised. Arian was not a man to sit and wait.

"Hey," Larent said, pulling Collette's attention to him.

"Hey," Collette replied.

Larent smiled and kissed her softly. "I love you," he whispered, pressing his forehead against hers. "I'm going to do everything I can to stay by your side and fight with you, but if we get separated, I know you can handle yourself. Just promise you'll bring yourself back to me safely."

Collette smiled and kissed him again. "Didn't you hear? I just got married. I intend to celebrate with you for years."

Larent laughed. "When this is over, we should lock ourselves in our room for a week and just enjoy ourselves."

"At least a week," she promised. "I might let you out some time later."

"Oh, I'm going to need much, much longer."

"I'd give you whatever you wanted, you know," Collette replied.

"I just want you, Freckles."

"You've had me."

"And I will never get my fill," Larent replied before kissing her again.

When this kiss ended, Collette stayed close for several long seconds. "Be careful for me."

"Always," Larent promised. "Oh, hey. I want you to hold on to this for me during the battle." Larent reached into one of his side pouches and held out his wooden figure of the Lady.

Collette's gaze moved from the figure and up to Larent. "Should you not keep it?"

"I want you to have it so that if we get separated, I know she's watching over you. And you know, for luck." Larent grinned.

She held out her hand and took the figure, despite their vast differences in belief. "You're getting it back after the battle," she said.

"Of course, I am. At least until I turn it into a necklace for you to wear." Larent laughed. "Then I'll know the Lady is keeping my heart safe."

"A discussion we might have later," Collette replied. "But I have her for now."

Larent looked at Collette, studying her face with a soft expression. "Hey Freckles, tell me something?"

Éric made his way through the different groups of troops, barely noticing the other monarchs talking to those close to them, taking what time was given to them in case the worst could happen. Éric spotted his father talking to Rion, though he knew his father would soon take his place toward the front of the battlefield to rally the troops in a way no one but Faron could. He marveled at seeing Faron already present as Éric had left early so his parents could have a few moments alone. He'd promised them he would do his best to remain safe during the battle, and he planned on following through on his promise as much as possible. He also had Alaoin to keep safe and breathing.

Spotting the support tent with Fythias colors, Éric altered his direction to ensure those inside had everything they needed. Upon entering the tent, Éric was surprised to see Alaoin already there. He was less surprised to see Alaoin goofing off with some of the troops. Feeling his temper rise, despite knowing Alaoin was doing it for troop morale, Éric stormed over to his king. The troops, spotting him coming quickly, cleared out.

Alaoin turned to look at Éric, clearly surprised to see him storming over. "Yes?" he asked.

"Having fun playing around?" Éric asked in a tone so sweet he knew alarm bells would be going off for Alaoin. A part of Éric knew he shouldn't be so upset, but they were about to partake in their first war, and he needed Alaoin to take this seriously. To survive.

"Should I walk around brooding because I might die?" the king asked him with a roll of his eyes. "Is that what you want from me?"

"I would at least like for you to take this seriously. You could die today, Alaoin. I or my father could die today. Losing any of us would break my mother. The least you can do is try and take this as seriously as the other monarchs," Éric threw out.

"I am taking this seriously," Alaoin snapped at Éric. "Just because it doesn't manifest in the behavior you demand of me doesn't mean I am not taking it seriously."

Éric tried to take a deep breath but found himself instead taking a step closer to Alaoin, almost getting into his face despite their height difference. "Other than the council meetings and the three training sessions I had to drag you to, you've taken very little seriously since we arrived. How many times now have I had to come get you from an all-nighter at the taverns or fetch you from the gardens before you decide your

rooms were not good enough, females draped all over you every time? I'm lucky you were dressed from the way things have been going."

Alaoin surveyed him thoughtfully. "I think this has more to do with how I've spent my time than it does whether or not you think I've been serious enough."

Éric sputtered, caught off guard by Alaoin's insight. Because it was true. He was jealous of every woman Alaoin had been spending time with, but what had Éric expected? Why wouldn't people throw themselves at Alaoin? He was handsome, charming, witty, intelligent when he wanted to be, caring, and a good king. There was no way Éric could let Alaoin know he thought all of those things. "Don't try to change the subject. How you spend your nights wouldn't matter if you were more responsible about it."

"You're looking for reasons to be angry with me, Éric."

"I don't need to look for reasons. You hand them out like candy."

"I am sorry I failed to live up to your expectations, Éric," Alaoin said, frowning now. "Do not feel as though you must stay by my side when I am so lacking."

"Spirits dammit, Alaoin!" Éric shouted. "You're not lacking. You've never been lacking in anything our whole lives. If anyone is lacking, it's me. It has always been me. I just need you to be safe and to take this seriously enough to survive the battle. Survive, make it through this, and you can fuck anyone on the Spirits damned island. I won't say anything about it."

Alaoin just stared at him before finally shaking his head and turning and walking away.

"You're just going to walk away?" Éric asked, surprised. Alaoin had never walked away from him before.

Alaoin glanced over his shoulder and paused in his stride. "I'm not going to fight with you. Despite what you claim now, you've made it abundantly clear, for years, I do not behave in the way you wish me to. You're so outraged by my need to stay in a place of peace before battle, you decided it was appropriate to scream at me on the battlefield in hearing of Nereid, elf, and human alike. I have no desire to squabble with you further."

Éric looked away from Alaoin, embarrassment coloring his cheeks as he realized he had done such a thing. "I apologize, Your Majesty." Éric took a deep breath. "My actions were not well thought out. I will leave you to it and see you when the fighting starts."

"Éric, if you don't tell Alaoin you're in love with him, he's never going to understand why you're truly upset," Faron said from behind Éric in a voice loud enough he would be surprised if the entire battlefield hadn't heard.

Never in his life had Éric wanted to murder his father before. "I would appreciate it if you stayed out of this, Father. As I have told you before, Alaoin already knows." Éric shook his head and moved to go. He was sure he could find something to do between now and when the fighting started.

"I did not know, actually," Alaoin spoke up, bringing Éric to a stop. "Regardless, it's not an excuse for how you've treated me today."

Éric let out a huff of air. "I told you a few years back, and you nicely turned me down. But you are right. It has no bearing on how I treated you. I do apologize."

"You two are hopeless," Faron said.

Éric shook his head. "Father, please stop. I've made enough of a mess of everything. Now is not the time to delve into this."

"Having a real conversation with me would have been a better choice," Alaoin acknowledged. "You're right, though. Now is not the time. The ships are approaching."

"A conversation is pointless. You made your feelings clear years ago," Éric said with a shrug as he pulled his sword from

its scabbard. "Stay as safe as possible," he told Alaoin before following his father to where their troops were situated. He had no intention of allowing himself to go far from Alaoin, but a little distance wouldn't be the worst thing right now.

# Chapter Forty-Five

The ships drew close to the shore, and soldiers disembarked on small boats, closing the distance between where they made berth and the shoreline. As Aphros was the leader of the invaded Nereid people, he had been acknowledged as the leader of the battle. Riken and his horde would have come regardless of Collette's presence. She was simply a bonus to their ultimate plan.

A horn sounded from behind her position, Aphros's signal to prepare themselves. A hum of excitement rolled across the field, and the rapid splashing from before them identified the first of the Coralian and Azmarin soldiers as they made it to shore. A rallying cry began from the Fythian frontlines, traveling slowly through the ranks until reaching the battlements.

"Stand firm!" Aphros cried out as the Coralians surged toward them. The air filled with the clash of swords and steel, followed by grunts of effort and pain.

On the eastern side of the field, Whyldon engaged in a battle against a sturdy man who stood an inch or two shorter. Despite Whyldon's older age, his fluid movements spoke of years of training and instinctual reflexes. His sword slid into the opponent without resistance, and he yanked it out just as quickly before moving to the next person.

The archers from the battlements let loose a barrage of arrows. They found their marks on the approaching Coralian army, stopping the first line from reaching too far inland.

Collette's movements remained limited to the area, though she had her fill of components. Soldiers weighed down by armor and weapons in a way she was not tired easily from swings of blades and jumps and ducks from rogue blows. Collette lost count of the people she moved through, and glances for familiar faces between opponents told her they'd all been pulled in different directions with the flow of battle.

Minutes trickled into hours, and the fatigue of fighting, suppressed by adrenaline and the need for survival, licked at the edges of the fighters. The field, now more sparse, provided Collette with a moment to roll her shoulders, to breathe. Rion joined her, a cut on his shoulder, and his fair skin, beard, and hair dirty from battle. "You okay, Joss?" he said, voice rough.

"Perfect," she replied, her voice pitched upward so she could be heard. "Have you seen any of the others?"

"I saw Tolan not too long ago. No injuries," Rion recounted.

"Good," Collette said. Even with the distance between them, she'd be brokenhearted if he died. "His arena fighting probably helps."

"Probably," Rion agreed. He took a deep breath and raised his sword as an enemy soldier came toward them. "You good, Joss?" he asked.

"Yeah," she replied, and Rion nodded and went to meet the opponent, leaving her to deal with more immediate challengers.

More time passed, and the numbers standing on either side grew smaller, though Collette saw more Fythian and Nereid colors than Coralian and Azmarin. Still, she saw none of her people, a worrying thought. Nawalya, she hoped, remained on one of the battlements. Ceto was supposed to be beneath the water. The others, though, were less safe.

With more of the field now open to her, she moved forward, scanning the field for any signs of her people while dispatching any who dared come for her. As she moved closer to the shore, she saw the Coralian ships, some drifting away and others sporting noticeable damage. Ceto and her subsurface regiment had been effective.

"COLLETTE!" a deep, male voice screamed, one she didn't immediately recognize. She looked around, her eyes landing on Lord Riken Saullet strutting toward her as though she hadn't crushed his kneecap only months before.

# Chapter Forty-Six

"You bitch," Riken growled as he stalked closer to Collette. "I am going to gut you."

"You'd have to know how to use a fucking sword to gut me," Collette shouted back. "Or do you intend to have a couple of guards hold me in place again?"

"No. I think I'll do just fine against you on my own," Riken called as he drew closer.

Collette's grip on her sword tightened. She would not run forward. She would let him come to her. She could see Riken's eyes narrow in anger the closer he got, his movements smooth and confident, like he already knew the conflict would end in his favor.

As soon as he was close enough, he brought his long sword up and motioned her forward with his other hand.

"You beckon your queen?" she asked, taunting him, her sword raised in response, though her feet remained planted where she stood.

"You're not my queen. You never were. I thought you were more intelligent." He approached her, stopping within reach and shrugging. He feinted to her left, his sword positioned to strike, only to swing out with a dagger he'd hidden in his right hand.

Collette pivoted out of the way, dodging the dagger altogether while using her sword to block his own. Riken would have to do better. "You scampered back to Wild Run pretty quickly after your queen banished you from Quenall," she shot back. "Letting the likes of your bitch and Lord Crobán do the hard work. You never did like to get your hands dirty."

"It's called a strategic retreat." He struck out at her again. As she evaded his strikes, Collette noticed he made sure to stay out of range of her being able to kick him. "Lord Crobán acted on his own. If he'd been working for me, we'd have made sure you never got out of prison alive."

Collette laughed, harsh and mocking. "Right. You strategically stood by while Rhoslyn got married. I completely believe you."

"You have to admit, until recently, it worked beautifully. She is running the country, and when I return, your brother will be beheaded for treason," Riken growled.

"If you're already trying to kill your supposed king, I can't say it's going well for you." Collette would have to consider the Zephraim situation later.

"Trying isn't a word I would use. Your traitorous brother is helping your precious little rebellion in Quenall. We will have his head and theirs," Riken spat before moving quickly, raining down a flurry of blows on Collette, more controlled and less arrogant than the last time they met. His other hand swiped out with the dagger whenever he thought he saw an opening. "I will kill you here, and Rhoslyn will kill your worthless brother, bringing an end to your entire line."

Collette's sword stopped a deadly blow from falling on her head, though the position left her vulnerable, and she winced as she felt the tip of his knife run down her side. She pulled back

in time to prevent the blade from going too deep. Despite the acute sting of her injury, she didn't give it much inspection. She could heal it, and she treated it like the merest scratch. "That all you got?"

Riken just smirked and advanced, his weapon at the ready as he struck out at Collette again. She blocked the swing, withdrew her weapon, and drove it at Riken, catching him off guard as the blade cut into his skin. He'd made it clear he wasn't playing anymore. Neither was she.

"Bitch," he spat. Ignoring the wound, he corrected his stance and brought his weapon back up, his other hand tightening on his dagger.

Their swords met again, a clash of steel and strength. Neither relinquished their holds, both pushing against the other. Using her shoulders and arms, Collette gave a mighty shrug against Riken, putting temporary distance between them. She repositioned her hold and struck again, cutting into Riken a second time.

Rage flitted across Riken's face as he darted back from her blade. He forced himself to get his emotions back under control. He moved into a defensive position, allowing her to take the first move.

She stepped forward, her footing firm but ready to move, and the tip of her sword pointing in his direction. Impatiently, Riken lunged forward, trying to knock her sword aside to once again strike at Collette with his dagger. Collette moved, angling her body so the knife soared past her, and she plunged her sword deep into his side. She pulled it out just as quickly, stepping back long enough to regroup before going for him again, wanting to deliver the final blow.

Collette's effort was thwarted as a group of men ran forward, a couple taking hold of Riken while others fought her back. She growled in frustration, but her focus became consumed by fighting off two men at once.

A vicious snarl roared through the air, so animalistic the men assisting Riken from the battlefield let go on instinct. The brief reprieve from the fight nearly landed him ass-first in blood and viscera, but Riken managed to stay up despite his injury. His sneer only grew more prominent as he glared in the little bitch's direction, fighting off two of his men with an impossible ease. He had the better trained army, filled with capable human men, yet they lost ground and soldiers with every passing second. Taking out an army of Mers shouldn't have taxed Coralian forces.

*How are we so underprepared? How has Collette garnered so much support?* He'd watched her throughout the fight, her swings and jabs strong and efficient. He'd already known her to be strong, and her tireless effort on the battlefield proved it. The bleeding wounds he suffered now further proved it.

He growled again as he was forced to sit down on a table near his tent while Mallan did his best to call a retreat of their remaining men. Even in the chaos of battle, his eyes never left the scene before him. The long cut he'd gifted her bled, but unlike him, her people had not forced her from the field. She took down a soldier wearing Coralian regalia and moved to another, and Riken swore he would break her.

He watched as a blond elf fought his way closer to Collette, his fighting style precise and measured, while to the right came another man, this one seemingly human with russet hair. His fight felt more desperate, wilder, and Riken could distantly hear Collette's name leave the man's lips. Realizing who the man must be to the fallen queen, an idea came to Riken.

"Get me an archer," he commanded.

*"COLLETTE!"*

Separated. They had all been separated early in the horrific battle. Larent knew nearly anything was possible on a battlefield, and Collette was more than capable of the fight, but the sight of blood oozing from a long gash reaching from side to hip had him carelessly moving across the battlefield toward her. He spotted Whyldon and Arian doing the same. He would reach her first, though. He had to.

"She's okay," he told himself as he ducked between a couple of fighters, neither paying him much attention. "It's a small wound. She can heal herself." Larent came to a stop as a middle-aged man approached him baring yellow teeth just visible beneath a dented and worn helmet which might have been decades old. One swing of Larent's gloved hand took the man out, though Larent forgot him before the body hit the ground. He would give respect to the fallen later. Right now, he needed to move.

Taking a deep breath, Larent planned out the most direct route before he resumed running. Cutting down every enemy soldier who got in his way, Larent felt more relief as he drew closer to her.

A handful of Nereid joined Collette, three fighting away the men targeting her while another two insisted she leave the field. She shook her head, gesturing toward the front lines with the end of her sword.

"Collette!" he called out as he approached, hoping he could convince her to go along with the intervening Nereids.

She turned to look at him, her beautiful face displaying her stubborn defiance. He found no surprise in it even though Larent would bet one of his limbs Arian would have something to say on the matter after the fight.

# Chapter Forty-six

He hurried over, closing the remaining distance between them, though when he spoke, he kept his voice raised so he could be heard over the noise of the battle. "I think Riken's men are retreating," he shouted. "We should get you to the medical tent." He removed one of his clawed gloves and offered her a hand, and she reached to take it as pain erupted, unlike anything he'd ever experienced before. He fell forward, caught in Collette's arms, struggling to breathe.

Blood splattered across Collette's face as the arrow made contact with Larent's body. The strong aim and solid arrow slid through Larent without meeting a barrier. Arian met them as Larent collapsed into her arms, and the two hurriedly carried him away from the battle.

"You are going to be fine," Arian practically demanded of Larent, his voice calm, though laced with tension.

Collette didn't see how. Fleshy bits clung to the arrowhead, and the thick broadhead left a sizable wound in its wake. Copious amounts of sticky dark blood pooled from Larent's body as they hurried to a safer place at the edge of the battlefield.

"My kit!" Arian called near one of the officer tents, and a young Nereid boy with dark black hair and purple glimmers on his skin ran to fetch the pack.

Rion jogged over, flanked by Ceto, Lynessea, and Jayden. "You're going to stop the bleeding before removing the arrow," the former guard said after a glance.

"I know," Collette shouted over the commotion of the field, her teeth gritted. She felt less capable of breathing than Larent seemed to, though a broadhead hadn't pierced her lung. She glanced over at Arian. "Help me get him seated," Collette said.

The blond elf nodded, and they lowered Larent into a sitting position. "Just stay with me, okay?" she asked of Larent.

A gasp of air had Collette looking over her shoulder to Lynessea, who covered her mouth.

"What?" Collette demanded.

"The arrow," Ceto replied, letting her now shaky hands ball into fists by her side. "It looks like it's covered in Veinfire."

Jaydon's eyes widened and he moved closer, his jaw-dropping in what Collette assumed was confirmation.

"What is Veinfire?" she asked as she went back to tending Larent's wound. She wasn't sure where to start, and the panic from Jayden and Ceto wasn't helping matters.

"It's a poison," Jayden said, dropping to a knee beside Collette. "Fast acting. Painful. Basically incurable. It's known to be impervious to most magic." He ran a finger along the protruding arrowhead without touching the traces of sticky black ooze. "You see how the blood doesn't want to mix with the poison?" he asked her.

"You are wrong," Arian interjected. "Collette, stop his bleeding. We can fix this."

"It doesn't matter," Ceto said, her gold eyes wet with unshed tears now. "The poison—"

"Shut up," Collette commanded the Nereid woman, and she pressed her hands against Larent's chest near the arrow's exit wound. Her fingers grew warm and tingling, but nothing else happened. She looked up, catching Arian's gaze with her own.

"Hey," Larent said, his voice weak and punctuated with wheezing breath. "It's okay."

Collette shook her head. "It's not, but you will be," she insisted, not knowing how she could possibly help him.

"Try again," Arian yelled. "Try again."

"It won't work," Jayden replied calmly. "All trying again will do is drain her, and she already has wounds."

Larent gazed up at Collette as Jayden and Arian argued. He cupped her cheek, the effort tremendous as his arms shook and his breathing worsened. "He–hey Freckles."

"Hey," she breathed out, pressing her forehead against his as she put a hand over the one touching her cheek. The touch-point kept her from trembling in fear. "Hey," she repeated, her eyes stinging with tears threatening to choke her. "You know you can't do this. You cannot leave me."

"'Fraid I–I don't have—" His words halted as he coughed, and blood appeared at the corners of his lips. He sucked in a difficult breath, wincing from the effort and pain. "You're—you're gonna be okay."

She shook her head, denying any reality where she could ever be okay again. "Not without you," she whispered. "I need you. I love you."

"I love—you t–too. You're going to—t–to be okay. Strongest person I know." He tried to smile, even in obvious pain.

"Please," she begged him, tears flowing in waves now. "Please don't leave me."

"Collette," he gasped as his thumbs brushed along her cheeks. "I will l–love you forever," he promised her. He took another ragged breath, shallow and weak. "H–hey Freckles," he added in a near whisper. "Tell me something." The corners of his lips barely tilted up before he drew his last breath. As his free hand slipped from her face to hit the cold, hard ground, Collette knew he was dead.

Numbness enveloped Collette as all the surrounding noise of battle faded around her. She couldn't do anything. She couldn't breathe or move or think. All she knew was he was gone. He was gone. Something, or someone, touched her arm as she felt her grip on Larent's hand slip away from her. She did not fight the thing intruding on her last moments with Larent, the thing pulling her away from him. She couldn't. Even the

high-pitched wailing penetrating her hearing could not bring her back to face the reality of her new world.

She turned to look at the person separating her from Larent, giving no mind to the cascade of desperate, grieving tears. *Faron,* her mind told her. *Faron? Where had he come from?*

"You can't stay out here," he said in a far too soothing voice for a man his size.

"You're injured. You're not thinking. Staying with him now will not bring him back."

Collette did not argue, letting the elf lead her somewhere, passing Aphros along the way.

# Chapter Forty-Seven

Seconds or hours might have passed before she realized she'd been led to a medical tent and was now seated on a wooden chair. Gazing around the small tent, she noticed she was alone, though she didn't question why. Looking down, she saw she was bleeding, and her brows knitted together in wonder of the injury before she vaguely remembered Riken and a sword. She pressed a hand on her side, the warmth and tingling barely registering with her. Her empty wrist, however, somehow alarmed her. She just didn't know why.

The tent flap shifted, and Tolan let himself inside. Tall, tanned, and handsome as ever, the former arena fighter was covered in the grime of battle, his body weary and his expression sorrowful. "How are you doing?" he asked, voice subdued.

Collette blinked. "What?" she asked.

Tolan's eyes widened in concern, and he carefully approached Collette as though he expected her to lash out at any moment. "Are you still bleeding?" he asked after surveying her. Slowly, she shook her head.

"Do you need anything? Water? Bandages?" Tolan asked, his hands moving as if to touch Collette before dropping back to his sides.

She didn't acknowledge his questions, not even with something as simple as a shake of her head. She looked up to meet his worried eyes. "Where is he?"

Tolan closed his eyes, pain flashing across his face. "They were getting ready to move him to the area where they're keeping the rest of the…" He trailed off. "They will keep him separated until they know how you want to handle everything."

Collette rose to her feet, still not feeling as though she quite existed in her body anymore. She strode from the tent, surprised to see evening approaching and the battlefield cleared of living soldiers for now.

"Collette, Collette!" Tolan called trying to get her attention as he followed her. "You need to rest. I promise you can see him later."

She didn't respond and continued her dazed march toward her goal. Although their side had been largely victorious, finding the dead, laid out in neat rows, gave the queen no trouble.

Soldiers dressed in the rich colors of Nereid, Fythias, and Collette's Coralian purples carried the dead from the field. She knew the faces, both of the dead and those laboring as quickly as they could in the limited daylight.

"Collette," said a voice, and Collette saw Whyldon approaching. "Why are you out here?"

"Where is he?" Collette responded as Tolan caught up.

"Collette, we can come see him later. Please come with me," Tolan said, trying one last time to get her away from so much death.

Nawalya appeared at Whyldon's elbow and glared at Tolan before reaching a hand out to Collette. "Come, I will take you to him."

"Nawalya, she shouldn't…" Tolan was cut off by Nawalya's sharp retort.

"Shut up, Tolan. You are not helping. Either come with us, or go elsewhere, but shut up."

Thankful for the intervention, Collette allowed Nawalya to guide her back to Larent. As they walked, she didn't miss the other woman's puffy red-rimmed eyes. The grief others would inevitably feel seemed obvious now, but Collette had no room in her body to offer condolences. She had no desire other than joining Larent, and she wasn't entirely certain the desire only encompassed seeing him again.

Nawalya held Collette's hand the entire time as they walked to a small tent. Outside, Arian was on his knees, face buried in Thomas's chest, his body shaking in silent sobs. Nawalya pushed the tent flap open, and there he was, laid out on a pallet as if sleeping. Jayden looked up from his seat near Larent, his own eyes slightly puffy. He stood immediately upon seeing the two women.

Collette pulled away from Nawalya and ignored Jayden as she approached Larent's body. The arrow had been removed, and a patch was placed over the gaping hole in his chest. His face and hands had been washed, leaving him with the appearance of benign sleep. Collette swallowed, forcing herself to remain in a state of numbness. She didn't want to confront the pain, not now, not when she knew there was so much left to do.

Reaching out, she ran her fingers along the line of his stubbled jaw, brows furrowing over the strange warmth of his body. Surely, he should not be warm. He'd died hours ago.

"I put a stasis spell on his body," Aphros spoke up from behind. She had not heard him enter. "I doubted you would want to leave him here, especially when you plan on one day returning to Coralia."

When Collette said nothing, Nawalya responded to Aphros in a low voice. "I am sure, when things are more … settled, Queen Collette will be grateful. I know his grandparents will certainly be."

"Where is his bracelet?" Collette asked, her eyes now locked on the bare wrist which, in the early hours of the morning, had held the weaved ribbons from their marriage. Her eyes traveled to her own, realizing what had seemed so wrong earlier.

"His bracelet?" Aphros repeated, confused.

"Larent doesn't wear jewelry, Collette," Nawalya said slowly. The worried glance she shared with Aphros was not missed.

"He did as of this morning, Nawalya," Thomas said quietly as he entered the tent.

Arian followed behind the other man, his grief-stricken demeanor evident in his expression and his looks. Covered in blood and grime, the usually bright blond hair appeared nearly black. His sooty face highlighted the tear tracks, and his red swollen eyes glistened as though he could resume his desperate sobs at any moment. Without a word, Arian lifted a blood-stained hand to Collette. In his palm was the item Collette had requested.

Spotting the now unraveled bracelet, Nawalya let a curse slip from between her lips, horror and realization settling on her features.

Collette greedily plucked the item from Arian's hand, bringing the grubby ribbons to her chest. She closed her eyes, taking a deep breath as her tears began falling again.

Unlike normal, Arian didn't hesitate. He pulled Collette into his arms and sobbed with her. Again, time passed without Collette being able to track its length. She thought she might do nothing else but cry until she lost the very ability. Even when her latest rounds of sobs slowed to a quiet, sad flow, she stayed encompassed in her chosen brother's arms.

# Chapter Forty-Eight

Faron didn't remember the path he took leaving the battle-field to the very well-guarded room Sabine had chosen to stay in while the battle raged. His mind did not guide him to a decision nor tell his feet to move. All he knew was the bone-deep need to find Sabine, to see she was safe.

Watching Larent take his last breath and the subsequent breaking of Queen Collette's spirit all too well reminded Faron of the night when Sabine had been poisoned. The night when he thought he'd lost her and the rest of his family shortly thereafter.

So lost in his spiraling thoughts, Faron barely recognized the force he used to throw open the door to Sabine's room, let alone the resulting crack in the once sturdy wall. He crossed the room to her, not feeling as though he could possibly breathe until her small, soft hands were pressed against his chest.

"What's happened?" she asked, her question alarmed even if her voice soothed him. "Éric is well?" Thankfully, she didn't resist their closeness or pull away because he knew he was filthy from battle.

Faron nodded and pulled her closer, burying his nose in her hair, letting the scent calm him. "Larent is dead," he said hoarsely. He had spent time with the shifter, and from his observations, the man had a large heart, a sense of humor to light up even the darkest moments, and he had loved Collette with the same intensity Faron loved Sabine.

"That poor woman," Sabine replied, mostly to herself. Her arms circled Faron's waist, the increased closeness a much-needed balm to his frazzled mind.

"He took an arrow to the chest. He might have survived it, but the arrow was coated in Veinfire." He didn't have to remind his wife of Meri, their dear friend, losing control of her magic, nor the physical havoc it caused her.

Sabine pulled away enough to look up at him, horror on her face. "Was the arrow properly disposed of?" she asked.

"I don't know. I didn't stay long enough to find out, but Ceto and Jayden knew what it was, so I assume the Nereid know how to handle a dangerous poison."

Sabine nodded and closed the space between them again. "Perhaps we should have shared with them," she said after a few minutes.

Faron took a step back from Sabine, moving so he was now grasping her arms, not wanting to be physically apart from her just yet. "No. It puts you at too much risk, especially when Coralia is coating their arrows in Veinfire." The thought of what could happen to Sabine if anyone found out their secret chilled his bones. He would do anything to keep her safe, even betray their hard-earned alliances if needed.

"I understand the risk," Sabine argued. "Trust me. I was there when we went through it, but what do you think is going to happen with Collette now? Do you think she's going to have the will to keep fighting? We could have helped to prevent her pain."

Faron shook his head. "Collette will continue. She has a strong spirt. Taking her kingdom back may be..." Faron trailed off, his lecture about why it was safer for them to continue hiding what they had done coming to an abrupt halt as he realized exactly what he was doing. "Forgive me. I am trying to dictate what we do instead of having a reasonable discussion with you. A trait our son seems to have inherited in spades."

"Given how often you forget yourself, I doubt he had much chance to do otherwise," Sabine remarked. No hint of anger showed in her expression, but their years together allowed Faron to know he'd irritated her.

"I am sorry. If you still wish to tell Collette, the choice is yours, and I have no right to demand your silence." He moved to wrap his arms around Sabine once more. Thankfully, she allowed him. "Watching her hold him as he died was a horrible reminder of that fucking ball."

"I survived, though," she reminded him gently, reaching up to cup his cheek. "And we took the steps we needed when I was recovered enough." She sighed. "We should have said something, though. Nothing we went through can bring him back, but he might not have died had we spoken up."

"They could both be dead now. Either way, you're right. We should have told them." Faron sighed into her hand. "Let me get cleaned up, and I'll make up for my lapse of judgement. We can talk about how our son greatly offended Alaoin and figure out where we go from here."

Sabine nodded, evidently still unhappy with him. He'd do what he could to further apologize. "You've had a long and difficult day. Go take care of yourself. You need it."

Faron nodded and headed to the washroom, his head filled with thoughts of how to make it up to his wife. He couldn't help but wonder if his dreams would be filled with the sound of battle and a young queen's desperate screams.

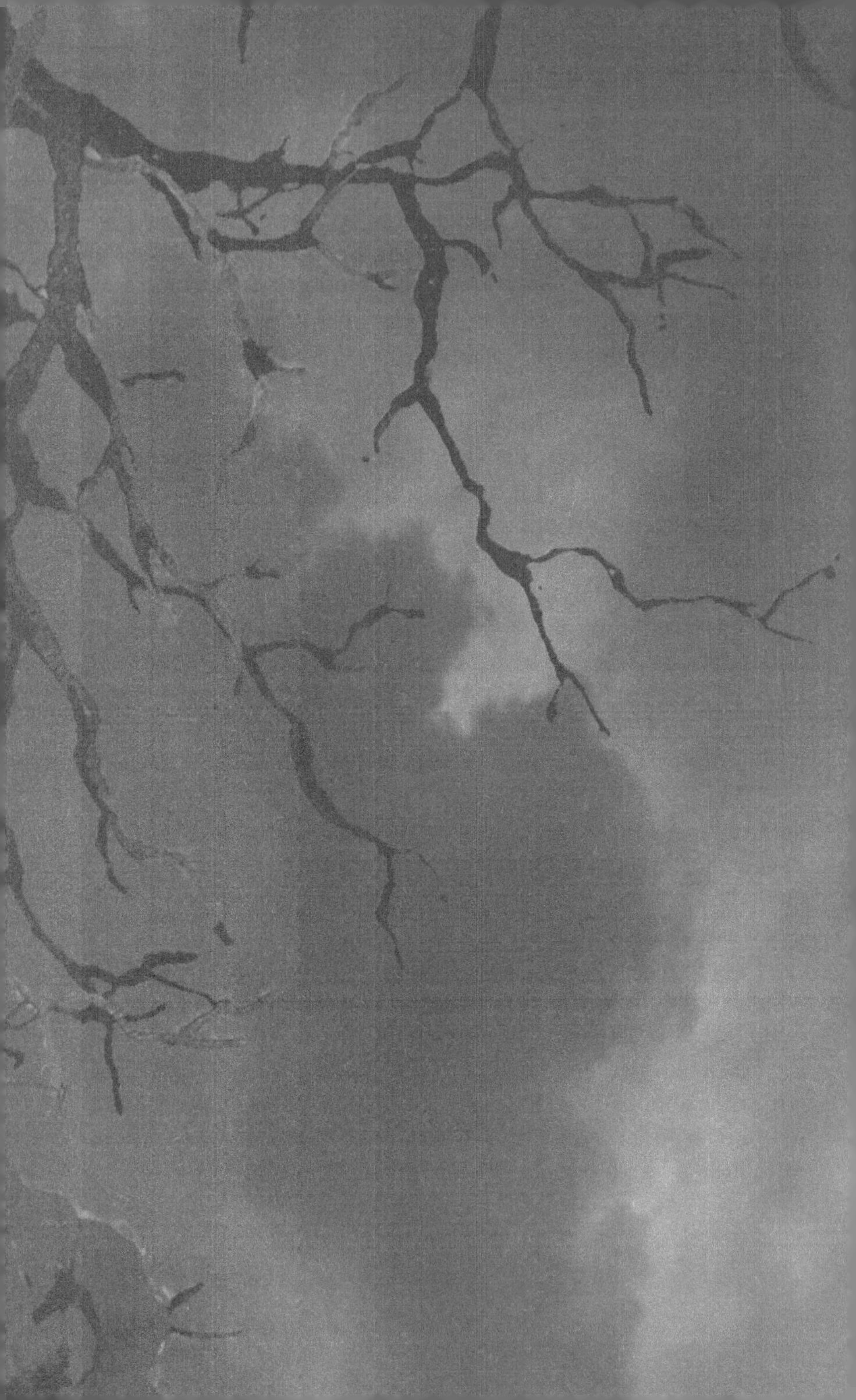

# Book Club Questions

1. Aphros, Alaoin, and Collette are three very different rulers. Who do you believe is the most effective leader? Why?

2. Tolan and Collette manage to reconcile in this novel. Why do you think Collette decided to forgive him?

3. Sabine clearly holds a great deal of power in Fythias. Why do you think she doesn't want to rule?

4. Is Riken hypocritical when agreeing to have a magic healer heal his knee? Why or why not?

5. Is Mallan a trustworthy ally? Do you think he desires the Azmarin throne? How should Riken respond to him?

6. If you were Thomas, would be patient with Arian when he becomes demanding, or do you think Thomas is too tolerant? Why or why not?

7. How would you describe the differences between Coralia, Azmarin, and the Nereid islands? Other than geographical, what are some of the reasons for such distinct locations?

8. Do you agree with Aphros's suspicion about Collette's connection to the Nereid? If not, what theories do you have?

9. Would you have agreed to be Marked like Collette did? Why do you think she questioned her worthiness for the honor?

10. What secret do you think Faron and Sabine are keeping?

# Author Bios

Kate Jenkins enjoys writing fantasy, sci-fi and romance as much as she enjoys reading them. She lives in a small town in Idaho with her autistic teen who is her whole world, her parents, and between them, four dogs and six cats. When not hanging with her son, she loves gaming, especially first-person shooters and asymmetrical horror games she can play with friends. She's a K-pop enthusiast and harbors a secret love of K-dramas and Anime, much to her mother's displeasure as she's slowly being sucked into them with her. Her favorites tropes are currently enemies to lovers, there was only one bed, coffee shops, time travel fixes it, and soul mates/soul identifying marks. She is hopeful one day she can talk her co-author into writing these with her.

Morgan Moreau is a passionate writer whose literary interests span various genres, showcasing a love for the imaginative realms of fantasy, historical fiction, crime and mystery, as well as contemporary stories. Morgan's affection for *The Little Mermaid* profoundly influences multiple aspects of her life including her vibrant red and purple hair, mermaid tattoos, and a growing collection of mermaid memorabilia. Morgan also holds a deep affection for pirates, especially those who "wear fine things well," though those in possession of jars of dirt will always hold a place in her heart. She lives in Alabama with her dog Scarlett, and she looks forward to adopting more puppies in the future. Her current passions include higher education, animal rights, and watching the 1995 *Pride & Prejudice* at least once a month. In addition to her current literary loves, Morgan is a fan of vampires, pirates, mermaids, and superheroes, and she hopes to incorporate them into future works.

A sneak peek from the upcoming sequel, *Legends of Coralia: Restoration & Ruin.*

"I'm going to Quenall," Collette announced, her position near Larent's body unchanging over the last hour. All of the members of her travel party, and the friends and allies they'd gained from the Nereids and the Fythians had joined her to sit vigil in the tent. Larent's body lay on a cot, hands resting by his sides, eyes closed, and russet hair smoothed back from his face. Someone had washed the dirt and blood of battle from his face and neck. With Aphros's stasis spell, his body remained as warm and limber as if he were still alive and just sleeping.

Muted alarm rose, though Collette paid little attention to the words. Instead, her fingers carefully focused on plaiting the ribbons of Larent's bracelet around the gold bangle belonging to her mother. She had no idea where her own now lay, but she would not lose his.

She didn't look up as careful steps approached her or pull away from the rough hand now on her shoulder. A smaller hand than she expected but calloused and firm. Surprisingly, when the person spoke, Thomas's voice was closest to her.

"I know losing Larent is hard," he said gently.

Collette knew he wanted her to speak, and a couple of times, she opened her mouth to try, only to close it again. Her eyes stung far too much, so she focused on her ribbon braiding, pausing occasionally to brush away the silent tears that fell down her face.

Thomas took her silence as an invitation to continue. "I know you've already suffered your fair share of broken hearts these past months. It's appalling how much you've suffered, how much you keep bottled up."

"I'm going to Quenall, so it doesn't matter," she replied, knowing her voice didn't sound like her own.

"You're not going to Quenall, Joss," Rion said, rubbing at his gingery beard. He sat in a far corner of the room, legs stretched out in front of him. He'd shed his armor, though the pile of metal remained within reach. "They'd kill you before you stepped foot in the city."

Collette looked over at her former lover, her expression void of humor or sarcasm. "Either I am your queen, in which case I shall do what I want, or I am not your queen, and you cannot stop me anyway. I am going to Quenall, and I do not need permission."

Whyldon stood, his blue eyes concerned, and he approached Collette as though to reason with her. "Why Quenall?" he asked. "To go after Riken? There are better plans to draw him out."

"I don't give two shits about Riken," Collette replied. "Not right now, anyway."

"Then you don't need to go to Quenall," Rion argued.

"I'm going to Quenall so I can bring him back," she said simply. Silence followed her explanation. She knew the others in the tent probably thought she'd finally lost her mind, but she didn't care.

A sneak peek from the upcoming spin-off series,
*Vassetre: Choice of a Duchesse*

Faron released the ornate door handle with a low growl. The elf's long, black, wavy hair fell forward as he pondered the solid door blocking his entrance. Faron knew he should return to his post. He knew he shouldn't be upset because, once again, Her Grace had locked the door to her rooms.

Stubbornly, she had not complied with his request to keep the main door to her suite unlocked, no matter how many times he gave it. "It is for your safety. I need unhindered access to your main space." And yet, now the door was locked, and Faron firmly believed her motivated by a heightened desire to vex him.

He might have walked away, grumbling and promising to address his concerns come morning, but a noise—not quite a crash—sounded, leaving him concerned. He pressed his lips together, thinking. The sound might have been nothing more than a dropped book or a stubbed toe as she accidentally collided with furniture. Neither event would justify more action. Just as he decided to wait, another crash, followed by a shout, reached his ears.

"Oh, you fucking bitch! I'm going to kill you!" shouted an unfamiliar voice.

Encouraged by the clear threat, Faron acted. Backing up, he braced himself and put all his considerable strength into kicking the door down. Once, the door barely budged; twice, the hinges groaned. With a third kick, the door budged. A fourth kick, and the door was done, breaking at the lock and hinges.

Unsheathing his sword, Faron strode into the duchess's private greeting area, a beautifully decorated room meant for tea with friends, and through the opening to her lounging room.

The sounds of struggle grew clearer the farther back he moved, and he sprinted toward the bedroom where she must have been.

Less effort was needed to access this space, and though he barreled through the door prepared for battle, he came to a stop as he spotted a nearly naked Duchess Sabine, wearing only the sheerest white chemise, straddling what appeared to be a young child. The poor excuse for clothing did nothing to hide the swell of her perfect pale breast or the rosy buds beneath the fabric. The fabric of the chemise bunched around her, showing off her long creamy legs.

She held a plain dagger against the child's neck, her other hand wrapped around the child's left hand which had been trying to go for a dagger just barely out of reach. Sabine used her larger stature and weight to keep the child on the floor.

Faron was about to ask why she was holding down a child when he took in the culprit's ears and face. She was no child. Just an unusually small elf.

"What the fuck?" was all Faron could say.

## Discover more at
## 4HorsemenPublications.com

**10% off using HORSEMEN10**